XX

ANGELA CHADWICK

dialogue
books

DIALOGUE BOOKS

First published in Great Britain in 2018 by Dialogue Books

10 9 8 7 6 5 4 3 2 1

A CIP catalogue record for this book
is available from the British Library.

Hardback ISBN 978-0-349-70024-3
C-format ISBN 978-0-349-70025-0

Typeset in Berling by M Rules
Printed and bound in Great Britain by
Clays Ltd, Elcograf S.p.A

Papers used by Dialogue Books are from well-managed forests
and other responsible sources.

MIX
Paper from
responsible sources
FSC® C104740

Dialogue Books
An imprint of
Little, Brown Book Group
Carmelite House
50 Victoria Embankment
London EC4Y 0DZ

An Hachette UK Company
www.hachette.co.uk

www.littlebrown.co.uk

For Lucas

The Interview

'After years of controversial research, scientists at Portsmouth University's Centre for Reproductive Medicine have this morning announced plans to create IVF babies from two women. They're pushing for a change to the Human Fertilisation and Embryology Act that will make it legal to fertilise an egg with genetic material from a second female.'

The presenter's face is unnaturally still as he reads from the autocue. 'With us this morning is Professor Becca Jefferson, the scientist leading the research into so-called "ovum-to-ovum fertilisation". Professor, tell us how it works.'

The professor is sitting up straight, knees together, hands folded in her lap. She gives the presenter a warm smile. 'Thank you for inviting me here today. Our new technique actually has a lot of similarities to a regular IVF. We harvest egg cells from two women, then we extract DNA from the nucleus of one and inject it into the other. By stimulating this combined cell with an electrical current, we start a reaction very similar to natural fertilisation. The egg divides in two and the resulting cells continue to divide until we have blasto-cyst – or embryo.'

The television station runs a short video: an

electron-microscope view of an egg cell, pitted and grey, being punctured by a fine needle. Then, time-lapse footage of dividing cells within a Petri dish, the nuclei stained, the cell walls accentuated by a blue backlight.

'These are human cells,' the professor explains. 'Up until now, we've had to terminate our test embryos at fourteen days. But we'd like to see a change in the law that will allow them to be implanted and, ultimately, to be born.'

'I guess the question that people at home will be asking,' the presenter says, 'is: why?'

'People were asking that back in the seventies, when IVF was being trialled for the first time. And the answer remains the same: there are couples out there unable to conceive their own children via natural means. Now we have the technology to help them overcome this barrier and create a family – of course we have to use it.'

'Your announcement made reference to the fact that children conceived through this technique will always be female.' The camera lingers on the presenter's face for a moment, capturing an expression of gentle concern.

The professor shifts in her seat. 'Yes, that's right. Most cells in the human body contain a pair of sex chromosomes – an X and a Y for males, an XX for females. But sex cells – ova and sperm – only contain one half of the pair. Egg cells always carry an X, but sperm can carry either an X or a Y.

'During natural fertilisation, the baby receives a sex chromosome from each parent and its gender is determined by whichever chromosome the fertilising sperm is carrying. But because egg cells always carry an X, ovum-to-ovum fertilisation can only ever lead to baby girls.'

The presenter's eyes are lit with mischief. 'So, in theory, us males could be phased out, then?'

The professor laughs, but it doesn't reach her eyes. 'I think that's highly unlikely, don't you?'

Chapter 1

The woman behind the desk sighs when I ask whether Professor Jefferson is available. 'The professor won't see anyone without an appointment. Are you a journalist, by any chance?'

I smile. 'That obvious, is it? I take it I'm not the first?'

She snorts. 'No, my love, you're not. It's been a busy day. You're number eleven – a new record. One of them pretended to be her sister.'

'I'm local, from the *Portsmouth Post*. Is there any way . . . ?'

The woman smiles and shakes her head, her gold hoop earrings swaying heavily.

'Is Professor Jefferson actually here today, or has she gone up to London?'

'Sorry, darling. You've got to ring the press office. You got their number?'

She's clearly been well briefed, so I nod and smile my goodbye. It's what I expected, and what Matthew, the news editor, must have known would happen when he sent me down here. We've been calling the press office daily, and every time we get the same answer: *Keep checking the website: we'll upload a statement after the vote.* They're only giving interviews to the nationals.

I head back out into the dank afternoon. Across the road students are clustered under the awning of a café, huddled together smoking roll-ups in their too-thin coats. The sky is slate grey and the drizzle that's persisted all morning is thickening into fat drops. Heading around the block, I locate the entrance to the Centre's car park. There's a barrier, but I squeeze through on foot, pulling up the hood of my parka. Sheltering underneath a fire escape, I quickly check Twitter. The Lords are voting now, each of them opting to walk through one of two doors: the 'content' door if they're in favour of two-mother babies; the 'not content' door if they're against. The BBC reporter in the chamber tweets live updates as they pass. Two 'not contents' in a row, then a 'content'.

The average age in the House of Lords is sixty-nine. Attitudes have changed, but many of those in the chamber grew up in a time when homosexuality was illegal. Can they really be ready to hand reproductive autonomy to lesbians? My mind conjures expensive suits in navy pinstripe. Rheumatic joints. Barely concealed distaste. Preparing myself for disappointment is the responsible thing to do.

It was last May, on holiday in Crete, that I finally came around to the idea of having a baby. We'd befriended a young family; Rosie playing endless games of catch with their four-year-old boy while the parents basked in the sunshine. The child's delighted squeals made me look up from my P. D. James, and I couldn't help noticing the way his face perfectly blended his mother's lips and chin with his father's forehead. I'd never been gooey for kids, far from it, yet I registered a pang of sadness. What might mine and Rosie's child look like? Ovum-to-ovum fertilisation wasn't yet being talked about, so there was no good reason for me to think along those lines. But I let myself perceive, just for a moment, how wonderful it might be to merge with the one you love in this way. To raise a child that's half of both of you.

The couple had a young baby too, and Rosie cooed and fussed, prompting gummy smiles as she slathered factor 50 onto chubby little arms. After years of saying no, of wrinkling my nose and anticipating obstacles, I suddenly realised just how deep Rosie's longing went. It was in the way she smiled with her entire face, with her body too, as though she'd accessed a whole other level of purpose. This wasn't the first time I'd seen her interact with children – she was already godmother to two of our friends' babies – but it was the first time I realised how integral this care was for her. In not wanting a family, I'd been denying her the very thing that lit her up.

On the second to last evening we took an outside table at a beachside taverna. The sun was sinking into the sea, filling it with ripples of brightness as the sky deepened into a rich indigo. Rosie wore a sleeveless lilac dress, setting off her tanned shoulders. Her hair was loose; a mass of blond curls trailing down her back in a way I found distractingly sexy. I liked to lift it away and expose the nape of her neck, peppering her with light kisses.

My short, dark hair was un-styled and fluffy from the shower and I wore a long-sleeved shirt and combat trousers – loose, comfortable and mosquito-proof. I'd caught the sun, but my tan lacked the golden sheen of Rosie's; my shoulders and arms were densely freckled, my nose a sore-looking red.

'It was lovely seeing you with little Molly and Jack earlier,' I told Rosie. 'You're such a natural with kids.'

She took a sip of her house white, her eyes focusing on mine with a new intensity. The last time I'd let her see my indifference to motherhood, unwanted tears had slid down her nose – I'll never forget the pinkness of her eyes, the crumpling of her face. 'It's just us two, then,' she'd said. And I'd let myself believe she could be content. That thin little laugh she gave as she said she'd settle for a cat, or maybe a hamster – remembering made me feel ashamed.

I looked away, down at the checked tablecloth. There were a few stale breadcrumbs on my side of the table and I brushed them to the ground. Rosie was waiting for more.

'I think I've finally realised how important it is to you,' I said.

'Jules.' She reached across the table and took my hand. 'Don't worry, OK? I'm happy. I'm not going to pressure you . . . ' Her voice trailed off and she looked away, out to sea.

Something reckless was in my blood. Burgeoning possibility. I felt myself transcending the ever-weary practicalities that weighed in my chest. The lists. The household budget. 'I want us to be able to talk about these things,' I said. 'Before . . . I wasn't really seeing.'

She looked at me, her eyes startled but alive with interest, while the waiter came and placed my salad on the table and handed Rosie a plate of thick, buttery garlic bread.

I watched her bite into a slice, her fingers gleaming with oil. 'Seeing you today, with those kids . . . you actually made it look fun. Rosie . . .' My voice caught. 'If anyone's way is going to be right for me, it's yours. You'll be an excellent mother. You should have the opportunity. I see that now.'

She placed the bread back down on her plate and took her lower lip between her teeth. I wanted to reach out and cup her face in my hands, but was unable to move. The relief of telling her something I knew she so desperately wanted to hear made me feel shaky, as though I'd done a long run on an empty stomach.

'Jules, are you sure . . . ?' she whispered. 'You're not just saying this because you think you have to?'

I shook my head, closing my eyes for a moment. Childcare costs. Depleted sleep. No energy left for making plans, nurturing ambitions. And, on top of all this, the Man. The stranger we'd need, whose features would be present in our baby's face, who'd no doubt take on mythical significance to the child he fathered. But this was Rosie, who had such a talent for happiness. My deepest joys came in those moments when I surrendered to her. When I ignored my ever-cautious instincts and let her choose for the both of us. What a fool I'd been to agonise over this for so long. Her happiness would sustain me, would give me the strength I needed.

It's already gone 4 p.m. I have twenty minutes to get a reaction from Professor Jefferson and file the story. In reality, it's not going to play out like that. The Lords vote isn't going to be finished before the cut-off for our evening edition, so I'll have to write two alternate versions, both lacking reaction quotes. The daylight is fading; the rain has soaked my hair and my parka smells of wet dog. To stop myself becoming too cold, I walk the car park's perimeter, trying not to stand out. I notice that the cars closest to the building have been allocated slightly larger spaces than the others, and each one bears a squat metallic sign.

At last. Something promising.

'Reserved for DIRECTOR' the first sign reads. *Yes.* I bet one of these spaces belongs to the professor, media superstar that she is. She has to be one of the most important people working in this part of the university. Ha – eleven bloody journalists and I'm the only one to think of this.

I walk along reading each sign. Head of Clinical Practice. Centre Research Manager. I check Professor Jefferson's official designation on my phone, just to be sure. Professor of Reproductive Science – it's not here. *Shit.*

But there is a space that's missing a nameplate. It's occupied by a black Golf GTI, and at the top edge of the bay there's a small square hole in the asphalt. A sign has stood here until very recently.

Of course. Professor Jefferson's research must have attracted the attention of all kinds of crazies, as well as journalists like me. The removal of the sign must be a feeble attempt at anonymity. This is her. I'm sure it is. I peer through the car window, searching for husks of personality. There's a pile of journals on the passenger seat, an empty Starbucks cup. Nothing conclusive, but it's certainly worth waiting around.

The eaves just about shelter me from the rain as I position myself in amongst a cluster of skips and check the progress of the vote with cold-stiffened fingers. It's about halfway through, with those in favour of two-mother babies currently leading by just five.

Hope. It's the most painful of emotions. Nothing I can do will influence the outcome of the vote. I daren't let myself think of Rosie: of the recently purchased pregnancy books piled up on her bedside table; of the conversation we need to have if the Lords vote no. I'll have to talk about procuring sperm, be the one to firm up plans, so she doesn't feel the need to tiptoe around my hurt.

Matthew rings me, but I ignore him – listening to him sounding off about the lateness of the copy is time I could be using to write it. I start tapping out a 350-word 'nation polarised' piece that puts Portsmouth right at the centre of the international debate. I include two different opening paragraphs, one for victory, one for defeat. And I give over most of the story to the 'for' arguments, hoping that it's too close to deadline for the sub-editors to tinker with.

Once I've filed, I go back to Twitter and click on a video link. A seething mass of protesters are blocking off the road outside Parliament. The chant they've got up, 'No to O to O!' has a rolling rhythm, and people are waving their homemade placards in time. 'Honour thy father and thy mother,' one reads. 'Vote no! Keep Pandora's box closed,' says another. The camera zooms in on a brown-haired little boy atop his father's shoulders. He's wearing some sort of bib, like they used to hand out in hockey lessons at school, and on the back, in red marker pen, someone has written 'Endangered Species'.

Knowing it'll make me angry, I nevertheless follow a link to the website of the Alliance for Natural Reproduction, the ANR, immersing myself in an alarmist article about long-term population forecasts. Part of me is intrigued: just how have they managed to convince people that a 'yes' today will lead to a steep decline in male births? It seems laughable, yet so many do believe it.

The Centre's back door opens and a tall, shaven-headed man steps outside, illuminated phone pressed to his ear. 'Mum, I can't . . . what about Justin? Can't he . . . ?'

He hasn't seen me. I scratch my head and shift my weight from foot to foot, ostentatious movement to try to make it clear that I'm not hiding. The man's too absorbed in his call to notice.

'That's not true . . . you know I . . . it's just that today's a big day. Please, Mum, be reasonable.'

I feel like an eavesdropper now. I scratch my head again. Reach into my satchel and fumble around. I even mutter to myself, 'Where did I . . . ?'

The man wheels around, then visibly jolts as he spots me. He keeps his eyes on me as he concludes his call. 'OK, Mum, alright. I'll be there in twenty. I've got to go now. Don't . . . twenty. I'll be there in twenty.' He claps his phone case shut.

'Can I help you?'

I swallow. 'I'm sorry – I didn't mean to make you jump.' My voice is higher-pitched than usual. 'I'm a reporter for the *Portsmouth Post*, but I'm not just here for work. I was hoping to grab a quick word with Professor Jefferson. Do you work here? I really admire what you guys are doing—'

'Jesus!' The man laughs to himself. 'This really isn't the place. You had me shitting a brick for a minute there. If you need information, you should call the press office. We don't give interviews to people skulking around outside.'

'I was just wondering … hoping … if not Professor Jefferson, then maybe someone on her team? Even if it's just for two minutes after the vote.'

The man tucks his phone into the inside pocket of his tan leather jacket. 'The vote's just finished.' He tries to suppress a smile.

My breath catches. Can I bear to know? I want to close my eyes, take a moment to compose myself. Please. *Please.* I swallow. 'And what did they—'

'They voted yes. Just. Squeaked it by twelve votes.'

The sound that escapes me is a kind of relieved groan. I exhale as my body folds forwards and I press my palms against my thighs.

A small group spills out into the car park, several conversations at once, laughter. 'Hey, Scott, you coming or what?' a woman shouts.

The man looks over his shoulder. 'Can't. Got something to sort out. I'll see you tomorrow.'

The chatter becomes hushed. I sense a few glances thrown back in our direction, then the sound of car ignitions.

They voted yes. A pins-and-needles sensation fans out across my body. I never get the things I long for this deeply.

'They really voted yes?' I say.

The man smiles broadly and proffers his hand, as though he's made a conscious decision to give up whatever kind of stand-off we've been having. 'Scott Bishop. I'm on Becca's research team. She's not here, by the way.' He tilts his head, gesturing to the black Golf. 'That's mine. I pinch her space when she's not in. Good powers of deduction, though. I told Estates that removing the sign wouldn't fool anyone.'

'But they voted yes? For definite?'

'They voted yes, for definite.' A benevolent smile.

'You must be so pleased. I can't believe it.'

Scott fishes his car keys from the pocket of his jeans. 'Right, well . . . '

'Wait!' He can't go – there's still so much I need to ask him. 'Tell me what happens next,' I say. 'My partner . . . we want to do it this way.'

He smiles, but his eyes dart towards his car. 'There's a long road ahead before the technique becomes available. Years of clinical trials.'

'Yeah, I understand. But what about the trial itself . . . you must need people for that, right? Volunteers? My partner and I are healthy. I mean, I've just turned thirty-four, but I look after myself. And we're local, so coming to the Centre for appointments won't be a problem.' I'm pleading. *Breathe. Be calm.*

'We'll have details up on the website within a few weeks.'

'So – I'll . . . '

'There'll be a form to fill in. Then we'll follow up with health screenings. Look, I've really got to go – but all the information you need will be put online.' He unlocks the car, then pauses before clambering in. 'You haven't told me your name.'

'Jules. Juliet Curtis.'

'Nice to meet you, Jules. And try not to worry – the application process will be open and very, very clear.' He gives me a parting wave as he drives off.

I inhale sharply as I check the BBC website on my phone. *Lords narrowly approve creation of two-mother babies.*

Rosie picks up on the first ring. 'Have you seen ...?' she begins.

'I can hardly believe it. The Lords did us proud.'

'This is such a huge breakthrough,' she cries. 'For women everywhere.'

I smile. 'It went our way. It actually went our way!'

As I pass the front of the building I see a Sky News truck and attendant crew, along with a grizzled photographer, sodden cigarette between his teeth. I ought to be kind, tell him he's not going to get the shots he wants, but I don't think I can remove the smile from my face, and I don't want him to assume I'm being smug.

I think of Rosie. Remember the electricity that flashed through her eyes the moment she realised I was relenting. She's going to be an excellent mother, and it will be my child, my own child, that benefits from her care and love. The donor, that spectre I've been fixated on ever since Crete, is finally gone.

Chapter 2

The application forms become available for download in March, three months after the Lords vote. We set aside that very evening to complete the paperwork, hoping to be one of the first couples to get our application in. It's dark by the time I arrive back in Petersfield. But since tonight is a special occasion, I swing by the Chinese restaurant and pick up Rosie's favourites of Beijing duck, chicken chop suey and special fried rice.

She meets me in the hallway wearing grey jogging bottoms and, despite the flat being warm, two thick jumpers. Rosie can't stand feeling cold; her side of the bed is always piled up with extra blankets. 'At last. I'm starving.' She whips the takeaway bag out of my hand and passes me her tablet: 'Take a look at this snidey story in the *Tribune* while I dish up.'

Returning home, the sight of our living room will often give me a little pang. It was Rosie's place originally, an inheritance from her grandmother. We'd been together just over a year when the government introduced civil partnerships as a kind of alternative to marriage for gay couples. At the time, I wondered if this was something Rosie would want. But how could I find out, without exposing my ignorance?

She pre-empted me. It had been my birthday, my twenty-fourth. After a long, twelve-hour day we took a table at Marinella's, Petersfield's best Italian restaurant. Rosie's lips were shiny with gloss, her hair piled up on her head – effort she'd made for me. I still felt little stabs of joy at such a thing being possible.

'These civil partnerships are bollocks really,' she said. 'A timid gesture. A way of letting us have our own thing, without giving us marriage.'

I sipped my wine to hide my disappointment. It wasn't that I craved a wedding day, not at all. But such a legal arrangement would have given us permanence. Recognition.

She reached down into her bag and produced a thick, somewhat rumpled document. 'But I think your name should be on the flat.'

'Rosie, I couldn't. It's yours.'

'It's both of ours. It's our home. And if anything happened to me . . . We'll need to make wills, of course. And your name will need to go on the mortgage. But it's tiny, and I won't accept any money for it.'

All around us the sound of lively conversations, laughter, clinking cutlery. I didn't trust myself to speak.

Rosie reached across and caressed my forearm. She never cared if people turned to look, never cared about disapproval. 'I guess I'm taking for granted that you plan to stay with me,' she said.

'Rosie, of course . . .'

Her eyes were alive. And there was relief there. How could she have been in any doubt?

In the years that followed, I paid for redecorating. It was

the very least I could do. The carpet is now a plush damson and you can feel the expense every time your toes sink into its woolly depths. We have a sofa and armchair in black leather and an oak fold-out dining table tucked in one corner. Every detail is cut from the imagination of a much younger me, the council-estate kid, conjuring vivid pictures of what success might look like. What it feels like against your hands, against your body as you sink into it. Its fabric-conditioner smell. And as I sit in our living room, years later, gratitude still swells within me.

On the sofa, I begin reading the *Tribune* story. I know what to expect by now, but part of me is always searching for a glimmer of support that's never there.

A world without men?
Male-free baby experiment launches recruitment drive

Experts are warning of a serious population imbalance that will weaken the UK and leave our cities vulnerable to terrorism, now that university chiefs have been given the green light to create father-free babies.

Portsmouth University today began actively signing up lesbians for the controversial fertility experiment, suggesting that the world's first two-mother babies could be born within a year.

But their artificial methods have caused several leading sociologists to raise grave concerns around the impact on our communities. Dr Jasper Kronin, who specialises in analysing long-term population trends, estimates that the number of males being born in this country could decline by as much as 18% per cent in a decade.

'This could leave the armed forces, police and fire services with a huge recruitment problem,' he says. 'It's social engineering on the scale of Nazi eugenics.'

China and the United States are amongst the 17 countries to pre-emptively ban the procedure, with many more set to follow in the coming months . . .

Rosie comes in and places a tray on my knees. 'What really pisses me off,' she says, 'besides the Nazi reference, is the way they always say "experiment" instead of "clinical trial". Even the posh papers. Every single word they use – it's like they're deliberately trying to make it sound freakish.'

'Freakish sells papers.'

'I know. But it's so mean-spirited. They should be celebrating the breakthrough.'

'Fuck 'em,' I say. 'Let's take a look at the form.'

We swipe at the tablet screen in between forkfuls. The level of medical detail the university requires is unsettling and we quickly realise the application process represents more than a night's work – it requires hours of cross-referencing, calls to our GP.

'We need to decide on the birth mother,' Rosie says.

'I always saw you being the pregnant one,' I reply. 'You know that.' We've discussed this before, but Rosie can never quite believe I'm ready to forfeit the experience of a baby in my belly.

She fights a smile. 'But are you sure, Jules? I mean, do think about this – pregnancy is part of being a mother. I don't want to deny you . . . '

I lean over and plant a kiss on her temple. 'I have thought about it. It has to be you.' I don't add that when I imagine being pregnant my skin prickles and I feel a wave of nausea.

A flush of pleasure spreads across Rosie's cheeks as she continues reading. 'Family history.' She turns to me, worry flitting across her eyes. 'Are you going to be able to complete this?'

I look down at the screen. MATERNAL SIDE. Have any family members on your MOTHER'S side suffered from any of the following conditions. Give details as required. There follows a long list, spanning the conventional heart disease and stroke, along with more obscure conditions I've never heard of, like fragile X syndrome.

Rosie watches me intently. She's far more sensitive about my mother's death than I've ever been. I lost her when I was only a baby and I simply don't have the memories to wrap in sorrow. Putting my fork down, I reach out and lay a hand on Rosie's elbow. 'It's OK. Dad will help,' I say.

We visit my father the following evening. He lives in one of the town's small pockets of council housing; a miserable line of terraces with inadequate parking and pavements bespattered with dog turds, fag ends and gum. Even now, I feel traces of the shame I experienced on bringing Rosie here for the first time. I could see how hard she was trying to keep a neutral expression, to resist the urge to wipe the rim of her cup before she took a drink.

When my father opens the door I'm hit by the earthy-sweet

stench of cannabis. 'Hello, love.' His eyes are soft with good humour. 'And Rosie too. This is a pleasant surprise.'

'Alright, Dad?' He's looking unkempt – more so than usual. For some reason he always wears proper shirts with buttons, but tonight's light blue one is crumpled and has stains under the arms. His hair, still a youthful black, is greasy and reaches his collar. I ought to come here more. I always think this, but today his lack of self-care sets off a twisting in my stomach that makes the guilt all the more intense.

I head straight for the kitchen and put the kettle on as Rosie greets my father with a hug and awkward kiss on the cheek. I love her for doing this, even though I'm burning with embarrassment at what she must smell. I've brought a couple of peppermint teabags over, and Rosie hovers next to me as I make our drinks.

When we join him in the living room, bearing our steaming cups, Dad's getting his bong ready for another go. He gestures with his eyes but I shake my head and he goes ahead himself, taking a long, rattling pull. I usher Rosie into an armchair and perch next to her. The nicotine-stained wallpaper is coming away in great swathes and mould has blackened the wall around the window. It is painful to look at, especially with Rosie beside me, and yet in a strange way this place is still home. I spent a childhood wishing I lived elsewhere, but now, when I dream, I often find myself living back here.

Dad exhales a stream of thick smoke. 'Was in the Green Dragon, lunchtime. Bill was asking after you. Said the police were round next door again.'

I nod. Petersfield may be a quaint commuter town, but it has its underbelly just like anywhere else. People I've known since childhood are often helpful, showing me the stories hiding behind floral window boxes.

There's silence. I'm sitting up far too straight, so I consciously try to loosen my shoulders. Dad will be surprised to learn I'm even considering children. We've not talked about it lately, and before, well, we always spoke of childrearing as a trap to avoid. I remember his warnings about pregnancy, which started when I was about nine. He always had such intense concentration marked on his forehead as he evoked the life of drudgery, contrasting it with what could be mine if I spurned such responsibilities. Perhaps I should have shared my change of heart with him earlier, because now, in this moment, I feel as though I've let him down.

He sprawls back on the sofa as the cannabis hits his bloodstream. 'You know Bill's Sally? Husband left her. Shacked up with a little nineteen-year-old. Rabbits, these people.'

Rosie remains silent. I take a sip of my tea and scald my tongue. This is ridiculous; he's my father. A grandchild might be just the thing to splinter his loneliness, to make him want more for himself.

'Dad, I don't know if you've been following the news – the research they've been doing into two-mother babies at Portsmouth University?' I say.

His eyes widen. I sense Rosie stiffen. I want to laugh, break the tension that stretches between us all. But I have to see this through. 'Well, there's a clinical trial. And we're going to apply, Rosie and me.'

A long pause. The lines around his mouth deepen as he stares at the wall behind us. 'A baby?' he eventually says. 'You're telling me that you want to have a baby? Now?'

His mouth stays open; I see just how grubby his teeth have become, brown stains all along the gum-line.

I nod. Rosie's breath quickens.

'We need to keep it completely confidential, of course.' I'm trying a flat, professional voice now. I'm a child again, playing at being a grown-up. I feel myself blushing at the idea of my father knowing I have such things as egg cells. 'I mean – the odds are we won't get accepted. But if we do, there'll be media interest.'

My father rotates his plastic lighter in his hand, then looks at me – only me. His gaze has no room for Rosie. 'OK. Putting your sudden need for a child to one side for a moment, why this way?' He's regained control of his expression now. It's hard, like a slammed door.

'I . . . I know it must be a surprise. But having a baby is something we—' My voice cracks.

'They don't know it's safe, though. You'll be human guinea pigs. All kinds of things could go wrong.'

Rosie clasps my hand. 'Fifteen years of work have gone into this trial. There's been careful testing.' Her voice is clipped, the Home Counties accent exaggerated – this is how she talks when she's pissed off.

He acknowledges her with the briefest of glances, then turns his attention back to me. 'But why, Jules? Don't do it just to prove you can. I'm surprised that you'd consider something risky like this when there are hundreds of kids in care all crying out for a good home. If you want a baby so much, why not adopt? Do some good.'

I look away. I've had this argument with myself so many times. A few months back I did a series of features on the foster-care crisis in Portsmouth. The tragedy of unwanted kids, bounced from one place to another. And the heroics of some of Portsmouth's poorest families, opening up their homes to squeeze in one more. I remember sounding off to Dad about it. Moaning like anything about all the spare bedrooms to be had in this snooty little town of ours, while just half an hour down the road children were suffering. Yet from the very moment of my relenting, it was always the idea of Rosie's own child that sustained me. I don't know why. It defies all logic.

I still remember the day, two months after returning from our holiday, when we learned about Portsmouth University's research. Rosie was by that stage fully immersed in compiling plans for lesbian parenthood. She'd scheduled visits to two local clinics and acquired a stack of pregnancy books.

I'd just showered and was doing emails on the sofa in knickers and my ancient Oasis T-shirt, Rosie's feet in my lap as she flicked through the *Observer.*

'Jules.' She thrust the pages at me. 'Oh my God, it's a sign. This is how we have to do it.'

We read the article together, several times. Then we turned on the television, caught the professor on breakfast news and watched footage from her lab. A voiceover introduced us to a capuchin monkey named Ella, conceived two years ago via ovum-to-ovum fertilisation. Her brown eyes seemed perplexed as they assessed the camera, and as I watched her I felt a pang of moral queasiness at the generations of lives lived in cages. But my body was filled with a tingle of anticipation. More than that – a sense of rightness. This was my reward for relenting, for putting Rosie first.

She was in tears as she took my hand. 'What an advance this is for women and reproductive choice. You'll be able to get me pregnant, Jules. I'll be able to have your baby.'

Dad picks his silver tin up off the coffee table and extracts a lump of hash the size of a matchbox. He draws his eyebrows together as he runs the lighter flame along one edge and begins preparing his bong for yet another round.

'This trial is such a good opportunity for us,' I say. 'Now the technology's here ...'

Rosie looks down at the threadbare carpet. I feel a pang of regret about bringing her. If she wasn't here I'd feel able to shout, to snatch away his tin and not hand it back until he listened. And I'd admit things: the antipathy I'd felt – and at times still do feel – towards wailing, shitting babies. The fear, always in my heart, that one day I'll end up an estate mum, that somehow it's always been my destiny. And he'd be different too. It's as though there's a tacit agreement between us, to not show our true camaraderie to other people. Not even Rosie. If I'd come here alone we would have argued, debated, perhaps had a smoke together. Maybe he'd still struggle to understand, but I'm sure I would have left knowing he supported me.

'This is about us being able to have a baby just like any other couple,' Rosie says. 'Our baby – half me, half Jules.' She turns to me. 'The forms ...'

I quickly rummage in my satchel for the printouts. My dead mother's health is a topic that requires delicate handling. I need to regain control of the conversation. 'Dad, the reason we're telling you about this now is because we need help with the application. They need a full medical history – information on both parents.'

My father closes his eyes for a moment, pain etched across his face. I feel a twist of compassion. It's been more than three decades since my mother was hit by a car, but his sense of loss is fresh and self-renewing.

'If you could just take a look . . . ' I go over and sit next to him. Bong breath and stale sweat; it's an effort not to wince. I try not to feel shame at Rosie's gaze, soft with pity. How very different these two loved ones of mine are. Yet both are so essential.

'We need to know if there are any conditions . . . ' I feel as though I'm punishing him.

He turns to me, eyes shining – from embryonic tears or cannabis, I can't tell. 'I'll help you. I'll go through the forms, give you all the details I can remember, of course I will. But Jules . . . think again, please. I'm all for scientific progress, but this . . . this is going so far off course. I mean – two women? No man involved at all?'

'Dad—'

'I can see you getting worked up over every cough, every childhood bug. You'll always be asking yourself: is this normal, or is it the first sign of some freakish new disease? The stress—'

'Dad, please—'

'And for what, Jules? For pride? Raising a child is what makes it yours. All this biological nonsense is irrelevant.'

Rosie is silent, her jaw clenched. I go back to her and put an arm around her waist.

'Well, I'm sorry you feel like that.' My voice is cold.

'Neil, this would be your grandchild. You understand that, right?' Rosie's throat catches, tears are close. 'Half of Jules's DNA – half of what makes Jules *Jules*. No different from a child she might have had with a man. Aren't you excited by that? A biological grandchild?'

He looks at Rosie for a brief moment, then turns back to me, slowly shaking his head. 'Jules, your mother wanted so much for you. She wanted more than anything for you to leave this estate and never come back. I swear to you. She used to give you pep talks while you were in your cot. "My daughter's going to have wings," that's what she used to say. Wings.'

As I look into my father's eyes, I'm able to imagine it, to hear my mother's long-silent voice. There's a heavy feeling in my chest, not loss exactly, but sadness. Mourning for possibilities never realised, for the life in which my father could have been happy. 'I'll pop in and pick the form up tomorrow, if that's OK.'

Rosie cuts in: 'But Jules has left this estate. I don't . . . what are you trying to imply?'

'Left the estate in body, but not in spirit.' He gives me a sad smile. 'Churning out kids, that's all the young girls here aspire to. Burgers and chips for dinner. Daytime TV. I thought you were different, Jules. I thought there was so much more you wanted.' He bows his head, scratches at his stubble.

Is this what he really thinks? He's shocked. Stoned. I mustn't take anything he says personally – I should know that by now. If I'd just prepared him, mentioned a few months back that we were looking into having a child. But I didn't. Some part of me wanted to postpone talking about it because

I knew he'd be upset. I'm showing him that I no longer hold his version of the world as sacrosanct. I'm rejecting the childhood lessons he took such pains over.

Rosie's face is white. 'Why would you . . . ? Jules is—'

'I'll swing by after work tomorrow to collect the forms.' I sound more composed than I feel as I sling my satchel over my shoulder. 'Thanks for helping us out.'

I usher Rosie out into the chilly March evening. She's shaking her head. 'I'm so sorry, Jules. I didn't mean to . . .'

'It's taken him by surprise,' I say. 'He'll come 'round.' I unlock the car but Rosie makes no move to get in.

'But to bring up your mum like that,' she says. 'And I still don't get what he's trying to say. You're a successful reporter – having a baby won't take that away.'

'I don't think—'

'And it certainly won't force you to come and live here again.'

My face feels hot. Something about the way Rosie said *here*, disgust inflecting her voice. She considers herself a liberal, but I always notice the way she flinches if anyone from my childhood stops me in the street to say hello, or to tell me about some parking dispute in the hope that the *Post* might cover it. I see her eyes widen as she takes in tattoos, beer bellies and bad dye jobs. This estate is in my bones, and while I may squirm with shame at times, I'll never disown it.

'He won't tell anyone, will he?' Rosie's voice is quiet, almost a whisper.

'God no!' I swallow. My flash of pique is gone and I'm on Rosie's side again. I feel her outrage on my behalf and I'm glad for it. 'He didn't handle it very well, but come on: he's my dad. I should have paved the way better. We've thrust this on him completely out of the blue.'

Rosie wraps her arm around my middle and gives me a little squeeze before we get into my Ford Fiesta. I've let her down. Until now the process has been infused with excitement and the prospect of against-all-odds victories. Perhaps it was inevitable that this happy stage would end, to be replaced by far more complex emotions. But I can't help feeling disappointed that my own father was the one to bring about the change.

Chapter 3

In May, with the arrival of the first cloudless days, we're invited to attend a selection day at the Centre for Reproductive Medicine. Rosie picks out the clothes I wear–blue skinny jeans and my newest black jacket. She insists on me abandoning my usual boots in favour of her red ballet pumps, which are now chafing my heels. And she makes up my face, masking the dark circles under my eyes with concealer, combating my pallor with a little blusher.

The waiting area is harshly lit, with white-tiled walls and rows of orange plastic chairs bolted to the floor. There's a medical tang to the air, the burning taste of antibacterial gel against my tongue. Rosie holds herself awkwardly, arms folded, back stooped. Her eyes dart around the interior, where five other couples wait. I should feel solidarity, sisterhood, but Rosie's nerves induce a new sense of competitiveness. I can't help estimating my rivals' body mass indices; speculating on the condition of their eggs. Another attendee catches my eye: she's Chinese, her black hair worn in a sleek bob. Her mouth twitches and there's an ironic glint in her eyes as she notices me observing her. I don't know whether or not to smile, so I quickly look away.

At last, a tall man in a lab coat arrives. It's Scott Bishop, the guy I saw in the car park on the day of the Lords vote. He gives me a friendly grin of recognition as he calls out names from a clipboard and I feel strangely elated, as though having met him somehow gives us a head start.

After a short briefing we're separated off in our pairs, with half the group sent for interviews, the other half assigned researchers for the medical. It probably isn't deliberate, but Rosie and I end up with Scott.

We stand against a height chart. We take off our shoes and are weighed. Callipers pinch our back fat. The worst part is the vaginal ultrasound. I go first, refusing to wince as the probe is inserted. It feels cold and intrusively solid. I'm breathing deep abdominal breaths, trying to relax, but my muscles tighten in an attempt to bar entry. I'm strangely bothered by the paper towel Scott's placed over my pubic hair, a laughable attempt to protect my modesty as I splay my legs.

When it's Rosie's turn to be probed I feel an unexpected enthusiasm for the pictures on the screen, staring at the pulsing caverns within her that have remained unknown to me even after all this time. She inhales sharply and I give her hand a sympathetic squeeze. We're mere animals in this room. Biological beings like Ella, the monkey which featured in the breakfast news report. Will our bodies be good enough? I think of my morning runs before work, the low-fat, mostly vegetarian meals I cook in big batches for the freezer. I'm not in my twenties any more, but I've tried so hard to stay healthy.

At lunchtime, we are ushered into the boardroom. We're unnaturally still, looking away in embarrassment each time we meet the gaze of a potential competitor. Up until now the day has been disarmingly normal. Not that having my vagina probed is normal, but there's been an efficiency to the medical, a routine-ness, as though we're merely replicating what heterosexual women go through in IVF. But as we gather in the boardroom, the significance of today becomes clear. Aside from Scott, there are no men present. We're here to make babies without men. This is Dolly the sheep territory – a whole new frontier – and Rosie and I are lucky enough to be part of it.

I feel queasy as I contemplate the buffet spread in front of us: plastic trays of sandwiches and slices of fruit; crisps in wicker baskets. The sandwich I sample is soggy with mayonnaise and I have to fight my gag reflex to swallow it down.

Whispered conversations stop as Professor Jefferson arrives, wearing an expensive-looking black trouser suit teamed with a red shirt and matching lipstick. 'Hello everyone,' she says. 'My name's Becca and I'm overseeing the clinical trial. We're holding several of these information days. As well as contributing to the screening process, they're designed to familiarise you with the steps involved in ovum-to-ovum fertilisation.'

There's a tautness to the atmosphere, as though we're all afraid of doing something wrong, of inadvertently revealing that we're not quite worthy of a place. I feel the heat of Rosie's thigh against my own and I take her hand underneath the table. She squeezes mine tightly, her palm hot.

'This is an exciting moment,' the professor – Becca – says. 'We've seen ovum-to-ovum fertilisation work time and again in animals. And our work with human cells has been overwhelmingly positive. Everything we've done here, over the last fifteen years, makes me confident that we'll soon be welcoming two-mother babies into the world.

'It's going to be tough. I'm sure you've all seen the tabloid coverage and will know that ovum-to-ovum fertilisation – or o-o, as they're calling it – has its vocal opponents. But what I hope to do today is equip you with the facts and separate the science from the speculation.'

She connects her laptop to a projector and images of single egg cells appear on the screen at the front of the room. She then shows us fused versions, followed by more substantial clumps of cells. A woman with short purple hair holds her phone aloft. 'Do you mind if I . . . ?'

'Of course, no problem. These images were all taken in the lab here – they're human cells, but up until the Lords vote we weren't allowed to let them develop beyond fourteen days.'

The cell clumps on the screen are indistinguishable from the images in Rosie's pregnancy handbooks. I feel strangely intimidated by Becca's achievement; she's created life in a whole new way, evolved the natural order. What might that feel like: knowing that your life matters in a way that few people's really does, that people hundreds of years from now might live differently because of you?

Becca works her way through the slides, talking us through the practicalities. How we'll be trained to inject each other with ovary-stimulating hormones. Check-ups and scans every two weeks. An uncomfortable procedure called egg harvesting. As she describes the fertilisation process – how the nucleus from one egg is extracted and injected into the other – a burst of singing floats through the room. It's faint, but definite. Hymn-like. The women around the table exchange glances, but Becca carries on, unfazed. 'So – I'm sure you've all got plenty of questions,' she concludes. 'Ask away.'

The purple-haired woman raises her hand. 'What are the risks?'

Becca presses her lips together and her eyes flit to the window. 'A very difficult question to answer,' she says. 'We've raised generations of healthy mice and monkeys, indistin-guishable from control populations.'

The Lord's my shepherd ... The singing is louder now. Purple Hair turns around and stares at the window, her fore-head creased.

Becca remains calm. 'But this will be the first time we implant human embryos. We've done everything in our power to ensure that the pregnancies and babies will be healthy. All our research indicates that we'll have a success rate very similar to convential IVF, but we're going into uncharted territory – I can't make promises.'

'But the papers are saying that the babies might have new genetic diseases,' the woman counters, earning herself a hos-tile glance or two from the other couples at the table.

'There's been a lot of speculation about that, much of it based on a misconception that our cellular fusion technique alters the DNA of the egg cells we use,' Becca says. 'I can tell you with one hundred per cent clarity that it does not. Whatever the tabloids say, this isn't genetic modification. We're not creating glow-in-the-dark babies.'

A few women, me included, titter for solidarity's sake. I'm remembering a front cover from the *Daily Sketch*: Becca's face and the word 'Frankenmum'.

'Seriously, though,' Becca adds, 'the Alliance for Natural

Reproduction have a roster of so-called experts all too willing to provide journalists with scary quotes. But I'd advise all of you, next time there's a worrying claim in the papers, to take a look at the credentials of the person making it. Are they employed by a university, have they been published in one of the major journals? If not, then you have to ask yourself what makes them qualified to comment. What data are they basing their opinions on?'

A different woman raises her hand. 'Why did they ban it in the States?'

'I'm not an expert in US health policy,' Becca says. 'But from what I gather, the opposition seems to be based around ideological concerns rather than anything to do with the science.'

The singing outside reaches a soaring chorus. I recognise the trilling of old ladies. Becca asks whether there are further questions, and clarifies a few elements around monitoring and medical care for trial participants. Then she takes a seat and Scott stands to address us. 'OK, so for those of you who had your medicals this morning, the final part of your day will involve individual meetings with members of our counselling team – your time slots can be found in your packs.

'You'll be collected for your interviews from here, while the other group goes off to have their medicals. Treat this room as a kind of base if you like, or feel free to nip out and get some fresh air. Although, by the sounds of it, we have a few of our regular protesters outside. Nothing to worry about. They turn up for a sing-song a couple of times a week – they probably haven't got a clue that we're doing screenings today.'

Purple Hair and her partner have the first appointments

with the counsellors, so Becca leads them away. There's a pause. An awkward stretching of legs, tentative glances around the room. Then Rosie and I join the surge of women making for the window. Rather than affording a view of the singing protesters, it looks out over the car park.

The woman I noticed in the lobby puts a hand on my shoulder. 'Let's go out the front. See if we can take a peek,' she says.

Rosie and I make quick introductions as we go down the stairs. The first woman is Hong Shu and her fresh-faced partner is Anita.

The singing is louder down in the foyer. *All things bright and beautiful.* Deeper tenors join the trilling. There must be a sizeable group. I'm tempted to go back, but Hong Shu is striding purposefully, Rosie right behind her.

'They're here because of us?' Anita's voice is shaky.

'Wait,' I say. 'Let's not confront them. If we go out the back of the building and walk round, we'll blend in while we take a look.'

Inadvertently, I've placed myself at the head of the group, showing them all out into the car park where I met Scott on the day of the vote, then around the side of the clinic. Pigeons coo from the guttering and I see that there are now security cameras on the roof.

There's what looks like a small encampment outside the Centre's glass doors, blocking off the pavement. Clusters of onlookers slow their pace to watch what's going on. There must be around fifty singers, their hymn reaching its soaring climax. A banner reads 'Honouring God's way. Trusting in Him to create our children'. In the corner of the fabric, in the now-familiar blue lettering, is the logo of the Alliance for Natural Reproduction. A white-haired woman, ivory blouse beautifully ironed and tucked into a tweed skirt, thrusts leaflets into the hands of passers-by. Even though it's May and the afternoon sun is bright, the protesters have lined the kerb with tea-light candles. A cheap attempt at spirituality.

This whole set-up is laughable; I should be cackling with derision. That's what these people deserve. And yet – their faces, the seriousness in their eyes – this isn't a social activity, simply capitalising on the boredom of a few pensioners. These people really believe that ovum-to-ovum fertilisation should be banned. They care enough to come here and make a spectacle. I've been reading about the opposition for months, but seeing the certainty etched upon these people's faces makes it real for the first time.

The hymn ends and a thin man with wispy hair addresses the crowd, his voice surprisingly deep and resonant. 'Join us in prayer.' The group bow their heads. A couple of teenage boys, in low-slung jeans and baseball caps, erupt into laughter as they pass by. I'm glad. *Please, let everyone mock these protesters, let them be laughed at, scorned.* Rosie clutches my arm. I turn to her, expecting to see hurt, but instead her eyes flash with anger.

'O Lord, we pray that You guide those involved in this terrible experiment back to the true path. We pray for Your mercy towards those who seek what is only Thine to give . . . ' A ripple of recognition makes its way through the group as one by one its members look up and see us watching them. Coming from around the back of the building has made no difference; it's obvious who we are.

For a moment no one speaks. I feel a flicker of fear at being part of the smaller group.

'Bigots!' Hong Shu calls out.

The protesters are uncertain. They've not planned for a confrontation; I see this in their darting eyes, their stiff shoulders.

Rosie strides towards them. I reach out to restrain her, but she's gone, Hong Shu following with a whoop of glee. There's a cluster of onlookers on the opposite pavement. Mobile phones are held aloft, snapping Hong Shu and Rosie as they approach the encampment. 'Fucking dykes!' someone bellows.

'I don't understand how you can be against more choices for women,' Rosie is saying. She's gone straight for the leader. His expression is disdainful as he assesses her, and it's this, directed at Rosie, that lifts me out of my strange bewilderment. If he touches her, I'll punch him.

'The Bible tells us—'

'Isn't loving a child the most important thing?' Rosie shouts. 'You're fighting the wrong people. Can't you see . . .'

The rest of the exchange is lost. There's shouting on both sides, and from passers-by, but we're outnumbered and quickly surrounded. An elderly woman tugs at my jacket. 'I'll pray for you,' she proclaims. I try to shake her off, but her grip is surprisingly strong. I cannot hit a pensioner – she's put me in an impossible position. I prise her fingers away, becoming less and less gentle as she fumbles and snatches. I try to push out of the crowd. I'm finding it hard to breathe. I can't see Rosie. Someone could have called the *Post* by now. This whole exchange could be uploaded to YouTube in just a few minutes' time.

I spot Rosie's hair and push through to reach her, taking her by the arm and ushering us both back inside the Centre. Her face is pink and she walks backwards, shouting over my shoulder: '... why won't you listen? It's not as simple as ...'

We're inside. I flash my visitor's badge at the two security men who've gathered by the door. The one closest to me is middle-aged, with a rotund belly and a moustache. He looks amused at what he's seeing, only half succeeding in holding down a snicker. My heart thumps as I lead Rosie deeper into the building. The contorted faces of the protesters, eyes glowing with the certainty of their own truth, continue to flash before me. We could have been hurt. And if we're accepted, will there be demos like this all the time? Will we have to fight our way past protesters to get to each and every appointment?

'Jules – what are you doing?'

'We've got our counsellor meetings in a bit. We mustn't get all riled up.'

'But we can't leave Anita and Hong Shu.'

'Hopefully they'll come to their senses and make their way back in too. Fuck.' My legs feel weak. Silly really, a group of churchy-types and their hymn books, that's all it was. But something about their conviction, their absolute belief that what we're doing is wrong, unnerves me.

Rosie puts a hand on my shoulder, forcing me to stop walking and look at her. 'We can't let attitudes like that go unchallenged, Jules. If we do, we become complicit.'

She believes that she can reason with people, change minds. I love her for it, but people aren't as rational and good-natured as she persists in believing. I look away, wanting nothing more than to close my eyes in a quiet corner. My mind is spitting out images of repercussions, of righteous expressions and placards, of a pregant Rosie being jostled.

'Jules? Are you OK? I should have ... that was scary.' She holds me and I let my body slowly loosen.

Hong Shu and Anita join us, breathless. Anita looks like she's fighting tears. 'They hate us,' she says. 'All we want to do is have a baby together.'

Rosie pulls her into a hug. 'Don't let them get to you. They're just small-minded busybodies who'd rather oppose progress than question their own values.'

'We should swap numbers,' Hong Shu says. 'If we're accepted we're going to need all the buddies we can get. Looks like we're walking into a right shitstorm.'

'Fantastic idea.' Rosie releases Anita and takes out her phone, and we each spend a moment going through the ritual of inputting new contacts. I won't be able to tell my friends at work what I've just been through, I realise. If we're accepted, these strangers will be the only people I can turn to.

Chapter 4

It's a Saturday when the letter comes, a rare weekend when both of us are off work. Rosie's in the living room with her friend Anthony, binge-watching episodes of some reality show while I cook a curry for lunch. When I hear the letterbox clang I go out into the hallway and spot the university logo on the envelope. There's a squeal of laughter from the living room. I'm tempted to rip it open now, alone, to process our fate privately. But Rosie will be hurt if I don't go and get her.

I pick the letter up and hold it to the shaft of light that comes through the front door's glass pane. The envelope is thick and brown: no possibility of a sneak preview.

With heavy legs I approach the living room. Rejection will ruin this weekend, this month, this whole summer. We'll have to put our disappointment to one side as we start making plans for alternative conception routes. And, later, we'll have to watch the news of two-mother pregnancies emerging in the media, trying to feel happiness for the women involved. Other women. Younger, healthier women. I peer around the door. 'Rosie?'

In our cramped kitchen – fragrant from the crushed

cardamom pods I've just added to the curry – I show her the envelope.

'Shouldn't we wait, open it after Anthony's gone?' I say.

'No. I can't bear to wait. And we said we'd tell Anthony if we got a place.'

'Well, we didn't quite agree . . . I mean, I know you're close, but it's not a confidence we can take lightly . . . '

She shoots me a frustrated glance and takes the letter from my hand. This is my news too – what makes her think that she can dictate the terms? I'm about to snatch the letter back, to say as much, but I notice the sheen of tears coating her eyes, the worry lines on her forehead. Anthony is important to her.

'Alright, then.' I put my arm around her waist. 'But just Anthony and our parents. No one else.'

She tears the envelope open and unfolds several sheets of thick letterhead with trembling fingers.

. . . delighted to inform you that your application has been successful. Please call the research team as soon as possible to schedule your Conception Planning Meeting . . .

We stare at the letter, both of us silent. I reread the whole thing several times – just to be certain. The envelope also contains a lengthy consent form, which falls to the floor as Rosie flings her arms into the air and screams. She turns to me and we embrace, we sway side to side. We're in. We are going to make a baby together – Rosie and me.

'I can't believe it.' Her voice is choked.

She looks over to the kitchen door and we pull apart. I follow her gaze and see Anthony leaning against the doorframe. He's thirty, like Rosie, but he still dresses like a teenager, in skater shorts that are constantly slipping halfway

down his arse. His hair is longish, always carefully dishevelled. 'What did I miss?' he says.

Rosie flies at him and envelops him in a hug. 'Oh Anthony,'
she cries. 'We've got exciting news and I'm so glad you're
going to be the first to hear it. We're going to have a baby!'

'What? You mean ... you're pregnant?' His brow
is furrowed.

My stomach lurches. Telling him is a mistake. I should
have intervened. Although I've tried my hardest to like him,
Anthony has never seemed like a fully grown-up person to
me. He still lives with his mother, never sticks at a job for
longer than three months.

'Not yet – but soon, I hope.' Rosie wipes her eyes with her
sleeve. 'We've got a place on Portsmouth Uni's clinical trial.
We're going to be one of the first couples to try ovum-to-
ovum fertilisation. Us. Can you believe it?'

'You can't tell anyone,' I say. 'We're keeping the circle of
people who know really small. It's literally just going to be
you and our parents. We can't have the press getting hold of
our names.'

Anthony stares at Rosie, his eyes wide, as though he feels
wounded in some way. 'You never told me you were thinking of this.'

Rosie bites her lip.

When she doesn't respond, he steps in closer. I feel my
body tense, but his voice remains gentle. 'Is it even right? I
mean, no men? What's it going to do to the world?'

'Anthony ...' Rosie places a hand on his arm.

'I've been reading about it – it's going to throw the population off balance. Make men a minority.'

'That's bollocks,' I say. 'Most of the population will carry on making babies the old-fashioned way.'

'And think of your dad, Rosie. Everything he's done for you. How he worships the ground you walk on. Saying babies don't need fathers is a slap in the face to him and men like him. It . . . it undermines everything.'

Rosie looks down at the floor tiles. 'Ant, even if we used donor sperm the baby would still be raised without a father. Our baby was always going to have two mothers – she or he was always going to be mine and Jules's.'

He turns to face me, his face flushed. 'How could you involve her in something like this? They don't know it's safe.'

'Now hold on,' I say. 'We've made an informed choice – don't be thinking you're the expert because you've read a few newspaper headlines.'

But he doesn't hear me. He's turned back to Rosie, placed his hands on her shoulders. The intensity makes me uncomfortable. In his eyes I'm nothing more than a twelve-year aberration. It's his own relationship with Rosie that's imbued with real permanence.

'Rosie.' His voice is tender. 'You're my best friend. I thought you'd at least talk to me about it. Didn't you owe me that?'

'It's perfectly safe, Anthony. And it's the right thing to do. How could I use donor sperm, knowing there was a way I could be having Jules's baby? This is such an important breakthrough for women – we have to be part of it.' Her voice judders – her happy tears have become tragic. I screw my hands into fists, draw myself up tall. We need Anthony gone; to rewind the clock, revert to our shrieking, jumping celebration.

He sighs and reaches up to adjust the stud in his ear. He's

got one of those silly ones, designed to create a giant hole in the earlobe. 'They're saying that the children are more likely to have genetic diseases. And they don't know what might happen to the women involved – you could be seriously ill. Damaged, even. You could miscarry. Imagine that, Rosie: imagine how upset you'll be.'

I inhale sharply. Rosie rests a hand against the small of my back as she faces her friend. 'Whoa. That's not nice. I don't need you quoting tabloid rubbish at me.'

'Rosie—'

She raises her palm. 'Stop. This is a happy day and you're ruining it. I think you'd better go.'

'Rosie – please.'

'No. Go. You're welcome back any time, but I'm not prepared to listen to any speculation about my baby's health. Remember that. Not now, not later on.'

'Rosie—'

'Jules and I have researched this thoroughly, and we know it's what we want.'

Anthony turns and leaves the room, head bowed. Rosie and I silently watch him fumble with his shoes, waiting to attempt a resurrection of our celebrations after he's gone.

But as he closes our front door behind him the atmosphere in our flat remains oppressive. Rosie leans into me and I stroke her hair, waiting for her tears to pass. I push and goad with my mind, willing the exhilaration back, but it's a shy animal, it won't be forced.

In the evening we head to Rosie's parents' house. Rosie believes that her mother, while she does a good job of hiding it, secretly dislikes the fact that she's gay. But I've never been convinced, and the way Elaine has eagerly followed the progress of o-o fertilisation makes it hard to believe. Even before the bill went through Parliament she knew that we'd be excited by the possibility. She questioned her GP, created a scrapbook of all the non-negative broadsheet coverage. When Rosie and I told her we were applying there had been tears in her eyes. Such a contrast to my father's stoned disappointment.

Elaine lives with Michael, Rosie's father, in a four-bedroom detached on one of Petersfield's newer private estates. Born in the age of development greed, the area is high density with tiny gardens and no pavements. But once you step inside the Barcombe home, all is spacious and tasteful – wood flooring, a refreshing lack of clutter, décor that's updated every three years or so to reflect whatever trends are appearing in the interiors magazines. Elaine always seems happiest when she's in her dungarees, her grey bob wrapped in a bandana, some new project on the go.

'Hello, loves,' Elaine says as she ushers us in. 'What a wonderful surprise.'

Michael is in the living room, newspaper spread across his knees, idly stroking Loren, their white Persian cat, who sits purring on a sofa cushion. He wears reading glasses with thick black rims and a khaki cardigan.

Rosie's face glows as she takes a seat on the cream sofa that looks out over the garden. I sense the battle within her – she wants to shout out our news, but there's another part of her that relishes the staging, that's determined to wait until her mother's finished sorting drinks for everyone and is settled in her armchair. When that moment comes she bounds up from the sofa: 'Portsmouth Uni accepted us. We got a place on the trial!'

Elaine puts a hand to her chest for a moment, then she's up too. Mother and daughter, hugging. 'Oh, I knew they would, I knew it. My girl – a baby. Oh, Jules, come here.'

I join the tangle, as does Michael. I'm not much of a hugger as a rule, but the Barcombes always make such a point of including me. These moments, when they show me they regard me as part of their family, never fail to give me a flush of pleasure.

The cat surveys us all with cold green eyes as Elaine dabs at her cheeks. 'Mikey – we're going to be grandparents. Can you believe it? Did they tell you when? I hope they don't make you wait too long.'

'We need to book a follow-up appointment,' Rosie says, 'but the plan is to get started straight away.'

We return to our seats. Michael is trying to maintain an upright, dignified bearing, but he keeps breaking into a smile. He looks so grandfatherly already, with his iron-grey hair, still thick, and the benevolent smile lines that make his whole face twinkle with goodwill.

'To tell you the truth, we were worried,' Michael says. 'We saw the piece in today's *Herald* and we supposed you must have heard already.'

Elaine chips in: 'I wanted to call, but your dad said you'd tell us in your own good time. If it was bad news . . . but it wasn't. Tell you what, I've got a bottle of champagne in the cupboard – I'm going to go and put it in the freezer, ready for a toast.'

'They might not be able to drink it, 'Laine. What do you say, girls? You allowed a drink, or have you got to be strict about that kind of thing from now on?' Michael's eyes glint – I can tell that he quite fancies a glass himself. But Elaine looks dismayed, as though she's just suggested something that will undo our success. 'Goodness, I didn't even think . . .'

'Well,' I say, 'a glass probably wouldn't hurt . . .' I look at Rosie.

'No,' she says. 'We mustn't. From now on I'm going to be like Jules: a hundred per cent healthy.'

'Of course,' Elaine says. 'That's very sensible.' She hurries back to her seat, folds her hands in her lap.

'What were you saying about the *Herald*?' I ask.

'Oh? You haven't seen it? Show them, Mikey. We were ever so upset. I don't think reporters should be allowed to do that sort of thing. Nothing personal, Jules – I know you'd never dream of being a spy like that.'

'A spy?' Rosie's eyes widen.

Michael rustles through the paper, proffering it to us open at a double-page spread. There's a large photo of two women wearing corporate-looking dresses and standing back to back, beaming at the camera. They look vaguely familiar.

Rosie gasps. I realise: it's Purple Hair and her partner, from the selection day. I am looking at a feature by Angela Simmons of the *Herald*. She'd hired an actress and they'd posed as a lesbian couple, submitting a false application to gain insight into the inner workings of the clinical trial.

'How could they?' Rosie looks at me, aghast.

Elaine bites her lip – I see Michael shoot his wife a worried glance. 'It's alright,' he says to the cat, stroking it behind the ears.

My face is hot as I try to take in the words.

How ranting about men secured my place on two-mother baby experiment

I meet Cheryl Bradley, the woman who is to play my lover, for a single hour ahead of our appointment at Portsmouth's Centre for Reproductive Medicine. Our 'relationship' is crudely summarised on a few index cards and we both hurry to memorise our fake milestones. We're intentionally provocative, keen to see just what vetting the university is putting in place – after all, the women in this trial will be world firsts. How do you assess whether someone is ready for that?

Our memorisation skills are sorely tested as we each attend interviews with the counsellors attached to the trial. I tell the woman assessing me that Cheryl and I have only been together for a year. That we're not sure about marriage, but we want to go ahead and have a child for the simple reason that we're 'not getting any younger'. I expect to be pressed on this point, but the counsellor appears to accept my lack of commitment without batting an eyelid, as though wishing to fuse your eggs with those of a woman you're casually dating is the most natural thing in the world.

When asked why I wish to participate in the trial, I tell my interviewer that I'm a feminist and that part of me dreams of an all-female society. I expect to be shown the door at this point – this sounds far-fetched and perhaps even a little unhinged to my own ears. But my questioner simply nods and moves on.

I'm going to skip ahead at this point and tell you

that after completing the vetting process (a process that unfortunately involved a vaginal probe – we'll come to that later), I was accepted. Let's just pause for a moment and consider what this means: the university is recruiting those who profess to dream of a man-free world, then equipping them with the means to make it happen.

'This is awful.' Rosie is shaking her head. I break away from the article – the descriptions of tests, speculation around how much money it must have all cost – and place a hand between her shoulder blades. Her eyes are dry, but there's a deadness to them, a forlorn expression I've never seen before.

Angela Simmons of the *Herald* – I look at her picture again. Her purple hair is styled differently, carefully blow-dried, and there's a professional polish to her make-up and clothes. She must have consciously tried to butch herself up for the information day. She looks younger than me, and she has a staff job on one of the broadsheets. It shouldn't matter, but it intensifies the anger.

I close my eyes. Surely the university wouldn't rescind our acceptance? They wouldn't be shaken enough to reconsider their processes? This is what the *Herald* is calling for: tighter oversight, a review of who's already been accepted. And yet the whole premise of the article is so ridiculous: can they really expect their readers to believe that there's some sort of lesbian operation at work, a masterplan to eliminate the male of the species?

'It's OK,' I tell Rosie. 'I'm sure this won't change anything for us.'

'But you poor things,' Elaine says. 'That journalist can't have any kind of a conscience. And what were the university thinking, accepting them?'

I sigh and place the newspaper down on the coffee table. 'We only have this one version of events. I don't believe for a minute that all the reporter did was rant about men. It was probably a very deliberate trap. One or two controversial statements buried in a very reasonable-sounding interview.' I find myself becoming even more angry. The planning it must have taken. The concerted effort put into ridiculing the trial that has given Rosie and me so much to hope for.

'You should write an article in response,' Rosie says. 'Show the world that we're just a normal couple. Set nights for grocery shopping. Watching TV on the sofa. Getting on with our own lives rather than hatching plans for a woman-only utopia.'

'What a wonderful idea,' Elaine says. 'Answer them back, Jules. You're so good with words.'

I look at Angela Simmons's smiling face and fresh rage boils up through me. How satisfying it would be to demolish her arguments. But at what cost? 'No,' I say. 'We need to be anonymous for as long as possible. If the media gets our names, there'll be a press pack outside our front door while we're going through the treatment. And it'll be a hundred times worse if Rosie goes on to become pregnant. The coverage will get really personal – they won't just be talking about the trial any more, they'll be talking about *our* baby, speculating on what might be wrong with it.'

Everyone is quiet. I look out across the garden, where a blackbird is tugging a worm from the lawn. In so many ways it would be easier to follow the donor path that lesbian mums have been taking for years. There would be no lies to tell, no terror of media discovery. I can't help thinking that a better lover would say *do it*. Take the simple option. *Have your baby with a stranger's sperm, and I will do my best to love it as if it were my own.*

But I imagine being told *he looks like you*, and flushing crimson, unsure whether to explain or let it pass. I see myself looking on as Rosie holds her baby, wondering whether whatever I'm feeling is normal, never being sure. And I feel my future dismay at the confused eyes of our child – always a little boy in these donor scenarios, for some reason – as he asks about his father. How will that not wound? How could I cope with this unknown man as a continued presence in my life? A hero figure. Someone who has a stronger claim than I do to Rosie's child. I want to believe I would do it for love. And I would have, had ovum-to-ovum fertilisation not been legalised. But now this option is available to us, anything else would feel like second best.

Chapter 5

It's a summer of hormone injections, of purple bruises spreading across my mid-section, of having to get by on just one coffee a day. They take seven eggs from me and twelve from Rosie; the sedative we're given prompts sprawling daydreams, but fails to mask the snipping sensation deep inside my body. Anita and Hong Shu's egg-harvesting is on the same day, and later the four of us sit in a café, snorting over the indignity of splayed legs and paper towels.

Rosie and I circle the day we're due to take the pregnancy test on the calendar in our kitchen. There's an author event at the bookshop where Rosie works that evening, so we agree to do it afterwards, last thing at night, in case the extra hours make a difference. Rosie's made a mental note to not drink too much water in the lead-up, adamant that her urine needs to be extra-concentrated if she's to believe the results.

Even though I promise myself I won't, my mind conjures snapshots of Rosie with our baby. Her peaceful expression as she holds a tiny bundle to her breast. Her soft singing, the usual combination of misheard pop lyrics and erratic humming. I imagine her chattering away as she pushes a pram, a tiny pair of eyes looking up at her. And I feel such a stab of emotion, as though her loving that tiny bundle somehow amplifies what she feels for me.

On the circled day, as the time for heading home from work approaches, my fingers are clattering across my keyboard in a desperate attempt to finish up the crime news in briefs. I keep looking over to the far end of the newsroom, where the section editors are sitting in a tight formation. Thankfully Matthew looks occupied – he seems to love nothing more than coming over with a surprise urgent assignment, just as someone is packing up their things.

But it's my mate Tom who approaches as I'm close to finishing. He perches on the edge of my desk. Even though he's in his late twenties, he gives the impression of having had a recent growth spurt that he's yet to fill out. He has chin-length hair, and large hazel eyes that make him appear perpetually startled.

'Early warning,' he says. 'The *Post*'s backing Richard Prior and going blue ribbon. Thought I'd get in and tell you before wank-chops over there.' He tilts his head in Matthew's direction.

Richard Prior is the Tory candidate for Portsmouth South's upcoming by-election. He's a vociferous campaigner for the Alliance for Natural Reproduction, and since Father's Day he's been encouraging Portsmouth residents to wear blue ribbons, to 'protect the next generation of baby boys'.

I roll my eyes. 'Well, got to resist the lesbian take-over, I guess.'

'Seriously, though,' Tom says, 'what's your take on the uni's research? It's weird, right? Creating a way to bypass men entirely? I guess I better pack away the old todger. There's probably going to be a lack of demand.'

I laugh. 'Oh, Tom, please. Surely none of your nineteen-year-old paramours are thinking of babies. Have some confidence in yourself and your abilities.'

He smirks. We both glance towards the editors' section. A tic developed by all the *Post*'s reporters.

'Did you see that piece in the *Guardian*?' Tom asks. 'One of their columnists says she's considering having a baby with a female friend. She had this whole thing about how the women in her circle are more likely to make committed parents than any of the men she's been with. And she's not even gay.'

I smile to mask a pang of remorse. Tom may be a hard-drinking Casanova-type, but he's a real friend: hiding my own involvement in the trial feels disloyal. 'It doesn't surprise me that the *Post*'s getting on the bandwagon,' I say. 'Prior's been clever – I heard him on the radio this morning, making out that the university's research funding is leaching money from local hospitals. The interviewer took everything he said at face value.'

Tom snorts. 'Well, I better let you get on. And – oh – be warned: I think Matthew actually expects us to wear those blue ribbon things when we're out and about.'

I should be thinking ahead to tonight, to the test. Cultivating calm and quiet so that later I can be strong for Rosie. But as I plough my way through the rest of the crime briefs, and knock out a quick piece on an upcoming fundraiser for the local hospice, my mind travels back to journalism college. The glow of burgeoning self-worth as our tutor Dave gesticulated with a jabbing finger, telling us that ordinary citizens were depending on us to root out corruption, to be good enough at our jobs that we were a deterrent to the greedy and power-hungry. Working at the *Post* for twelve years has taken the sheen off such aspirations. For years the sub-editors have been stripping away balancing statements and opposing arguments from my stories, making them louder and angrier than the material justifies. Moans become full-on outrage; parking disputes become wars.

After my first two years at the *Post*, once I'd earned my senior reporter's qualification and collated a nice selection of cuttings in a portfolio, I managed to get myself on the roster for Sunday shifts at the *Mirror*. The plan I set myself, back at college, was falling into place. Shifting would lead to a full-time job on a tabloid. A year or two of that, then I'd cross over to the broadsheets. And before long I'd be the political correspondent for the *Guardian*, the reporter sought out in the House of Commons bar, the one trusted with secrets, trusted to tell a story fairly and to tell it well.

But those *Mirror* Sundays changed everything. I'd often work so late that I'd miss the last train back from London and be forced to get the first train Monday morning, stopping at the flat to quickly brush my teeth and change my clothes, then flying down the motorway to work a twelve-hour day at the *Post*. I'd have to skip my morning run and guzzle a can of Red Bull before I dared to get behind the wheel.

My aspirations imploded in the freezing rain outside the house of a young female singer. I'd been tasked with keeping an all-night watch to see whether a particular ex-boyfriend showed up. So little time in my week to spare and here I was, waiting for hours in the dark for something that just didn't feel important. There was no inner questioning, no vacillation. The need to abandon this pursuit of a national gig was just there with me in the rain, a black certainty settling at the back of my skull.

And yet, sure as I was, it hasn't stopped me reliving that moment repeatedly in the years that followed. Could there have been a different path? Maybe life with Rosie had become *too* comfortable, softening me in some way. If I'd been tougher back then, what might my life be like now?

'Daydreaming again?' Matthew looms over me. He's tall and heavyset, puffing out his chest which makes him look strangely off balance. 'Crime briefs, Jules. Come on. Tonight's edition's got holes every-bloody-where.'

'Almost done.'

He wets his lips and taps his lapel where he's pinned a baby-blue ribbon. I've seen them on sale. *Donate a pound and help us ensure the next generation of baby boys has a place in our world,* the sales copy reads. 'Want to get yourself one of these,' Matthew says. 'Solidarity with the readership and all that.'

'What makes you think Portsmouth residents are so firmly in the blue-ribbon camp?'

'They're lapping Prior up.' There's a strange light in Matthew's eyes. I wonder what exactly it is that he gets from making me bite, from forcing a reaction then swaggering away. I'm supposed to get angry now. But I can do better. This paper can do better.

'You know' – I swivel my chair around so I'm facing Matthew head on – 'I've been thinking about his campaign . . .'

'I bet you have.'

'... and it feels like we're doing our readers a bit of a disservice. Prior's making all kind of claims. Jobs and hospitals – he works them into every interview – but no one ever unpicks what he's saying. We seem to accept his statements without really questioning them.'

'You're treading a fine line, Missy. Nothing wrong with how we've covered him. We're giving the readers what they want.'

'I'm not having a dig – I know he's always good for a headline . But I wonder – couldn't we explore the issue a bit more? I mean, the uni's partnered with an endangered-species charity – did you know that? Ovum-to-ovum fertilisation offers species on the brink of extinction extra opportunities to rebuild their numbers. Isn't that fantastic? There's so much more to it than people realise.'

'Jules, I get it: you're on the pro side. But Portsmouth residents won't give a shit about that. Not when jobs, hospitals and the future of our adorable baby boys are at stake.'

'But Matthew, you don't buy that crap, do you? Look at me and tell me you believe men are going extinct if we don't vote Prior in.'

He smirks, wets his lips again. 'Sounds to me like somebody wants the university to make her some lezzy sperms.'

'Oh grow up.'

'Ha. You do, don't you?'

'No, Matthew. I just thought I might be able to talk to the news editor about *news*. About alternative angles on a big global story. But I guess I better wind my neck in and finish off these crime titbits.'

*

I'm home before Rosie, who's texted to say that the author event is overrunning. I'm not often here in the flat without her, and tonight I welcome the solitude. How can you ready yourself for a result as significant as this? The tests we've been through, the procedures, the care of our bodies – it's unthinkable that we could have gone through all that, only for the hope to end tonight. Craving motion, I run a duster along the living room's dark wood surfaces, polish up the table and do a quick blitz with the Hoover.

Trevor, the bookshop's owner, drops Rosie home at ten. She's wearing a black and green dress over leggings, her chunky cardigan on top. There's a hardback book under her arm, and without knowing why I take it from her and look at the cover. *Waiting* by Kalika Sands.

'How did the event go?' I ask.

Rosie gives me a strange look, then reaches over and places a palm against my cheek. Closing my eyes, I take in the scent of her rose hand cream and let my body slowly unfurl as it absorbs her nearness.

'Let's do the test,' she says. She heads into the bathroom and unwraps the cellophane from a pink box, producing a long white stick with a pink cap on the end.

She hitches up her dress, pulls down her leggings, and lowers herself onto the toilet, giving me a thin little smile as she urinates over the stick. It's this attempt at bravery that finally wrenches something inside me. I have to hold on to the side of the basin.

She carefully replaces the cap, and lays the test stick down on the side of the bath. A brief glance at her watch. 'I can't stand here and stare at it,' she says.

She washes her hands and hurries into the kitchen, where we rest with our backs against the counter. At our checkups, Becca has been reassuring us that our chance of success is likely to be the same as a couple undergoing conventional IVF. But when I looked those odds up online, I found that a couple of our age would be barely scraping a one-in-three chance. Everything we've gone through – and for odds that make us more likely to fail than succeed.

I put my arm around Rosie's shoulders. I can't think of this. I've spent my whole life imagining terrible scenarios in vivid detail, but a negative result is something I just haven't let myself contemplate. It's too awful to picture such an outcome on Rosie's face.

Another glance at her watch. 'One and a half minutes.'

My body feels restless. It's as though on some primal level I'm craving something to do, a task, any tiny thing that might make Rosie's happiness more likely. My muscles are ready for anything except this powerlessness.

I think back to the first time I met her – when I was twenty-two and she was just nineteen. Back then I was curiously numb with regards to my own sexuality. I'd forced myself to try sex with a man once at university, and when it was as awful as I feared part of me was relieved. I could give up. Lead an insular little life with sealed edges.

The story that led me to Rosie was mundane – some kids had started a fire in a dustbin outside the community centre. But as this was in quiet Petersfield, in the northernmost corner of the *Post*'s patch, Matthew wanted a 'hooliganism shatters rural idyll'-type piece, and I'd been sent to speak to the residents of my home town. I knew the quotes I was expected to get, *that type of thing never happens round here, what's the world coming to*, and so on.

There was a well-presented block of flats next to the community centre and I'd methodically worked my way along, ringing doorbells. My hit rate had been fairly dire – the elderly residents had been trained never to open up for strangers. But on the upper level a dark blue door opened to reveal a young woman, perhaps a visiting granddaughter. She was slim but curvaceous, with full breasts and hips, wearing a simple black vest and cut-off jeans, bare legs and feet, toenails painted fluorescent pink.

'Hello,' she said.

'Hi, I'm from the *Portsmouth Post*. I'm doing a story about the fire over at the community centre. I was wondering if you saw anything, or if you'd noticed any gangs of kids hanging around there recently?' I was aware of embarrassment seeping into my voice. My navy trouser suit had seen better days and my feet were sweating inside horrible clunky boots.

The girl's eyes widened and a smile played at her lips. 'I've never met an actual journalist. Come in.' Before I had a chance to reply, she'd turned and was leading the way inside the flat.

In those days the sitting room was dated, its walls painted lilac and bisected by a floral-patterned border. There was a sofa and an armchair, both draped in a lacy white cloth, and a wooden shelf unit covered in china figurines took up a whole wall. I half expected to see a white-haired old lady huddled under a blanket, but I was alone with the girl who'd come to the door.

'Have a seat,' she said.

I lowered myself into the sofa, fiddling in my bag for a biro as the girl sat next to me.

'So, how does this work?' she asked.

I had the strangest desire to reach over and feel the texture of her springy blond curls. 'Let's start with your name and age.'

'Rosie Louise Barcombe. Age nineteen.' She smiled, as though pleased with the efficiency of her answer.

'And the fire . . . if you could tell me what you saw.' I shifted in my seat, flipped my notebook over to a new page.

'Oh – well, to be honest, I didn't really see it, not until after it was all finished, anyway. It couldn't have been a big fire, could it?'

'No.' I was supposed to follow up with another question, this wasn't enough, but my whole sense of the story was crumbling away. The flat was overly warm; the radiators were on when really the windows should have been open to let in the spring breeze.

'I remember you from school,' she said. 'You were three years above me. You won the fifteen hundred metres every sports day.'

I felt myself redden as I inspected her face again. Nothing clicked against my memories. How could I not have noticed such a girl? Hers was the kind of beauty that instantly drew the eye; that made you feel strangely glad.

'You don't remember me?' She looked disappointed, and I almost thought about lying. I gave an apologetic shrug. It was a big school, and maybe she was different back then.

'So, a reporter? I always imagined reporters to be older, for some reason. Middle-aged men. Is it a hard job to do?'

'Well ...' My face burned. 'The deadlines make it stress-ful, I guess.'

Her gaze was painful. It was as though I was knotted up inside, and being with her was somehow pulling the knots tighter. I looked away, casting my eyes around the room.

'This was my grandmother's flat,' she said. 'She left it to me. It's been three months, but I still can't bring myself to throw away her things.' Her bottom lip twitched and her eyes welled. I reached out and placed a hand on her arm.

'Have you ever lost anyone?' she asked.

'Me? Well, yes, but I was too young to understand.' I needed to get us back to the story. Or perhaps I should just leave – I was upsetting her, and it was clear I wasn't going to get the quote I needed.

'I've started categorising people now. Those who know what it's like, and those who don't. And I think to myself, those poor people, they have no idea what's coming to them. You think you can imagine, you think you'll feel a certain way – but you're always wrong.' She wiped at her eyes with the back of her hand.

I gave her arm a gentle pat. 'This will pass,' I said. 'Come on.' It wasn't like me, but I braved a hug.

She accepted this tentative offering immediately, arms around my neck, her body pressed against mine. I was aware of her breasts, could feel her ribs lifting with each breath.

My phone vibrated in my bag. The girl pulled away; just far back enough to look at my face. The story. That's why I was here. 'So – anyway – the fire engines ...'

She leaned forward and kissed me on the lips. My note-book slipped from my fingers as I found myself responding.

Responding to a woman kissing me. 'I . . .' I retreated, embarrassed.

'Oh. Oh God. I thought . . . I can usually tell. I'm so sorry.' Her face was still close to mine. Her cheeks were pink with humiliation, but there was something else written on her face. Could it be *disappointment?*

'I . . .' Again I tried to speak. Again I failed. What precisely was I turning down? My heart was thudding. Panic. I needed a moment to think, but something was slipping away. Here. Right now.

Her eyes roved across my face. 'This is your first time, isn't it?' She leaned in again. I was aware of her smile as her lips explored mine with a light pressure. Her hands cupped my face, and this time I let myself sink into the moment.

Another watch-check. Rosie swallows. 'It's time.' Her face is stricken as she holds my gaze for a second. Then she's charging into the bathroom to retrieve the test.

She picks it up and is instantly still, her back to me. I can't see the stick, wouldn't know how to interpret it even if I could. Every nerve ending in my body feels alive; I'm aware of hidden muscles, of the tiny hairs running along my arms.

'Rosie . . .'

Slowly, she turns around. Mascara-laced tears are trickling down the side of her nose.

'Oh, Rosie.' I step closer and hold her, running my hands along her shuddering back. 'It's OK, Rosie, we'll try again. I know how important this is—'

She pulls away. Holds the stick aloft. 'No . . . it's . . . I'm . . .' She splutters out a noise, half cough, half laugh. 'I'm so sorry,

I didn't mean to do that to you. It's positive. It's positive!' She wipes at her eyes with the back of her hand, sinks down onto the toilet seat and looks at me. 'Say something.'

I exhale. I feel strangely winded – those tears – I'd thought it was the end and I'd just begun to understand how inconsolable Rosie would have been.

'We're having a baby.' A smile spreads across her blotchy face. She springs up from the toilet and shouts it. 'We're having a baby!'

She throws her arms around me and finally the tension leaves my body. Our one-in-three chance has been realised. Rosie is pregnant with our little girl.

Chapter 6

The weeks leading up to our first scan pass quickly, but they have a blessed quality about them that I'll always remember. Rosie seems to radiate good health. Even though she's a long way from having a baby bump, her skin is silky and there's a surprising new maturity to her face.

The day after our own test we learn that Hong Shu and Anita had a positive result too, and so the four of us go for a celebratory dinner at an Indian restaurant. Ovum-to-ovum fertilisation works – we vacillate between giddiness and a kind of sober shock at this fact.

It would be very like me to immerse myself in statistics. To google health warnings and to sit, thinking of these, while Rosie talks through happy versions of our future. And yet I find that – temporarily, at least – I've shed such cautionary instincts. My baby is inside Rosie. My baby, hers and mine. And no internet research, no planning, can take the shine off such a marvel.

Even though she's younger, Rosie has always been a kind of guide for me. Her gentle presence has helped me find happiness in the most unexpected things. So many times I've resisted, and yet mostly I've been wrong to do so.

I think often of our first summer as a couple. The disbelief that someone like Rosie would let me touch her. The sensation in my stomach, teetering precariously between pain and joy as I ran my fingers along her contours, tentatively cupped a breast. Her breathing becoming heavy, turning into a gentle moan as I finally worked up the courage to slide my hand into her underwear. The intensity of her appetite, never tiring, was intimidating at times. How could I sustain such a thing? How would I ever be enough? The shame of being naked in her bed. Lying there stiff, mortified at my pallid flesh, the jut of my hipbone. She couldn't want to do this, not really. But she was persistent, coaxing. 'Relax,' she kept whispering.

I take a full day's holiday for our scan. It's scheduled for week seven of the pregnancy, and although Rosie's visited the Centre for a couple of check-ups, today is going to be the first time we see our baby. Because of the regularity with which protesters are now congregating around the entrance, Becca has issued us with swipe cards, so that we can enter the building via the staff door at the back.

When we make our way through to the foyer, we see a newly installed metal detector at the entrance, and two workmen in jeans and trainers are setting up what looks to be an X-ray machine for bags. One of the guards – the one with a moustache – nods at us in recognition.

Rosie looks bewildered as she watches the workers bolting the machine to the floor. 'Has it really come to this?' she whispers.

My mind flits over the online commentary, the outraged social media posts. 'It's sensible to take precautions.'

'But still. This is a university. A place of learning, not a military compound.'

I take her hand. 'Let's not think of that. Think about why we're here.'

Scott collects us from the foyer and shows us up to the second floor, chattering to Rosie all the while about *A Little Life*, the novel he's been reading. He ushers us into a white cube of a room, all gleaming tiles, with the same alcohol-rub smell that pervades the whole Centre. A technician, full-figured and dressed in blue scrubs, briefly looks up as we come in, then returns her attention to the ultra-sound machine.

'This is Claire,' Scott says. 'She'll be doing the ultrasound, but I'd quite like to stay, if that's alright with you?'

'Of course!' Rosie says. 'And I remember Claire – you did my egg collection, didn't you? I'm glad you're here, because I was so out of it that day, I don't even think I said thank you.'

Another quick look up, a silent half-smile.

'Hello, ladies.' Becca appears in the doorway. 'Gosh, it's getting rather crowded in here. Hope there's room for one more?'

Rosie greets Becca with a hug, then clambers onto the small bed next to the ultrasound machine. Anita's scan was yesterday, and everything was fine. But can there really be a baby inside Rosie? Already? It suddenly feels so implausible. My whole body tightens, resisting the idea of bad news.

'Jules?' Rosie gestures for me to come closer.

I take her hand and we watch as Claire smears lubricant over the ultrasound's probe attachment, getting ready to guide it in. We should be able to have normal ultrasounds soon, but for now, as it's very early in the pregnancy, Rosie has to be subjected to the vaginal probe again.

Scott and Becca inhale simultaneously as Rosie winces. I squeeze her hand and give my best reassuring smile, but she's looking away, over at the monitor.

'Is everything OK?' Rosie says.

Becca takes a step forward and places her index finger against the grey landscape on the screen. 'See that little kidney bean right there? That's Baby. Just the one, this time. Her heart is already beating – can you see?'

I lean forwards, and focus on Becca's fingertip. There, a speck seems to be waving back and forth, just slightly, like a filament of seaweed swaying underwater. That's a heart? That's life?

Becca goes over to the machine, standing over Claire as she fiddles with the settings, zooming in closer then clicking the mouse to measure lengths and widths.

'Congratulations to you both!' says Scott.

'Oh, Jules, look.' Rosie's eyes are welling up.

I inspect the screen. The back and forth of the filament is rapid, the rhythm strong and unwavering. My baby. Rosie is carrying my child. My mind seems frozen, unable to pluck any single thought from a fog of emotion. I look at Rosie again, the flush of her cheeks, the rapture in her eyes. It's impossible not to respond to her happiness. I go in for a kiss and for a moment her joy becomes mine.

'The persistence of new life,' Becca says. 'Isn't it wonderful?' She turns to Scott. There's a slight pause, and then Becca goes in for a hug with her colleague, laughing triumphantly.

'We've looked forward to this moment for fifteen years,' Scott says.

I look at the shape on the screen again. I made this. Her. This pulsing little sac is half me. I brush the tears from Rosie's face.

Once Becca has finished taking measurements and printed us a couple of images, Claire silently withdraws the probe. She must be around about my age but she has a hard, impassive face. She catches my eye, and there's something there, a moment of recognition that doesn't feel friendly. It's as though she's looked right inside my head and disapproves of what she sees there.

Should I be reacting differently? Is it unusual not to weep at such a time? I look at Rosie. Her eyes are still teary, and her face is pink. But when she looks at me I feel reassured: there's the same open trust that's always there. And yet more: she seems saturated with a new kind of joy.

'Let me take you both to lunch,' Becca says as we're preparing to leave. 'There's a lovely Italian place up on Portsdown Hill. Scott – you have to come too.'

'Oh yes, let's celebrate,' Rosie says.

'I can't,' Scott says. 'Promised I'd visit Mum this lunchtime. Jules, Rosie – I'm so happy for you both. You're going to be wonderful parents.'

We make our way to the restaurant in separate cars, my Fiesta following Becca's silver BMW. Although the leaves on the trees are starting to yellow, it's still warm enough to take a table in a pretty little garden at the rear. There are wooden benches, scattered rather than placed in rows, terracotta pots filled with late-blooming flowers.

Rosie takes the seat next to Becca and immediately starts gabbling her way through the menu, interrogating Becca about what dishes she ought to avoid. I sit back in my chair and observe them, Rosie making a mock gasp of horror at having to pass up goat's cheese.

Once the waiter has taken our order, I lean across the table. 'We really ought to be careful. The wrong person might overhear,' I say.

'Oh, Jules.' Rosie's voice is at full volume, loaded with laughter. 'I don't see anyone with a notepad here. People have their own lives to worry about – no one's listening.'

I turn to Becca. 'Everyone at the Centre signs a confidentiality agreement, right? Not just the researchers, but the nurses and cleaners – everyone?'

Becca smiles. 'We're as strict as any hospital; you mustn't worry. Your notes are password-protected, and besides – anyone who leaked anything would never work in healthcare again.'

'Sorry,' I say. 'It's just ... I can't stop imagining what the press would do if they got hold of our names.'

'Well, you're drawing more attention by whispering like that,' Rosie says it in a light, rather than a snappish, tone, but still I'm hurt. I look away, pretending to be distracted by a wasp. It's late in the season; its flight is drunken.

Becca reaches into her black leather tote bag and retrieves her phone. 'Speaking of the press – I need to give you my new number. A website published the old one last week and I was getting inundated with calls and texts. It was quite frightening, actually.'

Rosie looks shaken as she inputs Becca's new number into

her phone. *Good*, I think. She needed this reminder of just how serious our situation is, how many opponents are out there. And the moment the thought manifests itself, I realise that the old, cautious Jules is back. Perhaps it's for the best: the warm, breathless feelings of the last few weeks could have led to careless mistakes.

Becca places her forearms on the table and addresses both of us. 'So, have you thought about what you're going to tell people?'

'Sperm donor,' I say.

'We've told the real truth to our parents,' Rosie says. 'I can't wait to tell them we've got a heartbeat.'

'We should wait a bit longer before we tell anyone else you're pregnant,' I say. 'That's what people do, isn't it? Wait until the twelve-week mark? And we'll have to agree our story, in case anyone's particularly nosy. The name of the clinic, profile of the donor, that sort of thing.'

'Wow – you really do think of everything,' Becca says.

Rosie laughs. I try to let my shoulders loosen, to relax in my seat. I don't mean to be a killjoy, but that heartbeat – magnificent, yet so daunting – has reminded me just how much responsibility there is. How it's going to be my job to protect our daughter, to help her navigate a world where so many people believe she doesn't belong.

Our drinks arrive and Rosie starts bombarding Becca with questions about the trial: 'So how many babies will there actually be? We know about Hong Shu and Anita, but are there more?'

Becca picks up her napkin and spreads it across her lap. 'We have just the two pregnancies in this first round. But on a more positive note, we were able to successfully complete cellular fusion for nine out of the ten couples.'

Rosie gasps. 'So you're saying Anita and me – we're the only pregnant ones?'

Becca places a hand on Rosie's arm. 'These are the kind of stats we'd expect if we were working with conventional IVF. It's very positive news.'

'But I thought there'd be more women like me.' Rosie looks forlorn. I want to comfort her but my mind is racing ahead to the potential press implications. The fewer babies, the more newsworthy each of them will be.

'Our research partner in Newcastle is starting to recruit women,' Becca says. 'And we're about to start a new wave here in Portsmouth, so you'll soon be part of a much larger community.'

Our waiter arrives and hands pizzas to Becca and Rosie. The seafood linguine he places in front of me has a pungent fishy smell that turns my stomach.

'Any parmesan, black pepper?'

All three of us mumble a quick no.

'Come on,' Becca says, after the waiter has gone. 'This is a celebration. The trial is going well. You're going to have a baby.' She lifts her glass of white wine and thrusts it into the centre of the table. Rosie runs her index fingers underneath her eyes and then raises her orange juice, and I awkwardly lift my tap water.

As we eat Rosie and Becca start a tentative conversational to and fro, starting with Rosie's work at the bookshop and moving on to potential names. I'm surprised to learn that Rosie is considering Margaret, after her grandmother. I try to recall the little girl of my imaginings, to put the name Margaret on her and see if it fits. But she won't materialise.

'You know,' Becca says, 'it's a cliché, but nothing prepares you for having a child. Nothing. Just you wait – love like you've never known before. It makes everything worthwhile. When I first started out, my research was focused on unexplained infertility and over the years I worked with hundreds of couples – it was satisfying seeing how happy a child could make them. But I had no idea how it really felt, not until I had my own.'

'How do you balance children with your work?' I ask. 'I mean, it's hard for parents. Having to take time off, school runs . . .'

Becca's eyes shine. 'It gives everything so much more meaning,' she says. 'Knowing just what being a mother is like is what powers me through the meetings and tedious funding applications. I'm giving women the opportunity to feel like I felt – like I still feel, even now.

'And career-wise – well, I'm lucky, there's lots I can do from home when the children are asleep. My husband shares everything with me – he takes his turn staying home when they're poorly.'

I nod.

'It's normal to feel scared,' Becca goes on. 'I had days when I thought the whole thing was a mistake, right up into the ninth month. And the agony – the absolute agony – of even getting to that point. Women don't talk about it, but I spent years – whole years – not being able to decide whether to have a child or not.'

'Really?' Rosie's voice is high-pitched, incredulous.

'Oh yes,' Becca says. 'There was a raging war of pros and cons going on inside my head. But I'm not exaggerating when I tell you it was worth it. The sad thing is, though, the women I talk to about this can never believe me. Motherhood really is something you have to discover for yourself.'

She's looking at me as she concludes this little speech, and I can't help feeling as though I've been seen, somehow. As though Becca's been able to tell that I resisted the idea of motherhood for more than a decade.

Chapter 7

I acquiesce to Rosie's plans for a somewhat staged announcement lunch. The Sunday after the scan is her thirty-first
birthday, so we invite both families and Anthony around for
a roast. The morning is chaotic. Until now Rosie's nausea
has been light and episodic, but today she scrambles out
of bed, only just making it to the toilet, where she vomits
copiously. She's pale as she emerges from the bathroom;
her face is coated in a light film of sweat and a tang of bile
hangs over her.

'We could cancel lunch,' I say. 'Let you get some rest?'

I'm not looking forward to the occasion. I know the har-
monious picture Rosie has in her mind, but I also know that
my father will be awkward and uncomfortable. I'd rather tell
him about the scan privately, but Rosie would be hurt by such
a suggestion.

'I'll be fine,' Rosie says. 'I'll just lie down for another five
minutes. It'll pass.'

After she's fallen asleep again, I slip from the flat to get the
shopping under way. It's her birthday, after all, and while I'd
prefer a day of quiet solitude this family surround, this manufactured unveiling, is what she wants. So I'll brighten the

flat with flowers, stimulate her appetite with homely cooking smells and prod my father into being a well-mannered houseguest.

In Tesco I load the trolley up with the fizzy drinks and ginger biscuits I crave most when I'm unwell. As a kid I seemed to be afflicted by one bug after another, and these were the times my father never let me down. He'd tuck me up in bed, bucket placed strategically on the floor, Lucozade bottle within reach. His eyes would well at the sight of me, and I'd feel the full weight of being the only family he had. I remember how, with my childish lack of proportion, I'd solemnly promise him that I wouldn't die.

I select wrapping paper for Rosie's gift, a gold pendant in which I've placed a tiny reproduction of our scan image. I've adjusted the contrast, so that if you know what you're looking at, you can make out the outline of our baby's heart. It's a sentimental gesture, out of character for me, and when I think of giving it to her I panic and consider speeding back to the jeweller's to exchange it for something less loaded with expectation, something a little more fun.

Back at home I get the beef in the oven and peel and chop the potatoes. Rosie sips lemonade and nibbles at a couple of ginger biscuits, gradually becoming steady enough for a shower.

'Let me do something,' she says as she comes into the kitchen, hair in wet tendrils down her back.

I hand her the present, opening my mouth to say something, but failing to find the right words. The gesture is silent. I'm still not confident that the gift is right and I'm certain my face must be red. She'll be too polite to say if she doesn't like it, but she'll be disappointed, I know she will.

She opens the box and lifts the locket out with both hands. 'Jules, it's beautiful.'

She clicks it open without my prompting, and her breath catches as she realises what the image represents. She looks at me and I feel my eyes responding to her burgeoning tears. We kiss. Our life together, this flat, this very Sunday feels soaked with meaning, with the permanence of our life together. I'm no longer the shy young woman who lies in bed at night wondering how on earth this beautiful creature can love me, picturing in vivid detail the day when she tells me there's someone else. No, I'm someone different now, thanks to her. I'm confidently stepping into a new future with the woman I love, the woman who's chosen to make a child with me.

Anthony – back in our lives after delivering Rosie chocolates and a hugging apology – arrives as a trio with Rosie's parents. Elaine proffers an extravagant bouquet of flowers; Michael bears several bottles of prosecco and a clinking bag of high-end non-alcoholic drinks. I expect them to demand news, but they're restrained, perhaps sensing their daughter's need for staging.

My father – as always – is a good half an hour late. He brings with him the stale beer odour of the Green Dragon and a rich layering of bong and cigarette smoke. Handing him a bottle of Bud, I register his nervously darting eyes. He'd never admit it, but he's shy around the Barcombes.

Fitting all of us around our four-seater dining table is a bit of a challenge. We've pulled it out into the centre of the room and borrowed two chairs from Mrs Hamworth next door so that Rosie and I can perch at each end. I've put my father next to me, Anthony on his other side, the Barcombes opposite.

Once I've handed everyone their plates and squeezed into my seat, Rosie straightens in her chair. I see the corners of her mouth twitch as she takes a slow intake of breath – sure signs that she's getting ready to make her announcement. She's wearing a sleeveless red top and her hair is piled up on top of her head – she looks in so many ways like a natural leader, a matriarch taking her place at the top of the table, even though she's the youngest of us all.

My father is emptying the gravy boat onto his plate, but the Barcombes and Anthony are all rapt attention.

'Thanks for coming, everyone.' Rosie sits up tall; the paleness from earlier has gone and as she smiles her cheeks glow. 'We had our first scan on Friday and our baby has a heartbeat. I really am pregnant.'

Elaine is up. 'Oh, I knew it. My beautiful girl. Isn't it wonderful? Mikey, you're going to be a granddad.'

My father gives me a haunted look, but I turn away. I don't have the energy to try to manage whatever he's feeling, not today. I glance at Anthony – he's smiling, but his eyes are cold.

As everyone sits back down and begins eating, Rosie describes the scan and then gets up to retrieve the images Becca printed out for us. Her parents coo at the grainy pictures, while my father continues to eat with gusto. He can't be oblivious to the fact that he's letting the side down, but he won't even feign enthusiasm, won't do this one thing for me.

'We're not going to share the news more widely until week twelve,' I say. 'And – for the sake of privacy – we're going to have to lie and say Rosie was artificially inseminated with donor sperm ...'

Anthony laughs. 'Oh, Jules, no sperm at the dinner table, please.'

I fix him with a hard stare. 'We need to keep the number of people who know we're on the trial very small. It's really important that we all remember this and don't let anything slip. You've seen the way the media are treating the story.'

'You can count on us, Jules,' Elaine says. 'What's your due date?'

'Twenty-sixth of May,' Rosie says. 'She'll be a summer baby.'

Elaine chews slowly. I feel a pang of affection at the face powder nestling in the creases of her face, her smoothly blow-dried bob. 'Wonderful,' she says. 'Warm nights will make it so much easier getting up for the feeds. You'll have to invest in a breast pump. Express milk so that Jules can feed her too. It's important for the bonding.'

Michael blushes at the breast pump reference. I try to picture what Elaine's just described. Being jolted out of sleep by a screaming infant. Bottles of Rosie's milk lined up in our fridge. Milk coming out of Rosie! This is less than eight months away. This is what my life is going to be, and soon, so soon. I look over at my father and catch him regarding me with an amused expression. *Look at you, all middle class*, he's saying with his eyes. He looks as though he's tipped over into Drunk Neil. I need to be careful not to rile him – one of his tirades could spoil today for Rosie.

I lay my knife and fork down. I always find roasts too filling. 'When I say don't let anything slip, I guess what I'm really trying to get across is that you can't tell anyone at all. I'm sorry to have to ask you to lie, but if the press get our names we'll have photographers camped on our doorstep.'

'Have you picked out any names yet?' Michael asks.

Rosie smiles and shoots a brief glance at my father, noisily scraping up the remainder of his meal. 'Well, I did think Margaret, after Nana, but I was wondering, maybe Hazel.'

My dad's head jerks up. My mother was Hazel. Rosie means well, but my father will hate the idea. Hate that Rosie's lips even pronounced the name. 'Bit morbid,' I say, quickly and quietly, with a brisk headshake.

The Barcombes don't get the association and Elaine happily chatters away, throwing out suggestions – all the fad names: Ella, Evie, Maisie. 'How lucky you are, being guaranteed a girl,' she says.

Rosie's eyes flash. 'I would have loved a boy just as much.'

When it's time to serve dessert I spend longer than necessary alone in the kitchen, stacking the plates, dishing up the chocolate ice cream. The excitement of Rosie and her parents is so palpable; it shines from their skin, inflects their voices with song. But when I picture the post-birth life, a naked babe to clothe and feed, I feel the same confused fog as I did on Friday. I remember the persistence of the heartbeat and I try, so hard, to fill my body with remembered magic. It doesn't come. I am happy. Excited too, but just not in the straightforward way I thought I'd be. There's too much to worry about.

Dad is the last guest to leave. Rosie is in the bedroom taking a nap, and he stands next to me in the kitchen, swigging from his fifth bottle of Bud as I wash the dishes. 'My girl. Such a smart little cookie you were,' he says. 'I remember how proud I was when the *Post* first took you on. Only twenty-two. That big rape case they had you cover. I've still got the clippings.'

I think back to that time, the way my father tried to work my new job into his conversations with the long-haired men collecting their weekly eighth from our doorstep. Memories I hold tight to my chest. I know it's vain, but there's a certain status attached to being a reporter, even a local one. In the eyes of the people on the estate who'd watched me grow up, I became more significant. The skinny girl, school uniform always too small, clothes reeking of fags, now a reporter.

'I was so surprised when it didn't work out at the *Mirror*,' Dad adds. 'I could never understand why.'

I finish the cutlery and start scrubbing at the plates. 'The insecurity, Dad. Not to mention the hours. You have to start out doing shifts, and what with the *Post* and the commute . . .'

He makes a tutting sound. 'She wasn't prepared to support you, then, while you made a go of it? This flat falling into her lap, but she wouldn't let you jack in the day job?'

'You need to get that idea out of your head,' I say. 'It was *my* choice. Pushing for the nationals was making me unhappy.'

'But it was your ambition for so many years. I'm not getting at you, Jules. I just hate to think of you having regrets. Middle age sneaks up on you, quicker than you think.'

I finish lining the plates up on the rack, then run a fresh bowl of water for the pans.

Dad sighs. 'You made so much of yourself, really. It broke my heart, not being able to give you the Christmas presents you deserved. Not affording the school trips. As if losing your mother wasn't bad enough.'

I turn to him. 'You did the best you could. And I was happy – you shouldn't beat yourself up.'

He gulps from his bottle and we enjoy an amicable silence as I crack on with the dishes.

'Bloody snobs, those Barcombes,' he whispers after a short while. 'Petersfield people through and through. Can't see beyond the confines of this pathetic little town. You're part of it all now, I suppose. Being father or whatever you're going to call it to the Barcombe grandchild.'

'Dad, don't be an arse.' I reach for the roasting tin and pull it into the sink for a soak.

'They won't want me anywhere near it. I won't be good enough to be its granddad.' His voice catches and I look up in surprise. I'm about to tell him to stop being ridiculous, but his eyes are moist. He looks away.

'Come on,' I say. 'Do you really think I'd let them get away with nonsense like that?'

He puts his beer bottle down on the worktop, still not looking at me. 'You're different now . . .'

'Dad—'

'No. Listen. I'm proud. I really am. I mean – yeah – maybe you're not as high up in the world as your talents could have taken you. But you're a darn sight higher than me.'

'Dad . . .'

'I know it's not right, but every time I see you making conversation with those people . . . the fact that you even know how to talk to them . . . it . . . it makes me realise just how small I am. I know it. You know it.'

I dry my hands on a tea towel. I'm tempted to offer another beer, but that's the coward's way out. As I look at my father's lined face I conjure the younger version of my memories. The whites of his eyes clear, not yellow and veined like they are now. The stubble, black, free from the ever-multiplying flecks of white. I could roar sometimes at how it makes me feel, perceiving the inertia of his life in a way that I never did when I was young. He has the same sorrows as he did back then, but none of the joys. It isn't up to me to carry the burden of his unhappiness. And yet I feel it. It's a weight, pressing down on my heart. Every time I look at him the guilt comes back.

'You drink too much,' I say. 'You smoke too much hash.'

He sighs. For a moment I think he might be about to launch into one of his cynical tirades. But he continues looking down at the worktop.

'I know. You're right. Sometimes it's not even me. I don't know who I am, what I'm saying. And then I get scared. Because if not me, then who? Who takes over? What do I become?'

A coolness snakes its way along my back. Is this *it*, the call for help that I've longed for and dreaded all these years? What do I say? What *can* I say? I'm tired – too tired. I pat him on the arm. 'You're going to be a granddad – that's a reason to start looking after yourself better.'

He grunts and I feel a spike of fury. 'You could have shown a bit of excitement. It was humiliating, watching you tuck into your potatoes while everyone else was congratulating us.'

He regards me with soft eyes, lips pressed together in a pity-smile. 'I'm like you, Jules. I can't pretend. I was watching you. You're doing your best to hide it, but I can see you're struggling.'

'Don't be ridiculous.'

'I know I'm only a pisshead old hippy. But I've known you longer than anyone, Jules. To me you'll always be that girl whose every thought is written on her face. But it's OK.'

'I'm not *struggling*. There's just a lot to think about.'

'I can help you through it, if you'll just be honest with me. We can help each other. Like we always have.'

I pick up the tea towel. I'll dry the plates and put them away properly. The kitchen looks untidy when they're left on the draining board. I go about the task furiously, feeling my father's eyes on my back all the while.

When he speaks next, it's about the likelihood of rain.

Chapter 8

If Rosie had conceived a child by a sperm donor, this would probably be the point I started talking about it with just a few of my closest friends. So when I see that the sports desk is quiet, I head over to Tom. I'm strangely looking forward to his reaction. I'm not going to tell him about the trial, but I'm still going to have a 'sharing the news' moment that's all my own.

He greets me with a slap on the back. 'How's it going? You've been too quiet lately. When are you next coming out for a beer?'

I lean in. 'Well – it might not be for a while, actually. Keep this to yourself, but me and Rosie are having a baby.'

He stares at me. 'I have so many questions. None of them appropriate.'

I perch on the end of his desk. 'Donor. Rosie's the pregnant one. It's very early days and I'm not telling anyone at work besides you until we get to our twelve-week scan.' I feel a squeeze of guilt at everything I've omitted. Tom is far more trustworthy than Anthony. For a moment I imagine the relief of sharing the full story, of describing the protesters outside the clinic on the information day, admitting how angry I was with myself for feeling afraid.

'Wow,' he says. 'A real baby?'

'Due in May.' I feel myself smiling.

'So you'll be a proper grown-up? No more after-work drinks? It's hard enough dragging you out as it is.' He's about to say something else, but Elsa the receptionist is coming towards us, red-faced and out of breath from the stairs.

'No one answers their bloody phones any more. There's a chap downstairs, Jules. Asked for you. Says he's got a story, but he doesn't want anyone else. Only you. Rude, he was. Made me come up here.'

'I'll just grab my notebook and I'll be right down.'

We get plenty of walk-ins at the *Post*, people turning up with what they believe to be a story. These encounters mostly involve listening to prolonged moans about day-to-day gripes. But I go; I always do, just in case.

When I get downstairs Elsa directs me with a jerk of her head to a man standing to one side, idly browsing through last night's edition. He's average height, wearing a tan leather jacket and black jeans. When he turns I see that he's about my age; his light brown hair is cropped short and beginning to recede from his forehead.

'Ah, Juliet, I recognise you from your by-line photo. How are you?' He flashes me a warm smile.

'Very well, thanks,' I say. 'I hear you've got a story for me.'

'Is there somewhere we can talk, more privately?'

There's a wooden bench outside, currently free of smokers. I lead him to it and we both sit. I'm upright, pen poised against my notebook, trying to convey that my time is precious.

The man turns to face me. 'I'm authorised to make you a very generous offer, Juliet.' His voice is low.

'What do you mean?'

'I'm from the *Daily Sketch*.'

I draw myself up. The *Sketch*? A generous offer? Am I being headhunted? A tingling sense of possibility: a national job offer just as there's another mouth to feed. But – surely they don't usually send someone out to make the approach in person? And I've not broken any really big stories this month, certainly nothing that would make a red-top like the *Sketch* pay attention.

'I understand that you're a participant in a certain clinical trial. If you were to talk to us exclusively there's a lot we can do to help you. When I say generous, I'm talking five figures.'

Of course. I stand up. I wish I hadn't, it looks defensive, emotional. The trial. That's why he's here. But how? And so soon.

'I'm sorry, I don't know what you're talking about.'

The man remains seated, pressing his lips together in a caricature of pity. 'We have solid information. I'm going to have to run something, Juliet. Wouldn't it be so much better to be part of the piece? To be seen to be talking candidly, answering your critics?'

Critics. The pregnancy has been a secret shared with just a privileged few – but now I have critics? I've used the same line of reasoning myself to get people to talk. He says he has solid information. Where from? I can find out, I can navigate this.

Slowly, I pull air into my lungs. Delivery is everything. I have to project calm. Instil doubt. 'Tell me what on earth you're talking about. Where did you hear this rubbish?'

'We had a tip. You and your partner Rosie Barcombe got a place on the trial. Rosie's about eight weeks along. If you sign our exclusivity agreement we can protect you. Seriously, we'll station someone outside your home; we'll send any other press packing. We've got a lot of experience when it comes to protecting our interviewees. No one does it better than us.'

One of the sales reps approaches, fumbling with a packet of fags. I shoot her a warning look and she changes direction. 'Where did this tip of yours come from?'

Again, the pressing of the lips, that pained expression. 'I wish I could tell you, but we've got pretty strict policies. You're a reporter – I'm sure you understand. Now, why don't we start from the beginning?'

I have to make a decision. He's right: if the *Sketch* is confident their tip is sound, they'll run a piece with or without my cooperation. And yes, the piece written with my input will be kinder, as far as the *Sketch* goes. But then that would be it, our anonymity gone. Rosie, the bearer of one of the world's first father-free babies, will be public property. Regardless of this man's promises, she'll be sought out, commented on relentlessly.

'Juliet? Tell me what you earn in a year. I'd be right in thinking it's not that much? I remember my own regional news days all too well.'

'I . . . ' A tip. A tip is not the same as a bona fide leak with supporting documentation. There's a chance they don't have enough to run a story.

'Is this a political statement for you? I mean, experts have come out with some pretty scary projections. They're saying that by the time I'm in a nursing home, us men could be in the minority.'

Oh – the pain of hearing such nonsense. I've read every

news story, pored over Becca's journal articles. I could demolish every one of his arguments, I'm sure I could. But to do such a thing would be an admission. If Rosie and I don't comment, this could be parked, treated as speculation. It's a slim chance, but I have to take it.

'I'm sorry.' I fasten the button of my jacket. 'I don't know what you're talking about. I really can't help you.'

'Juliet, think again, for your own sake. We can make you comfortable. You could give up work for a while. We'd even put you up in a hotel if you needed to get away for a bit – you know how messy this is going to be, right?'

I shake my head and start walking back to the staff entrance. A broad-shouldered man with a goatee is in front of me. The sound of a camera's shutter. *Fuck.* I try to go around him. The photographer is shouting my name. The reporter is shouting my name. They're not going to accept this. They'll follow me inside, cross-examine my colleagues.

I don't have my bag, but my keys and phone are in my jacket pocket. They're all I need. Changing direction, I stride towards my car.

'Wait – just tell me why you put yourself forward,' the reporter shouts. 'Was it tough? Did they make you jump through lots of hoops?'

I'm at my car. Can I drive? My legs are shaky, I'm not sure I can manage it. A few more clicks of the camera and I'm behind the wheel. I crunch the gears and drive away.

I don't quite make it to the motorway before I have to pull over. I'm struggling to control the clutch; my legs are weak. A sharp pain shoots across my chest and blackness spreads at the edges of my vision. I've never passed out before, but I grip the steering wheel, sensing that a blackout might be close. I know I'm being pathetic, that I'm not helping. But it's a good five minutes before I'm able to move from my hunched position and continue the drive home.

Chapter 9

'Rosie?' I shout over the roar of the motorway traffic. I'm in the fast lane, pushing my ten-year-old Fiesta to a juddering eighty-five. 'Has anyone come to the shop asking about the trial? Any photographers?'

'Jules – goodness, you're not driving, are you? You know I hate you being on the phone when you're driving.'

'It's an emergency. The *Sketch* has got hold of our names.'

'What?'

'They've been to my work. I need you to leave the shop – they're probably on their way to you right now. Head home and I'll meet you there.'

'We're going to be in the *Sketch*?'

'Not if I can help it. But Rosie, you need to leave. Now. Tell Trevor you're not well. Get out of there and get home before they corner you.'

'But why do we have to run and hide? I'm proud to be part of the trial.'

I brake sharply as an elderly man in a dilapidated Nissan pulls out into my lane. 'Trust me, Rosie, there's a whole host of reasons for keeping a low profile. We'll talk about it later. Now please, go. If anyone's waiting at the flat ignore them and go straight inside. Don't answer the door to anyone.'

I throw my mobile down onto the passenger seat and flash my lights at the driver in front, who continues to hog the outside lane.

Twenty minutes later I'm backing the car into our parking bay and walking along the winding pathway to our block of flats. My skin is clammy with sweat; my shirt clings to my back. But aside from one of the downstairs neighbours walking her Yorkshire terrier, there's no one around. I take the stairs at a run and let myself in. Rosie meets me in the hallway. She listened to me: she's home, thank goodness. I pull her into my body, rest my head on her shoulder and inhale the bubblegum scent of her shampoo.

She laughs. 'This is all so dramatic. Luckily I was pretty queasy at work this morning. Trevor would never have believed me otherwise.'

My phone buzzes in my pocket. Probably work demanding to know where the hell I am. 'Rosie, this is serious.' I pull away and look at her. 'If the *Sketch* breaks the story, we're in trouble. There'll be reporters all over us throughout your pregnancy.'

The mirth drains from her eyes. 'What can we do?'

'We need to call Becca, let her know that our names have been leaked and talk through our game plan.'

'Do we *have* a game plan?'

My throat is dry. I'm still not sure what to do. It's hard to bring our options into cool, clear focus. My phone starts buzzing again. I draw myself up tall; Rosie needs me to be strong. 'You get Becca on the line, I'll deal with work.'

I have six missed calls from Matthew's extension and two

from a withheld number. I don't listen to the voicemails; instead, I compose a quick text to Matthew informing him that I have a migraine, that I need to lie down, that I'm very sorry. Leaving work without handing over is an unforgivable breach of the journalist work ethic. I remember Tom once vomiting into his bin, not permitted to leave until he'd finished deciphering his shorthand for me. But I can't worry about this now.

Rosie's through to Becca. I catch a few yeses, then a description of where we live. While I'm waiting, I call Hong Shu.

She's silent after I explain what's happened. A tiny part of me is hoping that she'll say the *Sketch* has been after them too. That we're not alone in this. I bite my lip as I hear her take a sharp in-breath.

'Oh, Jules, mate. I'm so sorry. If there's anything we can do to help, let us know.'

'Thanks – I don't think there is. Maybe just call me if anyone approaches you?'

'Of course. Stay strong, and send our love to Rosie.'

A chill creeps along the back of my neck as I realise what this means. Someone tipped off the *Sketch* about Rosie's pregnancy, but they didn't say anything about Anita and Hong Shu. If the leak came from a member of staff at the uni, they would have referred to two couples, two pregnancies – there'd be no reason to single us out. But it looks like the paper only knows about Rosie and me. The leak must have come from someone close to us. The circle of people who know we're participating in the trial is small: Rosie's parents, my father, Anthony. One of the people we trusted with our news has gone to a tabloid. Who? I can

dismiss the Barcombes immediately – they'd never do anything to hurt Rosie. And besides, they're exactly the kind
of people who'd take pride in screwing their lips tightly
shut and walking away if a reporter approached them. My
father is more volatile, true. And he does like sounding off,
especially when he's had a drink. But I was explicit about
needing secrecy, and if there is one thing I can be confident
in, it's his loyalty to me.

That leaves Anthony. He loves Rosie, I can't deny that.
But he's selfish. Impetuous. I think back to when he first
learned of our participation in the trial. In his confusion he
wasn't able to manage his expression and I saw, I'm sure I
did, how startled he was by the realisation that I wasn't going
away. That Rosie might bear my child and be tethered to
me for ever.

'Jules.'

I look up. Rosie's expression is serious, her eyes wide and
alert. 'Becca's going to come here. She's bringing someone
from the university's press office. They want to coordinate
with us. Agree a plan.'

There's a rapping at the door. Rosie instinctively turns to
go and open it, but I shoot out a restraining arm, just in time.
I inch backwards, press myself against the wall, and Rosie
does the same.

Another knock. Rosie raises an eyebrow but I shake my
head. The letterbox squeaks. 'Juliet, Rosie?' I'm pretty sure
it's the voice of the guy who approached me at work.

I compose a text to Becca: *There's press outside the flat. If
you have sunglasses or a hat in the car, put them on as a precau-
tion. Ring when you get here so we know it's you.*

Becca being recognised entering our flat would pretty much confirm the tip – I wish I had more time to think. The man outside calls out our names again.

'Can't we just tell him to fuck off?' Rosie whispers.

'He had a photographer with him. If we go to the door, they'll get more pics.'

'Well, what if we agreed to talk to him? We could explain why we're doing it, encourage him to write a half-decent story.'

I shake my head. 'This is the *Sketch* we're talking about. We could give the most rational, articulate interview and they'd still print a load of sensationalist bollocks.'

Rosie sighs as our letterbox squeaks. Heart thudding, I sneak a look and see a torn notebook page on the doormat. Absurd as it makes me feel, I drop to my knees and crawl across the floor to retrieve it.

We can go to £30k if you give us an exclusive interview and do a photo session. We're going to run the story anyway, so why not cooperate? If we work together we can make sure it's a nice piece. You've got an hour to change your mind, otherwise I'll just have to go with what I've already got. Please help me report this story sensitively.

The message is signed 'Shane' and there's a mobile number scrawled at the bottom.

He's probably gone back to his car to wait out the hour, but still I return to my position pressed up against the wall as I hand Rosie the note.

'Thirty thousand. Oh, Jules, think what we could do with that,' she says.

'It's too low a price for our privacy.'

She purses her lips, looking thoughtful. Thirty thousand. Neither of us makes that much in a year.

'So, who do you think it was?' I say. I keep my voice gentle. Because I know. Anthony. It could only be Anthony.

'What do you mean?'

'Someone who knows about the pregnancy called the *Sketch*'s tip line and netted themselves a hundred quid.'

'No!' She shakes her head violently. Perhaps it's cruel to keep pressing her, but she has to understand: Anthony is the only person it could be. She needs to sever all ties, bar him from our home so he can't do any more damage.

'I know it's hard to believe. But I called Hong Shu. The *Sketch* don't know about her and Anita. If someone from the uni sold the story, then the media would have their names too.' I move towards the living room, but Rosie is rooted to the spot.

My mind flashes to our unborn baby, our fragile little kidney bean, buffeted by chemical surges every time Rosie's emotions shift. This can't be good for her. I take Rosie's arm and steer her to the sofa.

'We've been so careful,' she says. 'We only told a few people. No one would ...'

'Anthony reacted pretty strongly when you first told him,' I say.

'Oh, Jules, let's not do this, OK? Anthony wouldn't do a thing like that.'

'But you don't know ...'

My phone goes and I see it's Becca. She's here.

Becca's colleague introduces herself as Caroline, before taking a seat on our sofa, uncapping a fountain pen and positioning a leather-bound notebook on her lap. Rosie sits down next to her and I arrange two of the dining chairs so that Becca and I can sit opposite.

'So, tactics,' Becca says. Something about her careful eye make-up, her stylish skinny jeans and boots, reassures me. 'How would the two of you like to handle this?'

'We're not commenting,' I say. 'And it would be really helpful if you at the uni could refuse to confirm that we're participants.'

'We've got a standard line about not discussing individuals,' Caroline says. 'But are you sure it's wise in this case? They have your names; why not turn the story into a celebration? I mean – it's a historic first. Surely I don't need to tell you what a step forward this is. What a breakthrough for gay rights.'

Rosie is just perceptibly nodding her head as she listens.

'Look,' I say, 'I know that from your perspective this is great PR.'

Becca interrupts: 'No. Don't go there, Jules. Our first priority is to your unborn child.'

'Well, I'm glad you've said that. Because the only way we're going to give that child any semblance of a normal life is by being boring bastards that don't give media interviews.'

'Your child is not going to have a normal life,' Caroline says.

Everyone is silent for a moment. Rosie folds her hands over her abdomen. Is this the first time she's made this gesture? I have the strongest urge to go to her, to hold her. But this conversation is important – I have to win the argument.

Caroline spares Rosie the briefest glance before continuing. 'I'm sorry, but it won't. This baby is a miracle child. People are going to be curious. Why not use the media? Speak out on your own terms. Not commenting is going to make it look as though you're ashamed.'

A tear runs down Rosie's cheek. 'We're not ashamed. We just want to handle this right.'

Becca extracts a packet of tissues from her tote bag and passes it to Rosie with a gentle smile. 'We'll respect whatever approach you choose to go with,' she says. 'Your baby, your decision.'

Caroline is undeterred. 'Look, we could do this well. I've got a contact on the *Observer*, she interviewed Becca, did a lovely piece. Let's call her so that there's another version of you out there – otherwise you're leaving people no choice but to get their information from the *Sketch*.' She sits back in our sofa.

Rosie's eyes search mine out. She looks thoughtful, curious. I see a flicker of resilience; it's in the twitch of her jaw as her mind conjures the highbrow story. Am I being unreasonable in vetoing this? I remember the steady wave of our baby's heartbeat, so beautiful and yet so fragile. It's down to me to protect her.

'No,' I say. 'I know a counter-story seems like the logical thing to do. But if we advertise ourselves as being willing to speak, then we'll just create more demand for follow-up stories.'

'Are you sure, Jules?' Rosie says.

I try to look confident. 'Maybe it's a nice idea in theory, and it might make us feel better about the situation we're in today. But longer term all it'll do is bring ten more journalists to our doorstep. You have to trust me on this. I know the media.'

Caroline inhales. 'Well, we'll do what we can to try and shape the debate. I'm speaking with Becca's research associate Scott, getting him trained up to do interviews so that we have a male voice on our side. But seriously – do spend some time thinking this over. You're going to have journalists outside your home for a while, even if you do stay quiet.'

'Caroline and I are going to leave the decision with you two,' Becca says. 'All trial participants are anonymous unless they explicitly choose not to be. I'll comment on the science if approached. But nothing more.'

'Thank you,' I say. I want them gone now. I want to be lying down with my eyes closed. Rosie and I need to savour these last quiet moments before our names are out there. Becca seems to sense this and hugs us goodbye. I shake Caroline's hand, then finally Rosie and I are alone again.

As the afternoon passes into evening we feign normality, heating up lentil and butternut squash stew from the freezer. Using my phone, I keep running searches on our names, but the results stay the same: the *Post*, Petersfield Book Club.

We attempt bed, too tense for sex. For Rosie, being pregnant is a distinct advantage: within half an hour of getting under the covers her breathing sinks into a steady rhythm. I keep my body still to avoid disturbing her as my mind turns over the possible angles the *Sketch* might take. I think of scenarios where they won't use the story at all. I conjure into being a burly news editor, a middle-aged man, as they so often are. I imagine him saying, 'Not enough here without quotes', or, 'Who wants to read about a couple of dykes?'

I wish I had a religious impulse; I crave the satisfaction of falling to my knees and begging for an intervention, but know it would be futile without the belief that someone or something is out there listening. Every ten minutes or so I carefully lean down to the floor and refresh the search results on my phone.

At 4.52 a.m. the story is posted. It's accompanied by a series of diagrams showing what happens in natural fertilisation compared to the o-o process. The sperm in the illustrations have smiley faces. The egg cells are sullen and intimidating, obese despots.

Global First as Lesbian 'Fathers' Child

A 34-year-old reporter from the posh commuter town of Petersfield in Hampshire is set to become the world's first female dad.

Lesbian Juliet Curtis (pictured, left) is taking part in a clinical trial at Portsmouth University. Boffins there have fused her eggs with those of her girlfriend Rosie Barcombe (below, left – they've lifted her Facebook profile picture.)

The *Sketch* can exclusively reveal that curvy blond Rosie, 31, is now two months pregnant. The baby – one of the first in the world to be conceived without male involvement – is due next May.

The shy couple declined to comment on the wacky experiment, but a spokesperson for the university confirmed that two women have been made pregnant without the use of sperm. 'Ovum-to-ovum fertilisation is a major scientific breakthrough,' she said.

Richard Prior, Tory candidate for the upcoming Portsmouth South by-election, said: 'The purpose of this bizarre research seems to be to do away with the role of dads altogether. With each generation we will see a steady decline in the number of baby boys, creating a huge population imbalance. We should all be very concerned about what this might mean for our national security and cultural institutions.

'It heaps insult upon insult that this research is happening in Portsmouth, one of the most deprived areas in the south, where our NHS hospital is in a state of utter ruin. The people here want their taxes ploughed into job creation and social services – not niche university projects.'

Millions of people are going to read this. Our lives, our aspirations, packaged up neatly, awaiting scorn and ridicule. Anger and self-pity are pointless, I know that. Our only option is to carry on – to go about our business and hope that curiosity quickly dies away. I'm certain we'll be door-stepped again as other news outlets seek to catch up, but we'll not speak, we'll not throw hissy fits – we will politely ignore those who harass us. A few paparazzi shots of us conscientiously looking away from the camera and, if we're lucky, the attention will die right down.

I just need to get through the next day at work (assuming my fake migraine hasn't got me the sack), reject any overtures to talk about it and get on. Tomorrow – today, now – will be the peak.

There's less than an hour and a half to go before I need to get ready for work. I'll forgo my precious run. I switch off my phone, roll onto my back and close my eyes. Now that I know the worst, I'm able to sleep a little.

Chapter 10

When my alarm goes off, Rosie is sitting up in bed reading the story on her tablet, her face pinched with anger. 'They're treating us like freaks,' she says.

'It's just the *Sketch* being the *Sketch*.' I put an arm around her. 'If neither of us talks to the press they'll run out of things to write about and the interest will die away.'

Rosie groans and closes her eyes for a moment. I know this expression; she's waiting for nausea to pass. But it doesn't, and she has to shuffle off to the bathroom.

While she retches, I make tea with two sugars and put three ginger biscuits on a plate, bringing them to her in the bedroom as she wraps herself in her pink dressing gown and collapses back into bed.

'What's Trevor going to think?' Rosie says. 'He's been so good about giving me time off – he'll be upset that I didn't tell him.'

'I'm sure he'll understand why. Give him a call in a bit; let him hear what's going on from you. I think you'll have to stay away from the shop for a few days. You'll be a sitting target for the media otherwise.'

She closes her eyes for a moment. 'So what do I do? Stay

in here all day with the curtains drawn? It's not right, Jules. We've done nothing wrong.'

'Invite your mum round. There's plenty of food in the freezer, so you won't have to go out. Anything you say to a reporter – any throwaway comment – they can print. I need you to remember that.'

'You're not staying? You're planning to go to work?'

I long to stay with her. I'm not sure she's strong enough to bear the barrage that's coming, and I want nothing more than to hold her to my chest, to shield her from the intrusion. But I need to think longer term.

'I have to go in,' I say. 'It'll be worse for me if I stay away. I don't trust Matthew – I need to see what's going on.'

She grips my hand. 'What about just for today? Just one day. Call in sick.'

I shake my head. A day's grace won't help the situation, won't lessen the scrutiny. And I can't afford to lose my job, not with a baby on the way.

She sighs. 'OK. But I'm not letting them make a hermit out of me for ever, Jules. Let's get today out of the way, then the two of us need to sit down and plan how we're going to fight back.'

My 7 a.m. start time foils the media: I'm able to get into work without encountering any photographers. The *Post*'s car park is quiet, so I stay in the Fiesta a moment while I brave a look at my work social media accounts. Even this early in the morning my timeline is filled with eccentrics from across the globe: some are content to call me an ugly dyke; others place me at the centre of a lesbian plot to eliminate men from the human race. But there's worse:

If men won't go near your dirty old cunt then it's a sign you shouldn't be having babies.

And worse again: *I wouldn't blame any man who put you back in your place with a good old-fashioned raping.*

I should be able to laugh at such things. It's so predictable, in its way. A few months back a female TV journalist was mooted as a potential replacement for a sacked presenter on a car programme. Social media instantly erupted with male fans of the show wishing her dead. And here I am, replacing men in the reproductive process. This day was always coming. Part of me has known it all along, and yet I was able to side-line the knowledge, to let joy at the scientific breakthrough suffocate my rationality.

My chest tightens. An image: Rosie, nauseous in bed, look-ing at these very same poisonous comments. I see her face in such vivid detail, the fury in her eyes. I shouldn't have left her. There's a risk that a day of door-knocks might rile her into doing something unhelpful, like trying to reason with one of the many reporters who'll base themselves at the flat. It's unsociably early, but I text her mother, sending a link to the *Sketch* story and imploring her to go to our flat as soon as she can. I list the reasons why it's essential to ignore the press, just in case Elaine shares her daughter's desire to answer back. For a terrible moment I think that I might cry, but I steady myself with deep breaths until the prickling behind my eyes goes away.

I put my tablet back inside my satchel and vow not to look at the social media nonsense again. It's unproductive, picking at a scab. I won't let these people sabotage my composure. A message from Elaine – she's going over to Rosie straight away. Good. Now I can face the day.

With what I hope is a blank face, I get out of the car and head towards the newsroom. I'm wearing my pinstriped trouser suit, picked out because it's the least faded and misshapen of my work clothes. I've styled my hair with a little wax, and although I never usually bother with make-up, today I've borrowed Rosie's mascara. My eyelids feel weighed down by it. I have a shaky, low blood sugar feeling from skipping breakfast and with each step there's a buckling sensation in my knees.

This is the easy part, I tell myself. Very few of my colleagues will have seen the story. Perhaps they won't hear about it until mid-morning, by which time my calmness, my normalcy, will make it very clear that we don't need to treat this as a big deal. My armpits are hot and sticky.

'Excuse me? Excuse me, miss?' A white-haired man wearing round spectacles is standing outside the staff entrance, barring my way.

'I hope you don't mind – I saw the newspaper article and I felt compelled to try and reason with you. Do you know that the word "father" is used eleven hundred times in the Bible?'

I give a weak smile and push past him. Absurd that I feel the blood rising to my face, that part of me feels guilty, even. But I can't stop, can't pause. Whipping my jacket off, I hurry up the stairs. *Relax that forehead. Lips tight together. Head up, but keep looking straight ahead.*

'Juliet!' It's Matthew. He turns and grabs my arm as I walk past his desk. I blink, looking down at his fingers, and he quickly lets go.

'In here.' He gestures to our glass-fronted meeting room, a tiny, windowless space containing a plain wooden table and three plastic chairs.

Neither of us sits.

'Do you want this paper to go under?' he asks. His eyes are hard pinpoints of hatred. It's not a rhetorical question. He is playing the schoolmaster role he seems to like so much and he expects me to answer.

'No.'

'Really? I find that hard to believe. Disappearing right on deadline yesterday – that was bad enough. But how do you think we look this morning? Take a look.' He proffers last night's *Portsmouth Post*. 'Tell me what's missing, Juliet. Tell me what story is not fucking in here.'

I don't reply. Instead, I focus on my breathing, on keeping my face still, on ensuring that none of the turmoil within me reaches my eyes.

Matthew flings the paper onto the table. When he speaks again his voice is low. 'It's humiliating – having a national scoop us to a story on one of our own reporters. You've made a fool of us. Everyone else is working their guts out to keep this paper afloat – and you're wilfully sabotaging us. You owe us all an apology. And when you've done that, you can help us claw back from this mess with a seven-hundred-word first-person account of this test tube baby nonsense. You're today's centrefold.'

He reaches for the door handle.

'Matthew, I can't,' I say. 'This is private.'

My face burns under his gaze. *It will get better from today*, I tell myself. *Tomorrow will be easier.*

'Oh no you don't, Missy. You're an employee of this paper – you'll write what I tell you.'

'If I was prepared to write about myself, I could ring up one of the nationals and get some proper money for it.' My stomach lurches – I'm shocked at my own nerve. But I will not be spoken to like a naughty schoolgirl.

Matthew's eyes harden, and when he speaks he pulls his lips right back, exposing his teeth. 'You – you check your contract. We own every word you write.'

I look down at the carpet tiles, a cheap grey synthetic that looks as though it would take your skin off.

'Sit down,' Matthew says.

I obey, thinking it might be easier to appear calm with the weight off my legs. My mouth is dry and I have to swallow.

Matthew doesn't sit. Instead, he steps in closer, towering over me. 'OK. I understand how awkward it must be for you—'

'If we give one interview, we'll—'

'—and I suppose I understand you wanting to protect your private life. But the story is out there now – you understand? Our readers will expect us to cover it. Answer the *Sketch* back through our pages. I could even stretch to giving you a column. An inside view of the trial. Your own personal soapbox.'

I shake my head. My life with Rosie is the most precious thing I have, something to be balled up tightly inside me, away from the petty sneers and degradations of my working world. I know all too well the careful selection of quotes that goes on, the twisting, the sensationalism. 'Matthew, there's nothing you can say that will make me write about it.'

'Then you're an idiot. We're covering the story regardless.'

I stand up. Matthew doesn't move, so I have to walk around him to leave the room.

*

From the glances and head jerks directed my way as I walk over to my desk, I'm left in no doubt that the story has made its way around the newsroom. They've probably all read the social media posts describing the anticipated satisfaction of knifing me in the vagina too. My face must be a mass of red blotches. But I can do this. I'll start the day with calls to the police. Then the fire and ambulance services.

Tom scurries in, late and clutching a coffee. A light pat on my arm as he passes. 'Hang in there, Jules.' Not a shadow of pique on his face for the lies of omission I've directed at him. I try to formulate an apology, but I'm too slow – he's gone.

As I approach my desk I see two yellow Post-its stuck to my screen and for a moment I feel a surge of gratitude. Messages! Stories! But when I get closer I see that neither of them bears writing. Each note features a crude drawing of a friendly, smiling sperm cell. Two desks down Kyle – posh, arrogant Kyle – is hunched over, his back heaving with laughter.

'Dick,' I say. I don't let the neutral expression on my face fracture for one instant as I tear away the Post-its, throw them in the bin and switch on my computer. While my elderly machine boots up, I call one of the police stations on my patch and begin taking down details of overnight vandalism and stolen cars.

It's not long before they send the *Post*'s only other female reporter, Abi Kaplan, over to me. She's twenty-two, with flame-red hair, and always moves around the newsroom briskly, face lit with excitement at whatever story she's working on. She's been here almost a year and often she'll stay even later than I do, seeking out new angles, holding out for the best quotes.

She stands beside me as I type. 'I've been sent to talk to you,' she whispers. 'Shall we go to the canteen, where no one's watching?'

I shake my head. The desk next to mine has been unoccupied since Will moved to London to shift on the tabloids, so Abi sits in his old chair, swivelling round to face me. I sense her awkwardness, and part of me wants to tell her it's OK – I know this isn't personal. But I don't trust myself not to cry. I try to keep typing, but the position of each letter on the keyboard sinks into a forgotten recess in my mind. My usual clatter becomes a pained tip-tap.

'They've put us both in a horrid position.' Abi keeps her voice low.

She'll be in for a bollocking when she admits she didn't get quotes. For all the confidence she projects in the newsroom, she's young enough and inexperienced enough to take each failure personally, to worry about not being good enough. With a twist of guilt, I remember that particular soup of concerns. I've nursed so many reporters through this moment, tried to lift their sagging self-esteem with carefully timed pep talks. But never Abi – I realise with a jolt that I've never made an effort with her. Perhaps she's simply never needed help. Or maybe I've finally become bitter, something in Abi's ambition and unstinting effort triggering it in me.

'Your partner, she looks pretty – pregnancy is obviously agreeing with her,' she says.

My fingers falter against the keyboard. I can't get another damn word out and Abi can see as much. Folding my hands in my lap, I turn to face her. There's hesitancy in her eyes and

I feel terrible at being so unhelpful. *Fuck.* It's so tempting to just grab my things and go home.

'We really ought to be friends, the two of us,' Abi says. 'The only two women on news, all the macho bullshit we have to deal with. And look what they're doing – they're pitting us against each other. You know as well as I do that they want a female by-line for this story so they can't be accused of being misogynistic. That's the only reason they sent me.'

'I know, and I'm sorry. I'm just not saying anything to anyone.'

'Well, I hate to say this, but I don't think you're being sensible. Matthew's not going to let either of us off the hook – you know they'll expect me to turn in my seven hundred words regardless of whether you speak to me or not. Please, think about it.'

I shake my head. She's right, but I'm still going to stick to my *starve the bastards of fuel* strategy. A flash goes off – one of the photographers has snapped me and Abi facing each other to create an impression that we're having a heart-to-heart.

'I find the whole prospect rather exciting,' Abi says. 'I mean, the tabloids are making a big fandangle about an all-woman society like it's some terrible thing. But imagine if they were right – what a different world we'd live in. No wars. Workplaces that get the best out of people. An end to dick-swinging hyper-competitiveness.'

I give her an apologetic smile and turn my attention back to my police story. 'I'm a no comment, I'm afraid. You're a great reporter but there's nothing you can say that'll change my mind.'

*

I manage to arrange things so that I'm out on the patch, covering a council meeting, when the evening edition comes out. After tapping the story out on my tablet and filing, I drive to the corner shop near our flat and buy a copy of the *Post* – something I've not done for years. They're trailing the story about me and Rosie as an exclusive on the front page; there's a teaser panel, a picture of me taken at a Christmas party around three years ago. *Inside the life of Juliet Curtis – the world's first female father-to-be.* I avoid the cashier's eye as I hand him the coins.

Back in the car, I look at myself on the cover. I'd noticed the camera just a second before the picture was taken, but had been too slow in turning away. It being Christmas, I was at least wearing a small slick of lipstick, along with my special-occasion top, a blue halterneck picked out by Rosie.

Inside, the feature is exactly as expected. Heavily padded to the extent that a well-trained reader will sense the struggle each of my colleagues faced in trying to remember anything noteworthy about me. Matthew gives an assessment of me as a reporter: 'I'd describe her as plodding rather than dynamic. But she's made steady progress as a journalist during her time with us.' Patronising bastard. I'm sure he enjoyed calculating what would cause me maximum offence, then twisting it into a sentence gleaming with surface-niceness.

Tom isn't quoted at all. I really must thank him because I know they'll have singled him out, put pressure on him to recall an anecdote, to describe our flat, or give up a few details about Rosie.

A couple of other colleagues describe me as hard-working but shy and private, implying that I'm secretive about my relationship – which I'm not. Overall I emerge as an underwhelming presence. Of course, this is what I wanted, to be boring and grey. To send a message: *No point being curious about me because there's nothing exciting to learn*. Yet, buried as I am under waves of tiredness, I still register a contradictory stab of disappointment that no one had anything better to say.

Chapter 11

There are four of them outside our block, all men, bantering at the top of their voices, no consideration for the neighbours even though it's after dark. Face still, eyes front, I stride towards the flat. They've littered the path with cigarette butts and discarded coffee cups.

'That's one of them, I think. Juliet? Juliet!'

I deliberately don't look, but I sense a flurry of movement, hear the clicking of expensive cameras. My face feels hot.

'We've got a very generous offer to put to you, Juliet.'

'Do you think it's right to try and do away with men?'

'Have you got anything to say in response to the threats on Twitter?'

Keeping my head down, I walk around them, no choice but to tread on Mrs Mallory's lovingly tended flowerbeds. Two of them follow me up the concrete staircase that leads to our front door. My instincts tell me to turn, to snarl a fuck off – but they want me to do that, their cameras are ready to capture every contortion of my face. Treating them as though they're invisible is the only option. Thank goodness I had the foresight to keep my keys in my hand.

I slip inside the flat and press my back against the door.

Home. Respite. The adrenalin that's powered me through the day, that's kept me upright in the face of hostile stares, leaves my body in a torrent. Something inside me crumples, and the need for Rosie, to be held by her, is so strong I almost gasp.

Anthony emerges from the living room, wearing a tight-fitting T-shirt bearing Thai writing and skinny jeans – the uniform of university students ten years his junior. I have to close my eyes for a moment; concentrate on each breath, on my legs, my middle. It would have taken so little to comfort me, and yet even this, a quiet hug, a moment of privacy, is denied.

'You're back,' he says. 'They've been banging on the door all afternoon.'

Rosie follows him into the hallway. She's wearing jogging bottoms and a thick roll-necked jumper; her unwashed hair is tied back and there are dark shadows under her eyes.

'How are you doing?' I ask, putting a hand on her shoulder.

Her eyes fill with tears and I see her swallow before she gives a brave little nod. 'OK. All things considered. Anthony's offered to go out and get us a takeaway. You must be starving.'

I turn to look at Anthony, watching for signs of guilt: a bobbing of the Adam's apple, a tightening of the jaw. But his face remains still. Could he really have betrayed us? It seems so implausible. But if not him, who? Out of everyone we told, he's the only person I can doubt.

'I'm exhausted, to be honest,' I say. 'Couldn't we just get something out the freezer? Have an early night?'

'I'll only be twenty minutes,' Anthony says. 'A nice Indian is the least Rosie deserves after the day she's had.'

'I had to go to work . . . I couldn't . . . ' Leaving her behind this morning was wrong. Of course I know that. But then, staying away from the *Post* would have been wrong too. None of today's choices carried a glint of a good outcome.

'Jalfrezi for you, Rosie? Poppadoms and mango chutney? Jules? What do you fancy?'

I meet his eye, watching for confirmation, for something, anything, that will let me be certain. His face is lit with his characteristic jolly energy. The optimism of someone who knows, whatever happens, his mother will always put a rent-free roof over his head.

'I don't want anything. I think I'm going to turn in.' Shooting Rosie an apology with my eyes, I shut myself in the bedroom.

I'd felt hungry on my way home, but now, as I lay down on the bed in my work suit, my stomach is clammed shut, resisting the very idea of food. I listen for the sounds of Anthony leaving, but his whispered conversation with Rosie retreats into the living room. Oh – how can she still be his friend? There's really no one else it could have been. Dad's reaction to the baby news wasn't what you'd call joyous, true, but it's unthinkable that he would betray me. We're each other's only blood relatives; the only people to know what life was like in our old family home after my mother's tragic accident.

Closing my eyes I conjure him working the frying pan, fag in mouth. We used to have a small glass table in the corner of the kitchen, and when I was really young I'd sit there while he cooked. I remember giving him a hard time because I wanted a McDonald's. It's all the kids at school ever went on about and I'd never even eaten there, not once. And so he sat me down and told me I was at McDaddy's. He put on this whole waiter act, laying out a couple of squares of toilet roll in lieu of napkins. Calling me Ma'am. What he dished up was essentially an omelette in between two slices of bread. But he added ketchup with a ceremonial flourish and told me it was an Egg McButtie. And, somehow, he made the best thing I'd ever tasted.

I have no way of making Rosie understand what it meant, to just be the two of us – father and daughter. Sometimes her face betrays pity as she contemplates how much I lacked as a child, compared to her. And yet no one was more loved than me. No one felt safer, more able to believe in the better life my dear old dad told me time and again was mine for the taking.

I sigh and reach in my bag for my tablet. I've not had any time to properly review the coverage since this morning. But I may as well know the worst.

The *Citizen*'s website carries an interview with someone I went to school with, who claims to be a good friend. They have a picture of her, Lisa Jones, all dolled up and wearing fake eyelashes. I haven't spoken to her for a good ten years, and we weren't particularly close back when we were at school.

'Juliet was pushing the political correctness agenda even before it was the fashionable thing. She always made a point of using the boys' toilets. I remember her saying at the time that she didn't recognise traditional gender boundaries, that she was making a statement.

'She wore trousers to school even though at the time they weren't permitted for girls.'

This is utter bollocks. I wasn't the kind of girl to make

points and I certainly never had the desire to relieve myself in the boys' bogs. Did Lisa Jones see the coverage about me this morning and recognise an opportunity? Or have the media been seeking out the Petersfield School's former students, taking any bullshit anecdote as fact?

The *Guardian* website carries a short interview with Scott. 'There's no need for men to feel threatened by this,' he says. 'It's a development, akin to the introduction of the pill, that should be celebrated for the choice it offers women.' He talks about the way heterosexual couples might benefit from the technique – for instance, the sister of an infertile man could donate an egg, creating an opportunity for family resemblances and genetic connections. But his interview is run alongside a piece on Richard Prior, where the politician once again manages to imply that the trial is somehow exacerbating social deprivation in Portsmouth.

There's also an article covering the decision of several Gulf States to announce that visit visas will not be granted to two-woman babies because of 'hitherto undetected genetic diseases that may put local populations at risk'. My baby hasn't been born yet, and already there are places in the world where she won't be able to set foot, her horizons narrowing before she's even taken her first breath. Have we done her a terrible disservice, conceiving her the way we did, letting her become a symbol? At the back of my mind, I feel the question forming: if we'd known that just two babies would be created in this first round of the trial, if someone had shown me today's coverage, would we have still gone ahead and used o-o to create our baby? I bat the question away. No good can come of examining choices already made.

Next, I brave another look at social media, the jaunty feed I'm forced to maintain for work. The *Post*'s masthead is my backdrop, and my profile picture has me giving a false, open-mouthed smile. A high proportion of the comments talk about my appearance:

Put us out of our misery. You're actually a man, aren't you? This is all one giant scam because you got the sperms.

How did you end up with a hottie like your missus? There must be a queue of men wanting to get her up the duff!

I screw my eyes tightly shut and make a snap decision to delete my profile, disappear from social media completely.

Later, after she's seen Anthony out, Rosie flings the bedroom door open. I know this mood; she's most likely furious with me for not feigning trust in him. But when she sees me on the bed she pauses and her posture softens.

'Jules? What is it? You look like shit.'

'Oh, nothing. I've just been looking at the coverage. I know how these things work, I shouldn't get upset.'

She sits on the bed next to me, takes my hand and presses it against her belly. She smiles and I feel my eyes moistening as I smile back. What should I be feeling right now? I'm too overwhelmed to register any kind of joy.

'Anthony's gone. We decided not to bother with a curry in the end,' Rosie says, releasing my hand and stroking my hair. 'Here – I know something that might cheer you up.' She reaches for my tablet and logs into Facebook. 'Take a look at this – *Sappho Monthly* have contacted me. They want to do a profile.'

'Oh Jesus – I thought you'd adjusted your privacy settings.'

'I have. But one of Ant's friends works there. What do you think? I know you're against us doing interviews, but this would be for their "Champions" segment. In their message they call me a pioneer. I like the sound of that. Better than "wacky experiment", anyway.'

'Rosie, we've been through this. If you speak to them it'll only feed the interest. We need the story to die away if we're going to have any chance of getting back to a normal life.'

She takes hold of my hand and kisses it. 'Listen, when our daughter is older, she's going to be trawling the internet, looking up everything that was said about her birth. Don't you want to be able to show her that we stood up for her right to exist? That we tried?'

It seems so impossible to imagine the baby inside Rosie as a young woman. Today seems to have made her less real in my mind: press strategies, the effort of holding my face still, have killed the magic of her beating heart.

'No, Rosie. I can understand why you'd want to do it, but you have to trust me – I've spent over a decade working in the media and I know how it works. Completely starving reporters is the only way we're going to be able to give our daughter a normal life. Later on, when we explain it to her, she'll understand that we had to keep quiet for her sake.'

Rosie sprawls back on the bed, then props herself up on one elbow. Our faces are just inches apart and I notice that, even though she's tired, her skin is different. It has a freshness to it; perhaps this is what they call the pregnancy glow. I find it unexpectedly moving, that she can look so pretty at such a time.

'Jules – can you just promise me that you're looking at the

big picture? I know you always want to do the right thing, but I can't help wondering: is this about you? You've always been a private person—'

'Rosie . . .'

She frowns. 'Because, even if it does bring a non-stop procession of photographers, I kind of feel as though we've got a duty towards the trial. To speak out and help people understand that this is about choice – no one needs to feel threatened.'

I sigh. 'What we need to do is prove who leaked the story so that we can stop him doing any more damage.'

'Jules . . .'

'Look, I'm sorry – Anthony's the only person it could be. I find it incredible that you won't even consider the idea.'

She gets up, tucking a stray curl behind her ear. 'Let's not do this. I'm hungry, you must be too.'

I stand, facing her. 'We can't ignore the fact that someone in our circle – one of a handful of people who we decided to trust the most – is willing to sell information about us.'

She goes out of the bedroom and across the hallway to the kitchen. 'You froze some of that risotto we had last week, didn't you? Shall we just microwave that?'

I follow her into the kitchen and watch as she rummages through the freezer and places a frosted plastic tub on the worktop. I place a hand on her arm. 'I do understand you not wanting to believe it. But there's a simple way to find out. Let's give everyone we know a very different, but specific, detail about the pregnancy and see which one finds its way to the press.'

Her mouth is open; her eyes lit with a new energy. 'You

cannot be suggesting ... Jules, I am not subjecting my best friend and parents to some sort of test. Jesus. Do you know nothing about how trust works?'

'Rosie—'

'No way. You need to drop this. Let me get to the microwave.'

I step aside as she removes the lid from the container and puts it in to defrost. We both look down at our feet as the microwave hums. I've always admired her loyalty, her insistence on seeing the best in people. But our situation is dangerous. Anthony's continued presence in our lives will bring nothing but pain. When we buy a new family home he could pass on the address; when Rosie goes into labour he might sell the news, ensuring the press pack is waiting for us at the hospital. He's never thought me good enough for Rosie. But doesn't he realise it's too bloody late to tear us apart?

I look up, about to explain, but Rosie gets in first. 'OK. Why Anthony and not your father?'

'Dad just wouldn't,' I say. 'If it makes you happy, I'll subject him to the same test, but you'll see—'

'We're not doing a fucking test!'

Rosie has never raised her voice to me before. The shock of it is like a lungful of freezing air. Her eyes flash. The microwave beeps, and then goes silent.

'You think because my father is poor, he must be the number-one suspect?' I remember his wounded expression when we spoke in the kitchen last Sunday. My only parent. Always so glad to see me after school. Always so keen to hear what I'd learned. The fact that Rosie can even suspect him makes me wince; it feels so personal. In her mind, my father dwells in an unsavoury place, one of failure and violence, of defeatism and sloth. Are there times when she looks at me and, seeing past the veneer of professionalism, believes that I belong back on the council estate too?

She sighs. 'That's not what I'm saying at all – I just . . . sometimes he doesn't seem as happy for you as he ought to be.'

A rare instinct surges inside me – I cannot be beaten. I will not let her have the last word. 'Because he lives in a dirty house, likes a drink, likes a smoke? It would have to be him, wouldn't it? Someone like that couldn't feel love and loyalty towards their only daughter. Oh no. That would be far too middle class.'

'You're angry and tired. Let's eat.' Still her eyes are lit with the conviction that she knows best. I want – I need – to see a softening of her expression. I am overwhelmed, unhinged by the need.

'I mean, a man like that . . . I'm surprised you think a tip fee for a story was enough for him. I'm surprised you haven't accused him of nicking things from the flat.'

She reddens as she reaches for a serving spoon to divide up the meal. In that moment her tears spill over. 'What are you trying to do, Jules?'

The remorse is instant. I wrap an arm around her waist, pull her into my body. 'I'm sorry. I don't know. I just . . . '

She lays her hand against the back of my neck. I feel a pang of relief. It's rare for me to go so far, to disregard consequences in a flash of hot anger. But perhaps, in some twisted way, this is what Anthony wants. I won't let him win. If he hoped his betrayal would break our relationship, then I'm going to prove him wrong.

Chapter 12

The next day, as I leave for work, I tape a note to the front door, informing journalists in black marker pen: *Neither of the inhabitants of this flat is prepared to give interviews. Please note this formal request to not disturb us. A continued presence here will be deemed as harassment and reported to the Independent Press Standards Organisation.*

I doubt that this will be effective – the IPSO Editors' Code of Practice is very much a voluntary thing, with no legislation to back it up. But still, I allow myself a moment of satisfaction as I stick it to our door. There are five different media outlets waiting outside, and my short walk to the Fiesta is captured by a television-camera, photographers shouting my name all the while. They close in as I pop the locks, shouting their questions. A frenzy of coffee breath, tangled arms and camera flashes. The instinct is to shrink, to flinch. But I make myself go dead inside. *In I get. Off I go.* The fuckers are reluctant to get out of my way, but I keep inching forward, revving the engine.

At work there's a handful of photographers outside, along with a TV anchor doing a piece to camera. The microphone she's holding bears the CNN logo. A reporter has come all the way from America. For me. How foolish to believe that yesterday was the peak. American press! Perhaps everything up until now has just been a prelude. I try to comfort myself with the knowledge that, had we given interviews, the attention would be even more intense. My *starve the bastards of fuel* strategy must surely start paying dividends soon.

Inside the newsroom my colleagues stare, amazed and perhaps even strangely envious of the attention I'm receiving, while Matthew's tone is more derisory than usual. When lunchtime comes around, I've had enough. I decide to do something I never do – take an actual break. Tom accompanies me to the canteen. It's a small room with white-topped tables and blue plastic chairs reminiscent of secondary school. There's a counter where a small woman with tight grey curls operates a tuck shop, selling a few sandwiches and the sugary snacks so beloved of those who need to eat on the go. I get a coffee from the ancient vending machine, and buy an apple and a KitKat. I take a table in a quiet corner while Tom carefully inspects each of the sandwiches, finally settling on a cheese baguette. Newsroom staff rarely make it down here, so most of the tables are taken up by the sales team, a different species with their immaculate grooming and upbeat chatter. I catch them turning to look every so often. *That's her, the female dad.* My first instinct is to wilt, to look down at the floor. But this is swiftly followed by something else: I won't call it strength, more a kind of stubbornness. I have every right to be here. Their stares shame them, not me.

'I need a favour,' I say as Tom sits down opposite me.

'OK.' Today he's stubbly and ruffled, like he's spent the night in a stranger's bed.

'It's a bit sensitive.'

'Well – you're obviously not going to be asking me for my sperm, so I guess I've got nothing to fear.' He takes a hearty bite of his baguette.

'I'm so sorry I didn't tell you the whole truth.'

'It's fine, don't worry. Looking back, I should have thought . . . I mean, of course lesbians are going to want their own biological children.'

'Well, I can't claim to speak for all lesbians. But it's right for Rosie and me.' I unwrap my KitKat.

'You're not worried about the health implications?'

I shake my head. 'I've looked closely at the uni's data, and although the process is a radical departure from everything we know, the animal babies they've created have all been normal.'

'There are scientists who disagree, though.' Tom holds up his hands. 'I'm not saying they're right. It's just, well, it's a debate that's going to rumble on and on.'

'So listen, only a handful of people knew that Rosie and me were signed up for the trial,' I say.

He nods as he takes another mouthful of baguette.

'We're looking at my dad, Rosie's parents and her friend Anthony – who, by the way, is the traitorous bastard who did it.'

Tom's eyes widen as he chews. A couple of pieces of grated cheese land on the tabletop. 'You're sure it's him?'

'Rosie won't believe it, though, that's the problem. So I'm stuck having to put up with this snivelly arsehole who still lives with his mummy . . .'

'I still live with my mummy.'

'Yes, but he's thirty.'

'I'm not much younger.' Tom gives a lopsided grin.

'Anyway, he hangs around our flat all the time. And I know he's the one who did it, but since I can't prove it, I'm expected to be friendly towards him. But I've worked out a plan. It will involve some amateur dramatics – you OK with that?'

Tom nods as he polishes off the last of his baguette.

I'm unexpectedly moved. Such easy acquiescence, such loyalty. Whatever happens, I have Tom as someone I can rely on. I sip my coffee, black and abrasive. 'OK. How about: someone saying they're a journalist knocks on Anthony's door and offers him five grand for an interview? You say that you've heard he's a very close friend of Rosie Barcombe and you're hoping to do a piece on what makes her tick. You promise him anonymity.'

'What do I do if he says "yes please"? I don't have five grand to hand him.'

'You'll do it, then? Oh Tom, I'm so grateful. Once he agrees, just say that you need to go back to your newsroom to get your editor to sign a cheque, and that you'll be back tomorrow.'

Tom looks up at the ceiling. 'Hmm – I think I'll say I'm from the *Tribune*. What shall I call myself? Maybe Calvin. Calvin Price. Sounds like a *Tribune* reporter, don't you think?'

I feel a pang of guilt – this plan is directly against Rosie's wishes. But unless I do something, her misplaced trust in Anthony is going to keep compromising our privacy.

'Here you are.' Matthew stands in front of us. He's wearing a red and navy striped shirt that hurts my eyes. 'What do you think you're doing? Who said you could hide away?

We haven't even got a bloody cover story yet. Get your arse back upstairs.'

Tom reports to the sports editor, so this is directed solely at me. I slide my uneaten KitKat and apple over to Tom and stand. 'My contract says I get an hour's lunch,' I say to Matthew as I walk away.

'Less of the attitude, Missy. And by the way – the *Citizen* have run a lovely piece on your dole-bludger father. Any comment?'

I don't look back.

'No? Didn't think so.'

I skim through the story when I'm certain no one's looking. It's something I should have predicted – an image of him leaving the Green Dragon, all greasy-haired and bleary-eyed. I left messages for him when the story broke, warning him about being doorstepped, but if I'd only calmly thought about what the press interest might mean for others, besides Rosie and me, I would have foreseen exactly this. *No wonder lesbian trial mum wants to do away with fathers*, the headline reads.

Dad didn't speak to the reporter, so they don't have much substance – only a few unnamed sources gloating over the fact that his last steady job was back in the eighties. They refer to him as a widower and single father, but in a way that implies he's somehow chosen this lot in life. Reading the article makes me feel the pull of my childhood home, and I decide to rebel again by leaving at 5 p.m. sharp. Perhaps now Rosie will be forced to admit that my dad can't be behind the leak. She's never been able to relax into his company the way I can – her comfortably off upbringing is far too great a barrier. But last night I was reminded of the thread of disapproval that runs through her uneasiness. That most middle-class of prejudices, the *anyone can pull themselves up by their bootstraps* narrative, so easy to believe when you're not the one who has to do it. Dad doesn't deserve this. He doesn't deserve any of it.

There's a photographer outside Dad's house, wearing a black beanie hat and combat trousers, leaning against an ancient BMW as he scrolls through his phone. He hollers my name when he spots me, thrusting the camera in my face, making me step round him several times as I approach my father's door.

Inside, the curtains are drawn. Dad drops himself into his usual spot on the sofa with a groan. 'How you holding up, love?'

I sink into my old armchair, keeping my parka on – in this house, central heating is reserved for sub-zero days. 'I'm so sorry about what I'm putting you through. That story – it was disgusting.'

'I'm a big boy,' he says. He nods towards the window. 'Although it's bad for business, having him outside. Fellas don't like having the press watch them buy their weed.'

'There's absolutely no justification for them harassing you like this . . .'

'Never mind that, love. Sit for a bit. Are Rosie and the baby OK?'

'As well as can be expected. It's all because of fucking Anthony. I'm sure it was him who tipped off the press.'

My father sparks up a fag. 'He's the one I saw at the birth-day dinner – no job? Correct?'

'Correct.'

'University-educated but still lives with his mum?'

I nod and my father tuts. I smile at this. I'm in the mood for a good, thorough slagging-off. If I'm to go home and enjoy a normal night with Rosie, first I need to vent some of the frustration that's clawing at my insides.

'He's had every advantage,' I say. 'Nice upbringing in a nice neighbourhood. Three years dossing around at university, even though his grades were nothing special. And now he's living rent-free. It makes me spit that someone could have so much and not make anything of themselves.'

Dad nods. 'Makes you wonder why Rosie likes him so much.'

'Loyalty, I guess. Been friends since infant school.'

He takes a drag of his cigarette and glances over at the bong in the corner of the room, but for the time being he resists. 'People outgrow each other all the time. I wonder what Rosie can have to talk about with him nowadays.'

I recall a hundred giggling conversations. Rosie and Anthony always appear to be having such fun in each other's company, but I've never been able to unpick why. For years I perched on sofa arms, perhaps overdoing my willingness to join in. And yet the substance of the conversation – if there ever was any – seemed to forever be just out of reach. I never found the things they laughed about funny. Rosie is a different version of herself with Anthony. Her laugh becomes shrill, sometimes spiteful. And at times I find myself wondering: where is *my* Rosie? Which version of her is most real?

Dad is looking at me. 'I'm scared,' I say. 'I keep telling myself that all this will stop. But there's a baby coming. A baby. And I'm going to have to be a mother to it and I don't know how. Not while all this is going on.'

He presses his lips together in a sympathetic smile.

'How was it for Mum?' I ask in a quiet voice. 'When she was pregnant. Was she frightened?'

He looks up at the ceiling for a moment. His hands are resting on the tops of his thighs and I see his fingers twitch. The nails are bitten; the tips are rounded and fat.

'Your mother loved every moment of it,' he says. 'You came as a bit of a shock. But it was like you woke a part of her that was sleeping. It was beautiful to see. Beautiful.'

I allow myself a moment to visualise it. Hazel Curtis. Only twenty. Hazel eyes like mine, light brown hair almost to her waist. I imagine her young hand resting against her belly. A delicate half-smile, as though she's remembering a special moment that's her secret, something she's never going to tell anyone about.

My father is assailed by a short bout of coughing. 'Suppose it's only natural that it'll be different for you,' he says. 'You haven't got the hormones and that kind of stuff going on.'

'Yeah.'

Eight months, I had with my mother. There are exactly four photographs of us together, taken in the pre-digital age when getting film developed was prohibitively expensive. Two taken in the hospital, my angry red face peeping out from a white blanket; my mother's smile wide and unselfcon-scious. Perhaps I imagine it, but when I look at those pictures I see a touch of possessiveness in my mother's bearing. She's holding me tightly, claiming me.

The other two were taken on the town's heath when I was several months older with sturdy arms and legs and a head of dark hair. In one picture she's lifting me up and our faces are close, my eyes staring into hers with a kind of fascination. I used to look at this photo a lot when I was little, trying to will myself to remember the moment. I never could. But the feeling it gave me – a warmth so intense that it came close to being pain – I was convinced it was a remnant, a shadow of what I'd felt then, as a baby with two parents.

The last image has my mother lying on her back, eyes closed, hair fanned out beneath her and me asleep on her chest.

Dad and I are silent for a while. If Hazel had lived, perhaps she would have given me things I've never realised were missing. Helped me understand what it means to be a mother.

My phone buzzes. A message from Tom. *Knocked on his door, made the offer & he told me to fuck off.*

I bite my lip. Did Tom definitely get the right house? This doesn't make sense.

'Alright, love?' Dad asks.

'Yeah. I better get going. Rosie's been stuck inside the flat all day.'

I'm photographed leaving Dad's house, and the paparazzo then tails me as I head home. Could I have been wrong about Anthony? Michael and Elaine wouldn't have been the tipsters, and it definitely wasn't my father. So that *only* leaves Anthony, whatever his reasoning. I should be relieved, I suppose, that for today he wasn't willing to share more details for more money. But I'm not, I'm confused. And more tired than I've ever felt in my life.

Chapter 13

The day of the Portsmouth South by-election arrives. Ovum-to-ovum fertilisation has come up repeatedly in campaign speeches, with Richard Prior now firmly established as the darling of the Alliance for Natural Reproduction. He's tapped into the city's own special variety of anger – he sensed a readiness to fight, and so he came to people with his cause and his blue ribbons and made them believe their sons were under threat. Because in so many ways they are. Not because of two-mother babies, but because of underinvestment, poor-performing schools and the cheapest heroin in the country. Because of the Saturday-night fights I'm always writing about, and the understaffing and long waits at St Luke's.

The voters now sporting blue ribbons won't read interviews with Scott in the *Guardian* – to them, he's just another over-educated liar. The threat they feel is real, even if the enemy they've conjured isn't.

Matthew saves me until last as he does his usual morning rounds, doling out assignments and demanding to know what leads reporters have for him. There's a spiteful gleam in his eye as he approaches and sits at the vacant desk next to mine. Looks like he's planning an extended visit.

'I'm giving you the election,' he says. 'Nice splash for you. I want talking heads from each of the polling stations ... '

'Am I really the best—'

' ... plus interviews with each of the candidates on their levels of optimism.'

'Matthew.'

'Then, you need to get down the Guildhall for live web coverage of the count. You've done election night before, you know the drill.' He smiles, but he doesn't get up. He's looking forward to the argument he knows will follow.

'You're putting her in an impossible situation.' Abi has rolled her chair over and is glaring at Matthew.

He turns to her, stony-faced, but she's undaunted. 'You can't expect Jules to interview a candidate who's campaigned on an anti two-mother baby platform. Let me swap with her. I don't mind a late one.'

A smile creeps across Matthew's face, but his eyes are filled with spite. 'Abi, my dear, ambitious as you are, you can't write every bit of news for this paper. And I do believe I'm the one who assigns the stories around here.'

I think ahead. Interviewing voters who care passionately about the trial when my picture is circulating widely in the media: it's a provocation. A trial participant interviewing an anti-trial candidate is a great news hook. The *Post* will be able to syndicate it across the nationals, make a few thousand. They're refusing to let me be the anonymous citizen I need to be if this story is to die down.

'Maybe I need to go home sick,' I say.

'Don't even think about it. There's already a written warning on its way to you for Monday's disappearing act.' He stands too close, his body looming over me. Wetting his lips, he lingers for another moment, perhaps a little disappointed that my complaints have ceased. Then he's gone.

'What a fucking joke,' Abi says. 'Talk to the union – surely he can't make you do this?'

I exhale. How memorable can a face be, when glanced at in a newspaper a single time? Perhaps voters won't know who I am. And when I interview the candidates I'll just say, 'I'm from the *Post*,' and not give a name. I'll do the minimum needed to not get fired; turn in turgid copy that's just about good enough. I won't let them win.

I look up at Abi. It's only 7.30 a.m. but her face is free from the tiredness stamped across the rest of the reporting team. 'I'll suck it up,' I say. 'But thanks for having my back.'

First stop of the morning is a polling station on a run-down estate. The houses in this part of the city were thrown up after the war, constructed from grey breeze blocks that conjure the Soviet Union of history textbooks. Locked together in tight rows, many have boarded-up windows or are decked out in graffiti. Penises are the prevalent motif.

I pull into the community centre and position myself outside the entrance with my notebook. A young boy, who should surely be at school, is riding a BMX bike in lazy circles around the car park. The rutted asphalt is dotted with patches of broken glass; there's an abandoned Rover, 'police aware' sticker across the windscreen. A sad little strip of garden runs parallel to the building, a grassy bank bedecked with burger boxes and beer cans.

The steady trickle of voters is mostly elderly. On average,

one in six is happy to stop and share who they're voting for and what they think are the important issues. I do four interviews, and even though one interviewee is wearing a blue ribbon, no one mentions the trial or shows any familiarity with my face. The tight knot in my stomach starts to unfurl. In this deprived part of Portsmouth the residents have more important things to care about than me and how I'm going about having a baby. These are my kin, in a strange way. I'm more at home here than I've ever been in my wealth-stuffed home town. Part of me will always associate Petersfield with not measuring up, with huddled groups of girls giggling at my clothes, with the humiliation of my maths teacher slipping me a jumper from lost property because he could see I'd long outgrown the one I was wearing. Here in Portsmouth there is no pretence, no fear of exposure. I'm surrounded by people who have it far worse than me.

A pair of potbellied men with matching shaven heads approach. Early fifties at a guess; one has a tattoo of a hawk on his neck.

''Ere – you're that dyke!' The one with the tattoo is speaking; he turns to his friend, who's rolling a cigarette. 'It's that dyke off the news, Phil. What you doing here, love? Looking for a fella? Want someone to show you what you've been missing?' He thrusts his pelvis forward and grabs at his crotch. Involuntarily, I take a step backwards. I despise myself for it. Stories of imprisoned reporters flash through my mind: faces swollen from beatings, executions in Syria. Lectures at college: *You go to prison for your sources. You rack up legal bills and lose your house to keep the whistleblower safe.* That's tough journalism. Not this.

I brandish my notebook. 'I'm from the *Portsmouth Post*. I'm covering the by-election.'

The boy on the bike pulls up to watch the exchange.

'Weh-hey!' This time it's the friend. He makes a grinding motion with his hips. 'She's come to find herself a real man before we go extinct.' The two men roar with laughter.

'Rug-muncher,' shouts the boy. 'Minge-licker.' His voice still hasn't broken, but he has one of those hard faces. A feral child. The men laugh even harder.

We've been conditioned to believe that things are getting better. Gay marriage. Ovum-to-ovum fertilisation. I look into the boy's eyes – there's no hesitation there. He must only be about ten, yet the views of his parents, of his friends' parents, are already entrenched. Deciding I've got enough material from this particular polling station, I walk back to my car. My eyes are stinging but I refuse to cry. I expected this. It's something I'm just going to have to weather.

For the remainder of the day I face intermittent ball-cupping derision across the city. People in groups behave the worst. You never can tell how someone will act from appearance alone – one of my fiercest encounters is with a sweet-looking old lady, shrunken and stooped, frosted pink lipstick, who shrieks at the top of her voice: 'Unnatural filth! Disgusting!' She seizes the attention of every passer-by and I can't help feeling ashamed.

In the evening I park up and approach the Guildhall, an imposing building in pale stone. There's a mini-demonstration on the steps. Perhaps thirty or so of Richard Prior's ardent supporters wave placards with anti-trial slogans for the sake of the camera crews prowling Guildhall Square. There are men and women, a mixture of ages, wrapped up tightly in coats and scarves as they line the route to the entrance, forming a corridor of hostile chanting that I'm going to have to walk through.

At the last moment I veer away, pull up the hood of my parka and carry on walking, entering a street lined with cafés and pubs. Even though it's a weeknight the pavements are alive with students. My nostrils are filled with a heady mix of aftershave, deep-fat fryers and cigarette smoke. I inhale sharply. The scent of youth, of normal life going on as usual. My city. My people. Every sickly tree, every piss-stench alley is as familiar to me as my own flat. This is my turf. How can they have stripped it of its comfort? How, in just a few short days, have they made it mean something else?

I stop and lean against the wall of a pub. If I'm recognised the media will bear down on me. I see it happening in my mind's eye: hyena pack, tearing at flesh, ripping and pulling and screaming with glee. I'm not strong enough. I'll crumple. Be seen crying on national television.

With shaky fingers I call Tom. 'I need to ask for your help again. I'm so sorry.'

'Jules?'

'Come and cover for me, please. I'll do one of your Sundays – whenever you want. Please. There's about ten different news crews – Al Jazeera's here, for fuck's sake. I'm not even kidding: Al Ja-fucking-zeera.' I'm being unfair. Reporters work too hard to be able to pick up the slack for their colleagues.

'Jules? I'm in the Nelson. With a lady.'

'Oh.'

'Mate? Is it really that bad?'

'I feel like I've turned up to cover a referendum on my own baby. There's a demonstration.'

A pause. The hyperactive beat of a summer hit thumps in the background. A shrill female laugh. 'OK, I'll come. I just need to—'

'You're drunk, aren't you?'

'Er . . . maybe a little bit.'

'Then don't worry. I don't like it when you drink-drive.'

'Jules . . . I just . . . Let me think—'

'No, it's fine, Tom, really. It was wrong of me . . . go back to enjoying your evening. I can do this.'

I breathe deeply as I hang up, then, without giving myself a moment to reconsider, I turn around and stride back towards the Guildhall.

My hood and brisk pace get me up the steps and into the building without a hitch. I'm probably the last person they expect to arrive. But once inside I can't keep my hood up without looking strange. Head lowered, I scurry into the main hall where the results of the count will be announced, one polling station at a time. It's a dimly lit wood-panelled room with a stage at one end and metal folding chairs in rows. Supporters of the various candidates stand in groups, chatting, while reporters conduct interviews around the edges of the room.

I take a seat in the darkest corner. What's the least amount of work I can get away with? At a minimum I need to maintain a live feed of the results, district by district. I'll need to identify myself to the candidates, get quotes from them as the count progresses to try to build anticipation on the *Post* website. Then, once the result is called, I need an interview with the winner and a couple of their supporters for tomorrow's paper.

I'm probably not going to be finished until midnight or thereabouts, but I can handle this. For the time being I'll avoid Richard Prior. My first interview will be with the Lib Dem candidate, Helen Gibbs. I know her from her work with various local charities. She's around sixty, wearing a teal skirt suit with short hair set in a wave very similar to Margaret Thatcher's trademark style. She's alone with her husband and as I approach I see her shoot a wistful look at the cluster of media around Prior.

'Mrs Gibbs? I was wondering whether you could spare a word or two for the *Post*.'

She stares up at me. 'Oh, love, you shouldn't be here.' She nods towards to Prior's supporters. 'That lot will eat you alive.'

'I don't have a choice, I'm afraid.' My voice catches. Kindness has no place. I'm in battle mode. 'So, are you confident?'

She shifts in her seat and is thoughtful for a moment. 'No. But don't put that. Let me think. Let's say: I'm disappointed that Tory scaremongering during this campaign has diverted attention away from the real issues. The impact of a single research project at the university pales in comparison to the larger issues of naval funding, housing and urban regeneration. How's that?'

I nod gratefully as I finish taking it down. Helen's eyes widen as she looks over my shoulder, and I feel a prickling sensation along the back of my neck. My presence has been noticed.

A tap on the shoulder: a young woman in a tailored grey dress, holding a notebook. 'Juliet? Hi! It must have been pretty hard for you during this election campaign. What are your thoughts on how Prior's manoeuvred?'

'I'm just here to report the results.'

'But you must have an opinion? The polls put the Tories in the lead. What will a Prior victory mean for you and your partner? Are you worried?' A flash goes off.

Movement. A parting of the crowds. Richard Prior is making his way towards me, hand extended, broad smile. My handshake is reflexive. Another flash. *Fuck*, I've just let myself become a photo op.

'Good to see you. Juliet, isn't it? How are you doing?' He's medium height, and stocky, with a full head of wiry brown hair. He wears a navy suit without a tie; his shirt is unbuttoned just low enough to ensure everyone can see the tattoo of an anchor on his collarbone. He makes a great deal of his past, working in the Dockyard, yet there's a definite political polish to his every gesture.

What an opportunity I've handed him. He can shake my hand, make his small talk. Show the watching media what a nice guy he is; how, despite his campaign theme, he most definitely isn't a bigot. My throat constricts. If I speak everyone will hear just how broken I feel. Why did I go along with this? I can't breathe. The fact must be visible to everyone around me. My mouth gapes open.

'Juliet, is there anything you'd like to say to Prior?' More journalists have crowded in; there are at least two cameras pointing at me.

'Now, now, let's not put her on the spot.' Prior puts an arm around my shoulders. The weight is hot and oppressive, and I wriggle free immediately. I have to get out of here.

'I'd just like to say that I have nothing personal against Juliet, nothing at all,' Prior says. 'But as a taxpayer I'm gravely worried. We don't know enough about this man-free technique, and there's a very real risk that Juliet's child – or her child's child – could have health problems the scientists simply haven't foreseen. Who is going to cover these medical expenses? I am. You are.'

'I ...' This is preposterous. I can't let him continue. But his audience is rapt.

'And it may not be politically correct to say so, but that's simply not fair. Invest in every child, not just designer babies.' He's been trained well, delivering his line with a suitably serious expression, no sign of satisfaction on his face, even though his body positively ripples with it.

'But that's preposterous.' Helen Gibbs has stood up. 'All Juliet wants is a family of her own. That's a basic human right, surely.'

Prior purses his lips and angles his head slightly. 'Family is at the heart of why this experiment offends me. Family is a privilege, not a right. It's something you work for, something you build yourself with two hands. It's time we stopped thinking of family as a commodity that can be bought and sold; something that can be manufactured in a Petri dish. We make our country a great place by making our homes great places.'

I wince as yet another camera flashes in my face. The journalists here are expecting to me to respond. And if I don't, I'm letting him win, no question. This confrontation will be reported and Prior will emerge as the victor. And the sad thing is, I've devoted hours – whole journeys up and down the A3 – to arguing everything out in my mind. To honing perfect one-sentence demolitions of every dodgy assertion. But where are these sentences now? Why has my mind become such a sucking void? Rosie will be so disappointed in me. I'm going to cry. I'm going to fucking cry.

'Ah, Jules, there you are.' It's Abi. 'News editor needs a word. It's urgent. Excuse us.' She steers me away, a hand on the small of my back.

Childlike, I go along, one foot in front of the other, trying to ignore the whispers and turning heads..

In a quiet set of ladies' toilets on an upper floor I see that my face is pink. My eyes are thankfully dry, but I look haggard, like a crime victim wheeled out for a police news conference.

'What are you doing here?' I ask Abi.

'Tom called. I'm so glad he did. It's a bloody circus out there. Matthew should be fired for putting you through this.'

I lean against the basins. How long would I have gone on standing in the hall, unable to speak as the media watched and waited? This is my life now. And I'm not up to it; I'm simply not up to it.

'I'm missing the count,' I say. 'I have to go back out there.'

'Oh, Jules, you can't. You'll be swamped again. Let me help you.'

'Matthew won't accept you covering for me.'

She reaches out and places a hand on my arm. 'He doesn't have to know. We'll be a tag team. Lock yourself in a cubicle and I'll go out and get you snippets. You've got your tablet?

Good. I'll drop off the quotes and you can bash out a story. We'll make light work of it between us.'

'But you're giving up your evening. Why? What's in it for you?'

The very moment the words come out of my mouth I know they're hurtful and rude. Abi looks wounded. But being rescued by a twenty-two-year-old – it just feels so degrading. In over a decade, this is the first time I've not been able to do my job. Even that awful night at the *Mirror*, I completed my assignment before I walked away. I've been spat at, punched, followed home by the burly sons of a rape defendant. And yet always in my core there was a kind of strength, a certainty in the rightness of my work.

Abi is trying to keep her gaze bright and optimistic, but she can't conceal the pity she feels. I wish more than anything that I could show her the woman I was, the reporter I've been. Make her understand that the version of me she's seeing now is an anomaly.

'Jules?'

'I'm so sorry,' I say. 'And thank you – to come out here without being asked. No one's ever done a thing like that for me before.'

Abi smiles and pats my arm, then hurries off to get her first round of quotes. I lock myself in a cubicle and allow myself the indulgence of tears.

Once tonight is over, I'll formulate a plan. Refuse to let Matthew bully me. I'll have that long-overdue think about my career. Find some direction. Rekindle the passion somehow. I'll be that fast-thinking girl in the lecture theatre, energised by the prospect of doing good work. Important work. The girl who looked around the room and said to herself: I will be the best. I will go the furthest.

Once tonight is over I will focus properly on our child. On shaping myself into the kind of mother I want to be. I'll be a better partner for Rosie. Try my best to make up for those days she's spent holed up in the flat.

I reach over and pull several sheets of toilet paper from the dispenser. It's scratchy against my face as I wipe my eyes, and it comes away black. Fucking mascara. Last time I bother with that.

Once tonight is over, things are going to be very different.

Chapter 14

Richard Prior wins by a narrow margin. From my toilet cubicle I hear the Guildhall erupt in cheers. It's torturous to have to write the story, to quote from his victory speech which he uses to demand a public inquiry into the supposed risks of ovum-to-ovum fertilisation. At least the campaign is over now, I tell myself. But I can't help worrying that Prior will become even more vocal, knowing he has such strong support.

In the weeks that follow, each time a new country pre-emptively bans the technique – Germany and Australia being the latest examples – he becomes the go-to interviewee, always ready with quotes about troubling population trends and frightening new diseases.

After the first week, groggy and nauseous, Rosie returns to work at the bookshop. Trevor lets her work out the back as much as he can, but she can't hide away all the time and the media run paparazzi shots of her standing behind the counter, pink jumper, hair tied back in a bun, smiling at a balding man as he hands over his credit card. In the *Sketch* she's pictured changing over the window display, one of her favourite tasks. She's standing up straight, eyes distant, thinking. Her stomach is circled and readers are invited to look for signs of a bump.

Trevor jokes that she's good for business. As well as journalists, curiosity-seekers come – older women who want to relive being pregnant, young feminists and progressive men delighted to hail an icon from their own generation. But there are other kinds of visitors: those who interrogate, who taunt, who sometimes leave Rosie no choice but to retreat to the storeroom. Trevor has had to call the police several times.

But, with the passing weeks, the media presence outside our flat starts to thin out. I'm able to resume my morning runs, but make a point of brushing my hair before I go through the front door, just in case. I go as far as wearing lipstick to work, but it doesn't stop the commentators shrieking in outrage at how someone as beautiful as Rosie can be with someone like me. Those election-night photographs, where I'm hollow-faced and gaunt, Prior's arm around my shoulders, are everywhere. And although I know I shouldn't read the comments, I can't help it.

On Twitter there's a #RescueRosie campaign. I suppose the participants would describe it as light-hearted. They detail their fantasies of luring her away, enticing her from her 'den of dykedom' with pretty dresses and dinners in fancy restaurants. But of course their attempts to be tongue-in-cheek are undermined by those who want to *impale the ugly one so hard that my cock goes all the way through her and comes out her mouth.*

A tabloid even unearths the object of my single sexual encounter with the male of the species – apparently I was vociferous as a lover, a claim downright hilarious when compared with the slow-death reality of the experience.

And then they give away our address. It's allegedly a mistake, the photo of Rosie leaving the flat, door number visible over her shoulder. The article doesn't say what road we live on, but there are plenty of articles out there that do. I complain, force the website to airbrush the photo; but I'm left wondering how many people have seen it, how many cranks have been able to piece together where we live.

We reach week twelve of the pregnancy. Our scans show a distinctly human-shaped being, well-formed skull, spindly little legs with feet at the end. Rosie tears up as we're able to make out toes. She starts to feel better: less sickly, more energetic. In bed she reaches for me and initiates sex rather than falling asleep straight away. Her appetite resumes and she's consumed by the need to snack at the strangest times. Often I wake in the early hours of the morning to the sound of the microwave. Our freezer stock of casseroles, risottos and curries is becoming depleted.

As the number of loitering photographers dwindles further, to the point where some days there's no one at all, my attempts to remain optimistic gain in strength. And as Christmas approaches, Rosie suggests that we start the search for a new family home. Having lived in the area all our lives, we know where the gangs of teenagers congregate, which roads are perpetually echoing with noisy exhausts, and which estates have a reputation for shoddy, thrown-up houses. Only two homes make it past Rosie's tough selection process and onto the viewing list. The first has no onward chain, but its décor is old and tired. There's eighties woodchip wallpaper throughout and the carpets are thin and need replacing. We keep our viewing short. Rosie makes a few upbeat references to location, but her lack of enthusiasm is obvious.

The second is an ex-rental in a quiet cul-de-sac near the heath. Here, the owners have done a quick patch-up job after their tenants left: new beige carpeting throughout and freshly painted magnolia walls. The living room is long and airy; patio doors open out onto a south-facing garden, not overlooked by any of the neighbours.

'There's room for a swing,' Rosie says. 'And we could get a table and chairs for the patio. Eat outside in the summer.'

The visit seems to pass quickly. We're careful not to show too much excitement in front of the estate agent, but once he's gone we sit in the car for a moment, reviewing the pictures that Rosie's taken on her phone.

'It's perfect,' she says. 'A garden for the baby to play in. And we can have a study as well as a nursery.'

'It'll be tough, taking on a mortgage,' I reply.

'Jules, you mustn't be such a worrier. We've got so much money tied up in the flat. It'll be a tiddly mortgage.'

I look back at the house. It's a semi. Room for two cars on the drive. The area itself is tidy and well-to-do-looking. A new Audi is parked outside the house opposite. Front gardens are landscaped, with evergreen shrubs adding little splashes of colour. There are a few Christmas lights dotted here and there, but nothing ostentatious or tacky.

But a mortgage and a baby? Two new sets of expenses all at once? We'll have to abandon thoughts of holidays – no more city breaks, no more Cretan sun. Dad's warnings begin to make sense. I'll be poor again, wondering whether I ought to be buying tinned vegetables for the curry rather than fresh.

'I've been thinking,' I say. 'I really don't know what I'm doing at the *Post*. I should just jack it in; get a PR job for more money and regular hours.'

Rosie reaches over and puts a hand on my arm. 'You don't have to do that, Jules. We're comfortable enough.'

'It's not that. It's . . . I mean, I'm almost thirty-five. Shifting on the nationals didn't work for me, so it's not like I'm going to climb any higher. Pretty much everyone at the *Post* only ever sees it as a stopgap. Except Matthew, perhaps. And I'd rather give up on journalism altogether than end up a bitter old bastard like him.'

'But the work's important to you.'

I look out across the street. A tall woman in an elegant bottle-green coat is supervising a young boy on a scooter. Does being a reporter mean that much to me? Or is it the idea of journalism that's sustained me so long? I remember locking myself in the Guildhall toilet cubicle. How broken I felt. My feelings may not have stayed at that high pitch, but something has definitely changed. *My* life has been written about – and poorly, most of the time. What public interest has that served? I try to bat the doubts away, but each morning, alone in the car, I recall the legion of dismayed looks that have greeted my doorstep arrivals over the years. I know now the sharp gut-twist of reading about yourself. Of wanting to hug your knees and shield your secrets, to keep the kernel of who you are safe from exposure.

Rosie kisses the side of my face. 'Don't make a decision you'll regret. We'll be just fine. I want you to be happy, doing work you care about. I've always admired how focused you are, the reserves of energy you seem to find.'

'I think they've been well and truly depleted this time.'

She lifts my chin, forcing me to look at her. 'Don't do yourself down. I've never known anybody with the capacity to work as hard as you do. I remember being astonished by how you managed everything – twelve-hour days, long runs, redecorating.'

I give a light little laugh and rest a hand on her thigh before turning the key in the ignition and driving us home.

Anthony is waiting outside our front door, wearing a sheepskin hat and high-end hiking jacket. He waves urgently.

'I've found out who did it,' he shouts as Rosie and I climb the outer stairs. 'I've pieced it together. I know who sold your story.'

As I put my key in the lock, I see that there's a copy of the *Post* in his gloved hand. My stomach tightens as I usher him and Rosie inside.

'What is it . . . who?' Rosie's voice is sharp. Her hand is on his shoulder as we stand in the hallway.

Anthony fumbles with the paper. He growls with irritation as his gloves hinder him, and he rips them off and flings them to the floor. 'Here.' He's turned to the sports section; his finger jabs at a photo of Tom. The tiniest of pictures, smaller than a postage stamp, accompanies Tom's story on Portsmouth Football Club's FA Cup prospects.

'Him,' Anthony says. 'He came to my house and offered me money. He said he was from the *Tribune.* He's a liar. He must have been looking for dirt he can sell. You guys need to be so careful.'

Rosie turns to look at me. For a moment I almost look away. I could pretend to be upset. Act as though I really believe it was Tom who sold our story. Avoid an argument that's going to upset us both.

'He works with you, Jules,' Anthony says. 'Did he know about the trial? Did you tell him?'

I see the disappointment in Rosie's eyes. She knows exactly what I've done.

'I . . . ' Do I lie? Dare I? But Tom – he was so ready to help, I can't stand the weight of blame falling on him. 'It seemed like a good idea,' I tell Rosie. 'Somebody betrayed us. I needed to find out who.'

Anthony lowers the paper and looks from me to Rosie and back again.

'So you set a trap? You subjected our best friend to a trap.' Rosie's voice is quiet. There's an enquiring edge to it, as though she's desperate for me to say no, to tell her it isn't true, that it's all a misunderstanding.

'Can someone tell me . . . ' It's Anthony again. It's too crowded here in this hallway. I take a step towards the living room.

'Ant,' Rosie says, 'thanks for coming over, but Jules and I need to talk right now.'

His brow furrows – he's piqued to be excluded from whatever drama is unfolding. 'I don't understand—'

'I'll call you later.'

Rosie and I remain still as he squeezes past us, the rustling of his coat the only sound.

He gently closes the door behind him.

'I—'

Rosie cuts me off. 'What the bloody hell did you think you were doing? How absolutely degrading. God, did you send Tom to my parents too?'

I shake my head. 'No. Just Anthony. I had to find proof.'

'And did you?'

'Well, no—'

'That's because it wasn't him.'

I lean against the wall. I'm overly warm; I should really take my coat off, but my arms feel too heavy. 'That's not true,' I say. 'There could be all kinds of reasons why he didn't take the bait—'

'Fuck you, Jules. How am I going to explain this to Anthony? *My girlfriend thinks you're a liar and tried to entrap you.* Jesus. You owe him an apology.'

I lift my hands to my face, pressing my palms against my temples. Is she right? Anthony seemed genuinely energised just a minute ago: not in a malicious way, but as though he was pleased to have helped. But then who else could it have been? That's the question I keep coming back to.

'I was only doing what needed to be done,' I say.

She snorts, shakes her head and walks into the living room without removing her coat. 'I'm not going to keep having the same conversation with you.' She sits on the sofa and folds her arms. 'Jules, I really can't understand why you're putting so much time and energy into this witch-hunt of yours. What's happened has happened. We're part of a ground-breaking trial offering women a new level of reproductive choice, and rather than celebrating that fact, you've got us holed up in here with the curtains drawn.'

I stand in the doorway. 'We've been through this. You don't know the media like I do.'

'You need to apologise to Anthony. What you did was an absolute insult.'

'Will you not even consider the possibility that he was the one who betrayed us?'

'No!' Two deep lines have formed between her eyebrows.

I shake my head and slowly retreat to the bedroom. Moments ago I was busy imagining life in the three-bedder by the heath. That optimism has dissolved now, replaced by a conviction that our lives, our hopes, have been irreparably weakened by the media scrutiny. One misstep, one wrong move, and our capacity for happiness could crumble into dust. I lie on my side, knees drawn up to my chest.

Perverse, that's what Rosie's blindness is: perverse. I screw my eyes tightly shut and try to quieten my mind. I make myself remember better times, the life we had before this motherhood quest. Rolling onto my back, I think of Rosie at twenty-four, a period of our life together that I often go back to, a time dense with happy memories. She'd just completed her masters in modernist literature and was embarking on a novel of her own. I'd come home from work and her fingers would be busy on the keyboard; she'd be leaning forward, eyes too close to the screen. She finished her first draft in just seven weeks, reddening with pride and apprehension when I suggested she let me read it.

'But it's still so messy,' she said. 'Everything in my head is so clear, but I always end up sounding like an amateur.'

On hearing this I steeled myself, ready to be encouraging and constructive, even if the manuscript was a struggle. But I found myself captivated by her tale, racing through the pages just like I did with the crime novels I enjoyed reading on holiday. The plot was fairly simple – a young woman becomes obsessed with the girlfriend of her school days. But there was such nuance: Rosie had given her characters inner lives of such complexity. The contradictory thoughts, the carefully constructed self-deceptions – I was amazed at the perception she was capable of. Up until then Rosie's life had been spent in one educational institution or another, with no specific career goal in sight. Yet her capacity to imagine was so developed, revealing a layer of wisdom that I'm ashamed to say surprised me.

In the weeks that followed I spent several evenings showing her how to edit. I pointed out redundant words, showed her how to flip a sentence to make it active rather than passive.

'But you've made it better – how could you see what I wanted to say?' she said. My chest swelled at her gratitude – I was thrilled at being able to help on a practical level. I even let myself daydream of her achieving literary fame. Perhaps, if she were to make some money from her writing, I could jack in the *Post* and try the nationals again. But properly this time.

Yet it seemed that once Rosie's ideas had been transferred to the computer during the tumultuous first draft, her passion for the story was expended. She took the job at the bookshop and enjoyed it, so completely. She always seemed bemused when I asked her what the *next step* in her career was going to be. And so draft number two was never finished. I wonder sometimes whether my pragmatic approach to editing might have killed it off.

Looking up at the ceiling, I ask myself: what is wrong with me? Why do I act as though being right is more important than the feelings of those I love? This is Rosie. We shouldn't be fighting.

I slide off the bed and head to the living room. She's still on the sofa, crying softly into the armrest. Sitting down next to her, I lightly place a hand on her back. My anger shatters like the brittle thing it is. There's room only for compassion and tenderness.

Testing Anthony was the right thing to do, but being right doesn't matter now. I fold my body over Rosie's, my chest over her back, hands round her front, underneath her breasts. Her crying develops a ragged edge, but her body melts into mine.

I need to do better by this woman. The question jabs at me: what do I feel towards this baby of ours? She has fingers, toes. At our scan I saw her move. But I can go hours where I don't think about her at all. It's the media intrusion that brings me back, reminding me of something that should surely be ever present.

Chapter 15

After several days of no media presence at all, we decide that yes, we can accept an invitation for a pre-Christmas get-together with Anita and Hong Shu. The last thing we wanted to do was lead the press to them, so we've been staying away from the world's only other ovum-to-ovum mothers-to-be. I'm impatient for their company. Hong Shu in particular, because, like me, she's having to engage with the pregnancy as an outsider. Perhaps she too is struggling with the reality of her baby. The joy of our positive pregnancy test already feels so distant. I'm unable to evoke those precious fragments of feeling that make an experience real for me, that let me remember with my body, not just my mind. If I'm able to talk about this with anyone, it will be with Hong Shu.

They live in Cosham, a self-contained pocket on Portsmouth's north side that has its own dilapidated high street lined with greasy spoons and charity shops. Hong Shu opens their door wearing a snowflake-patterned jumper and skinny jeans. 'Come in, come in.' She gives us each a smacking kiss on the cheek.

The homely smell of roasting turkey fills the hallway.

'You haven't gone to the trouble of a full-on Christmas dinner?' Rosie takes off her woollen gloves, unwraps her scarf.

Hong Shu nods. 'Why the hell not? You deserve a bit of pampering after the month you've had. Get yourselves inside.'

We follow her into an airy kitchen at the back of the house. It's large enough to accommodate a glass dining table, set for four and festooned with crackers and tinsel. A fat tabby cat is curled up on one of the chairs.

'You really shouldn't have gone to all this effort,' Rosie says as she greets Anita with a hug.

I'm startled by how different Anita looks. She's gained weight but it suits her – there's a healthy colour in her cheeks and her way of holding herself is visibly different; her back is straighter, her eyes shine.

At Hong Shu's behest, Rosie and I take our places at the table while she and Anita operate an efficient production line, filling a row of four plates. We watch in silence. Technically we've made up after last weekend's row. I agreed to apologise to Anthony, making the commitment carefully, without conceding that using Tom to test him was wrong. Rosie is disappointed by this, I can tell. We're both honouring our truce, but part of her is still indignant on her friend's behalf.

'So, how've you been?' Anita says once dinner is on the table. 'We've been seeing your pictures everywhere. I can't imagine what the last few weeks have been like for you.'

Rosie shakes salt over her roast potatoes. 'Jules was right: we just had to keep our heads down and weather it. They're starting to lose interest now. Finally.'

Anita pops a Brussels sprout in her mouth. 'We did think about going public. We felt so bad at all the focus being on you guys.'

'I'm glad for your sake that you didn't,' Rosie says. 'It would have been awful for you, and I don't think it would have lessened the intensity for us.'

Hong Shu looks up. 'Did you ever find out who gave the *Sketch* your names?'

I sense Rosie stiffen. 'No,' I say. 'We probably never will know for sure.'

'Scary, though, the way people have been responding,' Hong Shu says. Anita is staring at her. I know a warning look when I see one, but Hong Shu continues, oblivious. 'That new MP has been making a song and dance, hasn't he? He's planning a big rally in the city centre. Calling on the government to make o-o illegal. I sometimes feel like we're going backwards in time, not forwards.'

'I heard about the rally,' I say, turning to Rosie. 'But don't worry – the government can't give in to Prior – it'd be saying that mobs can rewrite the rule book.'

'But people believe the rubbish he comes out with,' Hong Shu says. 'I mean, every time he says something about health concerns my mum rings me up in a panic. She takes everything he says as fact because he's on the telly.'

'It won't be for ever,' Anita says. 'Our healthy babies are going to prove them wrong. Then we can all move on.'

'Have you guys seen that mad American pastor?' Hong Shu asks.

Rosie and I look at her blankly.

'He's got, like, three million hits. Here ... ' She produces her phone, placing it in the centre of the table once she's found the video.

An elderly man with staring eyes and flying spittle shouts at the camera. 'The Bible says honour thy father and thy mother. Let us be clear: thy *father* and thy mother.' He delivers his lines with vigorous arm gestures, unaware that he's bordering on parody.

Hong Shu cackles. 'Gold, isn't it?'

' . . . the perpetrators of this abomination will be delivered to the burning agonies of hell . . . '

'Turn it off,' Anita says.

The table is quiet for a moment, then Rosie sighs. 'I genuinely can't understand why people get so bothered.'

Hong Shu snorts. 'We're not dependent on men to drag a bloody deer into the cave any more. But they can't make babies without us. They need us, and they hate being reminded of it.'

'But it's not like every woman is going to do it this way,' Rosie says. 'All this rubbish about population shifts and men going extinct – why aren't more people challenging that? It worries me that people are so ready to believe such speculation and hype.'

Hong Shu flashes me a grin. 'I blame the media.'

Anita pats Rosie on the arm. 'We've started telling our friends, now that we're past twelve weeks. We said we used donor sperm. But, deep down, I wish people could know the baby's both of ours. It feels wrong, concealing something so wonderful.'

Rosie licks gravy from her lower lip. 'I guess, looking on the bright side, the media told everyone our news in one hit. Probably saved me hours of phone calls.'

As she says this I imagine the meetings that she would have

carefully choreographed. Dinners with friends, her smile as she announced that she had news. I feel a hot spike of anger at her being denied all of this.

'Whenever I saw your names in a newspaper,' Hong Shu says, 'I thought to myself: this could be us. And Scott – have you seen the way the commentators are laying into him? Scott, the nicest, most gentle man you could ever hope to meet.' She and Anita share a look of guilty relief, and everyone is silent for a moment.

We eat. We talk. As social occasions go, it's a good one, and much needed. Anita and Rosie compare sensations – breast tenderness, trouble going to the toilet and a plethora of unsuitable-for-the-dinner-table topics.

Once we've eaten our dessert of Christmas pudding and thick cream, Anita recommends a supplier of maternity bras and Rosie goes into the living room with her to browse websites. I'm glad that Hong Shu remains in the kitchen. I hang back and assume responsibility for making the coffee – decaf, naturally – while she stacks the dishwasher.

'So, how are you finding everything?' she asks me. 'With the pregnancy, I mean.'

I blow out my cheeks and shrug. How can I broach the strange numbness I've been feeling? I imagine Hong Shu confiding that she feels the same. The hug and whispered *me too*.

She laughs. 'It's strange, but there are times when I feel kind of envious of Anita. She gets to be so much closer to our child. She's the one that's growing her, nurturing her with her own body. I won't even able to feed her.'

'The baby will be half you,' I say. 'You'll be as good as any father.'

'But I want to be a mother.' She gives me a quick sideways glance. 'I know it's ridiculous to feel this way. But ... Anita gets to have this whole experience that I don't.'

'From what I've seen of pregnancy, I think it's an experience I'm happy to miss.' I remember Rosie's exhausted retching; the nights when I arrived home to find her collapsed on the bed, fast asleep in the clothes she'd gone to work in.

'And she has a nine-month head start when it comes to bonding with our baby,' Hong Shu continues. 'I feel like I'm being left behind. You're probably the only person who can understand ...'

The cat brushes against my calf. I don't know what to say. For me, it's a relief that Rosie is the pregnant one. It never occurred to me to want to have the child inside me, to want to shelter another life, have that responsibility. I picture myself pregnant: belly button sticking out, the sensation of something slithering around inside me. It's repugnant. I thought that Hong Shu – the only other mother number two in the world – might understand this confusion.

Her eyes are moist. 'Sorry,' she says. 'I don't resent Anita, please don't think that. I guess I just want more. Ever since the pregnancy test I've felt such a strong kind of love. You must know what I mean; I couldn't describe it to anyone that hasn't gone through it, but that tug. That feeling in the bottom of your stomach that this is the most important thing you've ever done.'

I smile and nod. I hope I'm convincing. 'Being part of the trial ...' I falter. 'I mean, for me, that's been amazing. We've been given an opportunity that generations of women before us never had.'

Hong Shu's expression is slightly confused as she looks at me. I don't know quite what I expected from her – but she's left me feeling as though I'm missing some primal instinct, some ingredient of real womanhood. Back when our child was a concept, a political victory, I'd been so sure of myself. I'd been able to visualise my fully formed little girl. But now she exists, I can't see anything more than the blob on the ultrasound screen. It's not only that my feelings are muted: something about the last few weeks has prevented me imagining my daughter's birth, her presence in the world.

Hong Shu puts an arm around my shoulders. 'It's going to be OK.'

I try to laugh, but can't quite manage it. 'I just ... the opportunity we've been given. How will we live up to it?'

She tightens her grip and pecks me on the cheek. 'By being ourselves. Raising and loving our kids like any other parents.' Her voice is rich with conviction.

I'm not going to get the relief I hoped for, the sweetness of a feeling shared. I turn the conversation back to the coverage; to how Scott is getting ripped to shreds on social media. It's painful to see Hong Shu's expression harden, but the shift in topic at least allows me to breathe.

Chapter 16

The Alliance for Natural Reproduction's national day of action falls on one of my working Saturdays. #ProudofOurSons is trending on social media, with celebrities, journalists and everyone else clamouring to post the most joyous family snaps. If the day's objectives were merely celebratory, I'd be able to laugh at this collective demonstrativeness. But the Alliance is demanding an immediate halt to any further ovum-to-ovum IVFs, pending a scientific and ethics inquiry. They've mustered a team of jobbing scientists to pick through Becca's research, and for the past few months they've been bombarding the media with shrieking press releases about unforeseen genetic diseases. Today's rallies – taking place in London, Portsmouth and Newcastle – are to demonstrate public support for a suspension of the trial. And the noise the media is making suggests that the public will be coming out in their tens of thousands.

Matthew tells me he's assigning me to cover the Portsmouth rally.

'Come on, be reasonable,' I say.

He frowns, but his eyes light up with relish at the confrontation to come. 'This isn't a request. If you want to keep your job, you'll do as you're told.'

The clattering of keyboards peters out, and across the newsroom I detect the sudden raised heads of avid listeners. Am I brave enough to resist? Immersing myself in a throng of people to whom I'm a symbol, a focus for disapproval and resistance, will surely be far worse than facing Matthew's ire.

Deep breath in, defiant lift of my chin, I meet his gaze. 'I'm not doing it, Matthew. It's unfair of you to ask me, and I think you know that. Put me on anything else.'

He wets his lips, does a quick scan to assess his audience, then lifts himself taller, sticks his chest out even further. Such concentrated loathing – on both our parts – turns the atmosphere brittle.

'Right. Pack up your things and get out of here. You're sacked.'

'You can't do that!' Abi shouts. Tom has somehow appeared at my side, hand on my shoulder. There's that despised prickling behind my eyes, but I will it to pass. I'm strong enough.

Another deep breath. I focus all my energy on banishing the threat of tears, and I smile. I actually manage it. 'Are you sure you want to do that, Matthew?'

'Should have done it years ago. Paper can't carry dead wood.'

'OK. But you realise that my first call, when I walk out of here, will be to the BBC? I don't have to remind you that I'm one half of the biggest news story in the city. I can get an interview with anyone I want, and I'll do it, I swear. I'll tell them how I was fired for not walking into a rally where I'm likely to be verbally abused. To be physically attacked, even.'

Tom's hand squeezes at my shoulder. No one in the newsroom is even pretending to work any more.

'You …' Whatever Matthew was planning to say next is

lost to a kind of growling sound rising up from his throat. The smirk is gone, his eyes are filled with loathing.

'What was that?' Not the slightest waver to my voice.

He doesn't respond.

'So, am I still fired?'

'We can swap stories,' Abi says. She inserts herself between Matthew and me. 'I'll do the rally. Jules, I'll give you a list of other bits – it's mostly Christmas fluff.' She looks up at Matthew. Her hesitancy, the fear that she's trying so hard to mask with confidence, makes my eyes sting. I shouldn't let her get involved.

'Fine,' Matthew barks. 'Suit your bloody selves.' He turns his back on me, and strides away. When he reaches Kyle's desk he stoops over and whispers something that makes them both laugh.

Tom and Abi are silent, guardians flanking me as the rest of the newsroom slowly gets back to work. Quickly I clasp both of their hands, giving them a fleeting squeeze before turning to my screen. I'm unable to speak, knowing that this isn't over. That I've most likely made things worse.

When I head out on assignment, there's a photographer waiting in the car park – the rally has upped my news value, bringing the respite of the last few days to an end. This paparazzo trails me across the city, his motorbike a constant presence in my rear-view mirror. My last stop of the day is a community centre, where a group of pensioners are method-ically assembling Christmas hampers to be distributed to Portsmouth's poor families. The table in front of them is covered with the random selection of items collected at food donation points: supermarket own-brand beans, multi-packs of crisps and lunchbox-size chocolate bars. There's a wealth of mince pies. Each wicker basket is festooned with a heart-achingly limp piece of tinsel. I introduce myself to the organisers and stand, pen poised, my anodyne questions at the ready. The fact that these people aren't at the rally makes me predisposed to like them.

In rushes the photographer, ferociously snapping, getting down on one knee to get the angles right. Backs straighten. Several of the pensioners quickly pat their hair, smooth their clothes. I don't have the heart to tell them that it's me, not them and their work, that's being photographed.

On my way back to the newsroom the traffic is heavy, snarling up the exit road leading off Portsea Island and reducing me to a slow first-gear crawl. I want to believe the drivers surrounding me are Christmas shoppers, leaving the city with present-laden cars, but it's likely that many of my slip-road companions were at the rally. I avoided the throng of protesters, only to become trapped amongst them later on.

It gets to the point where we stop moving completely. The photographer pulls his bike up alongside the Fiesta and takes a few snaps through my car window. But then he seems to get bored and weaves his way between stationary cars, out of the jam and away – most likely to start offering up my face to national news editors.

Although I've deliberately been ignoring coverage of the rally, I'm no longer able to resist the urge to find out how it went. Clicking on the BBC's report, I see that a couple of hours ago Guildhall Square was rammed tight with people, the crowd spilling out into nearby streets. The cameraman homes in on blue-ribboned lapels and bed sheets fashioned into homemade banners.

Stand up for Nature!

Say NO to Social Engineering

Firefighters against o-o

The square is festooned with Christmas lights, making the rally feel somehow like a festive occasion and leaving me with the unwelcome sense that Rosie and I have closed so many doors, excluded our baby from so many things by creating her the way we have. It's as though the camaraderie and sense of being right that radiates out from this square can never be ours. We've made outcasts of ourselves.

On the screen of my phone I watch Prior approach a microphone outside the Guildhall entrance, beaming down at the crowd from the top of the steps. His cheeks are pink with the cold, but his expression is one of real conviction. Not for the first time I wonder, can he really be a passionate believer in the Alliance for Natural Reproduction's work; or is he just someone who had the foresight to spot a cause that could win him a seat in Parliament?

A quick traffic check assures me there's time to watch a bit of his speech. He erupts into life, gesturing with his hands. 'As a father of two sons, the very concept of father-free babies, of women who can choose to turn their backs on mankind, leaves me feeling shaken and deeply disturbed. What kind of future will my boys have in a world where the natural order has been overturned? In a world where – to put it frankly – they may not be needed?

'We are perilously close to losing control. To allowing niche interest groups to dictate the shape of our society. To a world where my sons don't have a stake in the next generation. But we can say no. We must say no.'

A honking horn. I look up, expecting the traffic to have moved, but we're still stationary. To my left are two men in a blue Mondeo. The passenger is pressing his face against the window, waggling his tongue between two fingers. Looking away, I double-check that my doors are locked, then, throwing my phone down onto the passenger seat, I get to work reviewing the snippets in my notebook, underlining the best quotes, working out my intros to save me time later.

Back at the office, I efficiently plough through the stories, hoping for an on-time finish. I'm mid-way through my piece on the Christmas hampers when I'm distracted by Abi's raised voice. She's over at Matthew's desk, her face flushed.

'But you made it read like propaganda!' she yells.

Matthew gets up from his chair. 'Now, now, young lady. This isn't college any more. Everyone gets edited. That's how it works.'

'But those quotes added an extra dimension to the article. They deserved a place.'

'Our readers want a report on the protest. That was your brief. You had no business wasting time on irrelevancies.'

'This is bullshit,' Abi says.

'I beg your pardon.' Matthew's face is stern, but there's a

gleeful edge to his voice. He can deal with Abi far more harshly than he can with me, and he knows it. I should intervene – do something before Abi makes things worse for herself.

'You should be ashamed to be news editor of a paper that runs such one-sided pap.' Abi's voice is firm.

'Just who, precisely, do you think you are?'

'I'm a journalist, Matthew. And do you know what? I fucking quit.'

Somehow I've reached her. Placed a hand on her shoulder. 'Abi, don't—'

She turns to me, eyes blazing. 'I had some great quotes, Jules. An expert on population trends saying that the impact on gender balance would be negligible. How does that not have a place in the story, when Prior's telling everyone boys are going to become a minority?'

'I'm getting rather bored of this,' Matthew says, taking a seat. 'Abi, if you're going, go. If you're staying, I need filler items. No one goes home tonight until they've turned in five news in briefs.'

'Go fuck yourself, Matthew,' Abi says.

He looks shocked, but only for a moment. 'Right – pack up your things.'

'Oh – I'm going, don't you worry. I'm sick to death of the bloody boys' club you've got here. It makes me wish this male-free society wasn't just a load of bollocks. This paper would be a nicer place for a start.'

He grins. 'But what kind of news would you be putting out? Fluffy little featurettes. Pages and pages on hair straight-eners and Tampax. I've known all along that you couldn't hack proper news.'

Abi inhales sharply. I touch her arm. There are titters all around us. Tom catches my eye, then quickly looks away.

'Condescending prick,' Abi says, heading back to her desk.

Silently, I watch her stuff her black tote bag with all her old notebooks. There are loud conversations going on all around us. The atmosphere feels dangerous, but I also detect an air of hilarity rippling just beneath. Abi is so brave, so well-meaning. But it's precisely this that my colleagues find so funny. She doesn't cry, or betray any kind of emotion, as she leaves the newsroom for the last time.

'Abi, are you sure you want to do this?' I'm walking alongside her, seeing her to her car, hoping that I'm showing, in some small way, just how moved I am.

She turns to me as we reach her Micra. 'Bit late for that, Jules. The thing is done.'

'I hope—'

'I don't know how you've stood it for so long. I wanted to be a journalist ever since I was little, but I'm mostly embarrassed by the rubbish they put my name to.'

I feel as though I should be imparting advice about the quality of forbearance. Speaking of *sucking it up*, being a *good sport*. But the clearness in Abi's eyes makes me feel ashamed. I remember the purity of the fast, conviction-based decision. Those blessed days when right and wrong was something you felt in your gut. When the cloying mud of the middle ground could be deftly stepped over. When information brought clarity, not confusion. Looking at Abi, I see someone who is unspoiled. And I'm envious of this; envious of her bravery too.

'Call me if you need anything,' I say.

She smiles and holds my gaze. I wonder whether I should hug her; Rosie would do it, and would make it feel natural.

'Jules! Who's your pretty friend, Jules?' It's that bloody photographer from earlier.

Abi gives me a sardonic smile. 'They don't deserve you. I hope you realise that soon.'

Chapter 17

Days pass and I keep postponing having to apologise to Anthony until a rare reasonable-hour finish sees me back at the flat ahead of dinner. I'm not expecting him to be there, but he's on my sofa, wearing an expensive cashmere jumper with ripped jeans. His eyes meet mine with a look of distaste. How he's enjoying being the wounded party. Rosie smiles and gives me a meaningful glance. Her forgetting to mention that he was coming over wasn't accidental.

'Right, now you're back, I'm going to make dinner. I thought I'd cook tonight. Spaghetti bolognese, nothing fancy. No, you sit down, Jules. You're always waiting on me. Relax. Watch TV with Anthony.' She glides off to the kitchen wearing a satisfied smile.

I sit in her seat. Anthony is looking straight ahead at the television, where *EastEnders* is on, his face unnaturally still. He knows that I've been tasked with making an apology, and he's not going to make it easy for me.

My chest feels tight, as though some reflex of mine is squeezing at my lungs, trying to hold back the words. Sometimes I look at Anthony and I'm sure he was the one who betrayed us. It's there in the set of his jaw, the looks he gives me. I inhale. I promised Rosie. 'Look,' I say.

He slowly turns his head, trying his hardest to look wounded. For a moment, I feel a pang of uncertainty. Can I really be sure it was him, without proof? And if he isn't the culprit, then he must be so hurt by the loyalty test I devised for him.

'Listen . . . ' I try again. 'Sending Tom to you like that – it was out of order and I'm sorry.'

'So you accept that I'm not the leaker?' His eyes harden.

I don't break eye contact; I'm watching his face for the smallest slip of emotion. 'Setting a trap was completely wrong,' I say.

'But you accept it wasn't me who contacted the *Sketch*?'

If he really wasn't behind the leak, then he's right not to let this go. And I can't argue with the fact that he did send Tom packing.

'I accept it wasn't you.' I'm not sure I mean it. But the conviction I felt in the immediate aftermath of the *Sketch* story is gone too, replaced by a kind of hopelessness. Rosie and I won't be able to rebuild our lives if we can't even trust those closest to us.

Anthony gives me a wide grin, flashing his brace-straightened teeth. 'Good. Then I'm looking forward to putting this behind us. For Rosie's sake.'

I smile, my chest relaxing. At last this moment is out of the way. Picking up my phone, I scan the work emails that have come in over the last half-hour.

'It's been hard for me,' Anthony volunteers after a few minutes.

I look up in surprise.

He picks at his thumbnail. 'I mean – I was so happy, knowing that I could have been the one to help Rosie. And I would have been good. I really would have tried. I would have loved that baby, knowing it was hers.'

His cheeks are pink, the wounded expression gone, revealing something far more raw. There's a sharp twist, deep within my core, and I know that I'm not going to like what comes next.

'We both want what's best for Rosie,' I say, because it feels like a safe statement.

'Exactly. And with me as her donor there would have been no black holes. No sleepless nights worrying that she was carrying the child of some psycho. I would have been involved. A half-decent male role model, I hope.'

Leaning back on the sofa, I clasp my hands in my lap to stop them from trembling. *He thought he was going to be our sperm donor.* Was this just a fantasy of his, or did Rosie actually discuss it with him? She never mentioned anything to me; all our conversations before o-o were based on the assumption that we'd have to use an anonymous donor.

I inhale, trying to keep my expression neutral. 'So, that day we got the letter from the university – had Rosie given you any hint, tried to let you down gently?'

He lowers his eyes. 'No. I guess she felt guilty, poor thing. And I do understand. But I'd been thinking that I was about to become a dad. And it was taken away from me, just like that. I know I was supposed to be happy for you guys, but it was like a rug had been pulled out from under me.'

I feel winded, as though Anthony has delivered a sharp

kick. They must have come to some sort of secret agreement straight after Rosie and I returned from Crete. I was supposed to stand by, watch her nurse *his* child? Not a stranger's, but Anthony's?

He does a big stretch. Briefly checks his phone. 'That politician dude isn't letting up, is he? Although, to be fair, I do wonder sometimes whether there are women out there who won't be able to resist having a guaranteed baby girl.'

Slowly I stand, steadying myself against the arm of the sofa, leaving the room on weakened legs. In the kitchen Rosie is stirring at the bolognese sauce, a look of contented absorption on her face. A pan of pasta bubbles next to her, its starchy aroma filling the kitchen. From the moment I told her I'd changed my mind about children, I felt I'd brought us closer. My trust in her was absolute: I was letting her steer the course of our future, even though instinct and economics were screaming at me to take a different route. Perhaps Anthony misread the situation, interpreting Rosie's talk about donors as an invitation when it really wasn't. There must be an explanation.

'Not fallen out again already, have you?' Rosie says with a smile. Then, as she sees my face: 'Jules, what is it?'

'I just had the strangest conversation with Anthony. He seemed to think he was going to be our sperm donor.' I look up, and see the guilt wash through her eyes.

'I would have discussed it with you,' she says. 'I was going to. But then we learned about o-o and we were so focused on that.' She reaches an arm towards my waist, but I step back.

'But Rosie, how could it have ever have felt like my baby if his father was living five minutes up the road?'

'Oh, Jules, it would never have got to that stage if you were unhappy about it. Come here—'

'I need to go out,' I say. 'For work.'

'Jules.'

I shake my head. 'No, it's true. I forgot I was supposed to be covering something.'

She calls after me, but ashamed as I feel to be running away, I can't look back. There's no way I can sit in our living room, eating spaghetti bolognese, pretending not to be stung by their duplicity.

For want of anything better to do, I drive to the twenty-four-hour supermarket and walk up and down the aisles until I locate the baby section. I browse tiny little socks, tiny little jeans, and I will a new, more powerful feeling to emerge and replace the wretchedness. How could Rosie so radically misinterpret how I'd feel about Anthony being our sperm donor? Perhaps I place too much of a burden on her, expecting her to instinctively recognise my emotions. But I can't help thinking back to that night in Crete, when I offered up my acquiescence to children as a gift. There was such purity in the gesture, because my yielding was so complete, so selfless. To know now that Rosie followed it with secret discussions makes me feel as though she never really appreciated the sacrifice of my relenting.

But she is sorry. There is at least that. Nursing my hurt will serve no real purpose – we have so much to contend with and it's important that we face it as a unit. The woman I love is carrying my baby. I've secured a place on a ground-breaking trial; have an opportunity that generations of women could never have imagined. There is so much I should be looking forward to, and yet in recent weeks I've not had a moment to pause and appreciate such things.

I try now. It's quiet in this part of the supermarket. The harsh white light bounces off the floor tiles, making my eyes ache. Remembering what Rosie's mum said about investing in a breast pump, I take a look at the selection on display, reading through the different features. I look at feeding bottles, the overwhelming variety of teats on offer. Already I'm regretting the way I fled the flat. But the colour that rushed to Anthony's cheeks when he alluded to his and Rosie's child: that was real emotion. Seeing it made me ashamed at just how weak my own feelings were. *If I could reverse this baby, I would.*

I allow myself to hear the thought for the first time. And I recognise its truth. This is so much worse than feeling harassed and slightly numb. This is realising I've made a terrible mistake. I'm letting Rosie down. Becca and Scott too, not to mention our unborn child. I can't accept this. I continue walking the aisles. Inspect the teeniest, cutest little outfits. *Let tonight be an anomaly, please.* I'm upset. This can't be the way I really feel.

I arrive home around midnight. I'm expecting Rosie to be in bed, but I hear a commotion as I walk along the path leading from the car park to the flats. 'Listen,' I hear Rosie say, but her voice is then drowned out by the shouting of at least two other people.

I run. As I sprint up the staircase I see three figures outside our door. Young men, two of them wearing hoodies, the third a baseball cap. Rosie is illuminated in her dressing gown, hair puffed up around her face.

'Fucking lesbos,' one of the hooded figures is yelling. It's a young voice, but coarse. The boy it comes from can only be sixteen or thereabouts.

'Fuck off out of here,' I shout. All three turn to face me. 'Go on.'

'It's OK, Jules, we're just having a chat . . . ' Rosie says. I stare at her. The teenagers start up again, I can only catch fragments: *dyke conspiracy . . . need to teach you a lesson.*

There's broken glass outside our door, a beer bottle by the looks of it. One of the little shits takes his cock out of his jeans and starts waving it around. The others roar. Out of the corner of my eye I see Mrs Hamworth's lights coming on.

I'm too angry to be afraid. I grab hold of one of them by his sweatshirt and pull him away from our door. His eyes widen in surprise, then burn with hatred as his friends jeer at him.

' . . . everyone should have the freedom to express their sexuality in their own way . . . ' Rosie is saying. I love her for trying, but does she really think she can educate these thugs?

'Right – that's indecent exposure for a start, you little pricks,' I say. 'We'll combine that with criminal damage, with harassment. I'd start running if I were you: the police are on their way.'

'Jules!' Rosie shouts.

The tallest of the three squares up to me. I feel his breath on my face, smell the sourness of the lager he's been drinking. And my anger deserts me, replaced by a creeping fear. *Can I take him?* Perhaps one on one, but I'm not going to be able to fight all three and win. Any moment now they'll realise this.

'Go back inside, Rosie.'

'No, Jules . . . ' She steps out, barefoot, onto the concrete walkway, leaving our door wide open. There's glass everywhere; she's going to cut herself.

The jeering has stopped. Everyone is still as I stand nose to nose with the ringleader of the group.

'Everyone just calm down,' Rosie says.

The guy in front of me roars, and without thinking about it, without even conceiving that I might do such a thing, I shift my bodyweight backwards, then bring my head crashing forwards into his face. There's a sharp crack, and when I pull back his face is a bloody mess.

Everyone begins shouting at once. But my fear has gone. I feel strangely elated, as though I've accessed some hidden, primal power. I know that I can win. I'm protecting my family.

'Get the fuck out of here!' My voice rises above the confusion. And, strangely subdued, they retreat, hurrying down the stairs unable to muster any of their earlier swagger.

Rosie is pulling at my arm, trying to usher me indoors. 'They were just kids, Jules. What have you done?'

I follow her inside and bolt the door behind us. In the hallway I see that her eyes are wide with worry. 'They might report you. Jesus!'

'They won't want to admit what happened. They're probably shitting themselves.' I hear that cracking sound; relive the boy's shocked expression. I've never felt anything quite like the power I experienced in that moment. But already it's draining away. I'm having to suppress the urge to tremble. He was only sixteen or so, but he had a man's body, a man's strength. No, he isn't a victim – we were evenly matched.

'We can't go to the police now,' Rosie says. 'They'd end up arresting you.'

'They wouldn't have done anything anyway.'

Without eating the leftover pasta waiting for me in the kitchen, I get into bed and cradle Rosie's head against my chest. I know I won't sleep – I'm listening out for further trouble – but I feign relaxation for her sake.

'Are you OK?' Rosie whispers.

I remember. Anthony, the volunteer sperm donor. Fleeing from the flat, rather than having a conversation. Oh God, I'd allowed myself to forget, but now the knot is back.

'I'm sorry,' I say.

If I could reverse this baby, I would.

She runs a hand along my torso, up to my breast, drawing little circles with her fingertips. 'I should have told you. About the conversations I had with Ant. I was going to.'

'How could you even think it was a good idea? I mean, a stranger's child is one thing. But how could I be a parent to a kid when its dad was right here, dropping in whenever he felt like it?'

'It wouldn't have been like that.'

'The baby would have been more his than mine. That's what it would have felt like to me.'

'Oh Jules.' Rosie props herself up on her elbow, places a hand against my cheek. 'I'm so sorry.'

I swallow. Can I go further, tell her that I don't want this baby? Definitely not. This is a feeling that has to stay hidden until I can eradicate it. I think back to the happiness of earlier times and I feel a kind of pained disbelief that things can be so different now.

'Jules?'

I take a deep breath and give her arm a chaste little pat.

'It's OK, Rosie. Let's get some sleep.'

If I could reverse this baby, I would.

Chapter 18

We march towards our new family life, compiling shopping lists and researching childcare options. Rosie's parents oversee viewings of the flat, dealing with the local nosy-parkers and snooping journalists who outnumber serious buyers. We accept the first decent offer and solicitors get to work. I'm impatient to move. I never thought it possible that I could grow to dislike our home. But I'm finding it difficult to sleep at night; feeling as though I have to listen out for further trouble. The creak of the oak tree outside, our neighbour's late-night trips to the bins: such noises have me out of bed, peering through a gap in the curtains, scanning the street outside.

February takes us into new depths of winter. There's no respite from the freezing wind which blasts right through my parka whenever I'm out on assignment. My nose seems to constantly be running, my skin becomes dry and chapped. But the baby continues to grow. Rosie no longer fits into her jeans; her waist has thickened and there's a new roundness to her belly that she's always patting and cradling. Sometimes she'll take my hand and place it against our child's home. 'Take a moment to enjoy this,' she says. 'I can't wait to meet our baby, can't wait to see what she looks like.' At such moments I'm overwhelmed with dismay. I smile back at Rosie and I try, so hard, to share in her joy.

Rosie and I meet at the university for our week eighteen check-up. I have to rush back from an assignment, and she's there waiting for me as I arrive. Her face is pale, her hair pulled back into a messy bun. She fixes her eyes on the screen of her phone and holds herself still, as though deep in thought. Her shoulders, normally so elegantly sloping, are drawn up. I feel a pang of protectiveness, and with it something more wistful. I remember other Rosies. Carefree versions, her love and interest scattered across all manner of things rather than concentrated on a single being. And I ache from holding these memories so tightly.

She looks up. The way she parts her lips tells me she has bad news.

I greet her with a peck on the cheek.

'Jules ...'

'What is it?'

She hands me her phone. *Baby-experiment lesbians buy £350,000 dream home.* They have a picture of the three-bedroom semi with its rockery out the front and backdrop of conifer trees.

I sit down on one of the plastic chairs to read. It's a nothing story. They quote from the estate agent's website, listing the property's amenities. Some alleged expert spouts nonsense about nesting instincts, and how the move is *a natural step for Rosie and Juliet.* As ever, references to controversy, health concerns and opposition are threaded throughout the piece.

'How do they know?' Rosie whispers. 'Who told them?'

Anthony? Perhaps. But I don't have the energy for this fight. I return her phone without meeting her eye. 'It could be anyone. The estate agent, the sellers – we've got no way of knowing.'

'I can't help thinking we should have answered back, right at the beginning.'

'Rosie . . . '

'I know. You're the journalist, not me. But our strategy hasn't *worked*. The interest hasn't died away and it doesn't feel as though it ever will.'

I swallow. 'I know that's what it must feel like. But you can't compare the attention we're getting now with the absolute shitstorm we'd have faced if we'd spoken out and made advocates of ourselves.'

Rosie shakes her head. 'No, true – we don't know what that might have been like. But I'm sure I wouldn't be feeling as much of a victim as I am now.'

I'm about to put an arm around her, but Claire, the technician, emerges and shows us up to Becca's consulting room. There's a burly man stationed outside the door, chewing gum with an open mouth. He's dressed in a black suit and tie and I detect a smirk as he gives Rosie a brisk up-and-down glance.

Becca steps out into the corridor and ushers us inside, closing the door behind her. She wears a thick grey polo neck and blue jeans, teamed with her usual red lipstick.

'Was that a *bodyguard*?' I ask.

Becca gestures for us to sit, while Claire gets everything ready for the scan, laying a long sheet of paper on the bed, ready for Rosie to lie on.

'Well, I suppose, yes,' Becca says. 'Although they give themselves posh job titles these days. That's Dwayne. He stands outside when I go to the loo. Can you imagine? It's all rather embarrassing.'

Rosie hasn't sat down. She's regarding Becca with a puzzled expression. 'Are you in some sort of danger?'

'Lord, no. This is just my bosses doing what the insurance company tells them to. Now, hop up on the bed and we'll see how the little one is doing today.'

I search Becca's face for clues. Is she deliberately down-playing the situation? Her forehead is smooth and she wears her habitual smile. But I'm not reassured. A bodyguard? The threats against her have been constant – social media boils with violent comments and she once mentioned in passing that her kids had been taken out of school. But a bodyguard implies something more specific: a stalker, or religious extremists. How do you differentiate between the many threats embracing violence and the single twisted indi-vidual who might actually follow through? I haven't noticed any marked change in the commentary lately – it's been the usual *burn in hell/hope you lose the baby/protect our sons!* Yet, for a bodyguard to be standing outside, something must be different.

Claire smears ultrasound gel over Rosie's bump, and our daughter's form appears on the screen. I join Rosie in staring at her tiny body and I will closed-off parts of myself to open. Each time I come here I wait for a rush of feeling. It never comes, but I can't let go of the hope that one day it will.

The technician is watching me, and when I notice the attention she's paying, she neither smiles nor looks away.

Her gaze feels almost insolent. Is she seeing something in my expression that she disapproves of? She must be present at Hong Shu and Anita's scans, and perhaps she gets a whole other level of reaction from Hong Shu. I imagine her flinging out questions, her eyes welling like they did that time in her kitchen. It must be so much easier to like Hong Shu than it is to like me.

Rosie clasps my hand, and I see concern on her face as she looks at me. Smiling, I stroke her hair. I feel as though I'm playing a part, having to improvise because there's no time to pause, to reflect on exactly what the right feeling is, what the right expression should look like. I miss my mum, I realise. If I could only have an hour with the radiant woman in the photograph. If she could wrap her arms around me and whisper in my ear. Just a few words. Tell me what to expect. What I can give. It seems like so little, but in actual fact, it's everything.

Claire presses her lips together as she cleans the ultrasound attachment. Becca helps Rosie up from the examination bed, and gestures for us both to take a seat, but I can't help observing the technician: her gestures feel soaked in disapproval. 'Do people ask you about us?' I ask her. 'When they know that you work here, are they curious?'

She stops what she's doing and looks up, her face betraying nothing. But something is not right; I can feel her dislike of me. And the slight hint of amusement in her eyes tells me she knows I can sense it.

'We never discuss patients. Yes, people ask. But I don't admit to meeting you.' She gathers up her things, closing the door softly as she leaves the room.

'Jules, you made her feel uncomfortable,' Rosie says as I sit down.

Becca reaches over and takes Rosie's hand, gently separating her fingers. This happens roughly every other visit: a brief check for signs of swelling. And every time my throat catches at the intimacy of the gesture.

'So,' Becca says. 'Me and a charming young man from the insurance company have been having discussions with several hospitals. We want to get a sense very early on as to what they can offer in the way of security—'

'These conversations – are they linked to the presence of the chap outside? Has there been a specific threat?' I ask.

'This is more a case of the university recognising that your baby's arrival is going to be, shall we say, *of interest*,' Becca says. 'We have a responsibility to help you manage the situation and to make sure that nothing gets in the way of your care. I know it's a little early, but have you started to think about your birth plan?'

I'm about to ask where the hell Rosie's bodyguard is, if it's come to this, but Rosie gets in first: 'I suppose a home birth is out of the question?'

I look at her in surprise.

'The thing that worries me in a home-birth scenario,' Becca says, 'is that the press could present an obstacle in getting the help you need, should things not go to plan.'

'The press already have our new address,' I say. 'And they'll roughly know when the due date should fall. Come month nine, there'll be paparazzi trailing us twenty-four hours a day.' I imagine it: a hundred camera flashes as Rosie emerges through our front door on a stretcher, her face gleaming with sweat. I register an animal fear as I conjure the pressing crowds.

There's a pause. Rosie swallows.

'We've been approached by the Royal Free in London,' Becca says. 'They're one of the best-equipped hospitals in the country. And they have experience in dealing with high-interest cases.'

I picture Rosie on a hospital bed, a cordon of bouncers around her, checking the credentials of anyone who approaches. It's a scene I couldn't have possibly comprehended that summer morning when we first read about Becca's work in the *Observer*. If I'd known then where the journey would take us, I would have abandoned the idea. Raising a sperm donor's child would be less difficult, less heartbreaking.

Rosie places a finger between her eyebrows. 'I thought a water birth . . . '

'Very nice.' Becca smiles. 'How about I arrange a visit for the three of us? The chief exec is very keen to meet you.'

'But . . . I'm not sure it makes sense to look at a hospital so far away,' I reply. 'I mean, on a good day we're looking at a ninety-minute drive. But it could be three hours or more at rush hour.'

Becca sighs. 'That leads me on to my next point. How would you feel about a temporary relocation in the weeks leading up to the birth?'

There's a strange pressure in my sinuses. 'We're about to move house as it is,' I say. 'And we've got jobs – we can't afford to abandon everything. And we definitely couldn't afford to stay in London.'

'Don't worry about that,' Becca says. 'If a temporary relocation looks like the best thing, then the university will pay for it. I'm not saying that it is, but as you said, Jules, the press are likely to be hanging around as we get into month nine. It's something to think about. That's all. And in the meantime, we can explore what options are available more locally. I've had one of the private hospitals, Aspire Health, express an interest. So it's worth talking to them too. They've offered to put on antenatal classes for just the two of you.'

'Wow, I don't know what to say . . . ' Rosie's face is pinched with emotion. She looks down at her belly, then at me.

And perhaps because I realise I've already ruined the occasion, I ask the question that's been bugging me. 'When you say relocation, do you actually mean a safe house? Is that what things have come to?'

To her credit, Becca doesn't look away. 'Our security consultants want you to have the option to disappear, if that's what's best for you. But you get to decide – no one is forcing you to do anything.'

'And Anita – are you advising her to disappear too? Or do they get to have their baby right here in Portsmouth?'

'You know I can't answer that, Jules.'

'I know. I'm sorry. It's just – are there any other pregnancies yet? Do you think if there are enough pregnant women further down the line they'd consider going public as a group?'

For a moment Becca looks unsure, but she quickly smiles, looking confident again. 'They're doing well up in Newcastle. Seven confirmed pregnancies. But here . . . I mean . . . unfortunately there weren't any pregnancies in the second round. We were unlucky and didn't even have successful fusions.'

Rosie exhales sharply.

'Don't worry,' Becca says. 'That's how things go sometimes. Just like in nature, there's an element of luck involved.'

*

After the appointment, I drive Rosie to the station so that she can get the train home while I return to work. 'What do you think about the relocation idea?' she says.

'You mean the safe house?' My tone is snappish, and I instantly regret it. But I'm so sick of people not calling things what they are.

'I don't like the idea of being uprooted. But if it means we have peace and quiet, I think it's something we need to explore,' Rosie says.

I want to wrap her in my arms and sob and sob. In many ways the idea of a safe house is bliss. And yet, it would be an admission that things aren't going to get back to normal, maybe not ever. Our hope was to create a family, but we're slowly unmaking our lives, irreversibly stripping away the blessed routines that have made us so happy over the years.

'I guess we've got no choice,' I say.

Rosie gives me a searching look as I swing the car into a disabled bay and wait for her to get out.

'Jules, what's wrong? You were so on edge back there. That poor technician.'

If I could reverse this baby, I would.

'Jules? Talk to me. Have I done something?'

I shake my head, knowing that if I attempt to speak, I'll break down.

She places a hand against my cheek. 'I know it's overwhelming. But you're strong,' she says. 'And our baby is strong. Did you see the way she was bucking her hips? So strange, isn't it? She's inside me, but she's separate. She's her own person.'

I say nothing.

'Jules, if you won't talk to me, how can I—'

'Everything's fine.'

She's watching my face closely.

I try a gentle smile. 'I better get back to work, Matthew's going to have a shit-fit at how long I've been.'

'Alright, but Jules ... you can tell me anything. I want to help.' She cups my face and plants a hard kiss on my lips before getting out the car and walking away.

Chapter 19

A new week begins and I learn from a morning call to the fire brigade that there's been a house fire in Southsea. I book a photographer and head down there to knock on the doors of neighbouring homes and hopefully catch a few people before they leave for work.

The address is in a side street off the main promenade. This is an old part of the city, with narrow streets built before the advent of the two-car family, so I have to drive around the block before I spot somewhere to park. Gulls screech overhead as I walk to the house, and a charred, smoky fragrance hangs in the morning mist. My contact at the fire station told me the place is gutted: there were no fatalities, but the homeowner is in St Luke's.

A single police car is parked outside the burnt shell of the house. It's a semi, cordoned off with police tape. The front door, which opens directly onto the street, has been burned away, exposing blackened walls and crumbling plaster.

Three clusters of residents stand talking outside their homes, and a reporter from the regional BBC news is doing a piece to camera, her heavy foundation and shiny ponytail contrasting sharply with the wreck behind her.

I take out my notebook and jot down a few lines describing the scene.

'They reckon someone poured petrol through the letterbox. Terrible, isn't it?' A woman about my age has approached, holding the hand of a little boy dressed in jeans and a miniature Puffa jacket.

'Did you see anything?' I ask.

'I was woken up by shouting at around three. Poor chap was trapped inside. Had to clamber out of a top-floor window in the end. They took him away in an ambulance.'

'Do you mind if I quote you?'

'Where you from?'

'The *Post.*'

Her nose wrinkles slightly. 'I was just making conversation. Got to get the little one to nursery.' She turns and walks away.

Abi emerges from a front door further up the street and hurries over once she spots me. We've kept in email contact since her resignation, her energetic pursuit of freelance work prompting wistful admiration on my part.

'Hey. What are you doing here?' I ask.

'I'm reporting, same as you. The *Tribune* is interested.'

'In a house fire in Southsea?'

She screws her eyes shut for a moment. 'You don't know, do you? Shit.'

'Know what?'

'The neighbours told me the house belongs to someone who works at the university. They think he's involved in your trial.'

'Have you got a name?'

She looks down at her pad. 'Scott Bishop.'

I inhale sharply. Scott. Calm, efficient Scott, who patiently explains each test result, who reassures us that everything is normal before we even have to ask. Becca was always seen as the figurehead of the trial, the recipient of press criticism and hate mail. But in recent months Scott has had an increased media profile foisted upon him.

'Jules, are you OK? We're off the record now, you don't have to worry.'

I picture Scott's face. His frowning concentration. I never thought to ask him why he chose fertility as a research specialism. He's done so much to help us, but, more than that, he always seemed so interested. At each appointment he'd ask Rosie what her book club was reading, and I remember the little flush of pride I felt when he mentioned he'd read my court report on a recent domestic violence case. Why did we never take the trouble to ask him about his life outside the research centre?

Abi touches my shoulder. 'You knew him?'

I nod. I'm seeing his face, remembering the warmth of his voice, how he always sounded so kind, even when he slipped into efficient, medical mode.

'Christ. Come here.' She pulls me into a hug. Her narrow body, all hard angles, feels so different from the softness of Rosie. I have a day of work I need to get through. I cannot cry.

I wonder whether Becca has heard already, or whether if I call I'll be the one to break it to her. Was the fire some sort of warning? Or did a twisted individual light a petrol-soaked rag with the intention of murder? Does someone – still out there – hate the idea of two-mother babies so strongly that they'd be prepared to kill those involved? I think of Rosie, behind the counter at the bookshop. Regular habits, easy to find. Picture in the media, easy to recognise.

'Let's find a caff,' Abi says. 'Get ourselves a coffee. You've had a terrible shock. But we don't know it's connected to the trial, do we? I mean, it could be a personal thing. Or it might even be indiscriminate.'

I stuff my notebook back in my bag and retrieve my car keys. Whoever did this is still out there. I need Rosie out of that shop right now. And we need protection. We can't be alone in the flat, waiting for the next bad thing to happen. Not when there are people out there who would do a thing like this.

'I've got to go,' I say, hurrying back to my car.

I approach the shop from the opposite side of the road, and through the glass frontage see Rosie standing by the side of the counter. A tall, striking woman puts a hand on her bump; the two of them talk animatedly.

A pang of jealousy, so acidic, so poisonous, roots me to the spot. The woman has a pram with her; she's slender, with blond, straightened hair. Elsewhere in the shop, an elderly man is in the classics section, and two teenage girls inspect the 'new voices' table that Rosie takes such pride in curating.

Rosie looks up. She smiles and waves. She's safe. That's the most important thing.

As I go through the door, jangling the bell, the woman places a tote bag of books in the rack beneath the pram. 'Well, lovely to meet you,' she says to Rosie as she manoeuvres the pram. She doesn't look like a new mum taking an impromptu stroll around the town. She's applied make-up, accentuating

her eyes with kohl. Was this effort made for Rosie's benefit? Perhaps she came to the bookshop specifically, hoping
to see her.

'Let me . . .' Rosie dashes over to the door and holds it open.
The woman pushes the pram through, and at last is gone.

'Jules, what a lovely surprise.' Rosie heads back to the
counter and hugs me.

'Who was she?' I find myself whispering.

'Oh, I didn't catch her name. Lovely lady, though. Had four
goes at IVF before she conceived.'

The elderly gentleman approaches the till with a Wilkie
Collins novel. I stand to one side as Rosie serves him. 'Ah,
Armadale,' she says. 'You're in for a treat. Pop back in when
you've read it – I'd love to know what you think.'

The man beams at Rosie but his eyes are disappointed as
they take in my presence. I sense that I'm depriving him of a
long-anticipated chat.

'Do you think it's wise to let people touch your bump?' I
say after the man's gone.

Rosie grins. 'Well, actually, I wanted a second opinion. I
think I felt the baby move, Jules. I wasn't sure. It was kind
of like wind bubbles and I thought I might be reading too
much into it. But that woman said she thinks it's movement.
Can you stay a while? You might be able to feel.' The look on
Rosie's face is so impossibly tender. For a moment I almost
forget why I'm here.

But then I remember. 'Look, we need to talk. Is
Trevor around?'

'What? Yes, he's here. He's taking his break out the back.'
She draws herself up.

I should have asked about the baby, I realise. Made more of the movement. But I won't beat myself up over this omission – today there are more serious things to worry about.

'I think you need to come home with me. We ... there are things we need to sort out.'

She blanches. 'Sort out?'

'It's Scott. He's OK, I think, but he's in hospital. Someone set fire to his house. They haven't been caught yet.'

'Oh my God!' She presses both hands down on the counter. The two teenage girls turn to stare, but they quickly look away when they realise I've noticed.

'I'll get Trevor,' I whisper. 'We'll go home. I don't want you and the baby here while whoever did this is still out there.'

Inside the car, Rosie decides that we need to go to the police and ask for help. She's right. Name-calling thugs is one thing, but the idea of someone lighting a fire while we're sleeping is chilling.

Petersfield's own police station closed years ago, so I have to drive to Alton, a neighbouring town. We step through electronic doors into a crowded reception area. All the seats are taken, and still more people are standing, waiting to be taken off into back rooms to give their statements, fill in their crime reports. There's a strong smell of pine disinfectant, mingled with sweat and stale lager.

We join the queue for the reception desk. Despite the fact that there must be twenty people here, there's a strange hush. Grainy CCTV mugshots and posters about preventing car crime are taped to the walls. Ahead of us in the line, a tired-looking woman is listing items of clothing recently stolen from her washing line. It's wearying, and all at once so terribly sad. I know the local forces are under-funded: every week I'll get a call from a member of the public, incensed by a lacklustre investigation or a two-hour wait. But there's no choice – Rosie and I are dependent on whatever protection the police can provide.

From the corner of my eye, I notice a short, bald man pointing his phone in Rosie's direction. I turn and glare at him, but he surprises me by offering Rosie his seat.

I feel shaky as I continue waiting in line. Just the previous week I covered a murder trial. Liz Cartwright was the name of the victim. She ran away from a violent husband only to endure months of stalking and harassment. They played one of her 999 calls to the court and I'll never forget her panic-stricken voice. 'He's going to kill me. Do something, please.' There were twelve such calls over a three-month period. And while the police turned up here and there, dutifully filed their reports, no one took responsibility for protecting her.

Finally, I reach the front desk, and Rosie hurries over to join me at the counter. A grey-haired officer with a thick beard, looks up.

Here we go. I want to sound authoritative, but the quietness of the room forces me to speak in a lowered voice. 'My partner and I are involved in the ovum-to-ovum fertilisation trial at Portsmouth University. Our address has been published by the media, and we've been experiencing disturbances and anti-social behaviour.'

'You got a reference number?'

'Well, no. We didn't report them at the time. But that's not why we're here—'

'You didn't bother to report them?'

'We didn't think you'd be able to do anything.'

The officer gives an ostentatious sigh and scratches his beard. Rosie squeezes my hand. If I hadn't head-butted that boy, we'd have reported the doorstep harassment and perhaps there'd be a little more weight to our case now.

'One of the researchers' houses was set alight last night,' I say. 'And whoever did it hasn't been caught. We want to talk to someone about what protection can be put in place for us.'

I sense the listening ears all around me. There's not even a whisper now. But this humiliation is worth it, if it gets us what we need.

The officer does another of his sighs. 'I'm afraid that unless you've received a very specific threat, there's nothing we can do. Police protection is only offered in extreme circumstances.'

'Define a specific threat,' I say. 'An arsonist trying to kill a researcher on the trial sounds pretty specific to me.'

'As I understand it, that's just your theory,' the officer replies. 'It's still an active investigation.'

Rosie squeezes my hand. 'Come on, Jules, let's go. We should get in touch with the uni – they might be able to do something for us.'

Freeing my hand, I place my fists down on the counter. 'The arsonist wasn't going to leave a note explaining himself, was he? How can there be any other interpretation? Someone associated with the trial has been harmed. Think about it, please. Rosie and me – we're figureheads for this very unpopular science.'

The officer's eyes survey the room. His mouth twitches as he straightens his back, juts his chin forward. 'I'm afraid you can't expect the taxpayer to foot the bill. It was your choice to get involved with something so controversial,' he says. 'If anything happens, call us. We'll come out. We'll investigate, just like we would for anyone else. Now, let's get this queue moving again.'

He knows we're a target. I can see it in his face. Just like I can see how he thinks we deserve it. Fumbling in my bag, I produce my notebook. 'I'm writing down your badge number,' I say.

Back at the flat I get on the phone to the Police Commissioner's office and make a complaint, only to be told that the very best they can offer is to have officers 'look in' when they're on their patrols.

The university is slightly more responsive. Becca isn't there, but I speak to the dean of the medical school. Later, he calls me back with a promise to fund a high-tech intruder alarm system.

'What about a bodyguard?' I say. 'You've given Becca a bodyguard. Why not Rosie? I mean, she works in a shop. Any nutter could work out where to find her.'

'I've discussed it with the insurance company and at this stage their risk assessors don't feel it's necessary—'

'Don't give me that! Where was Scott's bodyguard?'

'They've assured me that they'll keep the situation under review. And we're committed to offering you a relocation further down the line, when your child is due.'

'But we didn't sign up to this. If we'd known there were only going to be two pregnancies, that all the publicity would be around Rosie and me—'

'I assure you, Ms Curtis, that we're taking the very best advice on this. You should speak to the police.'

I give up on the call. Rosie is standing over me, her hand caressing my shoulder.

'We'll be OK, Jules,' she says. 'Becca's sent us both a text. Scott's stable. Smoke inhalation and a broken leg. He's not in any real danger.'

'But he could have died. We don't know. Maybe that was the intention.'

She sits down next to me. 'Poor, poor Scott.'

I have to make her understand just how serious this is. The need to keep Rosie safe and happy has been the one constant through these turbulent months. I'm grateful for the purpose it gives me. I rub at my eyes. 'I think you're going to have to give up work.'

'No, Jules. We don't need to do anything as drastic as that. You're upset—'

'But any weirdo can work out where to find you, and you can't lock the doors; you have to let people wander in.'

'Trevor's there—'

'But what can he *do*?'

'Look, I'm not going to cower indoors all day. I shouldn't have to.'

I place a hand on her thigh. 'You've seen what people are capable of. Scott's lucky to be alive.'

She wipes a tear away with the back of her hand. 'Today was supposed to be a special day. I felt our baby move for the first time.'

I try a smile, wanting so much to feel something: an overwhelming rush of emotion directed at this child of mine would compensate for so much. But instead I keep visualising Scott's charred doorway.

'I was so excited about telling you. You haven't been yourself lately, and I thought that this would be the thing to put it right.'

We're both silent. Rosie searches my face, and I feel the scratchy sensation of tears – I have to try desperately not to blink. Keeping things from her goes against every instinct. But if she found out I was having regrets about the baby, she'd be devastated. Her view of me would be irrecoverably changed and it would be too late to unsay the words.

'Jules, what is it? You always said we could tell each other anything. What's really worrying you?'

'Scott was seriously injured last night.'

'It's more than that.' Her voice is sad rather than angry. 'I can't understand – we've never had secrets. But I know there's something and you keep on pretending that there isn't.'

I try pulling her into an embrace, but she's deliberately rigid. She won't drop her gaze, won't relent.

In the end, I'm the one who has to look away. I have to give her something, and so I go with what will hurt the least. 'I'm still ... I guess I'm still reeling from the idea that you lined up Anthony to father your baby.'

'Oh, Jules.' She wraps her arms around me.

I keep looking straight ahead. 'I know you apologised, and I don't mean to keep going on about it. But how was that ever going to be a good idea?'

'If o-o hadn't have happened, we would have discussed it. You'd have told me you hated the idea and we'd have moved on.'

Suddenly, I see how unnecessarily cruel I'm being. It's not

like I'm even angry any more – perhaps a little disappointed – but none of this is significant when paired with that terrible supermarket realisation: *if I could reverse this baby, I would.*

And the energy that this shame brings seems to demand an outlet. I kiss her, gently at first, then harder. I pull off her top, caress her breasts, so full now, and with a new firmness to them. She gasps, surprised, and I slide my hand inside the waistband of her leggings, rushing, trying so hard to silence everything in my head.

Afterwards, we lie on the sofa and she strokes my hair. 'Oh, I do wish the baby would move again. I want you to feel.'

I close my eyes and my mind skips ahead to the kind of excited reaction Rosie will expect. I'll have to muster the energy somehow. Place my hand on her abdomen and look enraptured. But if I tell the truth, what then? I imagine the incomprehension slowly coalescing into distaste, then perhaps fear. I'd reach for her, ready, in my panic, to retract the words. But she'd recoil from my touch. I know her too well.

Chapter 20

Moving day arrives. New house, new start. A cliché perhaps, but I'm determined to recapture the happiness of mine and Rosie's shared past. Anthony and the Barcombes have been enlisted to help. Elaine and Michael are based at the flat, while Rosie and Anthony unpack boxes at the new place. My role is to drive a hired van between locations.

On my second trip to the house, a photographer snaps Anthony and me as we unload the bed from the van. He's trampling our neighbour's garden and I feel the familiar bone-ache of disappointment: our infamy is already tainting our new home. They're not letting us enjoy a single day's reprieve. Anthony sticks his middle finger up at the paparazzo before taking one end of the mattress and helping me shuffle it through the doorway.

I hear Rosie calling from the living room. 'Ant! Come quick, she's moving right now.'

He drops his end of the mattress, putting me off balance so that I almost topple over. I'm stranded in the hallway, but standing on tiptoe I watch Rosie take his hand and place it against her belly.

They squeal in unison. 'Oh my God, Rosie, I felt it! That

little tap – that was an actual baby kick. She's so strong already.' His voice breaks and Rosie places an arm around him. This is how I should have responded, I realise.

'Hey,' I call. 'Kind of stuck here.'

Anthony dutifully returns and helps me inch the mattress upstairs. My forearms burn as we haul it into the bedroom and position it on the frame. We lock eyes for a moment, then hastily look away. I'm guessing Rosie has told him about my reaction to their sperm donation pact.

'I'm glad they caught those kids,' he says.

He's referring to the two teenagers who were arrested over Scott's house fire. When Abi called to tell me, she said it was *just kids*, as though expecting me to be relieved. But a chill swept through me. Children shouldn't feel such hate. What had these boys heard from their parents, to make them commit such a violent act?

I respond to Anthony with a vague smile and head downstairs in silence. Back to the van. I'm drawing a line. We're going to be happy in this house. Happy like before.

Click, click goes the camera shutter as I step outside, no doubt red-faced and dishevelled. A woman from further up the street goes by, walking a lively spaniel. I give her a wave, see her eyes widen as she takes me in, takes in the camera. She opts to blank us all, striding purposefully away.

When I arrive back at the flat, ready to load up again, Elaine and Michael are in the kitchen.

'But what kind of life is she going to have?' I hear Elaine say.

'Come on, 'Laine, pull yourself together. Jules will be here any minute.'

Quietly, I take a few steps back through the front door, then redo my entrance. '*Helloo*,' I call. 'How are we doing?'

They're resting their backs against the counter, where there's a neat row of boxes lined up ready to go. Michael flashes me a bright smile, but Elaine can't conceal the fact that she's been crying. Indeed, as soon as she sees me, she starts up again.

'What's wrong?'

Michael pats me on the shoulder. 'Nothing to worry about. She's just a bit worked up about those photographers that were here earlier.'

There had been two stationed at the flat this morning. Goodness knows why us moving house is considered such big news. While I was loading up for the first van run one of them shouted: 'Jules, your dad's been taken to hospital,' just to get me to look up. Dad was fine, of course; but for a few moments, until I clocked the photographer's smirk, I'd stood there, stunned.

Elaine steps forward and grips my wrist. 'I don't know how you've been tolerating it. And Rosie – she shouldn't be put through all this stress while she's pregnant. It's too much. It's really too much.'

'It's amazing what you can cope with, when you don't have any choice,' I say.

Elaine shakes her head. 'But is it always going to be this way? Is my granddaughter going to be followed around and photographed every moment of her life?' There's a strange energy behind her eyes and her tone is almost accusatory.

'I hope not.' As I say it, I register a cascade of images. Every doctor's trip documented and speculated on. Photographers arriving ahead of each birthday. The exhaustion of having to be vigilant all the bloody time.

'How can you stand working in the media when they're doing this to you?' Elaine asks.

''Laine . . . ' Michael shoots her a warning glance.

'It's OK,' I say. 'I guess I like to think that at least some of what I do is worthwhile. I mean, I've drawn attention to a fair few injustices. And I know I've made life better for some of the people I've written about.'

Elaine shakes her head. 'Is it true that they're going to make you go into hiding for the last month?'

'It's an option they've suggested.'

'Here,' Michael says, 'kitchen's done. Let me give you a hand with the boxes.'

By the time I drive off, Elaine's tears have dried and she's re-powdered her face. But as I head over to the house, I find myself replaying our short exchange. Was there blame there? The way she gripped my wrist, the desperate look in her eyes, made me feel culpable in some way.

We're all exhausted. And although I'm trying to fight it, I'm weighed down with sadness at having to leave the flat, at taking my last walk on the damson carpet. This was the first home I truly made my own. Its very walls hold memories of those early Sundays with Rosie. Perhaps I'm not the only one who wants to turn the clock back. Perhaps even Elaine would sacrifice her granddaughter for the life of before.

When evening arrives, I ache all over, but am pleased with the progress we've made. The security firm has been in to install the alarm system. And our boxes, while only half unpacked, are at least in the right rooms. We have a bed made up and ready to sleep in, and our television is in position.

While we sit on the sofa, delaying getting up to get dinner going, I tell Rosie about her mother's tears. She looks pained for a moment. 'Poor old Mum,' she says. 'She means well. And I don't doubt that she's really upset. But it's not directed at you – I'm the one she's disappointed in.'

'She loves you to bits.' I feel suddenly protective on Elaine's behalf, and I regret bringing it up. Perhaps all of us are feeling things we don't want, seeing things that aren't there.

'Oh, I know,' Rosie says. 'And I'm lucky, in so many ways. She really would do anything for me. But I know she'd prefer it if I wasn't gay.'

'You're being too hard on her. I've never seen the tiniest sign that she feels that way.'

Rosie smiles and puts a hand on my leg. 'It means so much to me that you love her.'

'She's always so warm and kind to me.'

Rosie smiles. 'When I was thirteen, my friend Chloe came to our house for a sleepover. She was the first girl I ever kissed. I'd spent months looking at her across the classroom, wanting to touch her. But Mum ruined everything by walking in on us.'

'You never told me that.'

She lowers her eyes, her expression sad. 'To be fair to her, I think Mum really did believe that all her shouting and screaming was going to help. She was worried about the life I'd have. But I'll never forget the shock on her face. The way she kept saying over and over: "Why can't you at least try to like boys?"'

'That doesn't sound like the Elaine I know at all,' I say. I'm thinking back to how welcome she's always made me feel. How, the first time I went over to the Barcombes' for dinner, I'd worked myself into a frenzy of nerves, but Elaine showed such genuine pleasure to meet me, that they were soon forgotten.

'She's come a long way. And I know how lucky I am to have a mum who always wants the best for me. But, as hard as she tries, sometimes I look at her and I see that part of her is pining for a more conventional family.'

I kiss Rosie's neck. This is how it always used to feel. Me and her. Talking freely, no topic off limits. We can start again, here in this place. If, this time next week, my feelings towards the baby haven't taken a more positive shape, then I'm going to be brave and talk to her about it. She'll be shocked, but I know she'll do everything she can to help me.

The doorbell goes. We look at one another, and for a moment I consider not answering – it could be a reporter with inane questions about our 'dream home'. I make a mental note to put up a discreet sign about not doing interviews, and haul myself up, answering the door with a friendly smile. I'm glad I made the effort to do so, because it's the elderly gentleman from next door.

'Hello,' I say. 'How nice of you to pop by. I'm Jules.' I put my hand out, self-conscious at how unnaturally bright I sound. But fuck it – this *is* going to be my dream home. If I want to be different, I have to act different.

The man gives my hand a brisk pump. 'Alf,' he says. He has wispy white hair and is dressed formally in dark trousers with a jacket.

'Can I offer you a cup of tea, Alf?'

'No, no.' He shifts his weight uneasily. I glance behind me. If only Rosie had come to the door instead; her natural grace is irresistible.

'I notice you had a spot of trouble earlier. Man with a camera.'

I sigh. 'Afraid so. I'm sorry if you were disturbed. I guess Rosie and I have become used to it . . . ' I trail off. Something about Alf's milky blue eyes is making me nervous. Perhaps it's the well-to-do feel of this neighbourhood. If he were a council estate pensioner I was interviewing for work, I'm sure we'd be gabbling away by now.

'It's the garden, you see. He's been all over my shrubs. Took me a long time to establish that border.'

'Goodness, I'm so sorry.'

Alf looks down at his suede brogues. I feel a pang of anger on his behalf – the arrival of new neighbours shouldn't have disrupted him like this. The bloody paparazzi have no consideration – most of them are freelance and accountable to no one.

I sigh. 'Listen, I don't know much about gardening, but perhaps tomorrow I could give you a hand putting things straight?'

Alf coughs. 'It's going to cost five hundred pounds to put it in order again. And that doesn't cover labour. That's just the plants.'

'Gosh. Five hundred pounds. I had no idea . . . did you speak to the photographer?'

'I'll get receipts. Do it all properly. But five hundred is my best guess.'

My mind is whirring. Is this man asking me for money? That's certainly what it's starting to feel like. I try to make a snap assessment of just how accountable Rosie and I ought to feel. The photographer was here because of us, but certainly not by invitation.

'Listen, Alf, I'm really sorry to hear this. But what with moving and everything, I'm not sure we can manage five hundred pounds.'

He frowns and rocks on his heels. 'It would be more if I decided to get a professional in. You should be grateful I'm prepared to do the work myself.'

'You should have taken it up with the photographer,' Rosie says. At last, she's beside me, her hand on the small of my back. 'I'm very sorry this happened, but we didn't do anything to harm your plants and I'm afraid we can't offer to pay for them.'

Alf flinches. He gives Rosie the up-and-down assessment that I'm so sick and tired of seeing, and his mouth lifts into a kind of sneer. 'I see. That's the attitude, is it?'

'It's really not our fault,' Rosie says. 'But let's not argue – come in and have that cup of tea.'

He snorts at this, then wheels around, scuffing his feet like a truculent teenager. 'Knew you'd be trouble,' he says, not looking back. 'Well – if that's how you want it . . . '

My heart is thudding as I close the door. I run my fingers around the newly installed panic button on the wall. It's one of five in the house, positioned so that you can press it while you talk to someone on the doorstep.

Rosie takes my hand. 'The fucking cheek of it,' she says.

I sigh. 'Now he's going to hate us.'

Chapter 21

Rosie defies the barrenness of the protracted winter. While the rest of us are grey-hued, veins visible beneath the skin, she radiates health – life blossoms in her cheeks and her face lights up with sudden smiles at the little kicks emanating from her ever-growing bump. We've been up to London to visit the Royal Free with Becca. Their head of security gave us a tour, showing us where police cordons would go and talking us through the credential checks they'd put in place to avoid giving away information to journalists posing as family members. We've also started attending antenatal classes at Aspire Health, our local private hospital, which also seems desperate to woo us for the birth.

Anita mirrors Rosie's ripening. She and Hong Shu don't dare to be seen out with us, but they invite us to their home for lunches and film nights. We're careful to make sure we're not being followed, never turning off into their road until we're certain that no reporters are behind us. Rosie's always so excited to see her developing shape reflected in her friend; they sit on the sofa together, comparing sensations, touching and prodding, part of a strange new fellowship.

But then the very worst happens. Rosie and Anita are

both twenty-four weeks pregnant. It's a drizzly Sunday, the anniversary of my mother's death. I'm planning to go to the cemetery with my father later that afternoon. It's a ritual we have – I remember holding his hand as a young girl, bored and impatient as he contemplated the grassy mound in silence.

Rosie and I are at home, eating toasted cheese and tomato sandwiches in front of the news, when we get the text from Hong Shu. Anita has gone into labour. For a moment we simply look at one another in shared incomprehension. I think of Hong Shu, how her eyes swim with emotion every time she speaks of their baby.

Rosie inhales sharply. 'We have to stay positive, for their sake. Babies can survive at twenty-four weeks. Becca will make sure they get the best care.'

'We ought to text back,' I say. 'God, what do we . . . ?'

Rosie places a hand against her bump. 'There's nothing. All we can do is let them know we're thinking of them.' Her lips quiver as a tear slides down her face.

I close my eyes. I feel unworthy, guilty that my feelings never matched the intensity of Hong Shu's. A cold feeling spreads across my back: might there be something wrong with the o-o technique? We're in a trial, after all. The term *uncharted territory* has been applied to our situation countless times.

I steal a look at Rosie. Although her face is blanched, she looks like any other pregnant woman. If something was wrong with the procedure, if she lost the child she's carrying, she'd be so broken. I take her hand and give it a squeeze, feeling a surge of love that I'm so grateful for. Yes, things have been difficult, but she's Rosie. I'd do anything to shelter her from such loss. And with this realisation comes a fresh awareness of the being inside her. It's a kind of mental force, an inner pushing of my will. *Survive. Live. Make her happy.* It's electric, lighting me from within.

It only lasts a second, because I realise: if Anita loses this baby, Rosie will become one of a kind. Our baby will be the first and only child born to two women. Her arrival was always going to be a global news event, but with this terrible tragedy the interest will escalate tenfold. 'We should call Becca,' I say. 'This is going to have implications for us.'

Rosie pulls away from me, eyes flashing. 'Jules – how can you be business-as-usual at such a time? Their baby—' Her voice splinters.

'I know, Rosie. And I'm so sorry for them. But this is serious.'

She runs the sleeve of her cardigan across her eyes. 'Unbelievable. If you realised how callous you sound . . .'

Winded, I remove my hand from her knee and look down at my half-eaten sandwich. The melted cheese has cooled and hardened into a chemical-yellow rubber that makes me nauseous. I stand up to take my plate into the kitchen. 'I just want to protect us,' I say.

She looks away with an angry sigh.

After stacking the dishwasher, I go back through to the living room. The sight of Rosie's pink, blotchy face, the curve of her spine as she radiates disapproval, makes something snap. Over the last few months every moment of my free time has been focused on creating the best possible future for our family, on navigating the glare of our opponents. I'm so tired of feeling like I'm failing to meet some kind of standard, an ideal of motherhood that comes instinctively to everyone else.

'I need to go and pick Dad up for our cemetery visit,' I say.

Rosie exhales and shakes her head.

I go out into the hallway and fight my way into my parka, tie the laces of my trainers. I will not be drawn as the bad guy. It's not wrong to think ahead to implications, to plan. Someone has to. And it doesn't mean I care any less. I'd do anything to spare Hong Shu and Anita some of the pain they must be facing.

My foot meets something soft and slippery as I step outside. I almost slide, but put a hand against the brickwork just in time. A dog turd. A large, sodden dog turd positioned in the exact centre of our doorstep. My breath catches as the stink of it hits my nostrils. I scan the street. Empty. But someone must have placed it here. For a moment I consider returning to the house, sharing my disbelief with Rosie. But I can't bear to return to the chill atmosphere of the living room. Instead, I hop round to the side of the house where there's an outside tap and rinse my filthy trainer. With a twig, I try to scrape the remnants from the deep grooves in the sole, retching as the force of the smell hits me afresh. Thank fuck there are no photographers here at the moment to capture this. Our garden shed is unlocked, so I use a spade to remove the rest of the shit from the step. My face is hot. I'm imagining eyes against my skin. The perpetrator's satisfaction as they watch the results of their handiwork from behind a net curtain.

Once I've collected Dad, I drive us out to the cemetery, which sits on a hill overlooking the town. 'Haven't seen you for a while,' he remarks. 'I've got used to checking the papers to find out what my girl's up to.'

'Then you'll know things have been hectic.'

'Shouldn't you be in full-on sprog mode? Boring me with talk about nurseries and the like?'

I turn into the car park. His eyes are taking in my expression. Without answering his question, I pull the handbrake and switch off the engine. I'm not going to pretend, not with him. Dad is the one person I can be sure won't judge me.

'Seriously,' he says as we walk to my mother's plot. 'What about the legendary maternal instinct? Has it started kicking in yet?'

I shake my head. For a moment I think of myself in the third person. *Jules Curtis. She tries so bloody hard. All she wants is to be loved and to do maybe one or two things in her life that are really worthwhile. But time and again she falls short of her own standards. Wretched creature!* I imagine the relief of unburdening. Of sharing this confused tangle of feelings with the one person who's inextricably bound to me, who could not, and would not, walk away.

'I don't have a maternal instinct,' I say. 'It's all Rosie. Christ, you know me. Do you think that some hormonal switch flicked and I went gaga for babies?'

I'm impatient for a reaction. Perhaps some part of me wants a gasp of horror. But Dad is silent. We've reached the grave. It's unmarked. We never had the money for a headstone, and over the years the mound has levelled out, the grass re-grown. As if to rebuke us, the graves on either side are carefully tended. To the left, a shiny black headstone marks the passing of Hubert Smith, dearest father. The grave is delineated with white gravel, and for as long as I can remember has always borne fresh flowers. Today a vase of irises stands next to the stone, petals quivering in the breeze. The plot to the right of my mother's has been completely planted over with tightly packed marigolds and begonias. The soil is always freshly weeded, the flowers well-watered and robust. I've never seen who does this, who sacrifices so much of their life in service to the dead.

My father's eyes are trained on the patch of grass that sits between them. I bow my head and am silent. This is where the broken body of my mother lies. When I was a girl I used to imagine the woman in the photograph, hair splayed out underneath her, sleeping peacefully beneath the ground. I had a toy bucket and spade, and I remember making secret plans to come here alone one day and scrape away the earth so that I could look at her. I was desperate for one real memory of her as a physical presence, as opposed to a picture.

Standing next to my father, I visualise the shattered bones under the soil. I try to feel a connection with this long-gone woman, who got to live a mere twenty-one years, but all I feel is my father's sadness. As in previous years, I wait a few moments, then leave him to his reflections, walking back to a wooden bench positioned next to the path. I watch dots of people making their ministrations and am aware of a loss that I can't fully understand. Perhaps the sadness of this place has coloured my character somehow. The atmosphere of graves and tears and flowers for those who'll never see them, never smell their fragrance.

I look over at my father and feel sorrow at never being able to hear the thoughts that percolate as he bows his head and feels the presence of his wife. But I know his reflections are something special, something rarefied. I feel sometimes that if I could listen in on the minds of those who come and pay their respects in this place, I'd be different, somehow; that my understanding of what it means to live and love would be deeper.

Now, sitting on this bench, an old feeling returns. One that has dipped and bobbed through my consciousness since childhood. A sense of being detached from the world. Of being excluded from some sacred communion of minds and hearts. I feel that anyone who was to look at me right now would draw themselves up in alarm, sensing the absence of some fundamental quality that binds human beings together.

After a while Dad walks over and we sit together in silence. His expression, while bearing the shadow of recent pain, has relaxed slightly.

'So,' he says at last. 'You're having doubts?'

'I don't know how I'm going to do it.' My voice catches. Dad looks at me in surprise for a moment, then puts his arm around me.

'Your mum really looked forward to you,' he says. 'Her whole pregnancy, she seemed filled with a kind of force.'

I try to smile. He means well. But it's exactly this talk of force, of excitement and anticipation, that leaves me feeling so inadequate. I sigh. 'I try and tell myself that motherhood is a myth perpetuated by the women's magazines. Nothing more. We did alright, didn't we? Just the two of us.' I rub at my cheeks. My exhaustion is somehow heightened. It's like I'm looking down on myself, amazed that I'm still awake, that I'm still finding the strength to plough through the days.

'Hey,' he says. 'Come on, you'll be OK.'

'I don't think I ever wanted a child. Not really. I just got swept up. The excitement of two-mother babies. Getting a place on the trial. And I knew how important it was to Rosie. I suppose I expected that the real feelings – the mother feelings – would come later.'

'We all do things for the wrong reasons. Nobody's perfect. Nobody's above making mistakes.'

'But perhaps nobody else has fucked up in quite such a spectacular way as me.'

He pulls me into a hug. I let the warmth comfort me for a moment. I meant so well. Every step of the way, I convinced myself I was doing the right thing.

'Rosie can never know. I have to pretend – act like I'm excited, like it's the thing I want most.' My voice is strangely high-pitched.

'You'll be alright, Jules.'

'I'm not going to be able to manage it,' I say. The thought of returning to the house fills me with panic. Running out on an argument was the wrong thing to do. What if Rosie won't forgive me? What if I go back and she isn't there? I ought to head home now, but I realise that I've actually enjoyed being here at the cemetery, that it's offered a moment of respite.

Dad gives me a gentle smile. 'You're strong,' he says. 'You'll survive whatever comes, I promise you.'

'And you? Are you excited?'

'No one expects it of me. But I do want things to work out for you. I want you to get your life back. Jules, you were so clever. I don't want you to waste any more days – you're capable of so much.'

After that we're silent. My mind revisits a plethora of childhood memories. The younger version of my father, face close to mine, eyes earnest. *I made a mess of things, Jules. But you don't have to. You make the most of your education, my girl. You do the things I wasn't able to.* I remember the feeling of burgeoning importance that such conversations used to instil.

My reverie is interrupted by Rosie calling. I answer quickly; my upbeat ring-tone feels sacrilegious in such a place. 'Jules, are you OK? I was getting worried.'

'I'm still at the cemetery.'

'Come home, Jules. I'm sorry. It's just ... Anita. It's too much to process. I'm so worried for them.'

I sit up straight and rub my eyes. 'Someone put dog shit on our doorstep.'

'Why the hell would they do that?'

'Oh, I don't know. Making a stand against the lesbian mafia, I guess.'

It's getting dark, I realise, when I end the call. Dad has stood up, ready to go. I probably shouldn't have answered the phone; it's broken some kind of spell. I'd felt on the cusp of something, as though I was about to grasp some shadowy understanding. But now it's retreated and my dad's bearing is frowning and impatient. The ritual is over for the year. Respects paid. And, once more, the forward march resumes.

Chapter 22

Anita's baby is stillborn. She dies in the birth canal, never breathes, never cries. We send texts. We send a card. And five days after it happens I get a call from Hong Shu. 'Anita wants to see you both.' Her voice is flat. 'We're still grieving, but it would mean a lot if you could come over. I know how uncomfortable this must make you feel—'

'Of course we'll come,' I say. 'If there's anything we can do . . .'

'It'll just be good to see you. Everything's OK on your side, I take it? With the baby, I mean.'

'Yes.'

Hong Shu's breath catches. She's trying so hard to master her voice. 'Sunday, then. I won't offer lunch – we're not really up to it. Come at about three.'

A pang of reluctance. How can we possibly help them in their grief? If there was some task I could perform, anything I could do to lessen their pain, of course I would do it. But all I have are words. And what could be more inadequate at such a time?

When I relay the invitation to Rosie she's propped up in bed, rereading *Sense and Sensibility*. Her eyes widen in alarm.

'Oh no, Jules, I really don't think I can go. What can we say to them? I'll feel like I'm flaunting my bump.'

I sit down next to her and take her hand. 'I know it's hard. But we can't refuse, not after what's happened. Anita specifically asked to see us.'

Rosie sighs and rests her other hand on the bump. 'She's really active tonight. Do you want to feel?'

I nod and place my hand on her belly. Sharp little punches. I try to imagine our lives in a year's time, the baby here with us, lying on her back, kicking her little legs in the air. I'm doing this a lot at the moment – imagining the baby into life, forcing myself to conjure scenes of tenderness and joy. It's my own way of responding to the tragedy, trying to assuage my guilt at having been spared such a loss.

'Jules?'

'Yes.'

'Our baby feels so alive, doesn't she?'

'Alive and kicking.'

'Nothing will happen? I really don't know how I'd cope, I want her so much.'

'She's going to be fine,' I say.

Hong Shu shows us into their living room. Cards line the top of their bookcase, the coffee table, the windowsill. Reminders of their loss are everywhere: they cannot have a single moment of respite, a single moment of forgetting.

Anita sits on one of their cream sofas, legs curled underneath her. Her face is blotchy; the dark circles under her eyes resemble bruises. On entering the room Rosie heads straight for her, closing her eyes as she pulls her into a tight embrace.

Hong Shu and I stand stiffly next to each other in the middle of the room. I brave a look at her face: the playfulness in her expression has gone and she looks as though she's aged ten years. The only part of her that seems alive is her eyes, which burn with indignation.

She turns to me and her lips twitch. She's going to say something but thinks better of it. 'Tea? Coffee?' she offers.

As I sit with a coffee cradled in my lap I wonder again: how can they bear to see us when their grief is so raw? Maybe the visit represents some step in their healing that Rosie or I couldn't possibly fathom. My whole body yearns to comfort, but I'm awkwardly drawn up, holding back because I simply don't know the right thing to do or say. Platitudes about finding meaning from tragedy rise up in my consciousness: half-remembered magazine articles, poignant lines from films. But everything is so inadequate.

'It was like food poisoning or something,' Anita says. 'All that morning I was on and off the toilet. But that's what the body does, Becca told me. It's nature's way of clearing you out so you can push.

'Anyway, about lunchtime I started to bleed. It wasn't heavy or anything, but when I called Becca she said to get down to St Luke's, just in case. My back was killing me. But it was my back, I mean . . . I didn't think it meant anything.

'Shuey met me at the hospital, and literally, the minute they showed me into a private room my waters broke.' Her ribs heave. I brave a look at her belly. It's flaccid, empty.

'It wasn't a gush like it always is in the films,' Hong Shu says. 'I just thought Anita'd wet herself.' Her jaw tightens. She doesn't look at either of us.

Anita blows her nose. 'The strange thing was – I felt fantastic. Your waters breaking unleashes all sorts of hormones and you really do feel good, like you can face anything. Honestly, Rosie – it's amazing how nature prepares you.'

Rosie attempts a smile, trying to restrain her tears.

'Our baby's heart was still beating,' Hong Shu says, in that same flat voice. 'We heard it. She was fine. Right up until the end, she was fine.'

Anita's eyes widen in alarm. She's been pacing herself. She's not ready for this part of the story and has to take a few steadying breaths.

'I had contractions. Just like a normal labour. It *was* labour. And I'd do it again: now that I've been through it, I'm not frightened. Your body really does know what to do.' Her eyes dart across the room.

I'm unable to bear the silence that follows. 'So what did the contractions feel like?' I ask.

I feel Rosie stiffen, but Anita seems grateful for the chance to resume the story.

'Oh – the strangest thing. Your whole body squeezes in on itself, as though you're throwing up and doing a poo at the same time. And that's the wonderful thing – like I said, your body purposefully clears you out beforehand. That's why I'd had diarrhoea all morning.'

I nod. I've never seen Anita this animated before. Her redrimmed eyes blaze. A chill spreads inside me. I know how this story ends. I'm terrified of getting to that point, of the horrors that Rosie will have to listen to, of the inadequacy of anything we might say or do.

'Five hours,' Hong Shu says. 'And her heart was beating

the whole time. It stopped in the birth canal. At the very last moment.'

Anita buries her head in Hong Shu's shoulder. But Hong Shu barely acknowledges her sobbing lover, makes no attempt to comfort her.

Rosie shifts in her seat, re-crosses her legs. I can tell that part of her wants to go to Anita again. That's the kind of person she is – other people's pain tugs at her, hurts her, even. But guilt is a powerful restraint.

I wonder whether we should leave. I go as far as thinking up tactful exit cues, but then Anita looks up. 'We named her Jessica. And she was perfect. There was nothing wrong with her, nothing. No one could tell us why she'd come so early. We wondered whether it might be down to how she was made – but she was a healthy baby. Or she would have been, if she'd come at the right time. I held her. I was like any other new mum, holding her baby. But my baby was dead.'

Rosie lets out a little gasp. This time she does get up and go to Anita, putting an arm around her and pulling her in close so that Anita's head is right up against the bump. I hope the baby is sleeping and doesn't taunt the bereaved with a kick. How upsetting this picture is. My ribs squeeze at Rosie's impulsivity, but Anita doesn't seem to mind. She cries relentlessly, as though Rosie has somehow conferred permission. I'm proud of Rosie for knowing what to do. But I find it too hard to watch.

I inspect the cards lined up on the bookcase. I hadn't known Hong Shu and Anita were such a popular couple. So many friends, but of all of them we're the only ones who knew their baby's true origins.

'The university took her,' Hong Shu says. The atmosphere in the room becomes taut. Rosie's face drains of colour as she looks up.

'What?' she says, a hand still on Anita's shoulder.

'It was in the agreement we all signed. I hadn't read the small print. But Becca was ready. Turned up at the hospital and just happened to have a copy of the paperwork in her bag. "In the event of a miscarriage or stillbirth, the tissue will be recovered by the university for research purposes."'

'They wouldn't let us bury her,' Anita says.

Rosie's face is blanched; she looks at Anita, then back at me. There's a plea for help in her eyes. This cannot be true. Becca wouldn't do such a thing.

'Look, we called you here for a reason,' Hong Shu says. 'You'll think we're mercenary, and I'm sorry. But we have to take any tiny little bit of good that can come out of this. The *Tribune* are going to give us twenty grand for the rights to our story. We've got an interview lined up for tomorrow.'

Saying nothing, I observe Anita's tear-streaked face. The grief is tightly packed into every muscle. I try to skip ahead in my mind. I need to be assessing what this will mean for Rosie and me. But my head fills with fog. *They weren't allowed to bury their baby?* We must have signed the agreement too, but the terms probably seemed so reasonable then, before our baby was even conceived. I picture a foetus on a steel worktop, scalpels at the ready.

When I look at Hong Shu again she lifts her head and shows me her hollow eyes. 'We're securing our future,' she says. 'We can't turn the opportunity down, we just can't. We'll want to try again – a sperm bank, probably. We can take something from this, do something for our next child.'

Rosie steps away from Anita. 'Let's go home, Jules.'

I expect protest. Entreaties to let them explain further. But they remain frozen on the sofa.

'Please,' I say. 'Reconsider. Telling your story will feed the media frenzy.'

Hong Shu bites her lip, looking at the carpet. Then, she jerks her head up and stares at Rosie's bump. She tries to keep her eyes hard, but she can't prevent me from seeing just how shattered she is.

I go to her, placing my hands on her shoulders. 'Please. They'll scaremonger, say the trial shouldn't have gone ahead.'

Hong Shu bats my hands away. 'Who's to say they're wrong? They let us hope, Jules. Six months. For six months we were thinking we were going to have a baby. We felt her move. We listened to her heartbeat. And now she's been taken away to be experimented on.'

'And I'm so very sorry. But the *Tribune* . . . I can't . . .'

Hong Shu turns her head to one side. Anita covers her face with her hands.

I linger for one moment more, then I place a hand on Rosie's back and we leave them to their silent grief.

Four days later the tabloid runs their piece, headlined **Lesbian baby experiment ends in tragedy**.

One of only two women to conceive via Portsmouth University's controversial ovum-to-ovum fertilisation experiment has lost her baby at 24 weeks, prompting fertility experts to further question the safety of the procedure.

Hong Shu and Anita are pictured on their sofa, wearing heavy expressions.

Later in the piece: *The tragedy means that 31-year-old Rosie Barcombe, a pretty blonde from Petersfield in Hampshire, remains the only pregnant woman from the first wave of the trial. If her baby is born it will be the first baby in the world to have no genetic father.*

If her baby is born? Is reportage like this actually designed to induce a miscarriage? For a moment I consider an official complaint. But that in itself would give them something to report on.

As I reread the piece I identify the heavy feeling in my chest as genuine sadness. Hong Shu's expression always took on such a dreamlike quality when she spoke of her future daughter. She had been looking forward to her so much, had imagined her new life as a mother in such detail. I remember just how shaken I'd felt on realising just how integral it was to her identity, how, like Rosie, she'd staked so much happiness on a future she couldn't control.

Chapter 23

As expected, Hong Shu and Anita's interview reignites the interest in Rosie and me. At least one photographer will follow me to work, then shadow me as I make my way through my twelve hours of assignments. And it's harder than ever to bear, because I know they're waiting for something to happen to our baby. They're making sure they're in position, in case there's a mad dash to the hospital, in case I have to lead Rosie from the house in a bloodied dressing gown.

The other day I had to knock on the door of a bereaved mother, knowing I was being tailed. The photographer waited at the foot of the garden, talking loudly on his mobile: 'Yeah. Still on her. She's gone to a house in Paulsgrove. Working, I think. Yeah, a right shithole . . . '

I turned to him: 'This is a death knock, do you mind moving away out of sight?' His response was to raise his camera and start clicking. For some reason shots of women trying to get the media to back off are all the rage at the moment. They always use the most ugly: mouth caught in a strange, contorted position, eyes wild with anger.

I had to knock on the woman's door knowing he was behind me, standing beside her broken gate. As I deployed my gentle reasoning: *a tribute, we'll celebrate your son's life, if you could spare just a few words* ... I knew I was exposing this grieving mother, hair un-brushed, jumper stained. I saw her face crumple as she clocked the photographer. And I'll never forget her high-pitched cry of misery as she shut the door in my face. I've always been professional, so careful not to be gratuitous around death. But this situation, and Matthew's refusal to take it into account when he gives me my assignments, makes it feel as though I'm leading a grotesque procession around the city.

A week after the *Tribune* story, Richard Prior approaches the *Post* offering an interview. And Matthew tells me, with some irritation, that the politician has specifically requested that I be the interviewer.

'You have to do it,' Rosie says when I tell her.

'But it must just be some twisted publicity stunt.'

'That doesn't matter. Make it backfire. Demolish him with your questions. Show him up for what he really is. This is our chance.'

And so I agree. There's a short exchange with his secretary: initially Prior wants to film me interviewing him, but I refuse. So he comes back suggesting an audio recording as a compromise, which I accept, making it clear that I'll be making my own recording too.

The night before, Tom and I go to the pub after work to prepare. It's quiet inside, a line of solitary men stare into their pints at the bar, and there are sullen clusters around each of the fruit machines.

While Tom gets the drinks I take a seat in one of the

tan leather booths. For each assertion Prior makes, I need to be ready with probing follow-up questions that expose the thinness of his arguments. Tonight Tom is going to be my stand-in, tasked with firing the ANR's flawed reasoning at me.

He hands me a glass of Diet Coke, a segment of lemon floating on top. 'Right then.' He slides into his seat. 'Assertion number one. Women, if given a choice, would choose a baby girl every time.'

'That's ridiculous – it's human nature to want to have a child with your partner. The majority of heterosexual women will carry on having babies the old-fashioned way. A preference for a girl isn't going to make them cut their boyfriends and husbands out of the equation by choosing o-o.'

Tom gives me a sardonic nod as he takes a sip from his pint.

'And look at countries where sex selection is widely practised,' I add. 'In India the birth rate is skewed in favour of boys. And in China the one-child policy led to millions of abandoned baby girls.'

'Nicely put,' Tom says. 'OK. On to argument number two. What if heterosexual women *don't* want to keep doing it the old-fashioned way?'

'That won't happen—'

'No, think about it.' He extends a hand as he speaks. 'A few liberal exceptions aside, I think we all accept that men are actually rather lazy compared to women. Especially where family stuff is concerned. There must be loads of women out there who are thinking, who will give my child the best life? Is it the guy I'm with? Or is it – say – my best friend since school, who I trust completely and has always been there when I needed her? Would my kids not have a better chance in life if I were to co-parent with her?'

I think back to Crete, to the moment that started all of this. The toddler Rosie befriended, his laughing face a perfect fusion of mother and father. Surprised as I was to find it, there must be some primal instinct in all of us that longs for this melding with the one you love.

'I don't buy it,' I say.

Tom runs a finger through the condensation gathering on his beer glass, and looks at me. 'That's because, in spite of everything, you're a hopeless traditionalist, Jules.'

'Ha.'

'No, I'm serious. Part of me is jealous of what you have with Rosie, of your faith in the happily ever after. But not everyone thinks like that now. We're programmed to want the best for our offspring. And I guarantee you, there will be an army of women out there who decide the best thing is a second mother.'

'You really believe that?'

His face is flushed. He meets my eye and then looks away, covering his embarrassment with a long slug from his pint. Can Tom really be *threatened* by o-o? It seems so absurd. Tom, who can pull within thirty minutes of entering a bar. Who wrinkles his nose at any suggestion he should settle down.

As he swallows, I find myself anxiously waiting. Will we simply go back to preparing for the interview, or are we going to explore this further? The kindest thing is to let him decide, and so I quietly wait. Out of the corner of my eye I see the photographer who's been following me all day go up to the bar and order a drink.

Tom sighs, putting his beer glass down on the table. 'Being in a couple isn't a prerequisite for raising a family,' he says. 'Now the science has evolved, who's to say that women won't decide to raise their children collectively? I mean, up until now women have had babies with men because they had to. No one can really know what they'll choose now there's another option available. We could end up with completely different child-rearing models.'

'Sounds pretty far-fetched to me, Tom.'

'And then, what would men actually be for? They could use us for sex here and there. But in today's world there's nothing women really *need* us for. I mean, take me for instance – I wouldn't choose to have a child with me.' His voice crackles with emotion.

I almost put a hand on his arm, but realise he'd hate that. I'm about to say something reassuring, but at the same moment I wonder to myself: what kind of father would Tom be? He's great company, and generous in so many ways. I imagine him holding a baby aloft, prompting squeals with vigorous bounces and silly faces; handing out Christmas presents he can't really afford. But would such responsibility keep him from the pub, from evenings with his mates that stretch into the early hours? I remember the times we invited him round: the chronic lateness, the driving home even though he'd had far too much to drink. And then there was that poor friend of Rosie's who was convinced she was in love, only to have her calls go to voicemail after he'd slept with her.

If I had to pick someone in my circle to raise a child with, someone other than Rosie, I'd never pick Tom. In fact, I can't name one man – aside from Rosie's father and my own – who'd do a better job than most of the women I know.

'Well,' I say, 'when the time comes to settle down, you can reflect on that. Do something about it.'

For a moment he looks wounded. I was perhaps meant to argue with him, to reassure. That's what he wanted. *Of course someone will want you – you're going to be a great dad.* But within a second, the expression is gone. He cracks a grin. 'OK. Number three. The o-o trial is diverting money away from St Luke's. What do you have to say about that, Ms Curtis?'

Throughout the evening, as we fling questions and answers across the table, I find myself revisiting Tom's point: now that there's an entirely new reproduction mechanism available to women, is it possible that we might start seeing a new kind of pragmatism? Might women reject romance, instead taking a far more outcome-focused approach to creating and rearing their children? Having babies seems to be the one arena that's always been so blessedly free from such calculation. I think of all the women I've encountered through the courts, tethered to unsuitable partners because of one moment – maybe lasting weeks, maybe lasting years – when everything seemed right and perfect. But these are the moments we live for as human beings. Like me in Crete, saying yes when there were a hundred reasons to say no.

The day of the interview is one of those March days that plunges you right back into winter. An icy wind whips up the drizzle, slamming it into my face as I step out of the car into the Victorian street where Prior lives. His house is on the corner of a long, three-storey terrace. Most of these properties were portioned off into flats years ago, but his stands proudly apart, the only one with a landscaped garden out the front. While he makes much of his time working in the Dockyard, he's spent the past ten years building up a rental business. Looks like it's doing well.

As the photographer who followed me here struggles to find somewhere to park, I hurry over and press Prior's doorbell. I'm ready, thanks to Tom. I've gone through all the arguments against o-o and I've memorised the facts and statistics that expose just how thin they really are. My article will show the world just how tenuous his grasp on the subject really is.

Prior comes to the door himself, and shows me through into a spacious sitting room that overlooks the back garden. The walls are festooned with pictures of his three sons at various ages. Broad smiles, muddied faces and football kits. There's an old-fashioned fireplace where a log fire gently crackles. On one side of the room, two large sofas upholstered in blue and white striped silk are arranged in an L-shape around a mahogany table bearing coffee.

Prior sits on one of the sofas and gestures for me to take the other. He's wearing jeans and an expensive-looking blue V-neck, his anchor tattoo protruding out of the neckline, as always. He pours two cups of aromatic coffee.

Taking my phone from my satchel I set it to record. 'You wanted to take a recording too?' I say.

Silently he pulls his own phone from his pocket and lays it on the table.

'You ready to get started?' I ask.

He nods.

'OK, then. Let's start with your swearing-in ceremony. What was that like for you?'

He leans back in the sofa, his legs wide apart, and gives a contented kind of sigh. 'It was a very special moment. I'd realised by that point that my mission was so much larger than I originally thought. It's no secret that I'm an opponent of ovum-to-ovum fertilisation and that I was elected on a promise to get it banned. But as I stood in that chamber – so familiar to me from the TV news – I asked myself: will a ban actually be enough?'

My stomach tightens at this first, early reference to the trial. I'm aware of just how alone we are, of the silence throughout the rest of the house.

I look up from my notebook. 'Go on.'

Prior stretches his head back and stares at the crystal chandelier hanging above us. 'I asked myself why my campaign resonated with so many people. People who feel like there's something broken in their lives. And then it became obvious to me: family.

'My voters are offended by this o-o experiment because it goes against their ideals of how families should be constructed. And they need someone who isn't just going to apply a sticking plaster. No. Something far greater is needed: nothing less than a national moment of soul-searching. Something that redefines what family actually means in the twenty-first century.' He straightens his neck so that he's directly facing me, and then smiles, showing me the gap between his front teeth.

Up until that point I'd let myself believe that this might end up being a typically oblique political interview. Plenty of stuff about values, but nothing of actual substance. This smile speaks of something different. He looks so incredibly pleased with himself. And there's a confidence there too. It feels as though he's *handling* me. The question I come up with next is probably going to be precisely what he wants me to ask.

Assuming a kind of bored confidence, I say: 'So tell me how this epiphany is going to impact on your work throughout the current session.'

There. A twitch of the chin. This is exactly where he wants to be in the interview.

'I'm drafting a bill to protect everything that's great about family and to give our children the very best start in life. We've let political correctness go too far, and it's time someone had the courage to start overturning a generation's worth of bad decisions.'

I look up, meeting his eye. 'OK. So what it is exactly that you think makes a family great? Could you be more specific?'

'A father and a mother, for a start.'

My breath catches, but I'm able to mask it. 'That's something many of your voters would say is simply untrue. Aren't you worried about offending the legion of hard-working single parents here in Portsmouth?'

'Study after study proves that I'm right, Juliet. I know it's not what you want to hear. But without a father in the home, teen pregnancies and delinquency rates go up. With a committed father in place, academic achievement improves and kids are more confident and sociable.'

'I can point to ten other studies that say otherwise.' My voice is becoming high-pitched. I remind myself to breathe, to slow down.

'All done by people with an agenda, no doubt.'

'I could say the same about the research you're citing.'

'Well, no doubt the bill will spark a national debate. Indeed, I'm rather counting on it. But I'm sure that it will make life better for children in Portsmouth and across the country.'

Taking a steadying breath, I will the heat to disperse from my face. I'm the professional here. I'm the one who's going to go away and write this up. I'll make the *Post*'s readers see how preposterous his assertions are. 'So. A bill that defines family as one man, one woman. OK. And if such a bill were to actually pass, what will become of those who choose to structure their families in other ways?'

'We'd need to review legislation around who can foster and adopt. Again, there are statistics that show this will be safer for the kids involved. But I'm a great believer in the carrot rather than the stick. So we'd put benefits and rewards in place for those who are devoted to raising their families in the best way. We want to give incentives for fathers to stick around. Decent tax credits for married couples, that type of thing.'

'Would gay married couples qualify?'

Prior presses his lips together and tilts his head to one side. 'You lost your own mother when you were very young, didn't you? It was in the papers.'

I hold my biro against my lip for a moment. 'That's got nothing to do with what we're talking about.'

'I'm sorry. Maybe it was wrong of me to bring it up. My point, that I was trying to make, is that your loss would have prevented you from experiencing life in a committed two-parent family. And perhaps, if you had experienced such a thing, you might put a higher price on it.'

For a moment all is silent. The thing no one has dared to say, but doubtless many have thought. *You don't know, Jules, you simply don't know the right way.* And I don't. What I've believed in, what kept me going through the o-o application process, was the idea that there's a multitude of different ways. That someone like Rosie would develop her own approach, and that it would be just as valid, just as competent, as the next person's.

Prior is watching me carefully. Why did he pick me for this? One of the nationals would have run an interview, easily. There must be some satisfaction for him in delivering his message to one of the people most upset to hear it. To know that I'll be heading back to the office in a bit, that I'll have to type up his words. Matthew's going to fucking love it. *Prior announces sweeping new family bill.*

I take a slow sip of coffee and place the cup carefully back down on the table. 'Does it not strike you as rather regressive?' I say. 'The nuclear family is of a different time, a time when a single salary could cover a mortgage. Things are different now. And the new family structures we're seeing weren't forced upon us. They evolved because people wanted them.'

Prior shakes his head. 'That's exactly the kind of thinking that got us into this mess. The idea that moving away from the past is always an improvement, even if it isn't. Hell, the traditional family might not be fashionable any more, but it's what scientists and psychologists will tell you time and again is best for our kids.'

'You say that the bill is currently being drafted.'

'Yes. And I promise you – once it's ready, I'm going to be camped outside the Bills Office in the House of Commons, demanding a reading. I'm going to make sure my constituents, all the hard-working people of Portsmouth South, get their moment. I'm going to make Parliament debate the important things for once.'

I reach over and stop the recording on my phone, holding it aloft so he can see what I've done. As I place it back inside my bag I ask: 'Do you really believe in this one man, one woman guff?'

He opens his mouth to speak, but I interrupt. 'Maybe I'm speaking out of turn here, but I've never had the sense that this anti-o-o rhetoric was coming from the heart. You're a clever man. You've owned the causes that get you the best reaction.'

A flicker of surprise passes through his eyes, and I know I'm right. He's not a believer. He's a politician. And as he struggles to compose his face, to reinstate the expression of utter conviction that's played out so well, I feel a spike of victory.

But just as quickly, it's gone. It doesn't matter what Prior believes. The response he gets from voters and the media will be just as roaring, with or without his real conviction to fuel it. He can mimic a believer very effectively. And that, at the end of the day, is what counts.

He's looking at me now. 'I'm surprised at your cynicism, Juliet. But I guess you are a journalist, after all.'

I flash him a bitter smile and gather up my things.

Before I even get back to the office, Prior has tweeted about our exchange: *Just announced my new family bill to Juliet Curtis. Read tonight's Post to learn more.*

By the time I arrive, two nationals have approached

Matthew, interested in syndicating the article. Those national by-lines, so important to me when I was younger, are now mine for the taking.

Matthew hovers over me as I write the piece up. I keep the tone neutral, letting the idiocy of Prior's statements shine through on their own. But I can't shake the knowledge that, across the country, he'll be admired for his brazenness. I'm helping reinforce the myth of the outsider. The fella with the guts to summon the journalist most likely to hate what he has to say.

Chapter 24

Prior's stunt pays off, with all the nationals – and several global outlets – covering our stilted little interview. As expected, the majority of the tabloids praise his nerve in giving me an interview, with many commentators hailing his proposed family bill as the kind of brave gesture we need to 'fix' society. A defiant middle finger to political correctness. The *Guardian* calls me to offer up a comment slot. It's the kind of gig I always longed for, and yet I know that I wouldn't be on their radar were it not for my reproductive infamy. No. *Starve the bastards of fuel*, that's still the strategy. Other, bolder reporters and activists will need to lead the way in opposing the bill. My focus has to be on creating some semblance of normal life for Rosie and this impending child of ours.

A terse hello, followed by hastily averted eyes, is the very warmest greeting we've received on our new street. Perhaps news of our refusal to compensate Alf for the damage to his garden has spread amongst the neighbours. The other morning a photocopied receipt lay on our doormat. It was from the local garden centre and included a long list of Latin-named plants, a bag of compost and a terracotta pot – with everything adding up to £423.67. Could one careless photographer really have caused that much damage? I find it hard to believe, but it doesn't matter, because it's not down to us to pay.

One night in week twenty-seven, Rosie takes hold of my shoulder and shakes me awake. I jolt up and switch on my bedside lamp. Tears and snot are streaming down her face. 'It hurts, Jules. Oh my God, it hurts.' Her face is red, crumpled.

I leap from the bed. 'Right. OK. I'll call the hospital ... where's ...?' I run downstairs, into the kitchen where my phone is charging on the counter. I yank it free and sprint back up the stairs.

'Where does it hurt?'

Rosie is sobbing so hard she's hyperventilating. I run round to her side of the bed and place a hand on her back as I scroll through to find the number for Aspire Health. My fingers are trembling.

'It's OK, it's OK ... ' The number rings. Rosie wails. 'What is it? Rosie ... I—'

'Aspire Health. Maternity Wing.'

I explain who I am. Answer the security questions. Rosie continues to cry out in pain, and there's a pounding on the wall. She must have woken Alf.

'Why don't you make your way in?' the woman at the other end of the phone says. 'We'll examine Rosie, make sure everything's OK.'

Ending the call, I cup Rosie's face in my hands. Force her terrified eyes to lock with mine. 'Listen to me. Everything's going to be alright. I'm going to get you to the hospital. But I need you to calm down. That's the only way we're going to be able to help our baby. By calming down.'

Somehow I manoeuvre her to her feet, help her shuffle down the stairs. I pull my parka over the top of my sleep T-shirt, slide my bare feet inside my trainers.

'It's happening to me,' Rosie cries as I pass her coat. 'What happened to Anita – it's happening to me too.'

I take hold of her arm. 'You mustn't think that. Everything's going to be OK. We're getting you to hospital.'

The security light comes on as we step outside. I'd been expecting at least one photographer, but thankfully no strange cars are parked outside. However, there's something wrong with the Fiesta: it sits lower to the ground because all four of my tyres are flat. They've been slashed.

'Fuck, fuck, fuck!' Rosie is doubled over, struggling for breath.

'It's OK. I'll … I'll ring the hospital. Get them to send an ambulance.'

I place my hand on the back of her neck and usher her back indoors as I make the call. She ignores my entreaties to rest on the sofa, remaining in the hallway, where she wraps both arms around the banister post and appears not to hear my murmured reassurances. Each minute stretches. Her rasping breaths fill my ears; her crying dampens down into short little whimpers. I circle my arms around her as she hugs herself to the post and a tear sides down my face and hits the carpet, a tiny dark spot on the uniform beige.

Is this what the end of the trial looks like? Has Becca failed? Perhaps the technique was never destined to work in humans. They were so careful to make no promises – *uncharted territory*, that was the term they kept using. I remember Anita's hunched body and blotchy face, the indignation burning in

Hong Shu's eyes. Will that be us tomorrow? How could I stand seeing Rosie in that state? I can't, I just can't. Our baby has to be OK.

I picture my feelings as an invisible force, enveloping Rosie and our daughter. If love alone could change outcomes, we'd be safe. This is the only thing I can do. This is all I have to offer them.

The first thing they do when we're admitted to the hospital is check the baby's heartbeat with a Doppler. Its steady rhythm fills the room, prompting a relieved gasp from Rosie.

'Ah, there we go. Nice and regular. No signs of distress,' the midwife says. She's disconcertingly young-looking, hair tied back in a neat bun. And yet she sets her face in such a practised look of reassurance. Confident smile, direct gaze.

I hold Rosie's hand; silent as the midwife lightly presses the bump, then examines Rosie between her legs.

'So, our baby's OK?' My voice is weak. 'Then, what ...?'

'I just need to finish the examination.' The midwife's voice is polite but firm, closing me down.

'Call Becca.' Rosie turns to me. 'I want her here. See if she'll come.'

'Of course.' I scuttle off into the corridor, glad to have a task.

This place is nothing like the local NHS hospital. The walls are papered with mint green and white stripes. They bear paintings, still lifes and pastoral landscapes, rolling hills and flocks of sheep. A tall blond man wearing a pinched expression passes me, clutching a Styrofoam cup, and heads into one of the other rooms. His footsteps make no sound – they've laid carpet, which takes away the horrible noise of echoing footsteps and rattling trolleys that I always associate with hospitals.

Even though it's the early hours of the morning, Becca answers her mobile, and while keen to reassure me that there are a plethora of innocuous reasons for a pregnant woman to feel abdominal pain, she says she'll come to the hospital.

'Stay positive,' she tells me. 'You've done exactly the right thing. And you're in the right place, where Baby and Rosie are going to get the best care.'

I pause for a moment before going back into Rosie's room, standing up tall and forcing myself to breathe, slowly and deeply. From further up the corridor comes a long, deep cry of pain.

The midwife greets my return with a reassuring smile.

'Is Becca coming?' Rosie demands.

I nod.

'Our consultant obstetrician will be along in a moment,' the midwife says. 'But I'm pretty sure what we have here is a trapped nerve. It happens. The tissues of the stomach are put under stress as they expand. Although it's painful for Rosie, Baby won't notice a thing.'

'That's great news,' I say.

I stroke Rosie's cheek. She's stopped crying and she's not as flushed as before. Her pyjama top bears a cartoon image of a smiling zebra and gives off the sweetish scent of her sweat. She looks at me, but her eyes are filled with impatience for Becca.

The obstetrician examines Rosie and confirms the midwife's diagnosis of a trapped nerve. Then Becca arrives, and, at

Rosie's demand, reviews the obstetrician's notes and confirms the diagnosis. All they can do for Rosie is prescribe paracetamol, a heat pad and rest. It seems so paltry given the pain she's in, but tears of relief run down her face.

The midwife withdraws, recommending a nap before we head home. Since we don't have the car, it's a sensible suggestion – I want to wait until six, at least, before we disturb Rosie's mother and request a lift. Perhaps we can make it back before the first photographers set up camp outside our home.

'Don't go,' Rosie says to Becca. Her eyes are large, shining with need.

Becca smiles and takes a seat in a comfortable-looking visitor's chair. 'I'm hoping this will pass quickly,' she says. 'It does for most women.'

Rosie reaches out and grasps Becca's hand. 'What happened to Anita . . .'

I notice a slight flush spreading across Becca's neck. I stand at the end of the bed, shifting my weight from foot to foot.

'Your baby is developing well.' Becca doesn't look at Rosie as she says this, I notice. 'You feel her movement. She's strong. Think of the thousands of healthy babies born every day. Don't let a tragedy distort your perception.' Her words are reassuring, but Becca's eyes have an opaque quality to them. As though she's trying hard not to give away what she really thinks.

'I might cut my hours at work,' Rosie says. 'That will help, won't it?'

My breath catches. I've been on at her for weeks, ever since Scott was hurt. Every time she's given me the same dismissal: *I won't be shut away.*

'How's Scott doing?' I ask.

Becca's smile fades as she turns towards me. Once again, I notice how tired she looks. And something more than that. That flush is still there. What does it mean? She seems agitated, but determined to hide it. 'Better,' she says. 'They've discharged him, but he has to keep going back to hospital for lung treatment. It's not a nice procedure . . . ' She looks down at the carpet, and her lips part as though she's about to say something else. Then, with a jerk of her head, she's looking back at Rosie, smile affixed. She places a hand on her shoulder. 'I think what you need is a nice long sleep.'

'Yes,' Rosie says. 'I'll be ready in a minute. But nothing's going to happen to our daughter, is it?'

Becca stands and pulls her black tote onto her shoulder. Her smile doesn't fracture, but she looks up at the ceiling briefly before she answers. 'There are no guarantees. But, statistically speaking, the most likely outcome for you and Jules is a healthy baby girl.'

As she gathers up her bag and scarf, I ask her about the seven o-o pregnancies in Newcastle. 'Are they . . . do they seem healthy?'

'Yes,' she replies. 'All doing well.'

'And have you attempted any more fertilisations in Portsmouth?' I'm watching her carefully, but she's reverted to calm, confident Becca.

'No. Not yet. But I meant to tell you, we had some lovely news from one of our charity partners. In Auckland they've successfully delivered a New Zealand sea lion conceived via ovum-to-ovum fertilisation. They're very rare – so it's a huge step towards their conservation.'

*

After Becca leaves I sit on the chair next to the bed while Rosie dozes. She would have been devastated at the loss of our child; all night long I've been desperate to spare her. But – what if this was all over now? What if this pregnancy – bringer of heartache and disruption – was gone from our lives?

Recognising these thoughts as the abhorrent, traitorous things they are, I screw my eyes tightly shut. But they will not leave me. I can feel the relief that would have been mine this night, had the outcome been different. I would have put everything into soothing Rosie's devastation, finding the strength to do so from the prospect of the baby-free months that stretched ahead. Now, sitting in this room, I sense the respite a tragedy would have brought me, and then I feel it flutter away.

The situation is of my own making. I have to do better. I force the images, will the elusive thing that's motherly love to fill me, to normalise me. The child in bed in our spare room, me next to her, turning the pages of a picture book. Wide-eyed excitement as I show a school-aged girl my by-line at the top of my articles. Rosie and I taking a hand each, swinging our child into the air while she shrieks with glee. I still can't see her face. These scenes from an imagined future are coming to me in words rather than in pictures. The feelings are absent, as they always are. Once again, I vow to be better. I do this so often now. Every day, it seems. And each time I lose a little bit of my ability to convince myself.

Chapter 25

The pain of the trapped nerve has eased within forty-eight hours, but Rosie remains cautious. She takes the week off work and calls for pizza deliveries while she lies on the sofa working her way through box sets. When I arrive home the sink is full of cups, marking visits from her parents and Anthony.

Knowing she's at home displaces the heavy and ever-persistent worry at her being so exposed in the shop. Trevor has agreed to Rosie cutting back her hours when she returns, and it feels as though we've entered a new, calmer phase.

But I'm worried. And though I'm careful not to give Rosie any reason to suspect, my mind keeps replaying her anguished wails. I remember Hong Shu's hollow eyes, Anita's shuddering body. And that flush at Becca's neck when she came to see Rosie in hospital.

What if the technique isn't quite working as Becca hoped it would? How much would she share with us, knowing that the worry would be bad for Rosie? I want to trust her – and she's been so good to us – but there's no escaping the fact that we are *test subjects*, rather than her friends. There is only one person I can talk to about this, someone I've longed to sit down with for a companionable picking apart of Prior's family bill: Hong Shu. For a week I agonise over it – we didn't part on good terms, and she's still going to be grieving. But then one day, my last story of the afternoon happens to be in Cosham, close to their house. I have no media tailing me, and so ringing their doorbell feels like the most natural thing in the world.

Hong Shu opens the door in what must be work clothes, a black pencil skirt and crisp white shirt. Her eyes widen when she sees who it is, and she silently waves me inside. Anita is on the living-room sofa, wearing navy jogging bottoms and a shapeless T-shirt. Her hair is greasy and she looks just as broken as before. We should have visited them. Never mind the *Tribune* interview, Rosie and I should have come back here, offered listening ears and solace.

I hug Anita. 'How are you doing?'

She closes her eyes for a moment. 'The same.'

'Can I get you anything to drink?' Hong Shu asks, gesturing for me to sit.

I shake my head and sit down in their armchair. The condolence cards have been taken down now, the room restored to its tidy elegance. There's an awkward silence as Hong Shu sits down next to Anita and folds her hands in her lap. How do I broach this? How can I ask them to relive their very worst experience?

'Rosie doesn't know I'm here,' I say.

Hong Shu looks at me curiously. It's heartening, a sign that the woman I came to like so much is still in there. But neither she nor Anita speaks.

'We had a bit of a scare a week ago – abdominal pains, had

to go to hospital. It was a trapped nerve, quite common. But when Becca came, there was something off with her. It's hard to explain – she was very calm, very *Becca*. But when I looked at her, I just got this sense that she was expecting something far worse. It sounds silly, saying it out loud.'

'What exactly did she say?' Hong Shu asks.

'Oh, it was nothing specific that she said. It was all in her face. She looked guilty – guilty at knowing something. I don't know . . . maybe I'm being paranoid.'

'But the baby's OK?' Anita asks.

'Yes.'

'Then what do you want from us, Jules?' Hong Shu asks. 'You'll forgive us for not having all that much sympathy to spare right now.'

I reach down and stroke the cat, but it walks away, as though offended. 'I know that,' I say. 'And it's not what I'm after. I suppose all I really want is the truth: is something not working like it should with o-o?'

Silence. Anita and Hong Shu share a glance, then Hong Shu slowly turns to me. 'We're not scientists, Jules. All we know is that the baby we loved was taken from us. She was real, and she looked perfect.'

'They said it was an infection,' Anita says. 'A common infection that led to a softening of the cervix. There was nothing we could have done. No way of predicting that this would happen to us.'

'But I don't trust Becca,' Hong Shu continues. 'All she cared about was taking our baby back to her lab. It was pretty fucking sinister. The fact that she had a copy of the agreement with her. Cold. That's what it was.'

I shift in my seat. How can I question Becca, whose life's work has been to offer choice to couples like Rosie and me? And all because of a change of expression on a harrowing, sleep-deprived night. But no new Portsmouth pregnancies on the second wave, versus seven in Newcastle – surely Becca must be surprised by that. And what tests, what research, could be so important that it warranted depriving Anita and Hong Shu of a funeral?

I sit back, try to relax my body. Maybe my own guilt is feeding this paranoia. Guilt at not connecting with my unborn child the way I should. How cruel of me to bring it here, to this house of mourning.

I look over at Hong Shu and try a smile. 'I suppose you saw the way Prior played me?'

Hong Shu's lip twitches. 'His family bill sounds like a return to the fifties. It'll never go through.'

'The media are certainly giving him enough airtime,' I say. 'You know, I gave my friend Abi a great story about how an endangered species charity are using o-o. Only one paper showed an interest, and even then they stuffed it in the back section.'

Hong Shu nods, but I can tell her heart's not in it. Our relationship is different now, perhaps it always will be. Her loss has re-drawn who we are to one another.

I reach for my bag. 'I'll leave you be,' I say. 'And sorry for springing a visit on you. I don't know what I was thinking. Silly really – I'm probably just reading too much into things.'

My heart is thumping as I stand. How can the ease we once shared be replaced by such fragility? There must be a way, some other way, of cutting through this awkwardness, of comforting and supporting.

'Bye then,' I say.

They both mutter a goodbye, but neither of them gets up to show me to the door.

Chapter 26

I'm at work, knocking out snippets of news gleaned from a morning at the magistrates' court. My notebook, dense with shorthand notes in blue biro, is next to my keyboard. As usual, I recall perfectly the scenes in court as I write. The one-word answers of the GBH defendant, the put-out tone of the businessman caught doing 103mph.

I sense Matthew behind me. He doesn't make a sound as he moves across the carpet, but his hostile presence sends a chill along the back of my neck.

'I've decided to return to the shop floor,' he says. 'Try my hand at a bit of good, old-fashioned reportage.'

I twist my chair around. 'Good for you,' I say. 'Wouldn't want you losing touch with how it's done.'

His nostrils flare as he gives me his most scornful up-and-down glance. At the edge of my vision I see Tom approach, then swiftly change direction when he clocks Matthew.

'So,' Matthew says. 'Any comment?'

'You'll have to be a bit more specific.'

He folds his arms and slowly his face lights up with a true smile, the corners of his eyes crinkling. 'On wifey's antics, of course.'

I'm still. Suddenly conscious of my face, I jam my lips together and try to relax my forehead, but in spite of my best efforts, my gaze wavers. I don't know what he's talking about. And he can see as much.

'Allow me.' I recoil as he reaches over and takes control of my mouse, bathing my face with stale coffee fumes as he brings up the *Express* website and clicks on an embedded video.

Every nerve ending in my body seems to crackle, but my thoughts are strangely clear. I will be still, silent, and I will not move my face.

I clasp my hands in my lap as I watch the black-and-white CCTV footage. It's Rosie and Anthony, stooped over, ripping up the newly re-installed plants in Alf's garden. They throw them on the ground, doubling over with giggles before hurrying back inside our front door.

What the fuck was she thinking?

'Hmm, let me think of an intro: *Juliet Curtis is stony-faced as she watches the childish antics of her pregnant lover,*' Matthew says. 'I wonder what title we should go with.'

I retreat as far into myself as I can go. He can look at my face, but my expression will give nothing away.

'Oh play along, Jules. This no-comment nonsense is getting rather tedious.'

I turn back to face my screen square on. I find my place in the story I'd been writing. Here we go. Magistrate's closing remarks. I resume typing. '*Your driving that day was irresponsible and reckless. It was pure chance that no one happened to be injured . . .* '

Kyle, in my peripheral vision, is shaking with laughter. They want an outburst. Shouted, unguarded comments, spit flying, face red. But I'm strong enough to resist such temporary satisfactions. If this job has taught me one thing, it's this: when circumstances require it, I can slip into a kind of robot mode. Never have I been so grateful for this skill.

On the drive home, I try to counter my hollow feeling with a little light praise. I did it. I got through the day. Rosie has sent a single text: *forgive me xx*. I didn't trust myself to respond, couldn't risk breaking the calm façade, disrupting the rhythmic rattle of my keyboard.

I still don't know what I'm going to say to her. Every time I think of that video, the ceremonial uprooting, the gleeful trampling, I feel a kind of exhaustion. There's nothing she could say that will soothe me or make me understand. She knows we're being scrutinised, and now she's shown the world just what a child she can be in Anthony's company.

And so, at the last moment, I decide I'm not going home. I stay on the motorway to the next exit, heading for Dad's place.

I blink several times when he opens the door. He's clean-shaven, the skin of his cheeks pink and sore, tiny little scabs on his neck. His hair has been neatly cropped and he wears a sea-green shirt that isn't just ironed; it's new.

'Alright love?' The same voice. The same beloved voice.

I step inside and go in for a hug. Not my usual greeting, but he squeezes back, the warmth of his body taking away some of the cold emptiness that seems to have settled inside me.

'Rough day?'

I grunt as I follow him into the living room. I'd planned to rant. But I realise I don't want to talk about Anthony. Or

Rosie. I want to forget about everything. To laugh, even, if such a thing is possible.

'New woman?' I ask, gesturing at his appearance.

He sinks into the sofa, eyebrows drawn together. 'Trying to sort myself out, Jules.'

I rest my head against the back of the armchair and close my eyes. I kick off my boots. 'Good for you.'

'I'm serious. If you ... I know I haven't always ...'

'Hey,' I say. 'I wasn't digging. No need to get sentimental.'

He bites his lip and his eyes shine. 'There's so much you don't know, Jules. Time and again I try to be someone different, I try to let the past go. But I always slip back.'

I sigh. I came here wanting nothing more than commentary on the goings-on at the Green Dragon, or maybe gossip about the neighbours. Is it wrong that the idea of my father wanting to talk tonight – really talk – fills me with weariness? I've imagined having the 'sorting yourself out' conversation with him so many times. But right now I'm too drained.

'Do you have anything that might help me sleep better?' I ask.

His eyes widen. 'Jules, you know I don't mess with chemicals. I get so angry when people lump the herb together with other rubbish. You should know better.'

I smile. *The herb*, always referred to with such reverence.

He lowers his eyes to the carpet. 'Listen ... I've been meaning to tell you something.' He swallows.

'Go on.' I look at him seriously. I need to stop being so selfish. If he does need to talk tonight, then of course I'll listen. It's not as though he has anyone else to turn to.

'I never told you about your grandfather. Never thought

it was something you needed to know. But when I'm gone, perhaps there'll be a time when maybe ... maybe you'll find me hard to understand ...'

'Gone?' This isn't the direction I expected the conversation to take.

'And then, well, I'd like to think you had the full picture.'

My phone vibrates in my bag, but I ignore it. Let Rosie stew. I look at my father's face. He has the same wide-set eyes as me, the same high forehead. Deep lines run between his nose and his mouth, giving him a sullen air. But he isn't sprawled across the sofa like he normally is; he's leaning forwards, hands on his knees. It fills me with a dread I can't explain.

He sighs. Closes his eyes and winces. 'I don't know why he singled me out. I was the middle child. An older and a younger brother. We've lost touch, I can't see them ... I'd have to say something. And how could I do that? David especially – he idolised our old man. I can't be the one to take that away.'

'You were an only child ...' I say. 'But you're telling me you had brothers? Where are they? Why don't I know them?' My chest feels tight. What possible reason could there be for the concealment? For telling me he was an only child, maintaining the lie for nearly thirty-five years?

'He made us box. Me and David. Two years older than me, he was. Bigger. Built different. Of course he won. Me outside, shivering in my pants and vest. Blood pouring out my nose. Then Dad, he'd give me a cuff for not standing up for myself. For being a sissy.'

'I ...' I'm about to ask him about his brothers again. But I stop myself. This is the first time my father has ever volunteered specifics about his childhood. He's given me plenty of generalities. *I was good at maths at school. We were poor.* But this is the first time he's ever shared what feels like a real memory. This is the first time he's ever evoked the shivering little boy he once was.

How could I have got to my age without questioning the gaps in my father's story of himself? I'm trying so hard to picture him as one of a group of small boys, but I can't manage it.

'I'm only telling you so you'll understand,' he says. 'I don't want sympathy.' He picks at a hole in the sofa's fabric, where yellow foam is jutting out.

My throat catches as I see him take a deep breath, steeling himself for whatever it is he's going to say.

'My old man used to visit me in the night. Not David. Not Victor. Just me. I pretended to be asleep. I was a bed-wetter and perhaps he thought . . . ' My father's Adam's apple bobs. 'Perhaps he thought I was so heavy a sleeper that . . . '

He bows his head. I stand, take a step towards him. But he springs up from the sofa and walks over to the window.

'Anyway.' He turns his back to me, stares outside. 'I'm not going to speak of this again. He's dead now. This is background, nothing more. But you have to understand . . . I couldn't let him near you. Couldn't let that man be your granddad.'

My body seems to demand the comfort of a hug. But the gesture is too cloying. My father won't welcome it. So I give him the lightest pat on the back. 'What's all this talk of being gone?' I attempt a laugh, but it sounds unconvincing. I'm dismayed by what he's told me. I always saw him as marked by the tragedy of my mother's death. But there was more to it. How could I not have realised? It seems so obvious now.

My head churns with questions. Where are my uncles? Do they look like my father? Perhaps I have cousins. I think back to when I was a student, how me and Dad would share a smoke in the evenings as I recounted the main points from whatever lectures I'd had that day. I thought we'd shared everything. Yet he must have made the conscious decision to withhold a part of himself every single day.

He puts a hand on my shoulder. 'You should head home. They were playing that video in the Green Dragon this lunchtime. I assume your visit was in aid of postponing a domestic?'

This time my laugh is bitter but genuine. How well he knows me.

Rosie rushes into the hallway as I arrive back, and I greet her with a kiss as though it's any other day. I'm unsettled by Dad's revelation. Why make things worse by launching into a full-scale fight? Pretending is so much easier. Pretending will at least allow me to rest, and try to make sense of everything that's happened.

Rosie takes my hands. 'I know it was a mistake.' Her chin wobbles. 'Shout and scream at me, I deserve it.'

I sigh and lead her into the living room, where we sit next to one another on the sofa. We've tried our best to make this room feel homely. Rosie's hung framed photographs on the wall: the two of us at her graduation ceremony, another where we're sitting in a taverna on holiday, leaning in to one another and smiling at the waiter wielding the camera. There's one of her and Anthony at a theme park, open-mouthed and screaming with glee.

I feel a rising pain behind my eyes. 'Just ... try and help me understand why, Rosie.'

She clutches at my arm. 'I know it looks bad. But, Alf, he's the unreasonable one. I know it was him that did your tyres – I can tell by the looks he gives me. And there's been more dog poo. I didn't tell you, because ... oh, and Anthony's car. He keyed it. I know it was Alf because when we went out there and found the damage he was watering his plants, all smug.'

'So you trashed his garden? You thought that would help the situation in some way?'

'What kind of freak has CCTV outside their house anyway? I mean, he's not a Russian oligarch. He's living on a bog-standard estate, filming everything that goes on outside his house. It's creepy. There's something very odd about him, Jules.'

'We're under so much scrutiny, I don't know how you—'

'Oh, Jules.' She reaches out and grazes my cheek with her knuckle. I close my eyes. Each time I think we're past the worst, something else rears up. As I sit, acting the forgiving lover, Rosie's hands on my skin, I remember the grainy footage. The flamboyant gestures, the teenage giggles. This side of her will always be there. Anthony brings it out in her.

I try to be fair. The media attention has left me exhausted; it must be far worse for Rosie, having to contend with it all while pregnant. Being at home, waiting for more dog shit or the next petty act of vandalism can't be healthy. Childish rebellion might even be a natural response.

And my father, I think again of the strange conversation we've just had. His own father *visited* him in the night. What does that even mean? Was it fondling? Rape? A question I can never bring myself to ask, and so I'll never understand just how deep the damage runs.

I have nothing to offer the people I love. No way of comforting them. The perplexity of not knowing what to do, the way it rises up through my chest and combusts into panic – these are the emotions that mark my life now. Ambitious Jules, shivering with anticipation in the lecture theatre, is gone. So is serene Jules, guiding her young lover through the editing of her novel. Tough Jules, knocking on the doors of criminals. I never took a moment to be proud of these versions of myself, to enjoy their perspective. Now they're gone. And I'm not sure what's left behind.

Chapter 27

The next morning an accident on the A3 has made me forty minutes late and I'm expecting a bollocking. But more than one person quickly looks away after meeting my eye and there's a hushed, expectant atmosphere. I think to myself: what now? More sperm Post-its? Or maybe there's been what the press would describe as *a new development*. Perhaps Richard Prior has written something scathing on his blog, or published more specifics about his family bill.

I steel myself. I'm getting so good at it. Firm, unmovable face. Lifted head. Eyes front. A bracing of the chest, deep breaths in and out. I will not pity myself. And, most important of all: whatever it is, I will not react.

When he sees me, Tom scurries over from sports. We meet at my desk and I bend down to switch on my computer as I say hello. I can feel everyone watching us.

'I thought maybe . . . I wondered whether you might stay home today.' Tom speaks in a low voice. There's a seriousness to his expression, which heightens my unease. But I won't let it show.

I smile at him and roll my eyes. 'What now?' There. To anyone listening, I sound supremely unbothered.

'Oh – you haven't seen? Maybe it's nothing. I should mind my own business.' His eyes dart around the newsroom. He gives my arm a little pat of goodbye, but then he changes his mind and grasps my shoulder.

'What is it?' I whisper.

Tom scans the newsroom again. Eyes large and perhaps even a little frightened. This must be bad. *Shit.*

He leans in. 'The *Tribune*'s website. But don't do it here. Take your tablet into the bogs, or head out to your car. If you need me, I'm here. Just say, and we'll go somewhere. OK?'

I give the slightest nod of acknowledgement. Tom turns and heads back to his desk, and I tap my password into my ancient PC. My movements are shaky and I get it wrong the first two times. Once I've completed this everyday task, I jerk my head up, as though suddenly remembering something important, and make my way to the ladies with my tablet.

In a locked cubicle I search the *Tribune*'s website for my name. I click on the link and am greeted with an image of my father, gazing solemnly at the camera. He's the tidied-up version of himself that I saw yesterday, face looking strangely exposed without his habitual stubble.

A Father's Anguish
Daughter involved in lesbian baby experiment for all the wrong reasons, says dad

Juliet Curtis, the lesbian 'father' involved in Portsmouth University's controversial two-mum baby experiment, has been secretly longing for the procedure to fail, the Tribune has learned.

In an exclusive interview, Juliet's father Neil Curtis
(55) told of his anguish over the experiment and how,
in his words, the pregnancy is a 'terrible compromise'.

I have to sit down. I almost drop my tablet as I lower the
toilet lid and take the weight off my feet. How could Dad do
this to me? I've warned him, so many times, of the mechanisms
of the press. How has he been stupid enough to get drawn in?
And to share such private things – there's no way this can be an
accident. *He's sold my story.* My own father has sold my story.

My pulse pounds in my temples. Rosie will see this. Jesus.
There's no way I can keep it from her. *Longing for the procedure to fail.* I didn't even say that. Can I make her believe
me? My stomach lurches and for a moment I think that I'm
going to be sick, but I shut my eyes and breathe deeply, until
I'm confident I can keep the bile down.

I read on, forcing myself to go slowly, to take it all in.

Years of single-handedly raising his daughter have
taken a toll on Neil, who admits to feeling 'constantly
worn out by it all'. Yet as he sits in his faded living room
he has a quiet dignity as he recollects how he begged
his daughter not to go ahead with the experiment.

'She told me about it very early on,' he said. 'I urged
her in the very strongest terms to reconsider. She'd
always rejected the idea of kids, so I found it strange
that she'd put herself forward for a trial like this.

'We joked at how it sounded like something from a
science fiction film – but underneath it all I could see
Jules was worried, just like I was. But she felt she had

no choice – her partner Rosie had pretty much given
her an ultimatum: babies or a separation.

So this wasn't a snatched encounter in the Green Dragon;
he must have given a full interview. I see it happening: the
journalist buying him a drink, suggesting sums of money. How
much had it taken? What thoughts went through his head as
he agreed a price? Could he have somehow convinced himself
that he was helping me? *Fuck* – it must have been him who
tipped off the *Sketch*. He listened to me blaming Anthony,
knowing all the while that it wasn't him. I have to close my
eyes to forestall tears. Nothing makes sense any more.

I struggle my way through the rest of the piece. It blathers
on about the trial in the derisory tone I've come to expect.
My father talks about how Rosie curtailed my career and
how the trial is ruining my life. Rosie is going to read this and
feel betrayed on so many levels. She'll think that every time
I'm alone with my father I moan about the pregnancy. That
I blame her for everything in my life that hasn't gone right.
But I've never said these things explicitly. My father has put
his own views in my mouth. The article says nothing of how
happy Rosie's made me. She'll think I don't love her. I have to
call her. I pat at my pockets then realise my phone must still
be on my desk. I can't go out there. Not yet. *Fuck*.

I stand up and grip the toilet-door handle as hard as I can.
My own father. Now his strange behaviour yesterday makes
sense. He was telling me about his past, getting in early with
a plea for forgiveness masked as a confidence.

There's a banging on the outer door of the ladies. Matthew's
voice: 'Shit on your own time, we've got a paper to fill.' A

theatrical gesture, put on for the admiration and snickers of the newsroom.

Replying is impossible. I have to stay very still, because if I move I know I'll lose control. My own father did this. My own father put me in this situation, hiding in the toilets at work while my colleagues read about my life in a national newspaper. He's undone months of *starve the bastards of fuel*. Given ammunition to Prior and his return-to-the-fifties campaign.

Slowly, I unlock the cubicle and go over to the washbasin. My neck and cheeks are flushed. I pull myself up tall and try to steady my breathing. Running the taps, I splash water on my face. I need to get this redness away; people might mistake it for crying. *Come on, Jules*, I tell myself. *This is the biggest test yet, but you can do it*. The anger slowly leaches from my bones, and with it my strength. How on earth can I make this right with Rosie? I can shout at my father all I want, but nothing will lessen her disappointment in me.

Somehow I make it back to my desk. I look at my phone, lying on top of my notebook. Perhaps if Rosie hasn't seen the piece yet I can prepare her, explain how my father has misrepresented our conversations.

'Juliet?' It's Matthew. 'I can guess what you'll say. But you know the drill: I have to ask. Any comment on today's piece in the *Tribune*?'

I refuse to look at him. I pick up my desk phone and start dialling the number of the local police station. Might as well get that motorway accident story done.

'No? Nothing to say at all? Well, we'll try the missus then.'

I drop the telephone receiver, stand up and shove Matthew

backwards, driving my palms into his chest, pushing him across the newsroom until he stumbles against Abi's old chair, falling onto her desk. His face is red, his eyes wide.

'You fucking failure,' I say as I stand over him. 'Lord it around as much as you want. But everyone is laughing at you, because we all know that none of the nationals would have you.'

He doesn't respond. He fiddles with his shirt collar as he eases himself up, but his eyes reveal his fear.

I turn back to my desk. A silent crowd has gathered. For a moment, no one speaks.

I hear a few clucking reassurances, followed by a dismissive grunt as Matthew forces the crowd to disperse. He'll be over in a moment to make his threats, but I don't care. I sit back down. Dial the police station's number again. Take down a few brief notes about the A3 crash.

And then I realise I can't go on. There's no drama. No sobs. I remain upright, posture excellent as always. But my screen is blank and my mind just can't form one blasted, pissing sentence. I'm falling apart. It's finally happened. The only way to handle it is to not move, to not draw attention.

I'm not sure exactly how long I remain this way. I'm vaguely aware of the paper's HR woman coming over. Then Tom, bending down and whispering, 'Jules? We need to get you home. I'll drive your car back to your place for you.'

I let him steer me out of the newsroom by the elbow, without even registering who's watching. Home is what I need now. Home and Rosie. I will curl up at her feet and beg her forgiveness. My father can rot, can kill himself by splurging the newspaper cheque on booze and drugs. It's Rosie I need.

Chapter 28

Tom backs my car into the drive and, without speaking, opens the passenger door and walks me to the house. There's the sound of a camera shutter, followed by Tom's sharp 'Fuck off and leave them alone'.

He hands me my keys, but the front door opens and Rosie is standing there. What must she think of me? I try to read her face, but she's not giving anything away. All I know is she's here, right now, and I have to say something, but I don't know what. A pat on my shoulder and Tom retreats.

'I . . . ' What can I say?

She takes me by the arm. Ushers me inside. She knows, then, why I've come home. She's seen it. Read my father's exaggerations. Learned of my conflicted feelings in the worst possible way. My chest tightens, and with it comes animal panic at not being able to breathe. How can I make this right?

She closes the door behind us. That fucking photographer is still shouting our names.

'Rosie, I . . . '

She holds me to her. The bump presses against me as I bury my face in the black wool of her cardigan. What did she feel when she read the article? Did she reject my father's version of my doubts, or even now, as she holds me, is she suppressing her disappointment? I brave a look at her face but I see only tenderness.

'Jules, look at you – you're run ragged. A long sleep and a proper meal – that's what you need. No phone, no computer. Your skin is grey. I should have realised.'

I don't deserve this kindness and it fills me with a heavy sadness. We sit on the sofa. I've let myself become tired to the point of exhaustion. I'd dragged myself out for a run to start the day, and while my mind pushed, my legs struggled. It was so much more than straightforward aches and pains. It was a feeling of being entirely empty, of having no fuel left, nothing else to give. For a moment I'd been tempted to cut it short, but somehow I'd stumbled my way along the whole route.

'Put your legs up on me,' Rosie commands.

I obey, closing my eyes. 'You've seen it, then?' I say. 'How come? You should have been sleeping.'

She massages my calves. 'Bladder. And I do look at what they're saying about us from time to time. You're right about it not helping, but I still like to know.'

'The things my dad said . . . '

'Don't worry about that now. I'm serious about you getting some sleep. I want you to go back to bed, get a few hours in.'

'There's no way I'll be able to sleep.'

'Try. Then we'll have lunch together. Something hot and wholesome. You look like you've lost weight – I'm cross with myself for not noticing sooner. It's not like you had any excess pounds to spare.'

'Rosie—'

'You should have talked to me, Jules. I wanted to be there for you.'

Taking in the seriousness in her eyes, I realise just how unfair I've been. I railed at the childishness of uprooting Alf's plants, but isn't what I've done so much worse? I've introduced a kind of opacity to our relationship, kept my feelings hidden from the person who most wanted to help. As she unfurled with relief after her medical false alarm, I felt *disappointed. If I could reverse this baby, I would.* I clasp her hand and give it a little squeeze.

'Bed,' she says.

Lifting my weary body from the sofa, I go along with her instructions, plodding upstairs. *Please, let her forgive me.* I see how important it is for Rosie to take control, to bring me relief. It means she must still care. And if she does, I can face anything.

Sleep is impossible, but closing my eyes for an hour does bring minor respite from the headache pulsing at the front of my skull. The bedroom is quiet; I hear a faint television murmur from the living room and the muffled chatter of the odd passer-by outside our window. The scent of cocoa butter stretch mark cream lingers on the sheets and is a comfort.

But then my father's face rears up before me, the shame in his eyes as he mentioned his brothers, his reddened cheeks. Did he betray me for the sake of a few thousand quid? I don't want to believe it; I want to think that he spoke without thinking of the consequences, that he'd been drunk or that he's been misquoted. But he hasn't called, hasn't even tried to explain himself.

I conjure the more familiar version: him on the sofa with bong-softened eyes. I remember how I used to feel as a child on our country walks, my hand in his, the certainty, instilled by him, that I'd grow up to become someone important. The idea that my past could be a lie induces a new kind of pain, running deeper than anything I've known before.

Rosie comes into the bedroom bearing a steaming plate on a tray.

'Lunch in bed. Let's prop you up.' She rests the tray carefully on the bed and fusses at the pillows. I'd actually started to drift off, but I sit up as eagerly as I can muster and inspect the meal: a reheated portion of the vegetarian chilli I'd made two weekends ago and frozen. 'You eat half,' I say.

'Oh, I'm doing a whole one of my own. It's in the microwave. I'm having lunch in bed too – perk of being pregnant.'

She disappears and returns with her own tray, settling it uneasily on her bump and eating with gusto. I'm not hungry at all, but I take a few tentative mouthfuls, to please her.

'I'm probably going to get the sack,' I say. 'I made a bit of a scene at work.'

'They don't deserve you, Jules.' She speaks with her mouth full. 'The fact that you've kept working ridiculous hours, even with everything going on, is nothing short of superhuman.'

The chilli is making my nose run. My mouth is dry, and swallowing each forkful is an ordeal. But I keep trying, to please her. 'What else could I do, Rosie? Journalism is all I know.'

'Maybe it's time to try another paper. I know you love the

writing, but you've not been happy at the *Post* for years now. Why put yourself through it?'

'Well, it might not be my choice to make after today's little outburst.' I sigh.

We're quiet for a moment. Rosie continues to eat enthusiastically, our daughter's appetite seemingly all-consuming.

'I guess I should go round to Dad's later on. Give him a chance to explain,' I venture.

'Why on earth would you do that?'

I look at her: two anger lines between her eyes, lips stained with tomato sauce.

'We need to sort this out. I need to understand how it happened.'

She reaches across and rubs at my arm. The tray looks even more precarious; any moment now that chilli is going to be all over the bed. 'Oh, baby.'

'What do you mean by that?' I put my cutlery down, all pretence at eating abandoned.

'Jules – you must see now. Maybe it's time—'

'We can't know. Not for certain. I know how it looks, but it might just have been him sounding off, thinking he was involved in some sort of philosophical debate. Maybe he didn't realise his quotes were going to be printed.' My voice sounds thin and unconvincing. That new shirt, the fresh shave. I remember his pinched expression, the far-away look as he spoke of his own father *visiting* him – surely he's not that rehearsed a liar? But he'd had thirty-five years in which to tell me, and he only did so at the moment of his betrayal.

Rosie takes another quick forkful. 'Do you think that's

likely? I mean, I'm sure you were clear to him about how the media works – you certainly were with me.'

I bow my head. There's a prickling sensation in the corners of my eyes.

'Oh, Jules.' Rosie lunges in for the full hug, and that's it, plate upended, chilli all over the bedding.

I spring up. 'Don't worry, I'll get this sorted,' I say.

Duvet cover and sheets changed, I pace about the house for a bit. Rosie keeps beckoning me to join her on the sofa, and in the end I give in and watch a couple of episodes of *War and Peace*. She places her legs in my lap and I massage her calves while she works her way through a tube of Pringles. When the credits roll, she flicks the television off and turns to me. The room is lit by a single corner lamp. The darkness and silence outside make it feel as though we're in the small hours, even though it's still early. 'Listen, do you feel up to talking about that *Tribune* article now? It's alright if you don't, we can wait until you've had a proper night's sleep.'

I take her hand. 'Let's talk.'

'The things your father said – it's normal to have doubts, you know. It's just important that we're honest with each other. You can say anything to me. Anything.'

I stroke her hair. She wants so much to help. I imagine the relief of letting it all out, holding her tightly as I admit how I wanted to reverse our baby. How I've changed, am no longer able to feel joy in the usual things, doubting every decision I make. This is the candour Rosie wants and deserves. And yet I know my lack of feeling would horrify her. What kind of woman decides she doesn't want the baby she planned?

Months of preparation went into Rosie's pregnancy. Medical checks. Consent forms. An opportunity hundreds of women applied for and were denied. Rosie would be rightly angry, exasperated that I'd done so much to ensure this baby is half mine, only to not want it. She deserves more. I will get past today and things will be different. There will be no terrible feelings to confess because I'm going to annihilate them.

'He's a liar,' I say. 'I mean, he knew I was anxious about the publicity, about the life we're now having to lead. But I never said I didn't want the baby. He's twisted everything. You have to believe me. I really do want her.' I reach over and place my hand on the bump.

Rosie's eyes tear up, her breathing is raspy, something Becca has reassured us is perfectly normal at this stage of pregnancy. 'I'll be honest with you,' she says. 'When I heard about Scott, I found myself regretting the baby. I still loved her, don't get me wrong, but I was so aware of all these different lives being turned upside down. I felt like a prisoner in the flat. It didn't last, but that's how I felt at the time.'

'Completely understandable,' I say.

She keeps looking at me. Beneath my hand, still resting on the bump, a robust kick.

'So you mustn't beat yourself up,' Rosie continues. 'Because I'd understand. I've always been proud of how honest we are with each other – I'd hate to think that anything could change that.'

Her eyes demand further confidences. But Rosie's moment of regret pales next to the months of numbness, to the growing realisation that I don't want the baby.

She sighs. 'It's hard, isn't it? You can't help comparing

yourself to other people, wondering whether what you're going through is normal.'

She places her hot palm against the back of my neck. 'And there's an ideal. Impossible to live up to. You're made to feel as though you should be happy every single moment. And if you're not, you're failing, you're ungrateful. Each time I've had a single negative thought over the last few weeks I've pictured Anita's face and felt guilty. It's made me crazy.'

Again, that soulful look into my eyes. The plea to share. But she doesn't know just how bad it is, how twisted my emotions have become.

'I'm so angry with my father,' I offer. 'And I'm angry with myself for not seeing what he was. For struggling to believe it, even now.'

Rosie sighs again and adjusts her position on the sofa. 'We all think things we're not proud of, Jules. Sometimes, when I'm overtired because the baby won't let me sleep, I think to myself: if I can't handle this, a bit of nocturnal kicking, then how am I going to be able to look after a tiny baby?'

I lean across and kiss her on the cheek. 'Come on,' I say. 'You're going to be an excellent mum.'

Rosie bites her lower lip, disappointment in her eyes. She must want more from me. She probably expects that she'll be able to forgive whatever it is I'm holding back from her. But she won't. She'll realise that she doesn't really know me. That I'm not a good person.

We've had enough upset. We need to get past this moment, and concentrate on the better life that's ahead of us. For the first time since reading my father's story, I feel confident about how to handle things.

'We should have an early night,' I say.

She sighs. I think she's about to say something, but then she presses a hand down on the arm of the sofa and eases herself up. Bed. A night's sleep, an end to this terrible day. Then tomorrow we can begin again.

Chapter 29

The following day I wake at my usual 5.45 a.m., even though I haven't set an alarm. It's a drizzly morning and a cool wind batters my face as I run. The mornings are gradually lightening; hopefully soon I'll be able to shed my tracksuit top and replace my leggings with shorts.

I feel fresher today. I nod at the odd solitary dog walker as I do my loop around Petersfield's lake, then run along the avenues of large detached houses that flank the town's outer rim. As I approach the road leading back to our estate, I quicken my pace, feeling more awake, more alive than I have for weeks.

But in the shower, as I soap the mud spatters from my ankles, anxiety overtakes me. I'll almost certainly be summoned by HR. Matthew will insist on penitence for yesterday. They'll expect me to plead for my job, perhaps even agree to a hideous 'Juliet speaks candidly to the *Post*' piece – and all for a burger flipper's salary.

It's not worth it. The realisation is sudden and unequivocal. I'm not on a pathway to a better reporting position, and I gave up my dream of the nationals some time ago. So why continue? I love the writing, but for years now I've known that I'm collaborating in the debasement of my profession. Why rush to start my twelve or thirteen hours at 7.30 a.m. sharp? Why not take the kind of job where I can leave on time and enjoy evenings that stretch out for a full five hours or so? Why not create extra time in my life to be a better partner? The futility of staying at the *Post* is now so palpable that I can barely believe my choices of the past decade. Why have I kept plugging on? Why? The Jules who'd believed, who told herself so many times she was on her way to something better, is unrecognisable to me.

And suddenly there's no longer any rush to be out of the shower, to be dressed and downing a coffee, getting into the car, hair still wet. I'm free. I almost tremble with the joy of it as I towel myself down. Free to live like other people do. Cooking meals with Rosie, evening strolls, having more than ten minutes at a time to read a book. I picked one of the most difficult career goals for myself, and the years that followed have been punctuated by disappointment. The revelation of not trying, of only worrying about making the best of today, makes my head reel. This braver version of me is going to make everything OK.

I take my time over breakfast, making proper coffee with the percolator that normally sits unused in the cupboard and slathering crumpets with cashew butter. Then I go up to our third bedroom, which we're using as a kind of office. I log into my work email, ignore the unopened messages and write out my resignation, effective immediately.

Buzzing with adrenalin, I retrieve my CV and set about bringing it up to date. It doesn't take long, what with me only having the one job since graduating from my journalism training. I put together a list of the seven PR agencies within a forty-five-minute commute and start on a covering email. *I'm looking for a new challenge in the private sector and would be delighted to discuss my skills and experience further.*

'Shouldn't you be at work?' Rosie stands in the doorway in her dressing gown, her eyes sticky from sleep.

Now begins the first morning of a new attitude, a new life. I spring up and give her a kiss. 'You were right, Rosie – now is the time for a new beginning. I've quit. No more twelve-hour days for piss-all money.'

She massages my shoulder. 'I'm so pleased for you, Jules. They didn't deserve you.'

While she's in the bathroom I make us both cups of peppermint tea and put some toast on for Rosie, knowing she'll be hungry. The prospect of a full day ahead, no work, time to make plans, leaves me feeling dazed.

She comes downstairs and eats her toast on the sofa. The living room smells of peppermint, but underneath it I catch the damp smell of the T-shirt she's slept in. The strangest things can prompt such pangs of love.

She looks up at my face. The morning light highlights the dark circles under her eyes, the new lines around her mouth that make her look more mature. 'We need to talk about what happens next,' she says.

I sit down next to her. 'I can't believe I just did it, quitting like that,' I say. 'But it feels so right. I'll look for a stopgap straight away, make sure we've got money coming in. But longer term I think I'll definitely opt for a PR job. Regular hours. Better pay. Perfect for when Baby arrives.'

Rosie chews her toast. 'In your dad's article, he says I held you back in your career. Is this what's happening now? You're giving up on journalism because I'm pregnant?'

'What? No, Rosie.' I wrap my arm around her. 'I told you – the stuff he came out with was bollocks, utter bollocks. You know what he gets like when he's been drinking. And PR – well, it's just going to be more practical at this stage in my life.'

She moves out of my embrace, lays her plate on the coffee table.

'Jules, last night I gave you a chance to be honest with me. I really wish that you'd taken it.'

'I did, Rosie. You're letting my dad get to you. He's winning, you're letting him win.'

'But you haven't left me any choice but to believe him. You don't talk to me. You never really tell me how you feel. His version is the only one I have.'

'I have been truthful with you. I've had a few wobbles along the way, but I've always wanted this baby.' My heart swells as I tell the lie. But I sound convincing, I'm sure I do.

Rosie stands up. 'You say that, Jules, but I don't know . . .' She puts a hand to her forehead, screws her eyes shut.

I stand up too, take hold of her wrists, kiss her lips. She doesn't respond to my touch.

'When you felt the baby move – what was that like for you?'

'What? Exciting. I mean, of course it was.'

'When was it? Do you remember? Do you remember the first time?'

'I . . .' I remember a long succession of hand-on-the-belly moments. Teaching myself to coo and smile. Which one came first? *Come on*, I have to remember.

Rosie sighs. 'You don't remember because you haven't been paying attention. I've been so stupid. Why? Why didn't you tell me how you really felt?'

'Rosie, don't cry. Sit down, this can't be good for the baby.' I put a hand on the small of her back, try to steer her back to the sofa, but she won't move. She jerks her head away so that she doesn't have to look at me.

'Why are we fighting? This should be a happy day. I've made a decision that I should have made a long time ago. This is going to be a new life for us and all I want to do is make you happy.'

She doesn't answer. The set of her mouth is tired, dejected. It's me that's made her feel this way, but with time I can put everything right again.

When Rosie speaks at last, her voice is a whisper: 'I won't ever be happy if you feel the need to lie to me. What kind of relationship is that? I don't understand you, Jules. Sometimes I think you don't see me as I really am, you don't take me seriously.'

I reach out and clasp her hand, holding it between both of mine as though it's a small bird I'm trying to stop flying away. 'Rosie—'

'I need some space, Jules. I need to get my head around all this. I think I ought to go and stay with Mum and Dad for a bit.'

'No, Rosie, please.'

'I don't want to hurt you – not after what you've just been through, I really don't. But I need to think. If you can't be honest with me, then what does all this mean, what kind of relationship do we really have?'

'But you can think here. Rosie, don't go.'

'It might only be for a little while. I feel terrible—'

'I know I've let you down. But I can change. I'll do better. I'll be more involved. The twelve-hour days – you don't know what that was like; it didn't leave room for anything else. But that's finished now. Things will be different.'

Rosie retrieves her hand and brushes away a tear that's snaking down alongside her nose. 'I'm so sorry that your father betrayed you. I'm trying not to . . . I'm not saying that this is it, that it's over. I think we both just need some time apart.'

'You're bored of me. Pragmatic, methodical, boring old Jules.'

She reaches out and puts a hand on my shoulder. 'It's this – this is the kind of thing . . . ' She turns to leave the room. 'I'm going to pack a few things. You can call me whenever you like. It's just . . . I don't know if I can be in a relationship where the person I love doesn't quite see me as an adult.'

She leaves the room and I sit back down on the sofa, hands on my knees. My neck slackens and my head lolls forwards. I need to rescue the situation, but what can I say? If it's honesty she wants, then what is my truth? That I mistook excitement at o-o and the clinical trial for actually wanting a baby. That I felt strangely menaced by the heartbeat. That I honestly can't remember when the baby first moved. That for a small moment I saw miscarriage as a way out, a chance to start again.

I focus on each breath, trying to subdue the heaving of my chest. After a while Rosie comes into the living room, bag slung over her shoulder, and says goodbye with a kiss to the top of my head.

This is it, my last chance to try to keep her here.

I look at Rosie's belly. Her bump is so neat, almost as though she has a football under her jumper. I try so very hard to feel something, anything. *That's her DNA and mine entwined*, I tell myself. I think of the wholehearted way she throws herself into the games of children. I try to imagine the face of our daughter, half Rosie, half me.

She's gone out into the hallway. *She has grown that child within her own body. Being a mother is part of the fundamental way she views herself.* I try. I try.

I hear her zipping up her jacket. The click of the latch as the front door is opened. *She wanted to give birth to my child. To raise my child. Is there any greater compliment she could have paid me?*

The bang of the door closing behind her.

Chapter 30

Two weeks pass, in which Rosie lets me see her just a few times. I've taken a job as an office cleaner and I go round to Elaine and Michael's after my shifts, reeking of artificial lemon. We talk logistics: hospital visits, antenatal classes and car-seat options. I make a point of asking about the baby, but there's always a cold formality to Rosie's replies. She won't let me kiss her. Each time I ask when she's coming home she answers me with a quiet *I just need time, Jules.*

During my cleaning shifts, as I scrub kitchen surfaces and empty bins, I wonder how much the baby has moved that day, whether she's let Rosie sleep. Although I dread sleepless nights and feel no excitement at the idea of nappy changes and feeds, I am starting to feel something. At first it was simply perceiving an absence. An unexpected source of sadness during a time of far deeper grief. But I realise it's more than that: it's a protective instinct, rising up within me. Which is a start, I suppose.

I don't know if I can be in a relationship where the person I love doesn't quite see me as an adult. Was Rosie right when she said this? Of course I see her as an adult, but perhaps there were times during the pregnancy when I'd dismiss my concerns, or opt not to share things with her. I thought I was helping, making life easier. Everything seemed to be passing in such a rush. I told myself that if I could take care of matters, there was really no need for her to worry.

And perhaps this process of closing myself off, and diminishing Rosie in the process, was something that started even before the pregnancy. I think back to all those questions I answered with a quick 'fine'. When did I start doing this? I want to beg forgiveness for each and every one. This fortnight has brought a new clarity. I've always been aware of the extra strands of happiness that she wove into my life. But perhaps there were moments when telling myself I was doing things for Rosie made me feel better about the choices I made. The *Mirror* didn't work out because I didn't want it to. It was no one else's fault. Rosie never held me back, never moaned or berated me for not being around. Staying at the *Post* was my choice, not hers. It was so easy to create an alternate version of my life in which I'd never met her, in which I was a success. But this was a fantasy. I chose the life I had. I chose Rosie. And it was the best decision I ever made.

The tabloids are filled with news of our separation: *Shock split for two-mother baby couple* screeches the *Citizen*. Angela Simmons of the *Herald* – our information day mole – writes a sanctimonious opinion piece: *As I highlighted at the time, Portsmouth University was slapdash in its approval process for the trial, accepting couples without testing their commitment to raising a child in a two-parent family.*

Richard Prior is quoted extensively: 'This goes to prove exactly why we need a family bill. It might not be fashionable to say so, but all the research shows that traditional structures are what work best for children.'

Once it's clear I'm definitely not returning, the good old *Post* joins the party with a *Juliet Curtis in Office Meltdown* feature. Several 'sources close to Juliet' speak of how I've 'unravelled' in recent months, and how the pressure led to a 'violent outburst'. They don't quote Matthew; he must be too proud to go into victim mode. I can't help smiling at the idea of him being pressured to tell his story, *for the sake of the paper.*

And, most hurtful of all, Hong Shu goes on breakfast TV. She wears a jade-green dress and heels, dabs at her eyes as she speaks of her loss. I'm frozen as I watch her, the slight stoop, the red rims to her eyes that not even studio make-up can conceal. 'I just . . . ' She's overcome for a moment, and the camera shifts to the presenter who's nodding with his head tilted to one side.

'I just find it so hard that someone could go through the whole process, all the happy milestones, the scans, the first kick. I don't understand how someone could feel that, and not want their baby. I . . . ' Hong Shu trails off, shaking her head.

I sit on the sofa, staring at the television for a long while after that. The crackle in her voice, the deep lines on her forehead, they tell of an ever-present pain. She must have been shocked, and so disappointed, when she read my father's interview. I want to explain, to call her and hear her voice. Yet the shared experiences that once held the promise of a great friendship have come to an end. Another person to add to the list; another person I wanted to draw close but ended up estranging myself from. There are only so many places I can put the blame: the demands of the *Post*, the stresses of the trial, my father being a traitor. These all contributed to the mess I'm in. But it goes deeper: there's something wrong with how I am, with my decision-making during stressful times. Understanding this, and doing something about it, is going to be the key to rebuilding.

Abi sent me several chin-up texts in the aftermath of my father's interview, followed by an excited voicemail telling me that one of the PR firms she freelances for is interested in taking on some additional support. We arrange to meet at one of Petersfield's more upmarket bars, somewhere my dad would never venture (*Full of stuck-up toffs*, he'd say). I set out an hour early. Since the Fiesta's tyres were slashed, the university's security firm has installed a high fence and lockable gate, which at least stops photographers from coming to the front door. There's an encampment of journalists on the pavement outside. Some reporters have even brought little camping stools along with them to make the stakeout more comfortable, and they sit, smoking or checking their phones, oblivious to the hostile stares of my neighbours.

Everyone springs to their feet when I emerge through the gate. Cameras flash in my face. 'Are you and Rosie finished for good?' a reporter shouts. 'Is it true you don't want the baby?'

I set off at a run. Car engines start up. One journalist tries to run alongside me, quickly becoming out of breath as he shouts his questions. But I know this town better than any of them and head for the heath, where the drivers won't be able to follow and I can quickly become lost amongst winding footpaths. When I'm sure I'm no longer being followed, I shoot back onto the road and up a flight of steps onto an old avenue, where I put on the baseball cap I'd tucked into my jacket pocket and I make my way to the bar.

Abi is looking well. She's been working at the PR agency today and is dressed in a floral jumpsuit. Her flame-red hair has been cut into a sleek crop. She orders a plate of cheesy chips to go with her shandy. Thirsty from the run, I just order a juice.

The bar's interior is rustic, with large wooden tables and deliberately mismatched chairs; menus on recycled card boast seasonal, local produce. There are a few clusters of suited types taking up tables, along with a young man and woman clearly on a date and struggling to think of suitable conversation topics.

'The *Post* had the nerve to ring me after you quit,' Abi says. 'Offered me the chance to take my job back. They put it to me like it was a treat.' She laughs. 'I was so pleased you plucked up the courage to leave – they made it absolutely untenable for you.'

I smile. 'Well, as it turns out, cleaning work is almost as lucrative.'

'Needn't stick that out for much longer. This agency I was telling you about, I do two days a week for them, more if they're desperate, but they're looking for another freelance. Jules, it's such easy money – two hundred quid a day. And when I say day, I mean an actual day, like nine to five. It's so bloody easy – they genuinely reckon writing one press release per shift is a good productivity rate. The way I knock stuff out completely blows their minds. To tell the truth, I've started doing some of my other work in their offices – don't want to be too much of a show-off.' Her chips arrive and she sets about them hungrily.

'Thanks for thinking of me,' I say. 'It sounds great, and I'm in. As long as they don't mind me turning up in my shabby *Post* clothes for a while. Can't afford anything smarter just yet.'

'No bother – the way they see it, scruffiness makes you an *edgy creative*. And, actually, I don't think you'll mind working there. I mean, I've had to write some boring stuff about refrigerated trucks, but they have some interesting clients too. I was working for an animal charity today, did a story about golden lion tamarins.'

'And how's your journalism coming along?'

'Better than expected. A student website and an interiors magazine are giving me regular commissions, and I'm keeping a few of the tabloids supplied with nuggets of Portsmouth crime. I spend one afternoon a week on the business side, coming up with ideas, putting pitches together. Then the rest of the week I'm actually working on paid assignments. Not bad, eh? I'm probably earning more than Matthew.'

She finishes the rest of her chips and sucks the grease from each finger before getting up and ordering another round of drinks. 'So how are you?' she asks as she hands me a second juice, this time upgraded to include vodka.

'Just trying to rebuild,' I say. 'So I really appreciate the PR lead. Nothing's come of the CVs I've sent out.'

'You're a great writer – I always wondered why you stayed at the *Post* so long.'

'I guess it was easy to keep telling myself the barriers were too high. Pathetic, really. We could have made do if I'd gone freelance. It would have been hard, but if I wanted it enough ... '

'You're only – what, mid-thirties? Plenty of time for another go.'

I sip my drink. 'I'm going to do my best.'

'And the pregnancy? Is that going OK? Rosie can't have that much longer to go.'

I look down at the table. I don't want to offend Abi, and I long to believe that anything I tell her will stay between us, but perhaps I'll never be sure. My own father sold my confidences for money.

When I look up, I see that her eyes have a wounded look. She's seen my reticence, seen that I don't quite trust her. She tries to smile, makes a comment about the weather, about how it's started to feel like spring at long last.

She deserves better. I have to face down these uncomfortable moments and actually confide in the people I want in my life. Be open to what they have to offer.

'I haven't been able to get excited about the baby,' I say in a low voice. 'I know it's not normal. I was so careful to conceal it. But Rosie's left me anyway.' Saying the words out loud gives me a physical pain, a kind of scraping sensation on the inside of my chest.

Abi reaches out and puts a hand on my arm. 'It'll be OK,' she says.

How does she know that? I feel a surge of despair at the platitude. So much is beyond my control.

'Jules? Do you want to get out of here? Go for a walk? Or let's get another vodka down you. Tell me what you need – I want to help.'

I have to persevere. My willingness to change can't fluctuate with my moods. However much it hurts, I have to go on. 'It's just . . . I've fucked everything up. And the thing is, I know – I know how you ought to treat the people you love, so why can't I do it? Rosie deserves better, so much better.'

'But that's for her to judge. Maybe if you just talk to her—'

'What kind of mother will I be to our child? I . . . I've never seen it done, I don't know how. My own mother died before I could know her, and my dad – I always thought he did his best as a parent, but he sold my fucking story.'

What an outburst – there's so much Abi can do with what I've just given her, and she's at the stage in her career when it would make the most difference. But no – I won't let myself worry about it.

She gives me a reassuring smile. 'You'll get by, Jules. You're so strong, I always thought that. I'll never forget that time you had a go at Kyle for taking the piss out of one of his interviewees. You were so calm.

'You treated everyone with such a natural respect, whoever they were. You were Matthew's opposite, his antidote. That paper is going to go down the toilet without you there.'

I smile. I'd forgotten the mouthful I'd given Kyle.

'And, you know,' Abi continues, 'I always think of motherhood as one of those experiences that we build up too much. Magazines are always so ready to tell you how to feel, harping on about special bonds and bollocks like that. It can't be helpful. I guess it's kind of like sex. I mean, before you actually have it, you read all this stuff about how good it should be – and in films everyone's bouncing around screaming their heads off. The reality can never compete with that.'

I laugh. 'How did you get to be so wise?'

'Your baby is going to be lucky to have you. I'm sure Rosie knows that.'

I meet her eye. Her concern is hard to bear. But it gives me courage. The next time I see Rosie, I'm going to refuse to participate in cold, logistical chit-chat. I'm going to confess everything. Maybe my lack of feeling for the baby will scare her. But I'll be telling the truth when I say that, since she's been gone, I've missed the baby's presence in my life.

Chapter 31

I accept Abi's offer of a lift home, and watch her eyes widen as she pulls into my street and takes in the media presence. 'Jesus – how can you tolerate this?'

'Best just drop me off here. They'll hem you in otherwise. You can turn around over there.'

We part hastily, promising each other texts, and I walk the last few yards to the house. 'Who was that, Juliet?' one of the loitering reporters shouts. 'Got yourself a new girlfriend already?'

As I'm unlocking the gate, something wet blasts me in the face. The photographers closest to me step back and swear. Automatically my hands go up to protect my eyes and I let out a shriek. It takes a moment to process the fact that nothing is burning, and to detect the smell of urine. Someone has flung piss at me. My lips are wet with it. Shaking myself off, I open my eyes and am blinded by the flash of cameras.

'Sick. That's what you are,' a voice hisses. He's standing to my left, a short man, maybe around fifty, with wiry hair and a pointed chin. He's holding a flask. He must have saved up his urine, been carrying it around with him all evening.

I quickly snap a picture of my assailant with my phone and hurry through the gate, locking it behind me.

Inside the house, I rest my back against the front door and wipe my face and sodden hair with my sleeve. These clothes need to go straight into the washing machine, and I need a shower; then I ought to get my complaint in to the police. Since the fire at Scott's I've been fastidious at reporting every incident, collecting a notebook filled with crime reference numbers and the names of investigating officers. But for the moment my feet are heavy and I remain in the hallway.

'Jules?' The light comes on and I'm confronted by my father.

'Shit. What are you doing here?' Perhaps it's the unflattering light, but every crag of his face is highlighted; his eyes are deep pits.

'Jules . . . ' He reaches out to touch me on the shoulder, but I shrink away. 'I've still got the keys you gave me – I hope you don't mind. I didn't want to startle you, but I thought you'd prefer me to wait in here, rather than out there with that lot snapping away. You're wet, what happened?'

'You sold a story about me. You shared private things – with a fucking journalist.'

There's a pause. I shiver and wrap my arms around my middle. I must not weaken.

He looks down at the carpet where a couple of drops of urine have dripped from my clothes. 'I thought I knew what I was doing. I thought I could put the record straight, show the world the kind of woman you are – and yes, maybe earn myself a note or two. It was a snap decision. A bad one—'

'But I warned you, so many times—'

'You're upset. Let's sit down, have a cup of tea and a talk.'

His eyes plead and I want, in spite of everything, to make him feel better. But Rosie isn't here with me, and it's his fault.

'No,' I say. 'You shouldn't be here. You've really fucked things up. I told you we weren't going to speak to the press. You should have respected that. I suppose it was you who tipped off the *Sketch* too?'

'What? No. That wasn't me. Jules, you're my daughter. I told them at the *Tribune*, Jules. I told them how hard you work, how you've always looked after me. They made out in the story that all we talked about was you not wanting babies, but it wasn't like that. The woman was nice – we had a good chat. It was like she was interested in you for your own sake, not just for the trial.'

I sigh. 'You're not that naïve, Dad. Admit it was about the money.' My voice trembles. I can't go on with this conversation. I really need to be in the shower, washing the piss out of my hair.

My father is very still. When he next speaks his voice is quiet: 'You talk about money like it's a dirty word, but you and I both know it's everything in this world we live in. You can't know what it feels like to have every dream stamped on, to witness lesser people having it all . . . I could have been someone, if things had been different.'

'Don't give me that. You could have made something of yourself if you'd been prepared to work at it.'

My father sighs. 'It ruined me, living in that house, with him. He made me feel like I was nothing.'

I close my eyes and shake my head. I'm starting to feel pity, but I resist it. My father's sorrows, his broken dreams, are undoubtedly real. But he cannot use them as an all-encompassing excuse.

'I thought I was doing the right thing with the story,' he says after a pause. 'It was a mistake, but it was made with a pure heart.'

I reach over and hang my keys on their hook, take off my jacket and give my hair another rub with the dry fabric at the back. I can't look at him. If I do, I'll relent, and it's too soon. What he's done is too serious. 'The things you told me about your family . . . are they true? Did you really grow up in Leigh Park, like you said you did?'

A hand on my shoulder. 'Yes. Of course. There were things I couldn't . . . But I never made stuff up. There were parts of my life that had no place in my daughter's family history. So I made them vanish.'

'Your brothers – do you know what happened to them?'

He snorts. I risk a quick glance and notice a packet of Marlboros protruding from his coat pocket. He never usually smokes the expensive brands. These were paid for by mine and Rosie's story. I step away from the door, blocking off the living room and making it clear it's time for him to go.

'You wrote about David.' He takes out the packet and retrieves a fag, ready for the walk home. 'Assault charge. Four years ago now. I was flicking through the paper at the Green Dragon. Always look out for your stories. Always. And there was his picture, taken outside the court. Bigger, fatter, but the same sneer in his eyes. And at the top of the page: *by Juliet Curtis*. I wonder whether he ever realised it was his niece writing about him.'

I don't remember the story – there have been too many assault cases for that. I open the front door a crack, ushering him out. 'I've got stuff to do, Dad. I need a shower.'

'Jules, please—'

'Stop drinking. I don't care about the weed, but if drinking makes you lose control, then don't fucking do it.'

'A man has to lessen the pain—'

'No more hippy bullshit. Stop drinking. And maybe, in a while, I'll be ready to talk to you again. But not now. I can't do it now. I'm sorry.'

My father is looking at me, and when I meet his eye he gives me a firm little nod. The gesture isn't much, it certainly isn't a promise. But when I close the door on him, I somehow feel a little less broken.

Chapter 32

We have an appointment with Becca at the end of the week. I call Rosie, suggesting that I drive her, but she tells me that she's going shopping in the city with Anthony and will meet me at the Centre. They're sitting in the foyer when I arrive, deep in conversation. Anthony is gesticulating and Rosie's nodding at what he's saying. As I sign in at reception she looks up and her eyes meet mine. She seems to radiate good health, and although it's only been days since I last saw her, the bump looks to have grown – her maternity trench coat juts out further than ever. I feel a pang at this – not quite the blind affection that mothers are supposed to feel, but something more elusive. Rosie awkwardly gets up and comes over, greeting me with a chaste peck on the cheek.

The cleaning has left me with a dull ache in my lower back and – in spite of my extensive rubber-glove use – dry, chapped hands. I wish I'd made more of an effort, rather than throwing on my old combats and a grey hoodie. But Rosie knows me. She'd see right through any attempt to dress up. Until now I've never had to try with her. Never had to calculate, to wear the right things, say the right things to impress. We skipped the dating stage. I moved in with her a fortnight after

our first kiss. But now I'm awkward, still unsure what I have
to do to make this work.

'What's that smell?' Rosie says.

'Oh – lemon multi-surface cleaner. I can't get rid of it, it
clings to everything.'

She wrinkles her nose and laughs. 'Jules the cleaner. I can't
quite picture it.'

'How are you?' I ask.

'Good.' She looks back at Anthony. 'We've had a nice
morning out, haven't we, Ant?'

He grins in return. Out of the corner of my eye I see Becca
coming down the stairs, dark-suited Dwayne in tow. I bristle.
Anthony better not think he's joining us in the consultation
room. He stands up, as though he believes he might be.

Becca waves at us. I haven't seen her since before my
father's interview appeared. She's certain to have read it. My
stomach tightens with shame and I have to fight an urge to
look away.

'Ladies, shall we?' Becca gestures to the staircase.

'You alright to wait here, Ant?' Rosie says.

He nods, catching my eye. I shouldn't be so intolerant, I
tell myself. But he was the one who brought Rosie here today,
not me. I'm unable to be the bigger person in the presence
of such hurt.

When we reach the top of the stairs, instead of leading us
to our usual consulting room Becca peels off in the opposite
direction and ushers us into the boardroom. I'm surprised at
this, but we're only a month away from the relocation they're
advocating, so I'm guessing we're going to spend some time

talking about that. Sitting at the table are two men I don't recognise, and Scott, his leg in a plaster cast.

Rosie rushes over to him. 'Oh, how lovely to see you. How are you? Should you be back at work so soon?'

Scott gives her a wistful smile, but his eyes are troubled. 'I'm doing fine,' he says.

'Let's all sit down,' Becca says, positioning herself at the head of the table.

Rosie gives me a sideways glance as we both sit. The two unfamiliar men have oddly impassive expressions. One of them has a laptop open in front of him, the other a yellow legal pad and expensive fountain pen. They must be from the security firm.

'OK, introductions,' Becca says. 'To my left we have Chris Harpenden, dean of the medical school, and next to him is Alan Potter, our legal representative.'

There's a pause. *Legal representative?* In spite of Becca's composure, I notice that her hand shakes slightly as she reaches for her water glass. And – I realise in a moment of foreboding – she's in one of her trouser suits normally reserved for TV appearances, rather than the jeans she usually wears around the lab.

'Right.' Becca meets my eye. 'There's no easy way to say this, so I'm just going to be direct. I think that's always best. There will be time for questions afterwards – as long as you need.'

There's momentary silence in the room. Becca swallows. 'OK. We brought you up here to inform you that the trial has been compromised. We're currently investigating a mislabelling of patient ova.'

'We're so sorry this happened,' Scott says, prompting a sharp glance from the legal guy.

'What do you mean, compromised?' Rosie says.

Something cold spreads through my chest. The formality in this room is choking. I want to tell everyone to wait. To step outside and process what's just been said. *Compromised?*

Becca takes a deep breath. 'I know that you're friends with Anita and Hong Shu, and that they made you aware of their terrible loss.'

I quickly glance at Rosie. Her face is blanched. I want to comfort her somehow, but I cannot move an inch. If I do, something will fracture – I imagine myself melting, collapsing in on myself like a guttered candle.

'Well, subsequent testing revealed that the child Anita was carrying was not, in fact, biologically related to her.' Becca shoots a quick glance over at the legal representative, who gives her a faint nod. Her face is red and the carefully chore-ographed calm has gone.

She swallows and continues. 'The child she was carrying was the genetic offspring of Hong Shu and you, Rosie.'

I gasp and turn to Rosie, automatically putting my arm around her. She's holding herself very still, her forehead wrinkled in consternation. 'But . . .' Her voice is quiet. 'This baby. My baby. It's mine. Mine and Jules's, right?' She looks at Becca with pleading eyes.

'We can offer you genetic testing,' the dean says. 'Give you a definite answer.'

'So you're saying it's in doubt?' I ask Becca.

She bites her lip. 'I wish I could offer you more certainty, I do. It's up to you whether you want to take a prenatal DNA

test – which is an invasive procedure and does carry a risk –
or whether you'd prefer to wait until Baby is born. All we
know at this point is that there's been deliberate mislabelling
of the egg cells we retrieved. We're still unsure of the extent
of the sabotage.'

'Why would someone do that?' I ask.

The room is quiet. Again, I look at Rosie. There's a strangely
blank look in her eyes. I rub her back, but she doesn't respond.

'It's sick,' Scott says. 'I'll never understand what went on
in her head.'

'It was someone that *works* here?' I say. 'Who?'

'We're exploring the possibility of criminal charges,' the
dean says. 'So I'm afraid we can't answer that.'

'Who?' I ask Becca. 'Was it one of the technicians?'

Becca looks down at the table.

'It was that Claire, wasn't it? I knew there was something off about her, I knew it. Why did she do it? Did she
tell you why?'

Becca shakes her head, sorrow etched across her face.

'As I say,' the dean continues, 'there's an active investigation. We've called the police in and we really can't give you
any further details.'

I stand up. I have to. The anger is like a current flowing
through me. 'But, as of today, you're saying you don't actually
know whose baby Rosie is carrying?'

'Jules ...' Scott tries to stand for a moment, then lands
clumsily back in his seat with a grunt of frustration. 'God,
Jules, I can't tell you how sorry I am. But if it's any consola-
tion, any at all, there were only four sets of eggs in the lab
on the day yours were harvested. Yours, Rosie's, Anita's and

Hong Shu's. And we had robust processes in place – two scientists confirming the labelling. Secure storage. To mislabel even one set would have taken a huge effort – it could be that only the one sample was compromised.'

'And that's supposed to make us feel better?' My voice breaks. I've started to cry. From nowhere I conjure Rosie and Hong Shu's child. I see her as a little girl of about five, black hair, but thick like Rosie's. Gently sloping eyes and Rosie's dimpled cheeks. Rosie's little girl has died. The grief impales me and I double over.

I register Becca's arm across my shoulders, the light floral scent she always wears. 'We'll do everything we can. Whatever you decide to do about testing. And counselling. We'll make sure you get counselling. Anything you need.'

With a sudden chill, I remember the night Rosie was hospitalised, my strange conviction that Becca was withholding something. 'How long have you known about this?' I ask.

There's a pause. I hear Becca swallow again. 'We needed to know what we were dealing with before we worried you.'

'When you find out more, you have to tell us.' I wipe my eyes with the sleeve of my hoodie. 'Straight away, no hiding anything.'

'Of course,' Becca says.

'So can we ...?' Rosie's voice is still so quiet. There's no trace of tears, and for some reason that makes me feel so much worse. 'I just want to be clear. My baby. The baby I'm carrying inside of me. This baby is mine and Jules's?'

Becca's mouth falls open and she looks more crushed, more defeated, than I imagined possible. The two suited men exchange a glance. A soft medley floats in through the window: the local church group is back, singing their hearts out.

At last, it's Scott who answers. 'We don't know, Rosie. I think it very likely that it is, but I'm really sorry to say that, right now, we can't be certain.'

We leave the room in a daze. Becca sees us to the top of the stairs, continuing to talk of tests, of counselling, of giving us time to process the news. As we head down towards reception Rosie grabs at my sleeve. 'Please don't tell anyone about this,' she says.

I stop walking. This is such an un-Rosie thing to say. I'd assumed that she'd want to pour everything out to her mother, to cry in Anthony's arms. 'Come home with me,' I say. 'This is a lot to deal with. We should talk through what to do next.'

She takes hold of the banister and shakes her head. 'This is our baby, Jules. That's all there is to it.'

'Rosie—'

'Hurry up. I don't want Anthony to guess that anything's the matter.'

'But . . . You can't get in his car and act like nothing's happened. Come back with me. We need to talk about this.'

She shakes her head. 'There's nothing to talk about.'

I watch her muster a smile for Anthony, who waves at me as he leads her away. This isn't how Rosie behaves. Always, she responds in the most natural way, going wherever her emotions take her and not caring a damn for what anyone else might think. I'd expected tears. Rage. Anything but this muted denial.

I sink down into one of the orange chairs in reception, knowing that for the moment I'm incapable of driving. Incapable of walking, even.

Not our baby? Is this my fault? Retribution for all those *if I could reverse this baby, I would* thoughts? I imagine a tearful Rosie handing over a little bundle to Anita and Hong Shu, her dream of motherhood over. I'm going to be sick. And as soon as I think it, up comes this morning's muesli, onto the floor, splattering my combats and trainers.

A hush descends on the waiting area, but I feel no embarrassment. All I want is to close my eyes for a moment. And so I do, willing my thoughts to go quiet as my stomach roils and some kindly stranger comes along and places a wet cloth against my forehead.

Chapter 33

The silence of the house feels so oppressive that once or twice I peer through the bedroom window, just to get the reaction of the press outside. A flurry of camera clicks and shouted questions. Reassurance that life is carrying on.

'Leave it, Jules,' Rosie whispers when I ring her that afternoon. She refuses to discuss what we've been told and what the implications might be, cutting the call short, leaving me alone with the news. I call in sick for my evening cleaning shift and pace from room to room, movement the only outlet for my strange fog of emotions. I keep picturing that poor dead baby – Rosie's child by Hong Shu. A dusting of black hair, almond-shaped eyes and perfect, chubby arms and legs. Before, I'd felt pity for my friends, but nothing like this grief. Rosie's beautiful child, never taking a breath. Not being buried. Perhaps even now she sits in a jar in a cupboard in the lab.

And then there's disbelief combined with hot, potent anger. I imagine Claire deliberately staying late, sneaking into the lab and switching labels. Exercising a hate that she kept masked in front of others. What did she feel, each time she ran the ultrasound probe over Anita's or Rosie's belly, knowing what she'd done? Did she ever experience a twinge of guilt? Or did she revel in her secret? Only she can know how many eggs were mislabelled. Only she can know whose child Rosie is carrying.

Upstairs in the spare room, I pore over the ring binder containing all our documentation from the university. None of the fine print covers the situation we're in: there's no reference to misplaced eggs, nor to what might happen in cases of sabotage or malpractice. The internet is slightly more reassuring. I read about IVF mix-ups, black mothers giving birth to white children, institutional carelessness. Each of these tragic examples seems to suggest that in the UK, parental rights remain with the birth mother. If the worst has happened, and the child inside Rosie is not genetically ours, then it looks as though the law, at least, will be on our side.

Exhausted, I lie on the floor and stare up at the ceiling. I think back over the past few months, at how troubled I've been by my lack of affinity with Rosie's growing bump. By my inability to see past the press intrusion and visualise life as part of a new family of three. DNA didn't bind me like I imagined it would. Before, I anticipated a kind of resonance. A humming within my core, celebrating a connection almost holy in nature. The expression of my own mother in that handful of photographs – that's what I imagined for myself. Ownership. Certainty. I wanted what Rosie and Elaine have. The hand-on-shoulder moments, the subtle reading of moods. Communication without words.

And yet the key to all these things lay not in DNA, but in some hidden place that continued to elude me. The magic of bonding my genes to Rosie's was not enough to counter the upheaval we endured, and, more intimidating still, the sense that the life we shared together, the life of before, was over. But I was starting to feel *something*. A strange new longing to protect, which may have come too late, but was indisputably real. It's stronger than ever now. The baby inside Rosie needs an advocate – it needs certainty, to be protected from this mess.

I remember Rosie's sudden changes of expression as the baby moved, the gentle smiles, the yelp of laughter when she realised our daughter was hiccupping for the first time. Did this connection come from DNA? Or did it stem from the act of growing her child? I picture her sitting on her parents' sofa. What is she feeling now?

After a while, my phone rings and I see that it's Becca. I almost ignore her, but then I realise she might have news.

'How are you holding up?' she asks.

I grunt, lacking the energy to feign bravery.

'Jules, I'm so sorry – I know today has been an extremely difficult day, and I don't want to add to your distress. But we've been contacted by *Sunday Review*. The saboteur has given them an interview and they wanted a comment from the university.'

'Shit.'

'Our security consultants feel it wise to bring your relocation forward by a month. They're preparing a flat for you in Hampstead. You and Rosie can sit things out there, close to the Royal Free. I've already spoken to the team and they're happy for me to use their facilities for your check-ups.'

'Have you spoken to Rosie?'

'She's being picked up in an hour. They're planning to drive you separately.'

'An hour? We've got an hour to pack up and leave?'

'Your case manager is on his way to you now. He'll talk you through how this will work. It's your choice, whether to go or not, but I'd strongly recommend it.'

'What about our home? Who's going to pay the mortgage if I'm holed up in a safe house, not able to work?'

There's a pause at the other end of the line, then Becca gives a gentle sigh. 'I never for a minute imagined the trial would bring such disruption to your lives. You have to believe me, Jules. I expected scrutiny, but in my head I had such a different vision of how things would be.' Her voice splinters and my anger dissipates. Becca has been doing good work. Ground-breaking work that should have been celebrated, not reviled. This situation we're in is not of her making. And indeed, what use is blame now?

Twenty minutes later our case manager, Gary Williams, arrives. I've met him before, when he oversaw the installation of our home security. He's tall, with sandy-coloured hair, wearing a charcoal-grey suit and a red tie.

In the living room he produces a black folder stuffed with papers. 'OK. So the university are prepared to underwrite all the expenses relating to this property until a month after the birth. I have an agreement here.' He passes me a document. 'You just need to sign to say that you're happy for us to open your mail and that you'll provide a key and the alarm codes. We'll keep the house secure for your return.'

I stare at him blankly. 'I have a job interview tomorrow,' I say. The PR firm Abi put me in touch with. The easy money that was to mark a turning point in my life.

'Now, Juliet – may I call you Juliet?'

'Jules.'

'OK then, Jules, you're going to have to cancel. Or let's say, postpone. We need to get you relocated tonight, before the media presence intensifies even further. We can start making an assessment about visits and meetings tomorrow morning.'

'But ... I don't understand. We've been putting up with media intrusion the whole time – why do we have to run away and hide now?'

His face is still. No trace of exasperation, but nor is there a kindly smile, or even a sympathetic head tilt. 'The media is only one of several risk factors. We've been working with the police to monitor the more radical elements opposing the trial, and we're recommending a wholesale up-scaling of security. We're relocating Professor Jefferson and her family tomorrow.'

I bite my lip as I look down at the agreement. It already contains Rosie's neatly looping signature. What choice do I have? I sign, and on Gary's instruction I load up a suitcase with clothes and a random selection of books from Rosie's shelves. Then I surrender my key and am steered out through the gate and into a waiting Mercedes.

At just after ten in the evening, we park at the rear of a boarded-up pub. It's a three-storey building in ugly brown brick, on a busy London street. 'This is our safe house?' I say to Gary.

'Believe me,' he replies, 'you'll be more invisible on this

street than you would be in a secluded cottage somewhere. The back entrance is nicely tucked away.'

He unlocks the door and ushers me through, keying in a code in the hallway, then leading me up a narrow, musty staircase. 'You and Rosie are on the top floor. You have your own front door with cameras on it the whole time. My lot are in the flat beneath you. We've got cameras everywhere: back door, front door, stairwell. And we'll answer your buzzer, should anyone turn up trying to sell you double glazing.'

We emerge onto a small landing. The walls are magnolia and there's a horrible salmon-coloured carpet underfoot. Gary simultaneously knocks on the door and unlocks it with his key. It opens into a large living room where three tired-looking brown sofas are arranged around a TV set. On the walls, pristine rectangles mark where pictures once hung. There are empty bookcases, along with a dining table and six chairs, and throughout the room there's a strong odour of artificial lavender, not quite masking stale cigarette smoke.

Rosie is sitting on one of the sofas. She glances up as I arrive, then looks away without smiling. A woman in a dark suit, her black hair in cornrows, gets up and shakes my hand. 'I'm Jamila,' she says. 'I know it's been a long day, so we'll let the two of you get settled in. There's a phone over on the table. It doesn't dial out, but if you need anything just press zero and it'll call the team downstairs. There's a few basic supplies in the fridge – help yourselves for now, and we'll look at getting you properly set up tomorrow.'

Brief smiles, brief goodbyes, then Gary and Jamila leave us alone. As the door clicks shut my stomach unclenches and I exhale. 'Rosie.' I rush over to her and wrap her tightly in my arms.

She doesn't say anything, but she does at least soften her body in response. I close my eyes and drink in the feeling. This is the relief I've needed all day. 'How's the baby?' I ask.

Rosie pulls away and looks at me blankly. 'Still moving, if that's what you mean.'

I won't show that I'm stung. Whatever emotions are hiding behind her impassive face, she needs to get them out. She can fling all her rage, all the sadness, at me if it will help her. 'And how are you?'

She shrugs. Her pale complexion, the deadness in her eyes – she must be in shock.

'Rosie, this baby is yours. Ours. Regardless of what they say. Regardless of any test results. We chose to have her. She's growing inside your body.'

'I know that.'

'Good.' I squeeze her arm. 'Then nothing's changed.'

For a moment she looks as though she might say something. But then she changes her mind and looks down at the carpet. 'Do you want to take a look at the bedrooms and pick one? They're the same size, but you might prefer the one at the back. It's quieter.'

I swallow. How can she bear to be alone tonight? Am I really so very bad? Are we really so very broken? 'Rosie—'

'I'm tired, Jules. Leave it.'

And I do. Not by choice, but because I see that my persistence will only agitate her. Perhaps space is the best thing for right now. I set myself up in the back bedroom and pass an almost sleepless night. My father's interview made Rosie disappointed in me, but she's never shut me out like this, not ever. She's in shock, I keep telling myself. But a new fear makes its presence felt. *What if it's more than that? What if we really are over?* My mind rejects such ideas. Instantly. More than ten years of kisses. Of trips abroad. Of eating our meals next to each other on the sofa. With her I stopped being defined by my upbringing, by the smelly house I grew up in. For the first time in my life I felt accepted, as though I didn't have to strive for anything. I could simply enjoy each moment.

Such deep connections are surely meant to endure. But there's an acid presence in my belly that feels like truth, slowly seeping throughout my body, whispering, *It's over and you know it.*

Chapter 34

The technician looks very different out of her blue scrubs. She wears a sleeveless black dress and sits on the sofa with her legs primly crossed, hands folded in her lap. Her face has been carefully contoured by the studio make-up artist, and her straightened hair looks recently dyed. It's only her feet – in gold stiletto sandals – that undermine the professionalism she aspires to.

'So, Claire.' The male presenter blazes her with his smile. 'Talk us through what happened in the laboratory at Portsmouth University, back on the fourth of September last year.'

She looks at the camera. Tucks a few strands of hair behind her ear and takes a deep breath. 'I got into healthcare because I wanted to help people, and I thought at Portsmouth I'd be working with couples who struggled to conceive. Bringing joy to people's lives. But this – two-mother babies – it was unnatural. Wrong.'

The camera cuts to the presenter, who's nodding encouragingly.

'I suppose I felt trapped. I have three lovely children and I needed to keep bringing money home for their sake. I planned to look for another job, but in the meantime I told myself that going to work every day, even though I didn't agree with what was happening there, was the right thing to do. But on the fourth, something in me snapped. I didn't have a grand plan. I didn't even think about what I was doing. It was pure impulse.'

The presenter smiles. 'And just remind everyone of the significance of the fourth of September. That was the day Rosie Barcombe, Juliet Curtis and two other women had their eggs collected. Correct?'

'That's right. When the eggs are taken out of the body, they're mixed with fluids. You end up with what looks like vials of cloudy water. Later, in the lab, the scientists work to separate out individual egg cells ready for fertilisation.'

'And you intervened in this process?'

'It's supposed to be this highly controlled scientific trial. Two of us had to check the labelling of the samples before they were locked away. But there was a long stretch where they were unattended, half the staff had a key and there weren't even any cameras monitoring the storage area. I think, initially, part of me just wanted to draw attention to how sloppy they were being.'

'So – just to be clear. You knowingly switched the labels between samples?'

She dabs at her eyes as she gives the slightest of nods.

'And the security arrangements at the clinic enabled you to do so, with ease?'

'Exactly.'

'How many samples do you think you mislabelled?'

'It all happened so fast – I was acting on impulse. I'm really not sure.'

'To some people watching at home, your actions may be a little difficult to relate to,' the presenter says. 'Some may even call it sabotage.'

Even through the thick studio make-up, there's an unmistakable reddening of her face. 'But isn't what they're doing a far worse kind of sabotage? They're overturning the natural order, imposing their political correctness on all of us. What I did was reckless, but it was in service to a greater good.'

'OK – let's talk a bit more about the mislabelling. Many people will be asking about the child Rosie Barcombe is carrying. It's due in six weeks, I believe. Are you able to shed any light on its parentage?'

Claire's eyes widen. 'Like I say, it all happened so quickly. I really don't know.'

'And – I have to ask – do you have any regrets? The women involved have surely had their lives turned upside down by this revelation.'

She fixes the camera with a hard stare. 'I have three beautiful boys and when I look at them I can't be sorry. What world would they have grown up in if this trial had been a success? They'd end up in a minority.'

'But for Juliet and Rosie – two women who thought they were having a baby together – do you have any sympathy for them?'

'I'm a mother myself and I know what a precious thing it is to have a child. But the women involved in this trial are basically part of a science experiment – who would choose that for themselves and their children? How could you bring a baby into the world, not knowing what health problems you might be exposing them to? It's irresponsible and cruel.'

*

Rosie switches the television off and closes her eyes. I place a hand on her arm. 'She's off her rocker,' I say. 'And for all we know, she might only have switched one set of labels. Hinting that she interfered with more might just be part of her twisted game plan.'

'She doesn't seem clever enough to have a game plan, Jules.'

I say nothing to this. I ask myself quickly: does it matter to me, the fact that the baby might not be Rosie's, might not be mine? No. My body relaxes at just how sure I am. A child that grows up encircled by Rosie's love will be Rosie's child. Maybe it won't have her beautiful hair, but who cares? It will gain far more important things through being raised by her. Already Rosie has amassed a selection of story books; I imagine her delight in reading them aloud to our baby. She'll give each of the characters special voices and our daughter will wriggle with excitement.

'It really doesn't matter whose eggs were used,' I say.

She rubs at her face. She's wearing a clingy green maternity dress today, and there's the fleeting appearance of a tiny foot to one side of her bump. 'That's easy for you to say.'

I put my arm around her. 'It's true. The baby inside you has been part of our lives for a long time now. She's ours. No matter what anyone says. We're going to raise her and she's going to be our daughter. No test result could convince me otherwise.'

Rosie shrugs my arm away and gets up from the sofa. 'You've changed your tune.' She heads over to the dining table and opens her laptop.

We've been in the safe house for three days. Neither of us has set foot outside and the only people we've seen have been from the security firm. Our food is purchased online, and one of the team brings it up to us when it's delivered. Gary calls this an adjustment period. He wants the neighbours to get used to the comings and goings of him, Jamila and the four other members of our protection detail. I've begged to be allowed out for a run, but he's stubborn in his refusal.

Yet despite Rosie and I being at such close quarters, this exchange over breakfast TV is one of our longer ones. It's not that I haven't tried, but Rosie simply won't countenance talking about the baby or the future of our relationship, preferring instead to spend long silent hours at her computer. Yesterday I looked over her shoulder and saw search results for the technician's name. Claire Fenton. The woman has been embraced by the Alliance for Natural Reproduction, who are covering her legal costs and no doubt managing her interview schedule. In some quarters she's being hailed as a hero, with Richard Prior describing her as a 'victim of conscience'.

Since Rosie clearly isn't going to talk to me, I go over to the phone and call down to Gary. 'I really need to get out,' I say. 'Just a short run. I'll wear my baseball cap.'

There's a pause at the other end of the line, then a hard sigh. 'Alright. But only if I come with you.'

When I tell Rosie where I'm going, she looks stricken for a moment and I feel a pang of hope. 'I don't have to go,' I say. 'I can stay here if you'd prefer.'

'Of course you should go, don't be silly. Just be safe.'

The simple act of slipping into my leggings lifts my mood. It looks sunny out, so I opt for a vest, no over-layer, and I pull

my baseball cap down low. Gary meets me on the landing and
we set off towards Hampstead Heath at a brisk jog.

I luxuriate in the sensation of air rushing against my face,
of the sun on my skin and the rhythmic movement of my
body. Initially I keep my eyes down, terrified of recognition,
but before long I realise that here in London I'm just another
anonymous jogger. No one is searching my face. No one
expects me to be here.

On the heath, being near trees again, drinking in the green,
makes me feel as though I'm shedding layers of misery as I
go. It's a beautiful day and I am alive and I'm strong. These
are all things to be thankful for, whatever happens. I head for
a hillock, taking it at a fast pace. Gary's breathing becomes
laboured and he starts to fall behind.

'Hey,' he calls. I ignore him, drunk on the sensation of
strength and power as my heart thuds but my legs send me
happy little signals that they still have more to give.

'Hey!' he calls again, more sharply this time. I wait for him
at the top of the hill, admiring the cityscape below as I stretch
my quads. Rosie and I should have moved to London in our
twenties, I think. What stopped us?

'Don't do that again,' Gary puffs as he catches me up.

'I thought you security people were supposed to be fit.'

He scowls and leans forward, palms on his thighs, fighting
for breath. 'We're going to walk for a bit.'

'But—'

'If you want to do this again, you have to play by my
rules.'

I do a few more stretches, stifling my resentment. I am outside. I'm going to enjoy this moment. If only I can persuade

Rosie to get out of the flat for a little while, I'm sure it would do her as much good as it's done me.

Obediently, I walk at Gary's side as he dawdles down the hill, still puffing. 'I tend to focus more on weights at the gym,' he offers.

A cocker spaniel sniffs at my ankles, entangling me it its lead; its elderly owner laughs and gives me a cheery *good morning*, no trace of recognition on her face.

'Have you been reading about Richard Prior and his family bill?' I ask Gary. Prior's dominated the headlines; he's circulated a draft bill to the media and is now lobbying for a reading in Parliament.

Gary looks at me curiously and grunts a yes.

'And what do you think?'

'I do my job, regardless of the politics of a situation. I'm not paid to have opinions.'

'I know that. I'm not trying to trap you or anything. I'm just curious.'

He wipes the sweat from his forehead. 'Well, I suppose maybe there is something in it.'

'Go on.'

'He's done his research, hasn't he? And they say that kids with a male and a female parent are better off. I'm not saying you and Rosie won't do a good job – I'm sure you will. I just think this fella's right to focus on the statistics.' Gary says this in such a reasonable tone. There doesn't appear to be any homophobia at work, not that I can detect anyway.

'What statistics?' I say. 'I'm not offended, I just genuinely want to know. What specifically is convincing you that the traditional way is better?'

'Well, they're saying that kids with a mum and a dad do better at school, aren't they? They're less likely to go off the rails.'

'But who's saying it? Have you looked at the actual studies?'

Gary gives an awkward laugh that sounds more like a sigh. 'I knew this conversation was a bad idea. Two more minutes, then we'll jog the rest of the way.'

'I'll take that as a no, then.' I make sure there's a smiling tone to my voice. 'It's OK. I'm just trying to understand why so many people believe the arguments Prior and the media put to them. There are hundreds of sources out there that say something very different.'

Gary rolls his shoulders, cracks his neck. 'I only have time for a quick scan of the papers. And he always seems to know what he's talking about.'

We resume our run, heading back towards the old pub. *Seems to know what he's talking about.* I guess that, for most people, this really is enough. But how has it come to be this way? Can it really be that the charisma of the speaker is what wins an argument? Becca is a competent interviewee, but media outlets always put her in the position of having to defend the trial, and perhaps that skews people's perceptions of her and her work.

I think back over the coverage, right back to when 0-0 was first debated. The broadsheets gave detailed explanations of the science and explored both sides of the moral debate, interviewing a range of different sources. But the tabloids have, without exception, taken an 'anti' stance. The vast majority of people, who consume their news in flick-throughs and social media posts, will be thinking of the trial in terms of seismic population shifts and the draining of resources by a tiny lesbian elite. How do you go about changing the minds of such people? Certainly not through stories in the *Guardian*, which they'll never read. And people only ever seek out blogs that mirror their own points of view. On the surface it all seems so futile. Yet isn't this exactly the kind of dilemma that made me want to become a journalist in the first place?

I remember my dad offering me my first pull on his bong on my seventeenth birthday. 'The mind is ready at seventeen, not before,' he'd said. I'd felt privileged, excited even, but how I'd choked on that acrid smoke. We passed an evening cackling at the inanities he'd been exposed to in the Green Dragon that day. He recounted a monologue by one of the regulars, Bill Dorn, who spoke of 'foreigners stealing our jobs', even though it was apparent to everyone that Bill would be appalled if someone lined him up a nine-to-five.

I remember staring up at the ceiling, looking for patterns in the smoke-stained Artex swirls. 'I'm going to make them see,' I told my father. 'I'm going to revolutionise the media from the inside, make it serve the people again.'

Oh, such grandiose things I believed back then.

As Gary and I emerge from the heath and re-join the street, I feel a pang of nostalgia for the ideals of a younger me. Where are the journalists and editors who can encourage the likes of Gary and Bill Dorn to explore an issue just that little bit further? I spent years with the *Guardian* as my gold standard, yet had I got the job I wanted, I would have been no closer to my real goal. What drove me through my student days was the idea of informing people, of creating a hunger for information that could maybe break down allegiances and challenge long-held points of view.

I pick up the pace just a touch, hoping Gary will be able to stick with me. Ovum-to-ovum fertilisation is losing support. Not that it enjoyed much of it in the first place. Was I wrong to persist with *starve the bastards of fuel* for so long? Don't I have a duty to *do* something? I've been longing for the right spokesperson, the right campaigning journalist to come along and demolish Prior. But they haven't, not yet.

Perhaps the PR job was never meant to be my new start after all. Perhaps I was never meant to move away from journalism. I could instead try to change things, put everything into doing it better. I've spent enough years at the *Post* churning out stories that sometimes made me cringe when I saw my name against them. Now could be the time for something altogether more purposeful.

When I get back into the flat, Rosie's face is blotchy from crying.

'What's happened?' I envelop her in a sweaty embrace.

'The government's just announced an inquiry into the management of the o-o trial. There's a moratorium on any further implantations. They've killed it, Jules.'

'Fuck.' I squeeze her tightly and kiss her neck.

She pulls away. 'There aren't going to be any more pregnancies. This baby is going to be a freak for her entire life.'

'That's not true. There's Sweden. And Holland. And the Newcastle pregnancies – don't forget about them.'

Rosie shakes her head. I feel such a physical longing for her, to run my fingers across her skin. Taking comfort in each other would be the most natural thing in the world. I put a hand on her leg and start massaging, innocently at first, and when she doesn't stop me, I lean in to kiss her.

She slaps my hand away. 'For goodness sake, Jules. A quick shag isn't going to make me forget just how much you hurt me.'

'Then what will?'

She sighs and presses a hand to her temple. 'The fact is, I don't know. I don't even know if it's possible.'

Chapter 35

The first contact with our old life is a get-together with Elaine and Michael, two weeks into our safe-house stay. No one is allowed to know our location, so the meeting takes place at the hotel in Greenwich where the Barcombes have temporarily decamped.

'There were never less than five reporters outside our door at any one time. And we were getting letters, people writing the most horrible things,' Elaine says.

Their suite is airy, with a large window overlooking the river. It's roomy enough for a king-size bed, a sofa and a dressing table, where Elaine's expensive cosmetics sit in neat rows. I wonder whether my father has been exposed to similar levels of harassment. He'd never be able to pay for relocation to a hotel. Or at least he wouldn't have, had it not been for his *Tribune* pay cheque.

I took it as an encouraging sign that Rosie wanted me to join her for this visit, but her face is blank as she sits on the sofa, both hands folded over her bump. If this is shock, then surely it's gone on far too long. Nothing I say seems to reach her; it's as though she's forged a tough outer shell, which no words can penetrate. The ordeal of the last few weeks has turned her into someone different. What if the Rosie I've known and loved is gone for ever?

'So how've you been, girls?' Michael asks. He and Elaine are sitting on the bed; I've perched on the dressing-table stool.

'OK,' I say, when Rosie doesn't answer. 'I'm allowed out for a daily run, at least. And I've had lots of time for reading. Made me realise how much I've missed it.'

I've also been mining the internet for information on Prior, searching for a lead, the right quote, the right fact that will help me shape a story. My plans are vague, but each time I read about his family bill my muscles register a long-dormant purpose. *We make our country great by making our families great* – he repeats this relentlessly in interviews. And yet no one seems to probe what he really means; no one challenges him on the detail.

'You poor things,' Elaine says.

There's an uncomfortable silence. Rosie's shoulders are drawn up and she won't look at any of us.

'We read about the lawsuit,' Elaine says. 'That Chinese lady. So insensitive.'

Hong Shu and Anita have gone through the courts to apply for something called a 'declaration of parentage'. They want to force a DNA test, and depending on the results, seek custody of our baby. The solicitor we appointed tells us they're almost certainly going to fail – UK law is very clear in identifying the birth mother as the legal mother of the child she carries, and in cases involving IVF mix-up, the courts always rule in favour of the pregnant woman. This is *our* baby, mine and Rosie's. I feel enormous pity for our former friends, but tussling over an unborn child is only going to cause unnecessary pain. Perhaps when the shock has subsided they'll realise this. There can be no compensation, no recompense for the loss they've suffered.

'What are you going to do?' Elaine asks.

Rosie looks up. 'What do you mean?'

Elaine bites her lip. 'Surely you want to know?'

'Know what?'

With my eyes, I beg Elaine to stop.

'Well, whose baby it actually is.'

'It's my baby.' Rosie's voice is flat, but her eyes blaze.

Elaine gets up off the bed, joining Rosie on the sofa and taking her hand. 'Oh love, what a thing to happen.'

'Mum, don't. It's my baby.'

'But darling, it might come out half Chinese. Imagine how you'd feel, knowing that it might not be yours, or it might not be Jules's. I know it's hard, but you need to think about what you're going to do.'

'We'll support you, whatever you decide,' Michael says.

Elaine looks over at him, her forehead wrinkled, then turns back to Rosie. 'I can understand you not wanting to do a test when the baby is still inside. But when it's born, you'll want to know.'

Rosie stands. 'You'd love that, wouldn't you? A test result that put the baby firmly outside your family. I could hand it over and all this would go away. Hell, I could be *normal.*'

'It's OK,' I whisper.

'No, it's not OK. Mother here is seeing this . . . this tragedy as an *opportunity.* As a way out. No one will love this baby more than me. I grew her. She's mine.'

'Rosie, darling . . . ' Tears spill from Elaine's eyes.

'Let's get out of here,' Rosie says to me. 'Sorry, Dad, I just can't . . . '

She heads towards the door. I shoot a sympathetic glance back at Elaine, who's calling her daughter's name. And then I follow.

'She was only trying to help,' I say, once we're safely ensconced in the back of the Mercedes.

Rosie shakes her head. 'I mean, what does she actually think will happen? A DNA test proves the baby's not mine and I just give her up?'

'I don't think—'

'You need to stop romanticising my mother. I used to think it was sweet. But she's not a nice person. Not all the time, anyway.'

I take her hand. 'She loves you, though, Rosie. And even though she might be a bit clumsy with it sometimes, she only wants the best for you.'

She makes a sound somewhere between a sigh and a growl, and looks out of the window. We're passing a Victorian terrace. Its neat little line of chimney pots gives me a pang of affection; I really do love London. I wish we could stop the car, meander through the streets, drinking in the history. If only we could step outside our own lives for a few precious moments.

I glance over at our driver. He's focusing on the road and the partition between us is up. Perhaps now is the right moment to attempt a serious talk. At least here, Rosie can't retreat to another room.

'I've been thinking a lot about the conversations we had after my dad's interview,' I venture.

Rosie turns to me and inspects my face.

A pang of hesitation. But no. Holding back will serve nothing. She's listening – never a given any more.

'I did have doubts, about the baby. You have to understand, when we were applying I wanted it so desperately. The fact that you wanted to bear my child – there was no greater honour, Rosie. I felt secure for the first time in my life. I would have gone along with sperm donation, if it was our only option, but it would have left me feeling as though I was on the outside.'

'Jules . . .' Her eyes are teary. A departure from the emotional repression that's marked our time in the safe house. Is it wrong to feel a pinprick of hope at this?

'It's OK. It's the truth,' I say. 'But you wanted *my* baby. And so I went into it excited. I mean – fuck – what a scientific breakthrough! And we were going to be part of it, part of history.'

'We didn't know we were going to be the only ones, though.'

'No.' I sigh. 'The thing that scared me the most when you became pregnant . . . It wasn't doubts, as such. It was a kind of numbness. I expected more of myself. I mean, Jesus, what expectant mother is numb? And I tried, Rosie, I tried so hard. But perhaps willing excitement to come is precisely the most effective way to kill it.'

'And now?' Her eyes are expectant, her forehead creased. Vulnerability, combined with complete focus and attention. She looks like herself again; she looks like *my* Rosie.

'Rosie.' I reach across and gently lift her chin. 'I'm going to be completely honest with you. There were moments when I regretted our baby. When I thought we'd be happier if she'd never happened. But when you left, I really missed her. I found myself wondering whether she'd moved much, or whether you noticed her doing anything different. She'd become part of my life without me even realising it.'

The car slows. We've joined a snake of crawling traffic.

'And I feel protective. Really protective. I still think I'll be bloody hopeless, flailing around never knowing how to get her to stop crying. But I feel as though I could rip the head off anyone that wanted to hurt her. I've never felt that way before. Maybe I'll be a shit mother, but I'll be an excellent guard dog.'

Rosie straightens herself up. She smooths her hair and clears her throat, but the redness of her face undermines her poise. 'Why didn't you talk to me?' she says. 'I feel like such an idiot. I remember, right back at the early stages, Anthony said you didn't seem to be coping right. But I didn't believe him because I – stupidly – thought you'd talk to me if there was something wrong.'

'It was complicated, Rosie, I didn't want to admit the way I felt. Not even to myself.'

She shakes her head. 'Jules, you can't understand how it makes me feel, knowing that for months you were keeping things from me. I always thought we had a very different kind of relationship.'

'We did, Rosie. We do. This is just one blip. One fuck-up.'

'Jules . . .'

'Just tell me what I can do.'

'I read about your doubts in the *Tribune*. Just stop for a moment and imagine what that was like for me.'

My eyes are starting to sting. I blink. 'It must have been awful. I don't know how I let myself get into such a destructive place – the way I behaved . . . it wasn't me. That's not who I want to be. I'm going to do better, Rosie. I promise.'

She reaches across and gently brushes away a tear from my face. I place my hand over hers, and we're silent for a moment. Her eyes are soft now, and sweet relief swells in my chest. She still loves me.

'And if she isn't yours?' Rosie asks.

'After everything we've been through, I can honestly say that it doesn't matter whose eggs she was made from. We're facing the difficulties in front of us as a three. She's part of our family already. You've loved and protected her for all these months.'

'I don't know how I'll feel, Jules. If she isn't mine.'

'Well, that's really not surprising. It's a lot to take in.'

Rosie is silent for a few moments. 'But – I'm such a hypocrite. I was prepared to have a sperm donor's child. I was expecting you to raise a baby that you weren't related to. And now the shoe's on the other foot, I . . . ' She covers her face with her hands.

'Everything OK back there?' the driver asks through the intercom.

'Fine, thanks,' I shout.

I rub Rosie's back. 'Don't beat yourself up. You're going to be sucked into some pretty strange emotional states, but they'll pass. You have to believe that they will.'

She's crying too hard to reply.

'We can make a good life for this baby, Rosie. She's the child we planned and wanted. That makes her ours. Test results won't change that.'

She looks up at me with a tear-streaked face. 'But I'm not sure that I want her. Not if she isn't mine.'

'You don't mean that.'

'I think I do.'

I pull her in close, so that the side of her face is resting against my chest. Can she mean such a thing? Her emotional responses must still be coloured by shock. Over the years she's forged such an easy rapport with the babies of our friends, with the children of strangers. It's unfathomable that she could give birth to a baby girl and not feel something towards her.

But if she does mean it? I feel my protective instinct rising up within me. It will be my job, then, to look after our baby. To make sure she's cared for in the way she deserves. And I'll need to guide Rosie back somehow, make her see that this child can be her daughter regardless of her genetic heritage. I see now that the merging of blood that once held the promise of an idyllic future was nothing but a happy fantasy. We will make this child ours through love. And sheer hard work.

Chapter 36

A week passes. Rosie moves into the back bedroom with me. We make love for the first time in weeks. She instigates it, searching for my lips in the middle of the night, running her hands over my body, as though reminding herself of who I am, what I feel like. She kisses me hard on the lips, and neither of us speaks. It's as though a strange kind of masochism underpins our delight. As though we're scraping one another raw.

Other nights, she falls asleep with my arm around her. Or she'll lay her head on my chest and as I stroke her hair I can pretend that things are as they were. But this intimacy never transfers itself to the daytime. I've tried several times to continue the conversation we had in the car, to encourage her to articulate her feelings towards the baby she's carrying. But she shrugs my questions away. A new habit that she must have learned from me.

She still devotes hours to googling that fucking technician, and she refuses to leave the flat. Jamila has supported my calls for fresh air, but Rosie's having none of it.

I think hard about what might make her feel better, and in the end I settle on Anthony. How blessed I would feel to hear the giggling that once so annoyed me. I arrange everything with Gary, and Rosie and I are driven to a flat in Camberwell.

Anthony rushes at Rosie and envelops her in a hug. 'Oh God, Rosie, I missed you. Where are you living now? Are you, like, in actual hiding?' He ushers her into an imitation leather sofa, which squeaks as she sits down.

'I brought you presents,' he says, reaching into a Tesco carrier bag. 'I figured with all this time on your hands you really ought to get round to reading David Foster Wallace.' He hands her a chunky paperback. 'And I thought Baby could probably do with some chocolate.'

'I'll let the two of you catch up,' I say. 'I'll be in the kitchen.'

I've brought my laptop with me so I sit at the counter, looking back through my notes on Richard Prior. His entry in the MPs' Register of Interests shows that a company called Data Insights has been providing him with consultancy valued at ten thousand pounds per month since the beginning of his by-election campaign. On its website the firm claims to help its clients 'better understand the issues and concerns of your target market through complex analysis'. I would have just put them down as your average marketing agency, were it not for the fact that the sales copy repeatedly promises 'discretion' and 'confidentiality'. I've set up an email account and requested further info under an assumed name, but they're yet to respond.

When I look up the firm's New York premises, I discover that they share an address with American Freedom, a right-wing lobby group created by a prominent financier to 'put American values at the heart of our democracy'. Amongst other things, the organisation opposes abortion, stem cell research and ovum-to-ovum fertilisation.

If it transpires that Data Insights is linked to American Freedom, then US lobbyists have interfered in a British by-election; more than that: are supporting a British politician in his attempt to impose regressive legislation. I'm about to go and tell Rosie what I've discovered, but just at that moment I hear her laugh.

I exhale. What a longed-for sound. Perhaps her healing can only ever come in increments, but I'm now certain that bringing her here was the right thing to do. Anthony offers her something very different from what I can provide, but perhaps Rosie needs it. And maybe when our baby arrives she'll benefit from a little of Anthony's silliness too. I conjure our daughter in a laughter-filled room, watching the grown-ups, enjoying seeing them happy. This imagined child is dressed in little jeans and she listens carefully, her face hungry for knowledge.

After a while Anthony comes into the kitchen to put the kettle on. From the living room I hear the low murmur of the TV. Good – Rosie's not rushing to get back to our temporary home.

'How are you doing, Jules?' There's an unexpected seriousness to Anthony's face as he asks this.

'It's good to hear Rosie laugh again,' I say.

He stands a little closer, and whispers: 'I tried to ask her about what she'd feel, if it was . . . well, if the baby turned out to be another woman's. She just changed the subject.'

There's a tenderness to his expression that makes my eyes start to fill. Did Rosie mean it when she said she wouldn't want the child? She's not repeated the sentiment and the care she takes over her bump seems to tell a different story.

'I think that what she needs, more than anything, is a day off from thinking about babies and egg mix-ups,' I say. 'A day that's as close as possible to her old life.'

He gives me a grateful smile. 'She's going to be a wonderful mum.'

I draw myself up. There's that all too familiar pinching sensation in my chest as the vision comes to me: the two of them making their secret plans.

'I donated sperm last week,' he says.

I blink.

'Yes, Rosie found it hilarious too. But the truth is, watching the two of you, it made me realise just how important it is for me to be a father. Or not, *be* a father I suppose, but to feel like I have some sort of stake in the next generation. I hate the idea of dying one day and leaving nothing behind.'

I try to suppress a smile. 'If you want children so badly, why not settle down?'

He sighs. 'I'd be a terrible dad. Probably end up like my own father, fucking off and only showing an interest here and there when it suits him. I couldn't be an authority figure in a kid's life. Maybe I could have made it work with Rosie, but only because you'd have been there, balancing things out.'

My body relaxes, and I find myself becoming genuinely curious. 'So you saw me being the father figure, then? A disciplinarian who'd come home from work expecting her pipe and slippers to be ready?'

He laughs. 'Not quite like that, Jules. But you would have created structure, routine. And you will – for this baby.'

'You can still be involved, you know.' I hadn't planned to say these words, but they feel right somehow. Perhaps where children are concerned, the more influences the better. Hearing Anthony and Rosie laughing seemed to settle something in my mind. Anthony need not be a threat. He offers things that I can't, things that have a value all of their own.

He smiles back at me. 'That means a lot.'

'And you do realise, right, that there's no one way to raise a family? If you want kids, your way of doing it will be just as valid as the next person's.'

He shakes his head. 'For now, handing over my sperm is enough. I like the idea of lots of Anthonys running around. But I can't say I'd want to wipe their arses.'

I stare after his departing back, too amused to be irritated. Anthony's reference to his own father resonated with me. I spent months measuring myself against a perfectly calibrated idea of motherhood, and being continually disappointed. Could it be that Anthony has done the same with fatherhood? Perhaps he filled the hole his absent father left with images from films and magazines, creating an intimidating ideal.

I remember the prickles of resentment I felt at his ease in the Barcombes' house, his almost flirtatious manner with Elaine. Rosie accused me of romanticising her parents, but it strikes me now that Anthony did exactly the same. We both idealised the nuclear family, both felt tainted by our outsider status.

In the car on the way back to the flat, I tell Rosie about my investigations into Prior. She smiles and her face seems to carry some of her old energy. 'Jules, people need to know this. Do you think you can keep investigating, even though we're holed up?'

'I'll do what I can. There are lots of gaps I need to fill in before I contact Prior for official comment. It may take a while. But I'd love to have a story ready for when he finally gets a reading date for his bill.'

She clutches at my arm. 'Thanks for pushing me to come out today. I enjoyed myself.'

'Good.'

'Do you think we'll ever get our old life back?'

We. She's talking about *we.* I reach across and stroke her hair. 'Perhaps not. But we can try and protect what's important. Friendships. Family.'

She swallows. 'Do you miss your dad?'

My childhood home rises up in my imagination. I see my father alone on the sofa, subjected to continual raps on the door. 'Yes,' I say. 'Maybe he doesn't deserve it, but when I think of how miserable he must be, I can't help feeling sad.'

'Then you should see him. For your sake.'

I study her face. Her eyes are clear, alive again. She cares. She wants me to be happy.

'Maybe I will,' I say. 'But I think you should also see your mum.'

She sighs. 'I can't have another conversation about DNA testing.'

'Then tell her that. Let her know what your boundaries are. She'll accept it, I know she will. She'll be so grateful to see you.' I lean over and kiss her on the cheek. 'It's true, Rosie. It's up to us to protect those bits of our lives that are important.

Your relationship with your mum, for all your differences, has to be worth persevering with.'

She gives me a sad smile. 'I guess you really did mean it when you said you planned to change.'

'I did. Some good has to come from what we've been through.'

Chapter 37

When I call my father to set up a meeting, I ask him to take me to where he grew up. I'd always known that he was raised in Leigh Park – a housing estate infamous for its chronic unemployment and criminality. But if we're to continue our relationship I need him to share more specifics with me.

Gary drives me back down to Hampshire, but rather than risk a trip into Petersfield, we pick my father up at a nearby train station. He's waiting outside, wearing the sea-green shirt that appeared in his wardrobe after the *Tribune* interview. He stares at the car awkwardly, coming over only when Gary lowers the window and calls his name.

'Where we headed?' Gary asks as my father clambers inside. Dad retrieves a slip of paper from his shirt pocket and passes it to him. He gives me a nervous smile as he does up his seatbelt. I nod in return, not quite trusting myself to speak.

Is this a terrible mistake? This man listened to my confidences, the churning worries and insecurities, then sold them to a journalist. Even now, remembering what he did brings on a rush of pain and disbelief. Part of me still wants to be told it isn't true, it was all a terrible mistake. I think back to the meals he served me in our poky little kitchen; his attentiveness on our countryside walks, me babbling about school and him listening all the while. I can't comprehend the emptiness left by the destruction of these memories. So I'm left in a strange kind of limbo – feeling anger and love and pity all at once.

We drive to Leigh Park and pull up outside a concrete end-of-terrace house which has a small, bramble-filled garden out the front. The gate has been torn off its hinges and there's a boarded-up pane in the front door. Upstairs, the curtains are pink and a row of teddy bears lines one of the windowsills.

Gary waits in the car while Dad and I step outside. Being near this house seems to have a physical effect on my father; his form is hunched, smaller, as though something inside him is withering away. He opens his mouth as though he's about to say something, but his strength seems to desert him and he looks at the pavement with defeated eyes. What he told me about his own father was the truth. As I look at him now, I'm sure of this.

'Let's go for a walk,' I say.

Wordlessly, we head to the small strip of park at the end of the road.

'This is where I got high for the first time,' he says as we sit side by side on the swings.

'Do you know who lives in your old house now?' I ask.

My father shrugs. 'Can't be David. He was inside for a while. Don't know what Victor's doing. Maybe he managed to hang on to the place, but I doubt it.'

Could it be that those teddy bears belong to a young, unknown cousin of mine? Should I feel any kind of affinity for these relatives, this David, this Victor, who are bound to me by blood? I'd like to see them from afar, I think. Being introduced would be too much, but I'm curious about their faces.

I start swinging back and forth, remembering the very simple pleasure that can be had from playing on a swing.

'Jules, what can I do to make things right?'

It's a question I've asked myself many times, and the answer keeps changing. But right now my thoughts are clear-edged: for me to continue to share my life with my father, I need a commitment to full, complete honesty. The very same thing that Rosie requires from me.

'The *Sketch* story, Dad. I need to know. It was you, wasn't it? I know you denied it, but that was in the heat of the moment. I'm giving you another chance. Be straight with me.'

He looks down at his feet and bites his lip. I feel myself relaxing – he's not going to attempt to lie.

'Why?' I ask.

'I was drunk. I barely remember doing it.'

'That's all there was to it? You were drunk?'

A tear runs down his nose. It is impossible not to feel pity. Here's a man who lost his twenty-one-year-old wife, who became a single father in an era when such things were unheard of. A man who didn't feel able to tell a soul about his childhood abuse.

And yet. Pity has been my default position for too long, as far as my father is concerned. It's blinded me to his flaws, made me an accomplice to his excuse-making. I take a deep breath. 'I want my daughter to know her granddad,' I say. 'But she can never meet the drunk version of you – you have to promise me that.'

'Of course ... Jules, I—'

'You'll need to get your act together, learn how to be a decent houseguest.'

'Jules.' He retrieves his fags and lighter from his shirt pocket. 'I'm going to make everything up to you. I've been thinking – you're trapped God knows where, so let me get to work on the nursery. I've still got my keys to your place. I'll go in and decorate it for you.'

'You've never decorated in your life.'

'I'll figure it out. I want to help.'

I'm not sure whether this scheme of his will come to fruition, and I'll have to warn the security company. But we have so many other things to worry about – it won't hurt to let him try to make himself useful. 'OK. Thanks.'

He smiles gently, taking a drag of his cigarette. I stretch out my legs and start swinging higher and higher. Perhaps I resemble him in ways I've never really understood. When I reached my teens, I used to feel hot spikes of rage at his inertia. At how he'd always have an excuse ready as to why he couldn't find a job, or why it was too late for him to educate himself. Yet as I rise up and take in the concrete houses all around me, the graffiti and rusting cars, I realise that I too stayed where it was safe. I had a different work ethic, true, but I was all too ready to find reasons for not moving on, for staying in a job that I'd outgrown, sticking to routines that had long ceased to be rewarding. It's the first time I've made this link between me and him, but it doesn't intimidate me. It hardens my resolve. The next era of my life is going to be very different.

My father stubs out his fag and I let my swings slowly dwindle until I can rest my feet on the ground. 'You know, you were right,' I say. 'About DNA not being important.'

'Jules, you don't have to—'

'I thought it was. But, really, insisting on a biological connection is a strange kind of possessiveness. Loving a child is what really makes it yours. The raising of our daughter is what will make me and Rosie her parents.'

Dad smiles. 'Been a long time since I last saw you on a swing. But it feels like yesterday, sometimes.'

I meet his eye. In spite of his smile there's something so sad about him. He's a man whose joys have been too fleeting, whose adulthood was burdened with unexpected responsibility. Perhaps soon he'll be pushing another young girl on a swing. And this time he needn't feel so alone. He can savour the moments, knowing that all the joy and pain of raising a child will be shared with others.

Chapter 38

Just a week after the meeting with my father, he calls me
to say the nursery is ready. In truth, I'd forgotten his promise to decorate. He hasn't asked us about colour schemes
or anything like that, but if he's simply picked a shade
of paint, then applied it to the walls, a week would have
been enough.

In the safe house, we've settled into a routine of sorts.
Anita and Hong Shu have secured a June hearing date for
their parentage lawsuit, which at least means there is no further talk of genetic testing while the baby is still inside Rosie.
We have weekly updates from our solicitor – mostly proce-
dural. He takes great pains to be reassuring, but Rosie's eyes
always remain distant. It's as though her only way of protecting herself is to make a mental retreat whenever others raise
the prospect of the child not being hers. And that includes
me. Some of our old intimacy has returned, but when I talk
about the future her face instantly hardens.

It occurs to me that going back to our house – even for
a short visit – might help. Perhaps if she can just stand in
the nursery, the happy images that once filled her mind
will return.

Gary takes some persuading, but the fact is we've been in hiding for over a month now. His colleagues have been checking on our house, and he's forced to admit that the photographers have given up awaiting our return.

So, one bright April morning, we find ourselves heading down the A3 towards our home town. Rosie fidgets in her seat throughout the journey, her bump making it uncomfortable to stay in one position for too long. But she shakes her head when I suggest pulling over for a brief leg-stretch.

'When do you think your article will be ready?' she asks.

'Soon.'

Prior's bill is due to be debated in the House of Commons at the beginning of June. The papers continue to give him regular coverage, but, as yet, no journalist has reported on his links to Data Insights and right-wing American lobbyists. It seems inconceivable, but at this point in time the story is all mine.

'I do wonder,' I say, 'whether it might be better to simply ring the *Guardian* and give them what I have. They'll have more resources to put behind it.'

'Don't you dare. You've come this far on your own.'

My research has revealed that Data Insights and American Freedom have two board members in common. And I have a recorded phone call with a sales rep from the marketing firm outlining some of their services: they use thousands of social media metrics to build up voter profiles and help firms shape their messages to ensure they resonate with target groups.

On the call, I'd pretended to work for a prospective parliamentary candidate. 'So you guys can tell me what issues

voters in his constituency are most likely to care about?'
I'd asked.

'More than that,' said the sales rep. 'We can tell you precisely what language will *make* them care. We can tell you
what they're most afraid of, and how you can harness that for
your campaign with the right imagery and messaging.'

My next step will be to contact Prior for an on-the-record
comment. Then I'll have to act quickly to place the story.
I can imagine the tweets that will follow our conversation:
*Lesbian elite out to sabotage family bill! Opponents of traditional
families stoop to fabrication and lies!*

We pull into our old road, something about its conifer trees
and neat driveways tugging at my heart. How much optimism
this place represented when we first moved in. The street is
empty, save for Alf, who's in his front garden with his seca-
teurs. He straightens up and frowns at the Mercedes.

Rosie takes a sharp intake of breath. Our fence has been
covered in a mosaic of spray-painted penises and insults. I'd
had such high hopes for this visit, but Rosie looks fragile. Our
break-up, the Fiesta's slashed tyres – I can almost see these
moments flitting through her consciousness.

'Thirty minutes,' Gary says. 'I'm starting the clock.'

Alf saunters over as we step out of the car. 'Wondered
if you'd show your faces again.' He looks like such a sweet
old man with his milky blue eyes and thick white hair,
it's almost hard to believe that he's been the source of so
much trouble.

'Come on, Rosie.' I steer her towards the gate, but she
seems reluctant.

'Are you going to sell up, then?' Alf takes a step towards us.

Rosie takes an involuntary step back, and lets out a cry as she stumbles over the kerb, hitting the ground with a sharp smack.

'It's OK, I'm OK!' she shouts.

She landed on her side, breaking her fall with her forearm.

'Shit.' I crouch down next to her, fumbling for my phone, ready to call an ambulance.

'I didn't do anything!' Alf shouts. 'I didn't touch her!'

From the corner of my eye I register Gary coming over.

'It's fine, I'm OK,' Rosie says again. Already, she's shifted her weight, moving onto all fours, then slowly, deliberately, easing herself upright. 'See – just a grazed arm.'

Gary frowns. 'I think we should get you checked out.'

'I broke my fall,' Rosie insists. 'And we're here now, so we may as well do what we came to do. I'm not letting an old bigot like him intimidate me.' She looks over to Alf, who has retreated to his garden, pretending to be engrossed in his flowerbeds.

Gary sighs. 'OK. Thirty minutes.'

Unlocking the gate, the sight of my car on the drive gives me a little pang. Its faded red paint is coated in dust and bird shit. Indoors, we wash Rosie's graze in the kitchen, speaking in hushed whispers, as though we're visitors creeping around while the people who really live here are asleep in bed. What a mistake it was to come here today. The life we wanted to have in this place never materialised, and I realise now that it never will. Perhaps we won't ever be able to return. If we're to give our daughter a normal life, we'll have to move somewhere different, maybe even change our names. I make a mental note to talk to Gary – he used to work for the police, so perhaps he can tell me how it might work.

It's with a guilty heart that I go up the stairs. Whatever effort Dad has put into the nursery will surely be wasted. Rosie's progress is slow and panting.

'Are you sure you're OK?' I ask.

'Yes. And I just felt the baby move, so she's fine too. Don't worry, Jules.'

We step into a room of bright sunshine yellow, looking out over our back garden.

'Oh, Jules.'

The room hasn't just been painted. It's been transformed into a complete nursery. White gauze curtains hang from the windows and a cot sits in one corner. Dad has even gone to the trouble of hanging a brightly coloured mobile above it, and making it up with a pristine white sheet. Next to the cot is a comfortable-looking reclining chair in white leather – perfect for breast-feeding. How could he have known we'd need such a thing? And how has he afforded it? The *Tribune* money – it must be.

'Jules, look.' Rosie's looking inside a new chest of drawers. Neatly folded sleepsuits. Tiny little hats. She starts to cry. 'It's so perfect.'

I stand behind her and encircle her with my arms. It's too much. Within the space of just a few minutes we've been reminded of the inaccessibility of our old life. And now we're standing here, in a kind of dreamscape – a precise realisation of the nursery Rosie wanted and expected to have in this house.

The image of my father, unshaven, loading up a shopping

trolley with baby gear, is heartbreaking and wonderful all at once. This is his best side. The side that seemed so absent most evenings, as he sat nursing his bong.

'Our baby's never going to sleep in this room, is she?' Rosie says.

'No. But we can move all this lovely stuff to a new home. She'll still get to enjoy it.'

Rosie turns around and buries her head in my shoulder. 'Oh Jules.'

I stroke her hair. 'We'll create a good life for her. Wherever we have to go. We will.'

She kisses me. 'I can see how hard you're trying.'

'I just want us to be happy, Rosie.'

She looks down and places a hand on her bump. 'I know. And I'm trying too. I want more than anything to feel, to really *know* that this baby is mine. There are moments when I do. But other times . . . '

I grasp her hand. 'It's going to be OK.'

We're about two-thirds of the way back to London when Rosie lets out a high-pitched gasp. I'd started to doze, but I turn to her and see that she's put a hand against her crotch.

'I think . . . I—'

'Rosie, what is it?'

'I think my waters have broken. I'm all wet.'

'Shit. Gary – we need to get to the Royal Free.'

Rosie clasps my hand. 'It's too early.'

Panic rises within me as I make the calculations. 'It's going to be fine, Rosie. Thirty-six weeks is fine. You're almost full term.'

She takes a shuddering in-breath and closes her eyes. I'm trying to remember what we learned at our handful of ante-natal sessions. 'Deep breaths,' I say. 'Nice deep breaths.'

She opens her eyes. 'Jules, I'm scared. I'm not ready.'

Chapter 39

Rosie needs an emergency caesarean. The baby is in distress.

We're separated for a moment as they rush to prep her for the operation; I put on the scrubs and cap they give me, slather my shaking hands in antibacterial gel. A nurse leads me along a harshly lit corridor. I hear the agonised cries of another woman in labour. A young man pushes past me.

Up ahead I see Rosie being wheeled along on a trolley. I run to her. 'I'm here, Rosie, I'm here.' I take her hand.

'Jules, I can't feel her any more. I can't feel her move.'

Her expression is so defeated. I must have stopped walking because one of the nurses is chivvying me: '... need to get her to theatre.' Everyone seems to know their role apart from me. How can it be possible to want something so much, but to be so powerless?

'It's going to be OK, Rosie,' I keep saying. 'I love you. Everything is going to be OK.'

We get to the operating theatre. They're putting a blue curtain across Rosie's midsection, blocking our view of the lower half of her body. White light glimmers off the tiled floor. So many people. Plastic aprons. Movement and purpose. My teeth hurt from clenching my jaw.

'Hello, Rosie, my name is Alec and I'm your anaesthetist today ...' *Get on with it, Alec. Get on with it, everybody.*

I keep a tight grip on Rosie's hand. A stream of platitudes comes from my mouth, but Rosie is unable to speak, choking on her own sobs. I've never seen her so distraught. If our baby doesn't make it, will she ever recover? I can't let this happen. There has to be something I can do.

But none of this is within my control. 'It's going to be OK, Rosie, it's going to be OK.'

She doesn't feel the scalpel, but she winces as they pull the baby out in a swift motion. It all happens so quickly. Rosie's helpless crying is replaced by a sudden urgency. 'Is she OK? Jules? Jules, look at her! Why isn't she crying?'

I take a step to the side, so that I can see around the curtain. The surgeon is barking instructions to the nurses. My eyes are drawn to Rosie's stomach. Peeled-back skin, a pool of blood that a nurse is tackling with some sort of suction instrument.

Another nurse has our baby in a towel and is vigorously rubbing. So this is it, this is her. I glimpse waxy skin, sticky with muck. *She exists.* Rosie is shouting my name. The towel becomes filthy with bloody slime. The baby makes no sound – my ears strain and her silence stretches on for far too long.

No. This can't be. I can't turn back to Rosie, can't let her see on my face what I fear, what I know must be true.

And then my daughter cries.

My heart drops into my stomach, a flutter of ecstasy so acute it hurts. I go back to Rosie. Tears slide down her cheeks. I'm crying too, I realise.

'You did it, she's OK. She's OK,' I say.

Our child's screams fill the room as the nurse approaches with her. 'Let me see her,' Rosie shouts. 'Oh, my baby.'

'Just for a minute, then we need to get you stitched up.' The nurse lowers the baby down so that her face is only inches away from Rosie's.

And then, without me having time to think about it or prepare myself, the baby is placed in my arms. She's surprisingly strong as she wriggles and screams. Then she seems to find a position she likes, and while the crying doesn't stop, it tails off into a whimper. She's a little person. Not a concept. A little person who's come into the world terrified. The smell of the room, the bright lighting – all of this must be new and frightening. I clasp her tightly. Find myself uttering soothing nonsense as I look at her properly. She has a scattering of fine dark hair and as she cries she shows me perfect little gums. Her eyes are screwed shut, but periodically she opens them just for a second, as though she's plucked up the courage to peep at this new world of hers.

I look up from the baby, back at the bed. Rosie is watching me with our daughter, and despite everything that has happened to us she looks the happiest she's ever been.

Dazed, I walk the corridor with some half-formed notion of calls I need to make, people I need to share our news with. Rosie has managed to feed our baby for the first time, and now they both need to sleep. There are tasks I need to perform, but the list in my mind is a vague swirl.

My baby is here in the world, and as I held her the rush of pure, animal feeling that everyone talks about came to me. I am normal. And happy, so happy. From today my life can begin anew. I have faith that things will work out, that all of the possibilities in this tiny human being will be realised. Faith that we're going to be happy as a family of three. Never one to believe blindly, without weighing the evidence, I am awash with joy at the strange new confidence that's been instilled in me.

I call Rosie's parents, my father, Abi, Tom, Anthony. Bestow our good news like the gift it is. After, I head to the café, suddenly ravenous. There's a low murmur of conversation. Elderly patients with their middle-aged offspring. A couple of bleary-eyed new fathers. I order a large plate of macaroni cheese and a Coke, taking a seat at a corner table. I still have that swelling sensation in my chest, as though I'm on the cusp of tears. It feels as though it will never leave me.

As I eat, I brave a look at the BBC website and see that our baby's birth is already one of the lead items. The picture illustrating the story is of the Royal Free's entrance: there are crowd-control barriers up now, and a scrum of photographers four or five deep is being held back by the presence of uniformed police. This is beyond anything we've experienced so far. We're going to need a police escort to get past this lot. And I doubt our safe house will remain safe for much longer.

Soon I see Becca coming towards me, tailed by Dwayne. 'Jules – congratulations.'

I stand up and give her a hug. The physical contact prompts a few more tears to spill over, and I discreetly wipe at my face.

'Have you given her a name yet?' Becca asks as she sits down opposite me. Her face is lit with excitement, and there's something rushed and far less polished than usual about her appearance.

I shake my head. 'Have you been in to see her?' I say. 'She's so perfect. Six pounds one. Tiny but perfect. They had an incubator ready, but she doesn't need it. And she's feeding beautifully.'

'Yes, I've been in – taken the measurements and pictures that we need. She's an angel. I'm so happy for you both; I can't believe this moment is finally here.'

'There's quite a press pack outside.'

Becca purses her lips and nods.

'How am I going to protect her from all this? She's so tiny. Any jostling . . . I might drop her.'

Becca laughs, but stops when she sees the serious look on my face. 'It'll be alright, Jules. The university will cover the cost of your security arrangements for the immediate future. I mentioned the phrase *duty of care* to my boss, and he's taking it very seriously.'

'Thank you. And not just for the security stuff – for making it possible in the first place, for giving us the opportunity.'

Becca reaches out and puts a hand on my forearm. 'I've got some good news. All seven pregnancies up in Newcastle are viable. The parents have been communicating with one another, and they've decided to go public as a group, to deflect some of the attention away from your little one.'

I inhale sharply. 'But don't they realise . . . They'll all be doorstepped, their lives will be turned upside down.'

'They've considered it carefully – they've seen the attention you and Rosie received, so this group announcement is a strategic decision. They're also mindful of that odious politician and his family bill, and want to do something in response to that. I'm hoping it will help you and Rosie – ease up the intensity.'

I nod. Diminished news value. Solidarity. I stop resisting the relief that caresses my heart. I'm right to have faith. During our pregnancy quest I've seen humanity's ugly side too many times. But people can be kind. Too often, I've let myself forget this.

'What are you going to do, now they've suspended o-o?' I ask.

Becca places her palms on the table. 'I've accepted a job in Stockholm. I've got mixed feelings about it. Part of me thinks I should stay here and fight. Yet the pragmatic side of me knows I'd be facing years of uphill slog and unwanted attention. It's not fair on my family.'

'So, Sweden it is then.' I smile.

'Yes. Hopefully your little one will be joined by some Swedish pals in the not too distant future.'

Later, I creep back into Rosie's room. The baby is asleep and Rosie is leaning over her, stroking her fine, dark hair. 'She's so perfect,' she says.

I approach the cot and watch my daughter's little chest rise and fall. She makes a snuffling sound with each breath; it sounds warm and contented. Does she look like either of us? No. But she doesn't look like Hong Shu or Anita either. She is ours. The baby we were meant to have. Rosie rests a hand on my arm and I feel a thrill of pleasure. Our separation now has the half-remembered quality of an unpleasant dream. We've created a family together. I feel part of a unit now, here in this room.

I sit down next to the bed.

'What are we going to call her?' Rosie says.

'You liked Margaret, for your grandmother.'

Rosie tilts her head. 'No. It's not right. She doesn't look like a Margaret.'

'What about Emmeline? I was thinking we could name her after Emmeline Pankhurst.'

Rosie looks thoughtful.

'Is it too much?' I ask. 'It is, isn't it?'

'No. Actually, it's perfect. It's symbolic, but it's also a pretty name. Emmy. Baby Emmy. It suits her.'

I feel a flush of pride. I've been turning over name suggestions for the last couple of weeks, saving them up to offer to Rosie as a reconciliation gift. Emmeline was my firm favourite. Let the press have fun with it if they must, but I want my daughter to have a worthy name, a significant name.

Chapter 40

The next morning, while Rosie and Emmy are sleeping, I head out into the hospital gardens and call Hong Shu.

'I'm not supposed to speak to you,' she says.

'Don't hang up. Can't we just talk – like we used to?'

'You want me to congratulate you?'

'No. I can't imagine what you must be going through, Hong Shu, I really can't. But bringing lawyers into the mix isn't going to make things better.'

A woman in a floral dressing gown wheels her drip stand out through the door and lights a cigarette.

'That baby could be mine. Or Anita's. Why do you get to raise her? You didn't even want a baby.'

I take a deep breath. Pain is what's making her talk like this.

'I do want her,' I say. 'I want her more than anything. But you guys can be involved in her life. You should be.'

'How very kind of you.'

'You're going to lose your case. I don't know what your solicitor has said to you – I hope he hasn't given you false hope. The Human Fertilisation and Embryology Act defines the birth mother as the legal mother. You must know that.'

The line goes quiet. Then I detect a slight sniff. She's

crying. 'We'd begun to accept it, Jules. Jessica was lost to us. It hurt, but we could understand it. And then ... that technician. Can you imagine what it felt like to hope? To know that a baby of ours might still be alive?'

I swallow. 'I can't imagine. But I know that DNA results have the potential to cause even more pain. Drop the case, and let's talk about the role you can play in Emmeline's life. Rosie and I want you around. After everything the four of us have been through, we should be the very best of friends – not adversaries in a courtroom.'

Hong Shu sighs. 'I don't know, Jules. I really don't know where we go from here.'

When I return to our room, the Barcombes have arrived. Elaine sits in the visitor's chair holding a sleeping Emmeline. She beams at me. 'She's beautiful, Jules.'

I look over at Rosie. Her hair is rumpled and her face, while still heavy with sleep, bears a contented expression, as though she's forgotten her earlier rage towards her mother.

'She is,' I say.

Michael stands over his granddaughter, looking smitten. Emmeline seems so fragile in her pristine white sleepsuit, but the rise and fall of her chest is strong and rhythmic. It tells of resilience. How can a whole life, a universe of possibilities, be contained within such a tiny form?

After an hour or so I show the Barcombes the way to the café. As we approach its entrance Elaine grasps my sleeve. 'Are you sure you can't persuade Rosie to do the DNA test? Just for peace of mind. It's your right to know too.'

I'm winded. Elaine seemed to be the epitome of the doting

grandmother just now. I'd thought of this first meeting as a very special moment, one I would always remember. Can she have been scrutinising Emmy's face the whole time, looking for resemblances? Would she willingly give this grandchild up if the results showed that she wasn't Rosie's biological child? I don't want to believe such a thing, but now we're out of Rosie's room, Elaine seems restless. She wants to impose order, draw neat lines.

'You have to stop this,' I say. 'We've thought of her as our baby for so long; she grew inside Rosie's body. We don't want to know what her DNA says. It doesn't matter to us. I hope you can respect that. And I hope you can love Emmeline regardless.'

'But—'

'Of course we do, Jules.' Michael puts a hand on his wife's back and leads her into the café. As I watch them depart I see images of the hospital on the BBC news channel playing inside. The media are still camped out, waiting to get the shots of us taking our daughter home – wherever home may be.

Emmeline is still sleeping when I return to our room.

'There's press outside,' I tell Rosie. 'The first picture of her is likely to be worth tens of thousands.'

There's a defiant set to Rosie's mouth. 'No one is making money off of our baby.'

'The interest is always going to be there. I see that now,' I say. 'I got the whole approach to the media wrong. And you were right – it was partly down to me being a private person, wanting to avoid the attention. I should have stood up for what we were doing, let you put your head above the parapet and be interviewed like you wanted to be.'

'There's nothing to gain from beating yourself up, Jules.'

'Maybe not, but I can learn from my mistakes.' With my phone, I take a picture of our sleeping baby. Her delicate lips are slightly parted. You can see the blood vessels in her eyelids, tiny and perfectly formed.

I show Rosie. 'Let's put it on Instagram, with a message. I'll email the link to a few national picture desks – it will knock a few zeros off the value of paparazzi shots, give them less incentive to wait outside.'

A gleam of mischief in her eyes. 'Are you sure?'

'I am. Besides – I'm proud of our baby. I want to show her off.'

'Our baby. She *is* ours.'

'No question.'

We drift off to sleep, but in the afternoon, after Rosie has fed our daughter, we watch the world's media report our news.

It's fascinating to see what a snap of a cute baby can do. Throughout the pregnancy, Rosie and I were fair game. But perhaps chivalry isn't quite dead. Social media erupts with poisonous commentary, but the papers are disarmingly positive.

What a cutie! proclaims the *Sketch*. They talk of a *medical advance* rather than a *wacky experiment*. And Rosie and I are *proud parents* as opposed to *tight-lipped lesbians*.

The *Tribune* runs a ghastly summary of the trial, but they're no longer gunning for outrage like they were before. It's as if they know that any criticism, anything other than a joyous tone when talking about a baby girl, will alienate their readers. They cite our Instagram message in full: *Emmeline*

Curtis Barcombe, born to two mothers on 28 April at 12.02 p.m., 6lb 1oz.

The *Guardian* is billing her as the *baby girl who won over the critics*. And even Richard Prior tweets a message of congratulations.

I see that Rosie has started to doze off once more. Is our relationship fixed? Has she learned to trust me again? Our glances are stripped of self-consciousness. We touch each other constantly, like we always used to. And we have Emmeline. She is something we did together, a bond of flesh, regardless of her DNA.

The protective stirrings I've begun to feel are a surge now, and they encompass not only Rosie and our baby but the trial itself. How dare people sneer at this? I won't hide away any more. I will defend the right of other women to have children together, to utilise the possibilities offered by science, just as generations have before us. As soon as we're out of hospital I'm going to finish the story on Prior and his American funders. My name alone is enough to ensure that a national will take it, but I'm not going to wrestle with the ethics of that. It's a great story. A story that deserves to be told.

Epilogue

Four years later, we're living in an airy two-bedroom bungalow on a quiet stretch of the Cretean coast. The cost of security is cheaper here. We hired an unobtrusive twenty-four-hour detail to work with us: two broad-shouldered men and a muscular woman, all of whom regularly arrive for their shifts with homemade toys and the hand-me-down clothes of nieces and nephews. I'm convinced one of them is also slipping Emmy contraband chocolate, but my daughter is steadfast in her refusal to tell on her benefactor.

We have a little garden where Rosie has planted scarlet geraniums, rosemary and basil. There's a patio set, a table of latticed iron where I can sit with my laptop and write of my daughter's beginnings in the evening breeze. The commissions have been rolling in. Articles commanding five figures, followed by a book deal for six. I find that I like telling our story; I enjoy the space a book gives me. It took a while to train myself away from the 350-word prose punch-ups of the *Post*, but the importance of the task made me want to do it well. As she gets older, I want Emmeline to understand how she came to be. Of the love involved. I will be the person to tell that story – it's too important to leave to others.

Emmeline, your arrival made me more complete as a person. That's no sentimental reflection on motherhood. Insights did not come flooding in as I changed shitty nappies and defrosted expressed milk – if only they did. Rather, the circumstances of your birth forced me to question the way I organised my life, the way I treated those I cared about. I'm part of a web now, a web of people who are here to support you, but also to support me. I need other people. And there is nothing wrong with that.

There are now thirty-seven girls in the world who were made in the same way as you. We've met twelve of them, and I think of all of these girls as your kin. Rosie and I share a bond with their mothers that sometimes makes me want to weep with a sense of solidarity. We have an online message board where we share our experiences, along with pictures of our healthy daughters. We prove the scaremongers wrong, every single day.

Prior's family bill was defeated – narrowly. I like to think that my article on his campaign finance contributed to this in some small way. Yet the temporary ban on o-o in Britain has endured to this day. The ethics review still hasn't produced its final report and appears to have no sense of urgency. It's as though the issue has been conveniently parked until such time as public opinion changes. This has meant that Hong Shu and Anita's two children, Bella and Zac, needed to be conceived with donor sperm. But our friends love their children dearly, just as they love you.

Your first few days were chaotic. The release of your photograph did temper the media presence slightly, as did news of the second-wave pregnancies. But the attention was still relentless. We had to make our plans quickly. Where to live. What to do for money. After many discussions with our friends and with Becca, we decided to participate in a few, carefully selected media interviews and use the proceeds to

create a fund for your future. Then came the book offer. A different
life, away from Petersfield, became possible.

In Crete, my writing schedule adapted to the needs of a young baby,
then to the routines and games of a growing girl. We're blessed with
a year-round stream of visitors – Tom and Abi, Anthony, Becca and
Scott, Anita and Hong Shu. Even my dad was inspired to apply for his
first-ever passport. Rosie's parents have bought a holiday home fifteen
minutes away, in a neighbouring town. They're regular visitors, and
they dote on you. But there are moments, and I know that Rosie notices
them, when your grandmother searches your face so intensely that it's
clear she's looking for something. A genetic trace that still means so
much to her, even though she knows better than to say as much.

The advance for the book, supplemented by rent from the house
back in Petersfield, has given us financial freedom. But the publisher's
money, although very nice, was a secondary motivation. I'd spent so
long being desperate for privacy, but now I wanted to shout about
you, Emmeline.

There are days when I'm too tired to do anything other than plough
through a few tasks. Yet at other times I feel a twisting joy that skirts
so closely to pain that I find myself catching my breath. This is not
sentimental movie-love I'm feeling; it's far more complicated and it
runs far deeper. I'm so proud of you.

From talking to others, to Rosie, to Becca, to friends old and new,
I realise that my feelings are *normal*. Our family takes nothing away
from all those conventionally conceived kids out there. We may be
part of a long tradition of shaking things up, doing things differently – yet the routines that make up our lives are just as mundane
as anyone else's.

So, my darling girl, this is the story of you. Although I've behaved questionably at times, felt things I'm not proud to admit to, I've tried to be honest in my account. I think it's important for a woman to fully understand the forces she's up against in this world. There really is no point in showing things to be better than they are. But I hope I've shown you how endlessly adaptable and inventive love can be.

Acknowledgements

I must have been about five when I announced to my parents that I was going to be an author, and it was thanks to their encouragement that I felt able to pursue my ambitions, never feeling stymied by the relative poverty of my childhood. So special thanks to Elaine and the late Michael Chadwick.

Thanks too to Kim Chadwick for setting such an energetic example, and to Steve Cannings for helping me through each and every lapse of confidence along the way.

Writing was a relatively lonely process until I got to know the inspirational Jessica Jarlvi and my literary doula Kalika Sands. I owe a huge debt to these amazing women, whose insightful feedback helped me strengthen the book in countless ways.

Tobi Coventry and Rosie Welsh both provided helpful suggestions at the redrafting stage. And Orly Lacham-Kaplan was kind enough to read the manuscript and provide comments. Liberties taken with the science are entirely my own.

I'm in awe of Sharmaine Lovegrove – the driving force behind Dialogue Books – for the passion and enthusiasm she shows in publishing underrepresented voices. Having her as my editor has been a privilege, and I'm thrilled to be among

Dialogue's launch titles. Thanks to all Sharmaine's colleagues at Little, Brown; in particular Zoe Gullen for her meticulous yet sensitive copyediting.

I'll be forever grateful to my agent, Cara Lee Simpson, who has been a relentless champion for the book since it landed in her slush pile. It's thanks to her editorial insights and unwavering support that I can now call myself an author for the first time.

Bringing a book from manuscript to what you are reading is a team effort.

Dialogue Books would like to thank everyone at Little, Brown who helped to publish *XX* in the UK.

Editorial
Sharmaine Lovegrove
Simon Osunsade
Zoe Gullen

Contracts
Anniina Vuori

Sales
Sara Talbot
Ben Green
Rachael Hum
Viki Cheung

Design
Helen Bergh
Duncan Spilling
Charlotte Stroomer

Production
Nick Ross
Narges Nojoumi
Mike Young

Publicity
Millie Seaward
Grace Vincent

Marketing
Jonny Keyworth

Copy Editor
Zoe Gullen

Proofreader
Alison Tulett